TEXAS BRIDE

ROSANNE BITTNER

The characters and events in this novel are purely fictitious and the product of this author's imagination. However, said characters and events are based on the actual historical situation that existed in the Republic of Texas during the time in which this story takes place—1845—just before Texas statehood.

More from Rosanne Bittner

The Bride Series
Tennessee Bride
Oregon Bride

Full Circle
Until Tomorrow

Diversion Books
A Division of Diversion Publishing Corp.
443 Park Avenue South, Suite 1008
New York, New York 10016
www.DiversionBooks.com

For more information, email info@diversionbooks.com

First Diversion Books edition May 2014.
Print ISBN: 978-1-62681-374-8
eBook ISBN: 978-1-62681-283-3

This book is dedicated to the brave souls who settled the Republic of Texas; and to the equally brave souls who were forced to give up that same land to make way for the white man. In many ways both red man and white were right in their beliefs and actions; and in just as many ways, both were wrong. In retrospect, who can say who is to blame? All that is left is to forgive, to accept what is and look to the future … and to replace bitterness and hatred with acceptance and love.

Set not thy foot on graves;
Hear what wine and roses say;
The mountain chase, the summer waves,
The crowded town, thy feet may well delay.

Set not thy foot on graves;
Nor seek to unwind the shroud
Which charitable Time
And Nature have allowed
To wrap the errors of a sage sublime...

Life is too short to waste
In critic peep or cynic bark,
Quarrel or reprimand:
'Twill soon be dark;
Up! mind thine own aim, and
God speed the mark!

—from the poem "TO J. W."
by Ralph Waldo Emerson

One

A hot Texas wind blew the hemline of Rachael Rivers's dress, dusting the bottom of the deep blue skirt and spoiling the polish of her high-button shoes. It was a warm spring day, 1845, and Rachael was hot in her long-sleeve dress, but it was her best dress, and she had wanted to look nice for her homecoming. The dress fit her tiny waist perfectly, billowing below the waist with several slips beneath it; the perfectly placed darts of the bodice accenting her full, round bosom. Her blond hair was swept up under a small hat, part of its long tresses hanging in curls down the back of her neck.

Rachael ignored the heat. Her blue eyes saw only the inscription on the new gravestone beside her mother's.

HERE LIES JOSEPH RIVERS, KNOWN TO SOME AS RIVER JOE. BIRTHDATE UNKNOWN. DIED FEBRUARY 12, 1845. A GOOD HUSBAND AND FATHER.

Sand, carried on the wind, stung Rachael's pretty face. Texas was hard on fair skin, hard on everything. Rachael's mother, Emma, had been dead since 1840. She was only 30 years old when she died in childbirth, taking the baby with her. But she had left behind three sons and a daughter.

"At least they're together now," said twenty-year-old Joshua Rivers as he moved closer beside his grieving sister. "Ma and Pa didn't have a lot of years together, but they sure did love each other," he added.

Thirteen-year-old Luke stood across from his sister and older brother, sniffing and wiping at new tears that spilled out of big, blue eyes. He ran a hand through his dark hair. It didn't seem possible his father had already been dead for two months. Now, seeing Rachael grieving over their father, his own painful loss was reawakened.

Fifteen-year-old Matthew leaned against the big cotton-wood tree that shaded the graves. His thick, blond hair blew every which way, and his blue eyes were watery with tears that the boy was too stubborn to let fall. Luke and Matthew were both built big for their ages, good-looking young men who had learned about hard work early in life.

"If only I had come back sooner," Rachael spoke softly, hardly able to get the words past the painful lump in her throat. "I just never imagined a man like Father dying, Josh. He was so big and strong and able."

"I know," Joshua answered. "It got extra cold last January and the pond froze over. Pa went out to chop a hole in it for the horses and more ice broke. He fell right in. A couple days later he came down with a fever and he just never got better—got hit with a terrible cough to where he just couldn't breathe anymore. Maybe if Ma was still alive he'd have tried harder. But I think he just got so sick he started thinking about maybe giving up and going to be with Ma. He was never a happy man after she died anyway."

Rachael turned, half collapsing against her brother's chest. He hugged his weeping sister supportively. Joshua was tall and broad like his father, a handsome young man, with Joe Rivers's dark eyes and winning smile. His hair was a soft, sandy color, a grand mixture of his dark father and his blond mother.

"Go on about your chores," he told Luke and Matthew gently. "I know you want to visit with Rachael, but this is pretty bad news for her right now. Supper will be a better time to get your visiting done."

Luke fidgeted with a floppy leather hat that hung limply from his calloused hands. He came around to the sister it seemed he hardly knew anymore. "I'm glad you're home, Rachael," he said awkwardly. "I'm sorry about Pa."

Rachael turned to him, giving him a quick, tearful hug. She glanced at Matthew, who still stood leaning against the tree.

"We'll get reacquainted at supper, like Josh said," she told Matthew, finally finding her voice. "I'm proud of you and Luke both, for staying on here with Josh and taking care of the ranch. I know it's hard work."

Matthew nodded, quickly turning away to hide a tear that finally slipped out. He hurried off to do his chores, barking at Luke to come and help.

All four Rivers children were named after biblical characters. *"It's fitting,"* their mother had often said. *"I learned to read with a Bible, back in Tennessee when your pa and I lived among the Cherokee. The Cherokee raised your pa, even though he was white. They were family to him, so they became family to me, too."*

Rachael could easily remember Emma Rivers telling them stories about how she grew up, how she met Joe Rivers, things that happened back in Tennessee; how the Cherokee got sent away by the government; how she and Joe came to live in Texas to start a new life. That had taken great strength and courage, and the sons and daughter of Joe and Emma Rivers were nurtured to carry those same qualities, necessary characteristics for survival in a harsh land.

"Oh, Josh, I wish I could have been here," Rachael said. She took a handkerchief from the pocket of her dress and blew her nose.

"Pa would understand," Joshua answered. "Besides, you were doing what Ma wanted. She wanted you to go to that school back East. Now look at you, a fine lady, anybody can see. I expect my sister is the prettiest girl in all of Texas."

Rachael smiled through her tears. "That's what Father used to say to Mother," she said, her voice shaky. "Remember how he used to make her blush?"

Joshua grinned. "I sure do. Now you're doing it."

She shook her head, laughing and crying at the same time. "Josh Rivers. Don't you start."

Joshua folded his arms. "Well, the only thing I regret is that Pa can't see you now. You look more like Ma than ever. And Ma would be so proud to know you'll be teaching in Austin. You did right by her memory, Rachael, coming back here to teach."

Rachael wiped at her eyes, taking a good look at her brother. She had arrived at the Double "R" no more than a half hour earlier, paying the stage driver a little extra to bring her directly to the ranch after his stop in Austin. She had discovered the shocking news of her father's death upon her arrival. There had barely been time to visit with her brothers, or even to take a true inventory of how they had changed.

"And look at you," she said then. "Josh, you're a grown man."

"Three years can make a big difference. You've changed a lot, too, you know. You left here a shy, sixteen-year-old girl. Now you're a woman."

Rachael sniffed, studying her brother lovingly. "Now what, Josh? You moving into town?"

"Heck no. Pa loved this ranch. We're staying right here on the Double 'R.' We helped Pa enough over the years to know what to do."

"But the ranch has never brought in much money, Josh. The weather is so unpredictable. A crop can be wiped out overnight, cattle can starve, let alone the problems with Indians stealing the strays. That's what I worry about most—the Comanche renegades."

Joshua shrugged. "Pa was a hell of a fighter, and so are me and Matt and Luke. We all can handle our repeaters just fine. We'll handle those skulking savages."

"Josh! You know Father never would speak of them that way. You know how he felt about Indians."

"Comanche aren't like other Indians. Pa liked to think they were—said they were just afraid of losing all their land and all. But I rode on a patrol once last year with Jason Brown. He's a Texas Ranger now. Did you know that?"

Rachael stiffened. "No," she answered, wiping at her eyes again.

"We rode out to check on other settlers," Joshua continued, "and I saw what the Comanche did to a nice family north of here. I tried to tell Pa about it, but he just said I have a lot to understand about Indians and why they do some of the things they do. Then he went into that story again about what happened to the Cherokee. 'It didn't do them any good to try to keep their land the legal way, the peaceful way,' he'd say. 'Other Indians know that, so they're going to fight their own way to keep what's theirs.' But I'll tell you, if you saw what I saw, you wouldn't have any sympathy for the Comanche."

Rachael frowned, blowing her nose once more. "Why on earth did you go riding off with Jason Brown? He's an Indian hater, Josh, and you know it. Of *course* he's going to show you the worst. I never liked him much, and neither did Father."

"Well, maybe now that you're older, you'll change your mind. Jason asks about you all the time, Rachael. He never forgot you. And he's a good man, a capable man and a good Ranger."

Rachael turned, looking at the gravestone again. "I don't want to think about him right now, Josh. I just want to think about Father. Do you mind leaving me here alone for a while?"

Joshua put a hand on her shoulder, squeezing gently. "Sure. I'm sorry you had to come back to this, Rachael. I reckon you have a lot to think about right now. I'll be up at the house." He patted her shoulder and left.

Rachael gazed at her parents' graves, as tears stung her eyes. "I did it, Mother. I'm a teacher now, just like you always dreamed and planned for me. I know how much importance you put on a formal education. Now I have one, and I'll be teaching other children."

A hawk drifted overhead. Rachael glanced up at a wide, blue white sky. She wondered if she was crazy to come back to Texas, to leave the comfortable, convenient lifestyle she had enjoyed back East. But she had missed her family; wanted to see them all again. More than that, Austin was a city that was growing fast, and it was rumored that as soon as Texas became a state, which was expected to happen within the year, the town would become its capital. There were a lot of children in the Austin area who needed schooling.

Rachael had kept in touch with Lacy Reed, a friend of the family who owned a boardinghouse in town. It was Lacy who had written Rachael to tell her Austin had built a school and that another teacher would be needed. They had already hired a male teacher, but he spent a lot of time riding a circuit around Austin, visiting outlying ranches and teaching children who could not get to the school in town.

To Rachael's surprise and delight, those in charge of setting up an educational system for Austin's youth had approved of allowing her to come there to teach. Rachael didn't know if it was because she was from Austin, or if it was a matter of desperate need. She knew only that she was being given a chance to teach. She realized there were plenty of other places in this desolate land where teachers were needed, but since this position was close to her family Rachael was more than happy to take the job.

She bent down, touching the earth over her father's grave. New grass had begun to grow there, but the dirt was so dry Rachael wondered how the little blades had managed to take hold.

"I'll do a good job," she promised her parents quietly. "I'll make you proud of me." She sighed deeply. "I loved you so much, Father. I'm so sorry I didn't get back in time to see you again."

She broke into new tears. The wide, quiet land around her only enhanced her own lonely need to see Joe Rivers just once more. But that would never be. She breathed deeply to regain her composure, reminding herself life must go on and she had a job to do now. She would spend some time with her brothers, then get back to Austin and get to work. School would soon close for the summer, but there would be time to get to know the children before the next school season opened.

She rose, wiping at her eyes and looking toward a corral where Luke and Matt were trying to rope a mustang from amid its wild friends. She could not get over how her younger brothers had grown. Joshua was right. Three years could make quite a difference.

She turned back to the graves. "I love you both." She walked toward the house then. It stood there as she had always remembered it—a moderate, white frame house that Emma Rivers had strived to always keep tidy in spite of the Texas dust. Rachael had tried to do the same after her mother's death, until she had left for St. Louis at sixteen. Joshua stood on the slightly sagging front porch, watching her approach. Rachael could feel only pride at how her handsome brother had grown and matured. This was the first time in her life she had seen him as a man instead of as a boy.

She moved up the creaking wooden steps, facing her brother. "I'd stay here and keep house and cook for you and the boys, Josh, but I have to be near Austin."

Joshua nodded. "That's for sure, and it's fine with me, Rachael. The horses and cattle are enough attraction for them renegades. One look at you and they'd kill us all to get to you. You're better off in town."

Rachael blushed slightly, looking away. "I wish you'd sell this place and take jobs in town too, Josh. Father was probably right about the Indians having reasons for what they do. I can't really say they're wrong myself. But at the same time, I don't want anything to happen to my brothers."

"Actually, it's been pretty quiet here. A few renegades show up once in a while wanting some tobacco or some food. I don't worry much about them anymore. We can take care of ourselves."

She faced him, smiling. "I'm not saying you aren't capable, Josh, but I can't help worrying. After all, you're all I have now."

"Oh, I don't know. You did good on your own back East. And now you're an independent woman with a job and all. Besides, you sure won't have trouble finding a husband."

Rachael shook her head, folding her arms. "Don't be so anxious to marry me off."

Joshua moved from where he leaned on a support post and put an arm around her shoulders. "Where will you be staying?"

"With Lacy Reed."

Josh nodded. "Well, in spite of the danger, I hope you'll stay a couple of days, at least. The house could use a woman's touch."

Rachael laughed lightly, grateful for the diversion from her grief. "And you could stand to eat a woman's cooking, right?"

"That's for sure." Joshua stooped to pick up her bags.

"Maybe I should stay longer, Josh. I didn't expect to come home to a fresh grave. Maybe I shouldn't leave you so soon."

"It's okay. It's best that you go, much as we'd all like you to stay. I'll rest easier once you're gone and I know I don't have to worry about leaving you alone at the house while we go out in the fields. We'll try to stay close while you're here. In the meantime I'll have to figure out a safe way to get you back to town."

Rachael opened the front screen. The hinges squeaked, just as they always had. The familiar sound reminded her of girlhood days, when she would run in and out of the door to play or do chores. After she stepped inside the house she immediately realized how right Joshua had been. The place definitely needed a woman's touch. Dishes sat everywhere, some clean, some dirty. Clothes hung over chairs, and a vase of flowers long wilted sat on the table.

"Sorry about the mess," Joshua said. "We really can keep it pretty nice, but we've been awful busy lately—spring roundup and all, Rachael. If I had known you were coming—"

"It's all right. I understand. You go do what needs doing and I'll make you and the boys a real good supper."

Joshua set down her baggage, sighing deeply, a trace of tears in his eyes as he looked her over once more. "I'm glad you're back, Rachael."

Rachael smiled sadly. "I only wish I would have come back a couple of months sooner."

Joshua smiled through tears and quickly turned away. "I'd better get to helping Matt and Luke." He left, and Rachael looked around the main room of the little frame house. She ran her hand along the wooden table Joe Rivers had made with his own hands. She glanced at the coat hooks near the door to see that his doeskin jacket still hung where it had always hung. Joshua probably didn't have the heart to do anything with it. She walked up to it, touching the worn spot on one sleeve where his elbow had long ago wiped away the original light color of the pretty doeskin and had left a dark, shiny spot. Emma Rivers had made the jacket for her husband, using skins from deer Joe had shot for food. Rachael remembered how her mother patiently taught her how to properly dry and stretch the hide, how to smoke it to make it soft.

It seemed so impossible Joe Rivers could be dead. Such

men weren't supposed to die. But Texas had a way of claiming most living things prematurely, even men as strong as her father. She rested her face against the jacket, breathing deeply of its scent of the outdoors, of wild things, of leather and skins. That was the kind of man Joe Rivers was.

"Father," she whispered, the tears coming again.

Brand Selby peered from behind a boulder, his horse tied just below him on the other side of the ridge from which he watched the men below. Agony and indecision boiled inside the half-breed when he realized it was an old Comanche Indian man he saw hanging by the wrists from a cottonwood tree. The old man's shirt had been stripped off, and a white man lashed into him over and over with a bull whip, while two more white men stood nearby doing nothing. Each crack of the whip made Brand flinch. How well he knew that sound. How well he knew the pain of the barbed end of that whip!

Selby's grip tightened on the repeating rifle he held in his hand. He was tempted to use it on the three white men. It would be easy to hit all three of them from his perch above. But they were Texas Rangers. He didn't have to be close to know that. All he needed was to hear the snap of that whip to know it was Ranger Jason Brown lashing at the old man. The whip was Brown's specialty.

Selby would gladly kill the man, but life was hard enough for a half-breed who stayed on the right side of the law. Killing three Texas Rangers would mean being on the run the rest of his life, or being hanged if he was caught. No Indian wanted to hang. Hanging meant choking off the soul so that it could not get out of the body, and a man could never enter the afterlife. Brand was Comanche enough to believe that hanging was a very bad way to die. When he died, he wanted his soul to be free to join his ancestors.

Perhaps he could at least stop Jason Brown and the others below. Surely they were killing the old man. Brand prayed his own personal powers were strong, that his medicine was still good. As a younger man he had prayed and fasted for days in order to know the right way to lead his life. He still wore his medicine bag, which contained all his personal fetishes, those sacred items that made him strong and sure, including the clawed feet of a wolf that had given up its spirit to him after it attacked him. Brand had sunk his knife into the wolf, then properly honored the animal afterward, thanking its spirit as he cleaned the body. Now its skin made a fine warm neck wrap in cold weather; and its feet in his medicine bag meant Brand was blessed with the wise ferocity of the wolf spirit.

He turned and went down the back slope to his spotted horse, easing onto the animal's back with an Indian's agility. Some folks said he was more Indian than white. Brand himself had never quite been able to decide which. He had simply lived his life according to what seemed right at the time. It seemed now that men like himself and even the full-bloods were going to have to choose the white man's way in order to survive; but that did not have to mean giving up the Indian spirit.

He supposed he could pass for a white man if he would cut his hair and dress differently, for he had the white man's tall, slim-hipped build, broad shoulders and powerful arms. He had an Indian's high cheekbones, but his skin was dark from the sun more than from natural coloring; and his eyes were green. He had not been able to bring himself to cut his hair. It was another one of those things Indian men just didn't do. Somehow it seemed he would lose his power if he did such a thing. And when it came to dress, buckskin clothing and moccasins were so much more comfortable than white men's itchy shirts and hard boots.

He headed his gelding around rocks and boulders that hid him until he reached the sand below. Then he eased the animal around to where he was in sight of the white men. He raised his rifle and fired into the air, and Jason Brown stood still, his arm in midair.

"Let him go!" Brand ordered in a deep, commanding voice. His white mother had taught him how to speak the white man's tongue. As he rode closer, Jason Brown slowly lowered his arm. Selby recognized not only Brown, but also the two men with him, Jules Webber and Sam Greene.

"You're butting in where you don't belong, breed," the man told Brand.

"You will kill him. He is just an old man," Brand answered boldly, halting his horse a few feet behind the old Indian man. "Cut him down."

"Who are you to give orders to Texas Rangers, Selby?" Sam Greene asked with a sneer.

"Shut up, Greene!" Jason growled, his dark eyes fixed on Brand Selby. "This scum of a breed here can be mean as hell when he wants to be, and you damned well know it." Jason began rolling up the whip. "Cut the old man down."

Brand grinned softly. "You are a wise man, Jason Brown."

"Just patient. I'll get you one way or another some day, Selby—or do I call you Running Wolf? You ever make up your mind which it is?"

"Whatever name suits the moment," Brand answered, his voice cool and unruffled.

"Makes it easy for you, doesn't it, breed?"

Brand held Jason Brown's eyes. "No. It makes life a living hell." He turned his handsome green eyes to the old Indian man, who slumped to the ground as soon as he was cut down from the tree. "What did he do?"

"You know him?" Brown asked.

"He is Many Horses, and he is harmless. What has this big, bad Indian done that you must whip him to death?"

"He stole a calf that belonged to some settlers not far from here. We found him hanging the meat to dry—roasting some of it."

Brand looked down at the old man, then slowly dismounted, keeping an eye on the three white men. He walked closer to Many Horses, keeping his repeating rifle in his right hand. He bent his knees to get closer to the old man, rolling him onto his back and saying something to him in the Comanche tongue. The old man answered in a voice choked with pain. Brand looked up at Jason Brown.

"At his village the People are starving. He was going to take the dried and smoked meat to his daughter and her children. His son-in-law is dead and can no longer provide for his woman. The man had no brothers who would take her in." He rose. "I know the spring hunt was not good for the Comanche. It probably seemed to the old man that the white settlers had so many cattle, they would surely not miss one small one."

"Well, he figured wrong," Jason scowled. "You know the punishment for stealing cattle, Selby. The old man is lucky we just whipped him instead of hanging him."

Brand thought Jason Brown could be a very handsome man if his spirit were not so ugly. Jason was a few inches shorter than Brand, but well built, with dark hair and eyes, and a finely etched face that would look better if the man would just smile more. But Jason Brown seldom smiled, and what Brand hated most about the man was that he was an Indian-hater, with no really valid reason other than believing the white race was somehow superior to the red man. In Brand's estimation, it was very much the other way around.

"And you are lucky I have never told everything I know about you, Brown," Brand answered, his voice low and menacing, his grip tightening on the rifle.

"Take him, Jase," one of the others said. "He won't shoot back. He don't dare shoot at Texas Rangers."

Jason had already paled slightly at Brand's remark. He kept his dark eyes on Brand. "Never underestimate this stinking half-breed," he answered. The man nervously fidgeted with the handle of his whip. "You aren't a scout anymore, Selby. We could kill you right here and claim you were in on the rustling."

"You could. But one of you would die before I went down, maybe two of you. You want to guess who'd be first to take a bullet?"

Their eyes held challengingly, Jason nearly shaking with rage then, the color coming back into his face, only too much color now. "You sonofabitch!"

"You have no reason to harm me," Brand said calmly, enjoying the frustrated look in Jason Brown's eyes. "You wish that you could, but I am not one of your renegades, Brown. You can't even threaten me because I could destroy your career as a Ranger. Now I have even more on you—whipping a defenseless old man. The least you could have done was arrest him and take him in for a judge to decide his punishment; or you could have had him taken to Indian Territory. Rangers have rules, Brown, laws to be followed. You have a way of breaking those laws. If you aren't careful, it's *you* the Rangers will be hunting."

"When it comes to Indians, there *is* no law! It's each man for himself!"

"Not when you belong to the Rangers. You're a disgrace to that badge you wear. You were hired by civilized people who expect *you* to act civilized. Texas is struggling for law and order, especially with statehood just around the corner. I'm not your typical ignorant Indian, Brown. I know what's going on, and lynch mobs and mindless killings are supposed to end!"

"All Texans hate the Comanche! They won't give a damn about this old man!"

"Won't they? Leave right now, Brown, or I'll take this old man into town and show people the kind of justice you deal out."

Brown gripped his whip. "And what do I tell the settlers who lost the calf?"

"I'll pay for it myself at Ranger headquarters in Austin. I have enough."

"Do you now?" Brown sneered the words and backed up to his horse, looping the whip around his saddle horn. "And where did you get the money? *Steal* it?"

Brand straightened more. "I earned it working for a rancher over on the Brazos."

"Who the hell would hire a breed?"

Brand controlled his ire. "People who look at man as he is. I proved my worth and got paid for it."

Brown slowly mounted his horse. "Guess that explains why I haven't seen you around lately. That's just fine with me. You can go back to your Indian-loving boss."

"I've quit the job—saved up enough to get a little piece of my own land—bought a few horses from the man I used to work for. I was on my way to pick them up when I came across the familiar sound of your whip."

Brown scowled, then slowly grinned. "Yes, you know that sound, don't you?" His eyes glittered with hatred. "I'd love to let you hear it again—let you feel it again."

Brand did not flinch. "You would be very sorry this time."

Brown laughed lightly, nervously. "And what's this bullshit about buying horses and settling? You? Brand Selby? Settling like a white man?" He began to laugh, and the other two men joined in the laughter as they, too, mounted up. "And just where is this 'little place' you call home, Selby?"

"Just north of Austin."

Brown's smile faded. "I don't want you anywhere *near* Austin, Selby!" he warned.

"I can settle anywhere I please as long as I obey the laws and mind my own business."

"And why in hell don't you just go back to the Comanche?"

"That's none of your business. It's my life, Brown. Just make sure you stay out of it!"

Brown turned his horse in anger, making a full circle and prancing the animal a little closer to Brand. "And *you* make sure you stay out of Austin!"

"I will go where I damned well please. Now you get out of here and leave the old man to me."

Brown breathed deeply to stay in control. "Go ahead and nurse the worthless old bastard, Selby! I can't see anybody getting shot over an old man who's dying anyway. There will be a better time and place for you and me!"

"I can't wait," Brand said in a low, cool voice.

Brown gave the man one more challenging look, then turned and rode off, Greene and Webber following. Brand watched them cautiously until they were all out of sight, then set his rifle against the cottonwood tree and bent down close to Many Horses.

"I am sorry, old man," he told him. "I wish I would have come upon you sooner. I will help you." He moved an arm under the old man's neck and lifted him slightly, smoothing stiff, gray hair back from his face. "I'll take you back——" He did not bother to finish the sentence. He realized the old man was dead.

Brand just stared at his face for a moment, his eyes tearing and his throat aching. He gently closed the old man's eyes, then hugged him closer, gently rocking him. "Yes, I am sorry," he whispered. He threw back his head, giving out a mourning cry that from a distance sounded like a strange animal calling out.

They were dying, all dying, these last remnants of the Comanche. He had been watching it happen, feeling helpless, sometimes desperate. He had tried to help them by scouting for the Texas Militia, hoping to help ease the People into accepting reservation life. But it had hurt too much to watch the agony on their faces; and he could not help feeling like a traitor when he helped root out the renegades.

"Damned *tejanos*," Brand groaned. "Why must I carry their blood in my veins!" He slowly lowered the body of Many Horses, then turned and retrieved a small hatchet from his supplies to cut some slim branches from the cottonwood tree. "I will make a travois for you, old man," he spoke aloud, deliberately talking to keep from weeping. "I will take you to your daughter so that she can give you a proper burial. And I promise I will take the meat to them and find even more meat for them on the way."

Picking up the horses would have to wait. Mr. Kruger would understand. He was one of the few whites Brand knew who cared anything about the Comanche side of the settling of Texas. Kruger was a fair man—had given Brand a good deal on the horses.

He took a blanket from his gear and walked over to Many Horses, setting his hatchet down for a moment and covering the old Indian. "First I will take you home," he said quietly, his chest aching fiercely. "Then I will go back to the white man's world."

Two

Over the next four days after her arrival, Rachael occupied her time with cleaning, cooking, and mending; and spent her evenings getting reacquainted with her brothers. She was also reawakened to the difficulties of ranch life in a still wild and rugged Texas. After living three years in St. Louis, she had grown accustomed to a more comfortable existence. A woman could purchase anything she needed in St. Louis, could keep up with the latest styles, be a lady in every sense of the word. She could attend theaters and concerts. Doctors were readily available. Streets were bricked, and a woman rode in a carriage instead of on horseback.

Rachael had to grin at the contrast. She had nearly forgotten how hard life could be on a remote Texas ranch, and she respected her mother's memory even more. The woman had never complained when she was alive. She was happy to simply be with her husband and children, no matter what the hardships.

She sat down at the homemade wooden table, looking up at a penciled sketch of her parents drawn by a traveling artist. How beautiful her mother had been, how handsome her father. It hardly seemed possible three years had gone by since she had left Texas with Herm and Sarah Baker and their family. The Bakers had given up trying to make a go of it in Texas. Two of their six children had died, one of them only two months old. Sarah longed to go back to St. Louis, and so they went, taking Rachael with them on the promise to Joe Rivers that his daughter could live with them while she furthered her education.

Thanks to her mother, at sixteen Rachael was excellent at reading and writing, as adept as the formally schooled young people farther east. Emma Rivers had grabbed up every book that became available, either buying them or borrowing them from other settlers, from businessmen in Austin, anyplace she could get a book that might help her children learn more. But it had been hard to get the boys interested, with most of their time spent helping their father on the ranch; so it was Rachael who received most of the teaching, Rachael who had read the whole Bible twice, Rachael who wrote poems for her mother. Rachael would never forget the look of pride in her mother's eyes when she read the poems.

"Never forget that everyone has a right to learn, Rachael," Emma Rivers would tell her daughter. *"My pa chased away the only person who ever came around to teach young ones back in Tennessee. He wouldn't let me learn, but I had a terrible desire inside to read and write better, so I practiced all by myself. Then Pa threw out all my books—said learning wasn't for girls. Don't you let anybody tell you that, Rachael, and don't deny anybody else the chance. I don't care if they're man or woman, black or red or white. You know your pa and I don't judge people that way."*

Rachael's chest pained slightly at the memory. She still carried the old Bible that had belonged to Emma Rivers, and she thought how much happier her mother and father must be now, together at last. No one doubted the love Joe and Emma Rivers had shared.

The door opened and Joshua came inside, removing his hat and wiping sweat from his brow. Rachael glanced at him as though almost startled, his entry interrupting her deep thoughts.

"You look surprised," he said, hanging his hat on a hook.

"I was just thinking."

"'Bout what?"

"Just things—Mother, Father, things Mother used to tell me."

Joshua pulled out a chair and sat down. "Pa used to talk about you every night at the supper table, Rachael," he told her gently. "And when your letters came, he had me read them to him over and over. He never was real good at reading, you know. Anyway, he was so proud of you." He reached out and put a hand over her own. "Is there anything of Pa's that you want to keep? You can have anything you want."

Rachael shrugged. "Maybe his doeskin jacket—the one on the wall there that Mother sewed for him."

Joshua glanced at the jacket and its shiny elbows. "That old thing? You sure?"

"Yes." She continued to stare at her lap. "I put it around me earlier this morning, and it was like…" Her voice began to choke. "Like having Father hug me tight, having his… his protection, his love still with me. And it was like he was right here, Josh, right here beside me."

Joshua squeezed her hand. "I think I understand." He sighed deeply, rising. "You take it then. And I hate to say it, seeing as how we all enjoy your housekeeping and cooking and all, but you should go back to Austin pretty soon, Rachael. Every extra day you're here is another day of danger, not just for you but for all of us. It's better the Comanche don't see a woman around here."

"Oh, Josh, you're talking like the Indian-hating settlers who don't know one thing about Indians. You've been around Jason Brown too much, I think." Rachael rose and wiped at her eyes, taking the jacket from its hook and hugging it against her chest. She watched Joshua pick up the soup ladle and dip it in fresh chicken soup simmering on the cookstove. "Stay out of that soup. It isn't done yet."

Josh sipped some and smacked his lips. "Tastes done to me. Matt and Luke will like this." He put down the ladle and turned. "And don't be putting down Jason Brown. He's been out there, Rachel—seen things beyond description. You just don't know."

"I told you what I think of Jason Brown."

"Come on, Rachael. Give him a chance. It's been three years. Maybe you'll see he's different from what you remember when you were only sixteen. I reckon a nineteen-year-old woman looks at men different than a sixteen-year-old girl."

Rachael blushed slightly and carried the jacket over to the cot in the corner of room on which she had been sleeping. "Perhaps."

Joshua grinned. "Nobody special back in St. Louis?"

She laid the jacket on the bed. "Nobody special. I saw a

couple of young men, but none of them ever gave me that special feeling Mother said I'd feel when the right man came along." She smiled, sadly staring at the jacket. "She used to say she'd never forget how she felt the first time she saw Father, how she just knew she was supposed to belong to him. Even after all the years they were together, every time she talked about when she first fell in love with him, her eyes would shine just a certain way." She moved her own eyes to Joshua. "I'll never forget that look." She sighed deeply and folded her arms. "What about you, Josh? This place needs a woman. You're twenty years old."

He shrugged. "I figure me and Matt and Luke will work the Double 'R' into an even bigger spread, get to where we can hire more men. I've got no time to look for a wife, and when I do, I want to be a man of property, a man who can support her right, and I want there to be enough men on this place that she'll be safe."

Rachael nodded. "I can understand that. I hope all of us end up as happy as Mother and Father were. I guess to be loved like that is the most important thing in the whole world."

Joshua ran a hand through his sandy hair. "I guess."

There came the sound of horses' hooves then, and the mood quickly changed as Joshua ran to the door, opening it and grabbing a rifle that sat just outside. "Stay inside," he called to her, pulling back the hammer of the rifle and stepping off the porch.

"Joshua!" someone called out. Three men were riding toward the house.

"Jason! It's Jason Brown," Joshua told Rachael, setting his rifle aside. "I'll be damned! What great timing. Now you'll have safe escort back to Austin."

Rachael's heart fell a little. She had no desire to ride all the way back to Austin with Jason Brown. She stepped into the open doorway to watch as Joshua walked out to greet the three men. Matt and Luke rode in from another direction.

"It's Jason," Rachael heard Matt call to Luke. "Hey, Jason! We thought you were bandits come to steal away our sister."

They were all bunched together then, greeting one another,

shaking hands. "Your sister?" Jason asked. "She's back?"

Rachael quickly stepped back from the doorway so Jason would not catch her looking.

"Sure is. And wait 'til you see her!" Luke bragged. "Ain't a prettier woman this side of the Mississippi."

"I have no doubt about that," Jason answered with a laugh.

Rachael felt like hitting Luke for talking about her as though she had come back just for Jason Brown. He was the last reason she had returned. She hurried into the bedroom that had once belonged to her mother and father, patting the sides of her hair in the mirror and smoothing her skirt, yet wondering why she bothered. What did she care what Jason Brown thought of how she looked? She chided herself for the primping and walked back into the main room just as Jason and Joshua came inside.

"Rachael, you remember Jason," Joshua told her.

Rachael nodded, holding Jason Brown's eyes as the man slowly removed his hat. She thought him more handsome than she had remembered, but seeing him again did not bring that "special feeling" she had talked about moments earlier with her brother. She blushed, not out of any delight in seeing Jason, but rather the uncomfortable feeling he gave her as his dark eyes moved over her as though she stood before him naked.

"Well, I'll be…" Jason stepped a little closer, setting his hat on the table. "Your brother was right. There isn't a woman in all of Texas any prettier. Hello, Rachael."

She swallowed. How could she be friendly and yet make sure this man realized she had not returned for him? "Hello, Jason. You came back just in time. I need an escort into Austin, where I'll be teaching. That's why I came back, to keep my promise to my mother, and to see Father, of course."

Jason nodded. "Sorry your pa died before you got here. That must have been real hard on you."

She rubbed her hands nervously against the skirt of her dress. "Yes. Thank you for your concern." How she wished he would stop looking at her that way, as though he would like to own her. How did a woman turn away men like this without being rude? And yet she wondered if she was foolish to want to turn him away? He was indeed handsome and well built, and a capable man. He had to be in his late twenties already, maybe thirty, certainly of a marrying age. But there was something about him, an abstract quality that made her slightly afraid of him. Yes. That was what she remembered now. She had always been a little bit afraid of Jason Brown. He lacked that certain warmth that would make another person feel comfortable around him.

"Rachael, I can't say how happy I am to see you're back," he was saying. His eyes dropped for a moment to her full bosom. "And I have to say you're even more beautiful than I remembered."

She backed away slightly. "Thank you, Jason." She walked to the stove to stir the soup. "Are you and your men hungry? I'll have lunch ready soon. You're welcome to eat with us."

Jason stared at her as though transfixed. "We'd like that just fine, Rachael. And I'd be honored to accompany you back to Austin."

She refused to look at him as she stirred the soup. "I would appreciate it."

"We'll go in the morning if that isn't too soon for you. My men and I have been out a long time, and we're anxious to get back. Since your pa's death, I've made it a point to check on Josh and the boys now and again, what with Comanche and outlaws always on the prowl. That's why we came by."

"That's nice of you, Jason." Rachael set the ladle aside and finally met his eyes again. "I wish you could talk Josh into coming into town and giving up this place."

"Forget it, sis," Joshua told her with a grin. "Jason, I'll go finish up some chores and we'll help your men unsaddle and brush down the horses. That will leave you some time to talk to Rachael."

Jason looked at Joshua and gave him a wink. "Much obliged, Josh."

Joshua left, and Rachael could not help the anger she felt at his leaving her alone with this man. He was perfectly aware she had no desire to be alone with him at all. She turned back to the soup, adding some salt. "So, you've gone from the Militia to a

Ranger now," she commented.

"It's really about the same, just a little more organized. Somebody has to keep the law around here."

"I agree."

Jason ran a hand through his hair, suddenly realizing he needed a bath and a shave, and that his clothes were dusty. "I, uh, I'm sorry for the way I look. You know how it is out there on the plains."

Rachael stirred the soup absently. "It's all right, Jason. Please, sit down. Don't worry about your appearance. I'm from Texas too, you know. This has to be one of the hardest places in the country for a man to stay clean."

He brushed at the front of his shirt and ran his hands through his hair again. "Yeah." He pulled out a chair and sat down. Rachael set down the ladle and took a chair around the corner of the table from Jason.

"You, uh, you didn't get yourself hitched or anything like that, did you?" Jason asked her. "A man would be crazy to let you get away from him if there was any hope—"

"No, Jason," she answered before he could finish. "I'm still unmarried. But getting 'hitched' as you put it is not so important to me. I came back to teach, and to see my family, of course."

"How about me? Didn't you want to see me again, Rachael?"

There was such hope in his tired eyes that she didn't have the heart to tell him no. "As a friend. Yes. I thought about you."

He grinned, a handsome smile; but still the warmth was not there, and the look of possessiveness in his eyes still made her uneasy. He reached out and took her hand, but his own hand was cool and she could not resist the impulse to pull hers away immediately. He seemed to ignore the gesture. "I hope you'll let me call on you, Rachael, after you get settled in Austin."

She rose, getting down some soup bowls. "We'll see, Jason."

He watched her from behind, picturing how she must look naked, her breasts full and ripe for picking; her bottom round and firm; her golden hair undone and falling around her bare shoulders; her eyes closed in ecstasy as he took her. "Where will you be staying?" he asked aloud.

"At Lacy Reed's boardinghouse. I asked Lacy to hold a room for me."

"And you're *really* going to teach?"

Rachael caught the chauvinistic tone in the statement. *"Really,"* she answered with emphasis. "I'm as qualified as any man, and I love teaching."

Jason shrugged, rising from the table. "I don't doubt you are. It just seems like kind of a waste. Someone as pretty as you ought to be married and keeping her own house, having babies."

Rachael sighed impatiently. "There is plenty of time for those things. Right now I just want to teach." She walked back to the stove, stirring the soup angrily. "You had better go and wash for lunch, Jason."

He stared at her a moment longer, a sly grin on his face. "Still stubborn and independent, I see." He turned and walked to the door. "I really am sorry about your pa, Rachael. He was a good man. We went around a few times over the subject of Indians, but he was a good man."

Rachael faced him, thinking how different Jason Brown was from her father. "Yes, he certainly was," she answered. She turned away again. "I'll be ready to go in the morning," she added curtly.

Jason once more drank in her voluptuous beauty before he turned and left. Rachael walked to a window to watch him, struggling to find something about Jason that she could like, frustrated that she could not even name what it was about him that made her so uncomfortable. She watched as the men gathered at a stone well just outside the front of the house, pouring water from a bucket into wash pans that sat around the edge of the well.

"Run into much trouble out there this time, Jason?" Joshua was asking the man.

Jason rolled up the sleeves of his shirt. "Not too much. Came across an old Indian man who stole a calf from some settlers."

"You arrest him?" Luke asked the man, looking at Jason as though the man were some kind of hero.

"No. Wasn't worth it. We took care of it. He won't steal any more cattle."

Rachael felt an odd dread. How had they taken care of it? What had they done to the old man? There was a smell of cruelty about Jason Brown, a hardness that made her want to keep her distance.

"You think the breed will give anybody any trouble, Jase?" Jules Webber asked then. The man splashed water over his face.

"Hard to say about that one."

"Who are you talking about?" Joshua asked.

"A half-breed—used to scout for the Militia. I rode with him a time or two. Ornery as a wounded bear, that one. Brand Selby is his name. We had a little run-in with him. He told us he's settling north of Austin." Jason shook his head. "Only thing worse than a full-blood is a half-blood," he added. "Now there's one man to keep your sister away from."

"All she needs is a husband who is also a Ranger," Joshua joked.

Both men laughed lightly, and Rachael wished her brother would be more understanding of how she felt about Jason. She whirled and walked back to the stove, contemplating how delightful it would be to take Jason and Joshua's bowls of soup and dump the broth right over their heads.

"I don't need a husband of *any* kind," she muttered.

"You know where to find me when you come to town," Rachael told Joshua. She hugged him tightly, then turned to her two younger brothers, hugging them each. "You be good boys and help Joshua like Father would want you to do," she told them. "And be very careful. Watch out for yourselves."

"We will, Rachael," Matt told her. "Thanks for everything."

"I'll come back in a few weeks to put up some preserves for you like Mother used to do. Soon as the fruit and vegetables are ripe, I'll do some canning for you."

"Thanks, Rachael," Luke told her. "I miss that good jelly you used to make."

She stepped back to look her brothers over. In the short

time they had been reunited they had become as close as they had all been when Rachael first left home; closer, it seemed, now that their parents were gone.

"Once you get to town, you stay close," Joshua warned her. "Don't go wandering off alone."

"I won't," Rachael promised.

Rachael reached up to the horn of her saddle, putting a foot in the stirrup and swinging up into the saddle, then fidgeted with her skirt and petticoats to be sure her legs were covered. Jason Brown watched her mount up.

"You sure you wouldn't rather take a wagon, Rachael?" he said.

She looked at him with an air of pride. "Father taught me to ride when I could barely walk. Besides, riding is faster. This way we can make it by nightfall." She took a last look at her brothers—quiet and shy Matthew with his tousled blond hair; energetic and talkative Luke, his hair as dark as Matthew's was light; and Joshua, a man now.

"Good-bye," she told them, her eyes tearing. "I love you."

"Bye, Rachael," Luke answered. Joshua and Matt added their good-byes and Rachael turned her horse. She rode off beside Jason, the other two Rangers following behind, leading a pack horse with Rachael's baggage. Rachael thought how it seemed that lately her life was just a series of good-byes. She had an uneasy feeling, and she looked back once more at her three brothers, a terrible sadness moving through her chest.

"They'll be fine," Jason said.

She turned to look at him, thinking perhaps this feeling was due to having to ride with Jason all the way back to Austin.

"I hope so. I feel so guilty leaving them behind."

"It's what Josh wants. My men and I will ride back out in a few days and return the horses. So I'll be checking on them again."

Jason looked ahead, and Rachael took a moment to study the stern lines of his handsome face, the square jaw and proud nose. Today he was clean and shaved. "I appreciate your keeping an eye on them," she told him.

"You told me that yesterday." He turned to look at her. "I only do it because they're your brothers, Rachael."

Rachael caught the implication of his statement. "I know," she answered. "Jason, I have only been back a few days, and I haven't even started teaching yet. I know what you're trying to say. Just give me some time to get settled in and get used to being back in Texas."

He looked straight ahead again. "Are you glad to be back? You won't go back to St. Louis, will you?"

"I don't think so, at least not as long as Josh and the boys are here. I feel responsible to stay near them now that Father is gone."

"Good. But I wish you would reconsider teaching. It just doesn't seem right, a woman teaching school."

Rachael bristled. "I am doing what my mother would want me to do. There is no reason why a woman can't teach school. And you really don't have any right telling me what to do."

Jason looked over at her again, a possessive look in his eyes. "Maybe not. Then again maybe I do. You'll be all alone in Austin. *Somebody* has to look out for your best interest, and I happen to care about you, very much."

The remark seemed sincere, but Rachael felt frustrated, her feelings torn between anger and a feeling of obligation to be nicer to him.

"I'm sorry, Jason. I'm going through a lot of grief and a lot of changes to my life right now. I'm easily upset. But if you truly care about me you should understand how important teaching is to me."

"All right. All right. I give up! I won't bring it up again."

Jason rode forward, keeping his promise and saying nothing more about the subject. They rode on for several miles. A few times they dismounted and walked with the animals to ease their load, finally finding a shady grove of cottonwood trees near the Colorado River where they could stop to eat and rest the horses. Webber and Greene made a small fire and began to heat some beans and some biscuits Rachael had made just that morning. Jason insisted Rachael sit in the shade and do nothing.

"Me and my men are used to fending for ourselves on the trail," he told her. "You aren't along to be a cook. You're our guest."

Rachael glanced at the two men with Jason. She didn't like either one of them, but she told herself she was being too critical. Later, some of her apprehension diminished as she ate with them. They talked about how much Austin was growing and changing, just like all of Texas was changing. Soon it would be a state, and Austin was bound to be chosen as the capital. It had been the capital of the Republic off and on ever since it was first built for just that purpose. But opposing factions had wanted Washington-on-the Brazos or Houston to become the capital.

"It will be Austin," Jason said with no doubt in his voice. "No other city in Texas is prettier, nor planned as carefully as Austin has been. Houston turns into a swamp every spring, and it's too disorganized, too dirty, and too full of disease. Here it's clean, high, and dry."

"Except for being closer to the damned Comanche," Webber said.

"We can take care of the Comanche," Jason answered, a brittle ring to his voice. "We've done it before."

Sam Greene grinned. "Yeah, I reckon we have." He glanced at Rachael, looking her over. Both Webber and Greene seemed to prefer their unkempt look and had not bothered to clean up while at the Double "R."

"I think I'll go the river and wash my face," Rachael told Jason. "I'm so hot."

"Go ahead. Then we'll all rest a few minutes and be on our way."

Rachael rose, glad to walk away from them. Jason and his men watched her walk several yards down a bank to the river's edge.

"She ever going to marry you, Jase?" Greene asked.

Jason tore his eyes from her and looked back at his men. "Maybe."

Jules Webber sniffed. "Far as I'm concerned, you'd be

better off sellin' her to the Comancheros. That is one beautiful woman. She'd bring a pretty price."

"Shut up, Webber! I care about her."

"Maybe so. But it don't appear to me she cares much about you. After a while you're gonna get tired of her turnin' her nose up at you. Maybe then you'll see I'm right."

"Eat your damned bisquits and keep your mouth shut."

Rachael knelt at the water's edge, unaware of the conversation. She put her hands into the water, scooping some of it up and splashing it over her face. She had forgotten how hot it could get in this land, and how brutal. That was what Texas could be. But she was certain the brutality of men could be much worse than the brutality of the land, and she could not help wondering how brutal Jason and his men could be.

She splashed her face once more, then rose, about to turn, when she realized she was being watched. She stood frozen, her heart pounding as a man rode into view just on the other side of the river. She stared at him in awe, wondering why on earth she did not call out to Jason and his men. The sound of the rushing river drowned out the noise of the intruder's horse, yet she guessed he could probably move about without making any noise at all, for he was Indian! At least he looked Indian in dress, sitting on a painted horse, wearing buckskins, his hair hanging long. But it was not as black as Indian hair, and his eyes—they were green. He was an utterly beautiful man, and Rachael was shocked to realize she had even thought such a thing. His build was magnificent, his face perfectly etched, his whole demeanor proud and unafraid. He sported several weapons, and she knew she should be afraid, yet somehow she was not.

For a brief moment their eyes held; Rachael felt a wave of warmth she had never known before rushing through her body. She was amazed to find herself wondering if this was the unexpected feeling her mother had told her about. Surely not! She was staring at a complete stranger, an Indian, no less! Or was he? She had never seen a green-eyed Indian. Was he of mixed blood then? A "breed" as Jason called them with that ugly sneer in his voice? Was this the man Jason had talked about running into? Was he dangerous?

He broke his gaze to look past her, eyeing the three unaware Rangers. He smiled lightly then as his eyes moved back to her own, as though he knew he was playing a fine joke on the Rangers. Look how close he had come to the white woman they were supposed to be protecting. He could carry her off if he wanted, and they would not even know it! Yet she knew he would not do it; and somehow he knew she wouldn't call out.

Brand Selby was just as awed as Rachael. He stared at the most beautiful white woman he had ever seen. He had come to the river to water his horse, and there she was, splashing water on her face. He wondered who she was, what she was doing with the hated Jason Brown. He gave her a nod and turned his horse, riding off. He had delivered old Many Horses. He would go to Oscar Kruger's ranch now and get the horses he had purchased. But he would not sleep easily this night—not after setting eyes on the beautiful white woman with the golden hair.

Rachel stared after the stranger as he disappeared over a rise. It was several more seconds before she found her feet again. She put a hand to her throat, still amazed that she had not screamed for Jason, then turned and slowly walked back to the camp, sitting down in the shade. Jason looked over at her.

"Everything all right?" he asked.

She looked at him and nodded, then leaned against the tree and closed her eyes. She pictured the man she had just seen, realizing then how much he resembled her own father in build and looks. Joe Rivers had worn buckskins most of the time himself, and he was tall and broad like the stranger she had just seen. She peered around the tree trunk and looked down at the place where she had just been, wondering if the man had been some kind of vision or if he had really been there. Maybe the Texas heat was getting to her. For some reason she did not want to tell Jason about what she had just seen, even though it certainly seemed the thing to do.

She leaned back and closed her eyes again, unable to erase her vision of the green-eyed Indian on the painted horse.

Three

Rachael watched nervously as children filtered into the tiny schoolhouse one by one. She had been settled at Lacy's boardinghouse only three days, and after only one meeting with the circuit teacher, Mr. Dreyfuss, Rachael was left on her own.

Her emotions jumped from excitement to apprehension. This was her first true teaching assignment. She had lain half-awake all night, her thoughts wandering from how she would conduct her first day of teaching to what she should do about Jason, who had come to call on her every day since their arrival. She had also thought about the stranger at the river.

More and more children arrived, but before she could get started with lessons several adults, mostly women, made an appearance at the doorway, all eyes scrutinizing Rachael carefully.

Rachael suspected the purpose of their visit. She felt her cheeks burning as she faced them squarely, holding her head high in a display of poise and confidence.

"Can I help you?" she asked.

"I am Harriet Miller," replied a tall, robust woman dressed far too formally for a visit to the simple school-house. It was obvious the woman was wealthy and liked to flaunt the fact. "We just wanted to meet the new school-teacher."

The women's eyes showed their doubt as they moved over Rachael.

"Well, you're looking at her," Rachael answered. She told the children to be seated on benches and moved around the desk. They all obeyed, watching the pretty new teacher with wide, eager eyes. In the meanwhile Rachael approached the adults at the back of the room. "I am Rachael Rivers." She put out her hand, a friendly smile on her face. Harriet Miller could not help but return the gesture.

"I'm from the Austin area, you know," Rachael told them, scanning the small group and wearing a pleasant smile. "I studied for three years in St. Louis and passed all the exams that qualify me to teach. I truly appreciate your giving me this chance. I look forward to teaching here. It was always my mother's dream that I would be able to further my education and put it to use like this. She was denied the education she always wished she could have. I'm just sorry she died before she could see me fulfill her dreams for me."

Mrs. Miller nodded. "Yes, how sad. Some of those here with me knew your parents. We know quite a bit about you, both through knowing your family and through the résumé you submitted to Mr. Dreyfuss." A faint smile finally moved over the woman's lips. "We are the committee who agreed with Mr. Dreyfuss to give a woman teacher a chance, mostly because you are from Austin. Austin is a fast-growing city, you know, soon to be the capital of Texas. We like to think we are a forward-moving city, willing to try new ideas. We've come to welcome you. Do you mind if we observe you for a while?"

Rachael swallowed back a nervous dread. These people were doubting her ability. Her stubborn determination to prove herself gave her the courage she needed.

"Be my guest," she answered.

Mrs. Miller finally smiled fully. "Thank you." The woman turned and introduced the rest of those with her, all of them the more prominent people of Austin, businessmen and wives of businessmen.

After a few exchanges, Rachael quickly got the children in order and recorded all their names and ages. She passed a book around, asking each one to read from it.

Soon Rachael had the children organized into groups according to their learning abilities, each group participating in learning games. Even the older, more skeptical children were soon involved.

Rachael's heart swelled with the satisfaction of watching them. Harriet Miller moved toward the desk while all the children sat quietly reading, some of the smaller ones sitting in a corner making words with big, wooden blocks on which Rachael had painted letters.

"It's obvious the children like you very much," Mrs. Miller told her in a lowered voice. "I think we've seen enough for today." The woman put out her hand and Rachael took it. "We think you'll do just fine, Miss Rivers."

"Thank you," Rachael answered.

"I plan to have a formal get-together at my home soon where I would like more of my friends to meet you. I'll let you know when it will be. Welcome back to Austin."

Rachael breathed a sigh of relief. "That's very nice of you, Mrs. Miller."

The woman nodded and paraded out of the schoolroom, followed by the other adults. Rachael sank into the chair behind her desk, sighing deeply. She felt as though she had just passed the most rigorous exam of any she had ever taken. She sat there a moment, composing herself, then rose and walked to a window to look out at the sky.

Are you watching. Mother? she thought. She started to turn when she caught sight of a familiar figure. He was riding away through a stand of trees toward the back of the schoolhouse, a big man wearing buckskins, his dark hair hanging nearly to his waist from beneath a leather hat. Rachael frowned, watching him curiously, almost certain it was the Indian she had seen at the river.

A chill moved down her spine and she turned away. Calling the class to attention, she struggled to put what she had just seen out of her mind. But she could not help wondering what the Indian had been doing behind the school-house.

Rachael set down her cup of coffee, watching Lacy Reed knead some bread dough. The boardinghouse was quiet, the neat, two-story frame house empty except for Lacy and Rachael.

"My husband always liked to have people around. We had an even bigger house in New Orleans," Lacy was telling Rachael.

"For some reason we never could have children, so we made up for it by taking in people. Then Bob got the itch to come to Texas. Lord knows if I had known he was going to die in this godforsaken place, I never would have let him come." Her voice choked a little and her eyes teared, even though her husband had been dead for four years. "At any rate, I haven't had the heart to go back to Louisiana without him," she continued, breaking off some dough and dropping it into a bread pan. "He built this place and I just can't bring myself to leave it."

The woman moved her eyes to Rachael. Her eyes were still a bright blue, but surrounded by wrinkles. Rachael could see that Lacy was once a pretty woman, and her auburn hair was still thick, pulled up into a huge bun at the top of her head and showing just a little gray at the temples. The woman was tiny but solid, with a large bosom and strong-looking arms. She broke off another piece of dough with veined, wrinkled hands, and Rachael wondered how old she was. She guessed perhaps fifty.

"Oh, your mother would be so proud to see you now, Rachael," the woman was saying. "I remember her, even though Bob and I had only been here a few months when she died. We felt so bad for your pa. Everybody could see what a broken man he was after that. I expect he's a lot happier now." She dropped more dough into another pan. "I'm so glad you decided to stay in town. I'm real happy to be able to give you a room, honey. If there's anything you need, you just let me know."

"Thank you, Lacy." Rachael rose and poured herself more coffee. She felt comfortable with Lacy, felt she could confide in her, especially when they talked together in the big, warm kitchen, where Rachael often volunteered to help with cooking.

The other two boarders were men—Stewart Glass, a banker from the East staying only a few weeks to set up a new branch in Austin; and Bert Peters, a widowed settler who had sold his land and had come to town to work. The boarders' rooms were upstairs in the big, rambling house, while downstairs was a parlor, a dining room where the boarders all ate together and a library. Lacy slept in a small room behind the kitchen.

"Do you want me to cut the noodles for drying?" Rachael

asked, returning to the table with her coffee.

"Why, that would be real nice of you, honey," Lacy answered. She moved a huge glass bowl over toward Rachael, in which a warm, rising ball of dough sat waiting to be rolled flat and cut into noodles and dumplings. "How is the teaching going? You getting along with Mr. Dreyfuss? It's been nearly two weeks already."

"I hardly ever see Mr. Dreyfuss. He's usually out riding circuit. But he says he may have to stop for a while. There are too many renegades out there in the hills." Rachael set down her cup and put on an apron. "I think most of the parents have finally accepted me," she continued. "And Mr. Dreyfuss seems very happy to have me. The biggest problem is we never seem to have enough supplies and books."

Lacy chuckled. "That's Texas for you. Always short on supplies from the East."

Rachael pulled away some dough and dropped it onto the floured table, picking up a rolling pin. She thought again about the stranger she had seen across the river and again behind the school. She had never told anyone, but the memory of his face remained vivid, always there, especially at night when she tried to go to sleep. She turned the dough so that both sides were floured, then took a deep breath before asking Lacy her next question.

"Lacy," she said then. "I heard Jason talking about a half-breed who was supposedly settled north of town—I think his name was Brand something-or-other—Jason didn't have much good to say about him. Have you ever heard of him?"

"Oh, sure I have. Selby is his last name. I even saw him once, when I took old Betsy over to the livery for new shoes. There he was, standing just inside waiting for his own horse to get shod. Scared me at first—he's a big one, that man. I didn't even know right away who he was, not 'til Stu Bates, the livery owner, told me later. I just thought some Indian was standing there, and I was afraid to look at him again. But Stu, he didn't seem concerned, so I figured I didn't need to be either. I waited, watching Stu shoe that pretty, painted Appaloosa, while he just stood there real quiet like, saying nothing. Finally I couldn't resist glancing at him again, and you know what he did?"

Rachael stopped rolling the dough, moving her eyes to meet Lacy's. Lacy stood with a wad of dough in her hands. "That man smiled at me, and was I surprised—not just because he smiled, but because I realized then he wasn't any full-blood Indian. No full-blood looks like that, let me tell you. It might be sinful for me to say it, Rachael, but that man was downright handsome, and he had green eyes. I was so surprised by those green eyes, I guess it showed on my face and that's why he smiled. I knew by those eyes and his hair being brown and not black that he wasn't any ordinary Indian, and when he smiled..." The woman shook her head. "Well, I'll tell you, I felt things that a woman my age shouldn't feel. I'd never tell that to anybody else, especially with him being a half-blood. Most folks consider that the worst kind of race there is—the ones who don't really belong to one world or the other. And they say men like that can't be trusted— civilized one minute, wild as a polecat the next."

Rachael smiled to herself, feeling again the pleasant warmth deep inside at Lacy's description of Brand Selby. She would not forget the name after this. Brand Selby. It was a nice name. "What do you know about him?" she asked the woman then.

Lacy frowned, giving Rachael a cautious look. "Why are you asking, young lady?"

Rachael smiled outwardly, flattening the dough a little more, then picking up a knife to cut it. "I think I saw him once, Lacy. I didn't speak to him, but I saw him."

"Where?" Lacy wiped her hands on a towel, looking a little worried.

"On my way here with Jason. I was washing by the river and he just appeared without making a sound. It was the strangest thing that has ever happened to me." She put down the knife and met the woman's eyes. "For some reason I didn't call out to Jason. I just stared at him, and he stared back at me. What surprised me most was I wasn't even afraid."

"Hmmm." Lacy folded her arms. "I reckon it's a good thing you didn't call out. Jason Brown's got less use for half-breeds than he has for full-bloods. And there's some rumor about bad blood between them two, but I don't know what it's about."

Rachael returned to cutting the dough. "What do you think of Jason, Lacy?"

Lacy shrugged, picking up two pans of bread and turning to the stove. "He's a handsome man, that's for sure."

"I'm not talking about his looks."

Lacy opened the oven door and shoved the bread inside, then opened the wood-burning box beside it and added some more wood. Both women were already getting too warm from baking on what was going to be a very warm day. It was still early morning, and a day of no school, so Rachael had decided to get up early and help with the baking.

Lacy turned to face the younger woman, putting her hands on her hips. "I don't think I like him much," she told Rachael. "I know he's been coming here to see you, Rachael, but there's something about that man that gives me the shivers. And I have a feeling by the way he talks about Indians that he abuses the use of that badge he wears."

Rachael sighed, frowning. "I feel the same way. But he's so persistent, Lacy, and he really does care for me. Sometimes I think I'm crazy to not be able to think of him in a serious way. He's handsome, dependable, protective, capable. He's never done anything to frighten me, and yet sometimes I actually *am* afraid of him. Isn't that silly?"

"No. It's a woman's instinct. There's nothing wrong with that. You'll never go wrong if you follow your instincts. And don't ever do something for somebody because you feel like you owe it to them. Just because that man has a yen for you doesn't mean you owe him a thing. Besides, I don't doubt most of the eligible men in this town have a yen for you, as well as a lot of the married ones!"

Rachael blushed and smiled, and Lacy laughed lightly. "I don't mean to tell you your business, honey, but just be careful. You came back here to teach and to be near your brothers. That's enough for now. And you remember that Jason Brown can't stop you from seeing somebody else if you've got a mind to."

Rachael shrugged. "There really isn't anyone in particular I care to see."

Lacy nodded slowly, studying the girl as Rachael returned to cutting the noodles. "You sure about that?" she asked then.

Rachael looked at her in surprise. "Yes. What do you mean?"

The woman walked back to the table, greasing two more bread pans. "I mean you dropped the subject of Brand Selby kind of quick like. I didn't think we were through talking about him. You never said how you felt when you saw him—I mean, how you really felt. All you said is you weren't afraid of him."

Rachael shrugged. "What else do you want me to say? I saw a stranger on the other side of the river who was very interesting, to say the least. But we didn't speak or anything. I was just wondering if it could be the same man. After you described this Brand Selby, I realized it had to be him."

"And you haven't been able to get him off your mind ever since, right?"

Rachael blushed again, her hands suddenly feeling clammy. "I wouldn't say that. But I think I saw him again, riding away from behind the schoolhouse. That was the first day I taught. I've seen no sign of him since."

Lacy frowned. "Well, it's just as well. Remember he's a half-breed. Folks don't say what they say about half-breeds without things happening to make them believe that way. There have been half-breeds who proved to be worse than their full-blood brothers. And because they live in both worlds, they often betray one for the other. You never know if a man like that is going to be white or Indian."

"Lacy Reed, now you're talking like most other people around here. I didn't think you judged people that way."

"I don't. I'm just telling you how things are, Rachael. You can't judge anybody until you know them, and it's not likely you'll ever get to know that one. He doesn't often come to town, and even when he does, he knows better than to be caught dead talking to a white woman. Men like that get themselves hanged real fast for such things."

"Well, that just isn't right. He's a man—just a man—not a

half-breed. It's terrible to brand people that way. If he wants to talk to someone, he has the right to do it."

Lacy eyed her warily. "Let me warn you, Rachael, to get that one off your mind right now. You give him the time of day, and you'll be opening a kettle of trouble—and most of the trouble will come to that pour soul, not to you. This town would come down on him like the side of a mountain, and Jason Brown would send the first boulder tumbling."

"Jason Brown doesn't run my life." Rachael's eyes burned with a sudden feeling of sadness, her heart racing with a need to defend the stranger she didn't even know.

"Well, I'm not telling you what to do with your life, either, honey. I didn't mean it that way. I just care a lot about you, and I want you to learn to be careful, to think things through."

Rachael toyed with a piece of dough in her fingers. "I know." She met the woman's eyes. "And you were right. I haven't been able to forget about him, and I don't know what to do about it."

Lacy patted her arm. "Don't do anything. Just give it time. You're just beginning to get settled in here, and that doggone Jason Brown has you all upset with his pestering ways. You want me to turn him away the next time he comes calling?"

Rachael smiled sadly. "No. It's my problem, not yours. I'll just have to find a way to gently turn him away myself. He'll be going out on another patrol soon, and then I'll have some free time to think. He's not a bad person, Lacy; at least I don't think he is. But I just don't have that... that feeling for him that my mother always told me I would feel when I saw the man I knew I'd want to spend my life with. Do you know what I mean?"

"I know exactly what you mean. I had that feeling with my Bob." The woman returned to her end of the table, pulling apart some more dough. "I agree Jason is handsome, and he seems to be a good man—dependable and all that. But it's like your ma told you, honey. You've got to have that special feeling if you're going to be happy being a man's wife. I can't imagine anything worse than going to bed with a man I don't love."

"Lacy!" Rachael reddened deeply, cutting at the dough and unable to meet the woman's eyes.

Lacy chuckled. "That's all your mother was trying to tell you, honey. When you give yourself to a man you've got to feel good about him. You've got to want him same as he wants you, and there's nothing wrong or sinful about it. It's a natural thing, and it's good and beautiful. That's why it's so important he's the right man."

Rachael nodded, taking out some more dough. "I think I know what you mean." How, she wished she could forget about Brand Selby. "Don't ever tell anyone what I told you about seeing Brand Selby. Not everyone would understand."

"I won't tell anyone. You just remember I'm here, honey, anytime. You can tell me anything and I'll try to help and understand."

Rachael smiled softly. "Thanks, Lacy." She wanted to know more about Brand Selby—which one of his parents was white? Was he once really a scout for the militia? Had he ever lived with the Comanche? But asking questions would mean she was interested, and she must never, never be interested. She would not bring up the subject again. Besides, Jason was coming to see her this evening. She had to think about Jason, decide how she felt about him, what to tell him.

Jason followed Rachael into the parlor, watching the sway of her skirts, envisioning the body that walked beneath them. He wondered how much longer he could patiently wait for her to show some warmth and desire for him. He had seen her often over the past couple of weeks, had accompanied her while she shopped, dined with her, visited her often here at the boardinghouse. But she still treated him as a casual friend and nothing more.

"Lacy is bringing in some tea," she said and turned, watching him with the blue eyes that stirred his insides. If any woman was perfectly shaped and exquisitely beautiful, it was Rachael Rivers. She wore a dress today as blue as her eyes, and her long, golden hair hung loose, brushed back off her face and fastened with combs at the sides. She smiled, sitting down on a gold brocade settee and motioning for him to sit down beside her. "How long will you be gone?" she asked.

"It's hard to say. Could be a month, maybe more. Texas is big country, with too few men to keep order."

"I sometimes wonder how it can be done at all. It's good that there are men like you who are willing to go out and try to bring at least some sense of law and order."

He read a hint of admiration in her eyes, then wondered if it was only wishful thinking. "Will you miss me, Rachael?"

She reddened slightly, looking at her lap. "Of course. You've kept me occupied since I've been back—you and the teaching. It has helped me get used to being back here. The only problem is that after you leave, school will soon end. It's getting to be that time of year when children are needed at home to help with the planting and such, and it's too hot to expect children to sit still in one little schoolroom."

"Rachael, you know what I mean. Will you *really* miss me?" He reached out and took one of her hands. "The way I'll miss you—long for you—dream about you?"

"Jason, don't."

He sighed deeply, releasing her hand and rising. "What the hell—" He stopped mid-sentence as Lacy came in with a tray of tea.

"Hello, Jason," the woman said coolly, setting down the tray.

"Hello, Lacy. How's the boardinghouse business?"

"Full up, like always." Lacy glanced at Rachael, seeing a somewhat distraught look on her face. She reached out and patted the girl's hand and gave her a wink, then turned to face Jason. "How about the Ranger business? You going very far this time?"

"Making a wide sweep of all the settlers in kind of an arc around Austin from north to east to south. A lot of renegades and outlaws ride that border country between us and the Comanche."

"Sounds a little dangerous."

Jason glanced at Rachael, hoping she would worry. "Just living in Texas is dangerous," he answered, moving his eyes to

Lacy again. "But you're right. Out there it won't be any picnic. But I'll have help. I won't be alone."

Lacy nodded, putting her hands on her hips. "I suppose you'll have that ugly-looking whip with you, too?"

Jason flushed with repressed anger, his friendly attitude disappearing. Rachael watched in surprise, wondering why Lacy had made the remark.

"That whip is as much a weapon as my repeater," Jason told Lacy. "Like you said, it's dangerous out there."

"Yes, it is. But some men use that danger to satisfy their own thirst for power and adventure. And sometimes the line between lawmen and outlaws is mighty thin."

Jason frowned with irritation, glancing at Rachael and giving her a nervous little grin, then looking back at Lacy with the frown again. How he wanted to hit the nibby old battle-ax! "You got a bone to pick, Lacy? I would appreciate an explanation to that remark."

"Oh, I don't think it needs explaining, Jason. It's just that the other night one of my boarders heard one of your men talking about some of the things you've done with that bullwhip."

Rachael felt a chill at the gleaming hatred in Jason's eyes at that moment. His jaw was rigidly set in a mighty effort not to vent his wrath against Lacy in front of her. "I see no excuse to repeat such hearsay, Lacy," he almost hissed.

She held his eyes boldly. "I think there is. I've taken a sort of motherly attitude toward Rachael. I just wouldn't want to see her hurt."

"I would never hurt her," Jason spat back. "What I do in the line of duty and what I do with the woman I love have no relation. And I will thank you to stay out of it."

"Jason—" Rachael rose, going to stand beside Lacy.

Jason drew in his breath, struggling for composure, watching them both. "You can't believe the stories that come out of the mouth of a drunk man," he said then. "I don't know what your boarder heard, Lacy, but it was surely exaggerated. If I were stretching the law, I wouldn't last long as a Ranger."

Lacy grunted. "Depends who you pick to ride with you.

Pick the right men and they'll keep their mouths shut."

Jason's eyes glittered, and again Rachael saw a coldness in them that frightened her. "And certain other people should keep *their* mouths shut when they don't know what they're talking about," he growled.

"Stop it, both of you!" Rachael demanded, looking distressed.

Lacy turned and patted her arm. "I'm sorry, honey. I guess I have a way of talking out of turn." She looked back at Jason, grinning slightly. "Enjoy your tea," she added before exiting the room.

In the next moment Jason grasped Rachael's arms. "Rachael, I'm sorry. I don't know what that woman heard, but the way she made it look—it's not true, Rachael. I'm not mean and I don't break the law."

Rachael hunched her shoulders and pulled away, rubbing her arms as she turned her back to him. "What did she mean, Jason? What *do* you do when you go out on patrol?"

"My job, Rachael. That's all. Just my job! And I'm damned good at it or I wouldn't still be with the Rangers. Surely you know that." He stepped closer, again putting his hands on her arms, moving them up to her shoulders and massaging them lightly. "Damn it, Rachael, I didn't mean to be rude to Lacy, but she had no right saying those things in front of you, especially when it was hearsay from a drunk man. And especially when she knows I'm going away again."

He kept rubbing her shoulders, using more pressure. He was trying to relax her, but Rachael sensed his desire to squeeze harder, felt his anger. She could not help wondering just how much anger and force lay behind the handsome smile.

"Let's drink our tea and take a moment to think before we say anything else, Jason."

She gasped as he yanked her close. "Don't let that woman's lies make you think less of me, Rachael," he almost growled. "I love you! You heard me tell Lacy that, and now I'm telling you." He pressed her breasts against his chest, moving his hands over her back. "I love you," he repeated. "Can't you tell me the same?

Can't I at least have a good-bye kiss, a little hope to cling to while I'm gone?"

"Jason, I——"

He did not let her finish her words. His mouth came down on hers forcefully in a solid, pushing kiss. She wanted to pull away, to hit him, yet hated constantly hurting him. She tried to enjoy the kiss and let it linger for a moment in order to see if that magical feeling would come. But she felt only revulsion as he moved his head, touching her lips with his tongue and pushing as though trying to get her mouth to open. There was nothing gentle about him, and Rachael knew in that moment what Lacy meant about how difficult life had to be for a woman who didn't really want her husband physically.

She made a little whimpering sound and turned away. He kissed her cheek and her neck, apparently not even realizing she didn't like the kiss. Rachael felt a hardness as he pressed himself against her thigh and she pushed him away.

"Jason, don't!" She pulled away, quickly walking back to the settee, her breathing coming in quick little gasps.

"I'm sorry, Rachael," he told her in a husky voice. "A girl like you, she has to get used to these things. If you'd marry me, Rachael, I'd go easy on you, I swear. I love you. I'd treasure you. You liked that kiss. I could tell." He stepped closer and she kept her face turned away, amazed that he really thought she liked the cold, almost painful kiss. She put the back of her hand to her lips and he reached out and touched her hair. She jerked farther back, tossing the hair behind her shoulders.

"You had no right to kiss me like that. I didn't say that you could kiss me."

He just grinned, sitting down beside her. "A woman doesn't have to say it, Rachael. When she belongs to a man, he takes what he needs, and after a while the woman learns how to enjoy it. That's just the way it is, Rachael." He reached out and took her hand. "Please—before I go away—please say you'll marry me. At least say you'll think about it."

She met his eyes, her cheeks crimson. He seemed to have no conception of her real feelings, her revulsion. The hint of cruelty she had seen in those dark eyes moments earlier had again turned to the look of a little boy begging for a piece of candy. She sighed in resignation, turning and pouring some tea.

"Jason, I told you I just don't have the kind of feelings I need for marrying a man. But I respect your own feelings and I don't take your offer of marriage lightly, I assure you."

She put some sugar into his tea and stirred it, offering him the cup.

He took the cup and watched her pour her own before lifting the cup to his lips.

Rachael knew it was not likely her feelings would ever change, but she hated sending him off with no hope at all. She drank some of her tea.

"I will think about it, Jason." She relished the feel of the tea against her lips, as though the tea could somehow wash away his kiss. And to her surprise she suddenly thought of Brand Selby again—how warm and vibrant she felt in a quick moment from nothing more than a look. She turned to meet Jason's eyes.

"What did Lacy mean—about the whip?"

He shrugged it off, rising. "I don't even know. If it was true, I'd know what she was talking about." He faced her. "I'm telling you the truth now that whatever it was, it was a lie—from the lips of a drunk man." He put out his arms. "Look at me, Rachael. I'm just a man—a Texas Ranger. We live by certain codes. If I abused those codes, I couldn't be a Ranger. And here I am ready to ride out again—maybe to get killed—and you're worried about the lies of a drunk man, gossip handed to a busybody woman who is always trying to find out everything about everybody in town."

He put his hands on his hips. "I'll tell you what I use that whip for. It's to help bring in stray cattle for settlers. And sometimes we're riding in dangerous territory, where it's not wise to shoot a gun for fear a band of Comanche will hear the shot and come after us. In those times I can use the whip to kill a snake, or grab up a squirrel or a rabbit for a meal. I'm good with that whip, I'll admit that. But I don't use it to hurt people. That's what Lacy was trying to imply. My God, Rachael, do you really think I would do that? This is me—Jason—the man who has been coming to se you all this time with nothing but respect and patience—the man who goes out to check on your brothers for you."

Rachael sighed and rose, walking closer to him. "I'm sorry, Jason." She put her hands on his arms and leaned up to kiss his cheek. "There. It's not the kind of kiss you want, but I'm sending you off with one anyway, and with a promise to think about marriage, all right? And I really will think about you and worry about you. I'll pray that you come back safely. I wouldn't want anything to happen to you, even if all we ever are is casual friends."

He breathed deeply to keep from grabbing her up and kissing her again. How he wanted to do more! He took hold of her arms, forcing himself to be gentle. "We'll be more than friends, Rachael, I know it. You remember that I love you. You think real hard on it."

"I will. I promise."

He swallowed, studying her with eyes on fire with desire. "You watch yourself while I'm gone. Stay close to this place and don't go shopping or to the school except in the brightest daylight. And don't be wandering around after the sun goes down."

"I won't. Be sure to check on Josh and the boys for me."

"I will." He gave her a smile. "I have a feeling I should leave right now, while we're on good terms. I'm heading out in the morning before the sun even rises." He let go of her and walked into the hallway, taking his hat from a hook near the door. She followed him to the door and he gave her a smile. "Bye, Rachael."

"Good-bye, Jason. God speed."

He nodded, putting on his hat and going out.

Rachael stood at the door window, which was frosted with flowery designs. She peered through a clear section, watching him mount up and ride off, telling herself Jason couldn't possibly be as cruel as Lacy had hinted. She turned and looked at herself in the hall mirror, touching her lips where Jason had kissed her. Then she turned and headed to her room. She wished she could respond to his desires. But not only did she feel nothing, she had actually suddenly thought about a total stranger, a half-breed, no less. For nearly three weeks she had tried to forget about that day at the river, but the memory, and the feelings it stirred, would not leave her.

Four

Jason slammed Jules Webber up against a wall, his hands grasping Webber's shirtfront. "You stupid sonuvabitch!" Jason snarled. "It was *you*, wasn't it? I saw you drinking over at the Bull Run yesterday. You shot your mouth off about me using that whip on the old Indian man, didn't you!"

"I... I don't remember, Jase." Webber swallowed, staring at Jason with bloodshot eyes, his face sporting a stubble that needed shaving off. Jason jerked the smaller man away from the wall and shoved him into a chair. The two men were alone in the small building used for Ranger headquarters.

"You don't remember because you were too *drunk*!" Jason clenched his fists. "I could *kill* you," he growled. "And I just might do it! You know we can't have people knowing things like that. We've got a good thing going here, Jules! Don't destroy it by getting us knocked out of the Rangers! You want to lose that nice little nest egg you've got growing for you? You want to go back to Illinois where you're wanted for murder?"

"No, Jase."

"Then stay sober and stay out of the saloons! If we stay with the Rangers long enough, we'll be rich men. Do you want me to refresh your memory on the plan? We work both sides, Jules. We keep the Indians stirred up so they steal women, supplies, cattle, horses—trade them to the Comancheros for rifles and the Comancheros take the stolen goods to Mexico to trade for gold they use to buy *more* guns, and make a tidy profit to boot. We look the other way and keep the trouble brewing, and the Comancheros pay us for silence and for letting them operate in our territory."

Jason leaned close to Webber, resting his hands on the arms

of the chair.

"You and your big mouth could ruin everything, Webber! We get caught, it's all over. I don't intend to mess up on this, Webber. I need the money to marry Rachael Rivers. I can't give her everything I want on a Ranger's pay, so you watch yourself after this or I'll arrange to have the Comancheros take care of *you*. Understand?"

Webber's eyes widened and the man swallowed. "You wouldn't do that to a friend, would you, Jase? I didn't say nothin' about Comancheros or any of that."

"Don't say anything about *anything*! Just keep your mouth shut! And I don't call a man a friend who shoots off his mouth and gets me in hot water with the woman I love."

"I'm sorry, Jase. How was I to know it would get back to her?"

"People talk, you fool!" He sighed disgustedly and stood straighter. "I'm hoping not too much damage was done. We'll be riding out tomorrow. Maybe being gone for a while will cause any gossip you might have caused to blow over. Besides, most folks don't give a damn what happens to any Comanche, young or old. But if they suspected what we were doing, it's us they'll hate, not the Comanche! You want to hang, Webber?"

"No, Jase." The much smaller man seemed to actually shake, and Jason turned away in disgust.

"If that happens again, Jules, I'll let the Comancheros finish you off, I swear."

"I won't let it happen again. I promise."

Jason moved around behind the desk. "Be ready to move out in the morning." He sighed and sat down, putting his head in his hands. "I'm having a hard enough time getting Rachael to marry me, you bastard."

Webber ran a hand through thick, greasy hair. "You ask her again, Jase?"

Jason leaned back in his chair. "I asked her. She's at least thinking about it." He closed his eyes. "I swear if she doesn't say yes pretty soon I'm going to steal her away some night and take what I want by force. She'd learn to like it soon enough, especially when I show her all my money and how well I can provide for her."

Webber grinned. "Just get her a fancy brass bed and build her a fine house. Break her in good and she'll settle."

Jason's anger seemed to fade at the remark. "Yeah. I've won her brothers over. They probably wouldn't object. I kissed her tonight, Jules. And I could tell that's all she needs—just a little more kissing."

Jules Webber laughed lightly and Jason finally grinned. He couldn't imagine anything more pleasant than being Rachael's first man. Surely that was all she needed. After the first time she'd settle down. She'd find out how pleasant and sinfully delightful it was to be with a man. Suddenly, his smile faded and he eyed Webber with renewed anger.

"Don't you mess this up for me, Jules. I mean it."

"I won't, Jase. I won't."

"Go get some sleep. We move out early. And clean yourself up. You're a Texas Ranger."

Jules scratched his head. "I'll go over to Katie Doogan's place. MaryAnn will take care of me. She'll do more than give me a shave."

Jason finally grinned again. "Just make sure you aren't up romping with her half the night. We can always have our pick of the women the Comancheros have along to trade to the Mexicans. I want you bright-eyed and bushy-tailed in the morning."

"Sure, Jase. I will be." The man turned and hurried out as though glad to get away. Jason watched after him, his thoughts returning to Rachael. Sometimes when he took one of the stolen white women the Comancheros captured, he envisioned it was Rachael squirming beneath him. He had been tempted many times to take her that way—against her will. But his pride wouldn't let him. When he took Rachael Rivers, she would want him as much as he wanted her. He would make it happen somehow. Maybe when he returned from this trip she would be so relieved he was all right that she would fall into his arms and agree to marry him. The thought of it brought an ache to every nerve and muscle in his body.

Rachael tied on her robe and opened the door to her room. Lacy stood outside with a cup of hot chocolate.

"Still friends?" the woman asked.

Rachael smiled softly. "Of course. Come in, Lacy."

The woman stepped inside, setting the chocolate on a stand. "I wasn't sure if you were angry with me or not. You came straight up to your room after Jason Brown left. I'm sorry if I made things more difficult for you, Rachael."

"Things would have been difficult either way." Rachael sat down on her bed. "What on earth did you hear about Jason, Lacy?"

The older woman folded her arms and sighed. "Perhaps I didn't have any right repeating something that came out of the mouth of a drunk man."

"Father always said men usually speak the truth when they are drunk—say things they are afraid to say when they're sober."

Lacy nodded. "Makes sense." She studied Rachael a moment, true concern in her eyes. "Mr. Peters, the widow man, said while playing cards at one of the saloons in town, one of the other card players, a Ranger who rides with Jason Brown, joked about how Jason liked to use his whip on Indians."

Rachael closed her eyes and lowered her head. "What made him even mention it to you?" she asked.

"He saw Jason coming to call on you again. He came into the kitchen and we just started talking. He only brought it up because he was concerned for you. We're like one big family in this house, I guess. At any rate, he said he used that whip on some old Indian man who stole a calf. The other Ranger laughed about it like it was nothing, Mr. Peters said."

"Oh, my," Rachael sighed, rubbing her forehead. "When Jason came to my father's place before he brought me to Austin, he said something to Joshua and the boys about taking care of some Indian who had stolen some calf. The way he said it—I suspected something cruel." She shivered.

"Word gets around too much, Jason Brown will get kicked

out of that job of his. Then again, maybe not. Most folks tend to look the other way when it comes to dealing out punishment against Indians. But if it's true, it tells you what kind of man Jason Brown can be. And the way the man told it, if that Brand Selby hadn't come along, Jason would have whipped the old man to death."

"Brand Selby!" Rachael met Lacy's eyes. "He was there?"

"Came along and stopped it. Don't ask me how he managed to stop Texas Rangers without getting in trouble himself, but he did it. The way Mr. Peters says it, the Ranger talked like Jason is afraid of the half-breed. But he didn't say why."

Rachael rose, walking to the window. It was dark outside now, and she couldn't really see anything. She stared at the lacy curtains. "Somehow I can't imagine Jason being afraid of anyone." She sighed deeply. "How strange. When I left here I had never heard of this Brand Selby. Now it seems the man keeps coming into my life—not directly, but in a kind of haunting, abstract way." She turned and walked over to pick up the hot chocolate. "Thanks for thinking of me this way." She sipped some of the warm, soothing drink. "Lacy, it's almost a relief to know Jason is leaving," she said after swallowing. "Isn't that terrible of me?"

"It's not terrible at all."

Rachael set her cup down. "Jason kissed me tonight."

"He kissed you?"

Rachael blushed. "It was his idea, not mine. He practically forced it on me." She sipped more chocolate, moving back to sit down on the edge of her bed. "I didn't push him away at first. I wanted to enjoy the kiss, Lacy. But I didn't like it at all. The frustrating part is he didn't even realize I didn't like it. He said it just takes time for a woman like me to get to like things like that."

"Time! Honey, if he was the right man, you wouldn't need any time to wonder."

Rachael smiled. "Now you sound like my mother again." She shook her head. "He asked me to think about marriage while he's gone. I guess I'm just going to have to say it flat out when he gets back—I don't want to marry him, now or later."

She shivered. "He scared me, Lacy. I have a terrible feeling that Ranger was telling the truth."

Lacy put her hand on the doorknob. "Well, I don't blame you if you think of me as a snoopy old biddy, Rachael. I try hard to like that man, but I can't do it. Still, that didn't give me a right to butt in like that and spoil your evening. I'll try not to interfere after this. I apologize."

Rachael rose again, setting the cup aside. "It isn't necessary. You're just concerned, that's all." She folded her arms. "I just wish I could make Joshua see the kind of man Jason is. Joshua and the boys think he's wonderful. And I do appreciate Jason checking up on them like he does. But I don't want my brothers to be Indian haters. My father and mother wouldn't want that either. My father was raised by the Cherokee, and my mother came to know them as family, too. But Josh says there's a big difference between the Cherokee and the Comanche."

"Well, I expect there is on the surface—but not way down inside. The only difference I can see is that the Cherokee learned to accept what must be. Some of the Comanche haven't given up the idea yet of keeping this land for themselves. And the Cherokee have been Christianized and educated for years. The Comanche have all that ahead of them. I'm afraid a lot of heartache still lies ahead—for both sides. And once Texas becomes a state, Washington will start sending in soldiers and building forts. They'll soon take care of what's left of the Comanche." She opened the door. "You finish that chocolate. It will help you rest. We'll talk more another time."

Rachael nodded. "Thanks again, Lacy."

"No trouble." The woman left, and Rachael moved to her bed, bending over to blow out her oil lamp. She moved under the covers, stretching and settling into the feather mattress. As soon as she closed her eyes, the vision of Brand Selby returned. This time she saw him defending the old Indian. It would take quite a man to stand up to Texas Rangers—and quite a man to actually be feared by them.

Rachael placed a dozen eggs into the basket Lacy had given her. "I'll take a sack of flour, too, Mr. Briggs," she told the man behind the counter of the supply store.

Rachael felt better today, happy, free. Having Jason gone was actually a relief. She was being accepted as a teacher, making new friends.

"You got a way of getting all this back to Lacy's place?" Briggs asked with a grin.

Rachael studied her list, paying no attention to the scowl that came over Briggs's face as the door of the store opened. "Of course I do," Rachael was answering. "I brought Lacy's wagon. But you'll have to carry all these things out for me. Those men Lacy puts up certainly do go through the food." She turned to a glass jar of peppermint candy to her left. "Oh, give me a dozen or so of these peppermint sticks, will you? I use them as rewards for the children who do especially well."

Rachael looked at the storekeeper's face then, noticing he looked almost frightened. "Sure thing, Miss Rivers. How do you like teaching school?"

"I like it just fine, Mr. Briggs. I just wish more children would show up." She felt the silent presence then, turning to glance at who had just entered. A pair of green eyes met her own, and the sight of Brand Selby was too surprising to give her time to control the sudden flush that came to her cheeks. Her eyes widened, and she realized the man recognized her immediately as the woman by the river. He gave her the almost sly half smile again and she quickly looked away as the storekeeper shoved the candy into another of Lacy's baskets.

"You better not be eyeing young ladies like Miss Rivers, Selby," the storekeeper told Brand.

The remark only embarrassed Rachael, the embarrassment doubled by feeling embarrassed for Brand Selby. "It's all right, Mr. Briggs," she said softly, wondering how she had managed to find her voice. She was furious with herself for the way her heart was pounding and the clammy feeling that suddenly swept over her. "Be sure to throw in some tobacco. Lacy keeps it around for her gentlemen boarders."

"Yes, ma'am." The man looked past her at Brand Selby. "What is it you want, breed?" he asked.

Rachael felt him move behind her. Then he was standing beside her at the counter. She could smell leather and fresh air. She let her eyes move to view his dark, strong hands as they rested on the counter.

"When will the man be by from New Orleans—the one who comes up the river to buy horses?" Selby asked.

Rachael's surprise was enhanced by Brand Selby's clear English. Somehow she had expected him to speak in some strange language. The storekeeper turned and took down a piece of slate from the wall, laying it on the counter. "There's the schedule, Selby. Read it quick and get out of my store. You're upsetting the young lady here."

Rachael bristled at Briggs's assumption. "I'm not upset, Mr. Briggs," she said, irritation showing in her voice. "Go ahead and wait on this gentleman."

"Gentleman? Ma'am, you don't call a man like Brand Selby a gentleman. He's a breed. But don't you worry. Nothing can happen to you right here in broad daylight."

"Mr. Briggs!" Rachael's face was literally crimson. "I will thank you to keep such thoughts to yourself."

"Sorry, ma'am." Briggs cleared his throat, wiping at his brow with his shirtsleeve. "I didn't mean to offend or frighten you. What else do you need in the way of supplies?"

Rachael rested her hand on the basket. "Lacy needs a new pair of scissors—the best ones you have for cutting material."

The man nodded. "I'll have to go to the back for a minute." He eyed Brand Selby. "You watch yourself, mister. Get that schedule fixed in your head and get out of here. If you need supplies, come back later after the lady here has left."

The man turned and went through a doorway to a back room.

Rachael swallowed. "I apologize for his behavior," she said quickly, worried Briggs would come back before she had a chance to say it.

"I am used to it," he replied, an odd sadness in his voice.

Rachael turned and looked up at him. He was so tall and strong looking that he seemed to fill up the little store. Up close he was even more handsome than she had remembered, and his closeness brought again the strange warmth she had felt the first time. "You shouldn't have to get used to it. I think it's disgraceful the way some people act."

The hint of a smile came across his lips again. "You are the woman who was by the river."

She nodded, looking back at her basket.

"You should not be seen speaking to me," he told her. "Some people would say you're bad."

She rolled her eyes. "That's ridiculous. I speak to whomever I please."

He smiled more, but she didn't see it. To look at him made her feel too flustered.

"You teach school?"

"Yes," she answered softly.

"I saw you go there once, but you did not see me."

Rachael did not reply as he proceeded to move the slate in front of her. "Will you please tell me what it says?"

She frowned, looking up at him again, seeing a sudden embarrassment on his part. He apparently couldn't read the chart. She looked down at the slate, studying it a moment. "May tenth is the next date. That's next Wednesday. It looks like the man comes every four months. He doesn't come back again until the middle of September."

"Thank you, Miss… Rivers, is it?"

"Yes." She met his eyes again. Their eyes held for a moment as he reached over to take back the slate, his arm lightly touching her own. Briggs came from the back room then and Rachael quickly looked away.

"You got them dates in your head, breed?" the man asked Brand.

Brand nodded. "Next Wednesday he comes."

Briggs frowned. "How did you know that? I didn't figure you could read."

Brand shoved the slate hard in the man's direction. "If you

thought I couldn't read, then why did you hand me the slate?"

Briggs just swallowed, taking the slate and hanging it back up.

"You did it to shame me in front of the young lady," Brand answered for the man. "I am sorry I disappointed you, Briggs. When the young lady is finished, I need some supplies of my own."

"You got money?"

"You know I do. I've bought things from you before." Selby's voice was low and sure.

Briggs grudgingly shoved the new scissors into Rachael's supply basket. "Why aren't you with your Comanche friends, Selby?" he mumbled. "You didn't need to pick Austin for settling."

"I am as much white as Indian. And I have as much right to settle here as the next man."

"Half-breeds got less rights than full-blood Indians," Briggs answered. He turned to Rachael with a smile. "Anything else, Miss Rivers? I'm sorry for this man's presence. Maybe it's best you get your things and be on your way."

Rachael felt the slow burn of growing anger. "I believe you call yourself a Christian, Mr. Briggs. But the behavior I am seeing at this moment is as sinful as any I have ever witnessed." She picked up the basket of eggs. "Lacy said to put all this on her bill. I'll take out the eggs and come back for the other two baskets."

Briggs just stared at her dumbfounded as she took the eggs and stomped out the door. His eyes moved to meet Brand Selby's. Selby just glared at him, saying nothing. Rachael came back inside, and Briggs picked up one of the baskets. "I can carry them for you, ma'am."

"Never mind. You have another customer, Mr. Briggs, in case you didn't notice. I can take my own baskets."

She lifted the basket with both hands and walked out again. Brand Selby turned and leaned against the counter, folding his arms and waiting for her to come back. When Rachael entered the store she felt his green eyes on her as she picked up the last heavy basket. She wanted to look at him again but was afraid not for herself but for Brand Selby.

"Good day, Mr. Briggs," she said brusquely. She left then, and Brand watched through the windows of the double doors as she loaded the third basket and lifted her skirts to climb up into the wagon. She took hold of the reins and drove off, and the strange ache he had felt the first time he set eyes on her returned to tease him again.

He turned back to Briggs, who stood scowling, also staring after Rachael. The man finally looked up at Selby. "You keep your eyes off that young lady if you want to live long, Selby. She belongs to Jason Brown."

Brand slowly met the man's eyes. He had a lot of questions about that statement, but didn't dare ask them. To show an interest was to invite trouble. "I just want my supplies, Briggs," he answered, trying not to show his disappointment at the remark about Jason Brown and the young woman who had just left. Somehow he could not believe it. A perky, intelligent, independent young lady like the one he had just seen couldn't be interested in a bastard like Jason Brown. It didn't make sense. He chided himself then for even caring. The young woman was white. That's what he had told himself the first time he had set eyes on her. But ever since that moment she had haunted him, and from the look on her face when she first saw him in the store, he wondered if perhaps it had been the same for her.

Rachael scanned the reader that the children would be using, intending to write down questions she planned to ask about the stories. Finally she set the quill pen aside, and stared at a tablet that held only one question.

She couldn't concentrate. The encounter the day before in the store kept coming back to her—and the vision of Brand Selby. She wished she had never seen him, for she had just begun to get him out of her mind. And then there he was, like the other time—just standing there looking at her with those provocative eyes and that teasing grin. She hadn't told Lacy about seeing him. She couldn't yet—not until she decided herself what it was about the man that gave her these warm feelings and made her heart pound.

She sighed and leaned back in her chair. She had disobeyed the most important rule. She had stayed at the little schoolhouse until after dark. Leonard Dreyfuss had already left, and she felt a tinge of alarm then when she looked out the windows and realized just how dark it had become. She rose from her chair, wondering how safe it would be to walk home. It was true that people had been killed and robbed by Comanche after dark around Austin, and she chided herself for being so lost in thought that she had allowed the time to slip away from her.

She walked toward the doorway, taking her shawl from a hook nearby and putting it around her shoulders. She checked around the room to see that everything was in place, leaving her own material on her desk. She would work on the questions in the morning while the children read, if any children even showed up. She walked back to her desk to blow out the lamp, then turned to go back to the doorway. She would blow out the lamp near the door on her way out. She nearly reached the lamp when a huge figure moved from the outer entranceway into the main room, looming into the light.

Rachael gasped and stepped back, her heart pounding. At first all she saw was the buckskin clothing and the long hair. Her first thought was that a Comanche man had come to kill her, or do worse.

"I didn't mean to frighten you," came the voice. "I just thought I would wait until after dark, so no one would see me come here."

She stared in surprise, putting a hand to her chest. It was Brand Selby.

Five

Brand looked around the room quickly, his green eyes scanning every shadow and corner. "You are alone?" he asked.

Rachael just blinked, stepping back slightly. Her heart raced with a mixture of fear and excitement, and she drew a deep breath to control her composure, wondering if she should scream or find something to hit him with.

"Don't be afraid," he told her, coming farther inside. "I mean you no harm."

She moved a hand to her throat, absently fingering at the lace of her high-necked dress. "What is it you want, Mr. Selby?" She quickly moved farther back, edging her way around behind her desk.

"You remembered my name."

Rachael swallowed, taking on a casual air.

"Mr. Briggs spoke your name in the supply store." She wondered where she found her voice. He stood there tall and powerful. She realized the harm he could bring her if he chose. But again her fear began to subside under the soft green eyes.

"You didn't know my name before that?" he asked. "You didn't ask Jason Brown who I was, after you saw me at the river?"

Rachael frowned. "You know Jason?"

Her heart tightened and the fear returned for just a moment as a cold hatred came into his eyes. "I know him," he said, his voice lower, almost strained.

The whip! The old Indian man! Was the rumor Lacy had heard really true? Was Jason really that bad, or was it this man who was bad? As Brand's power seemed to fill the room, Rachael could understand why Jason could be afraid of him. She felt a need now to show him he didn't frighten her—more than that, a need to somehow let him know she didn't think Jason the better man. She chided herself inwardly for feeling a sudden defense of the half-breed before her. If he hated Jason, perhaps he had come to kill her because he had heard she was Jason's woman.

"I didn't ask about you that day," she told him. She gripped the edge of the desk, swallowing, looking straight at him. For a moment she felt as she would feel toward a wild animal. People said if you showed no fear around a wild animal, it would not attack. "I didn't mention you at all."

She saw the surprise in his eyes, combined with something close to admiration. "Why not?"

She could hardly believe she was carrying on a conversation with this stranger. Yes, he was handsome. But he was fearsome looking at the same time, standing there in his buckskins, a huge knife and a handgun at his waist, his dark brown hair hanging loose. She began to redden under his discerning gaze, and she felt an odd flutter deep inside as their eyes held, a warm dampness creep across her skin.

"I'm not quite sure," she answered. "You… looked Indian. You hadn't done anything wrong, and I know how Jason feels about Indians. So I said nothing."

"You speak of Jason Brown as though you know him well. Do you belong to him? Are you his woman?"

Her cheeks warmed with a pink glow, his remark surprising and embarrassing her. "It's really none of your business, Mr. Selby. But since you have asked, no, I am not Jason Brown's 'woman,' as you put it. We're just friends. Jason would like it to be otherwise, but I have no interest—" She caught herself, feeling ridiculous for sharing such intimate things with Brand Selby. "Mr. Selby, would you kindly state why you are here? You shouldn't be, you know. If anyone saw you here you could be in trouble, and someone will probably come along any moment. I should have left earlier. People will be worried about me."

The faint smile passed over his lips. "Yes. As well they should be. You are a most beautiful white woman. You should not be out at night. Some terrible, bad Comanche might murder you, or do worse. Those Comanche are a bad lot."

The words were spoken with a hint of sarcasm, and Rachael felt a smile tease her own lips. Brand Selby smiled even more, a broad grin that showed white, even teeth, a melting smile that brought the pleasant flutter to her insides again. Why was she smiling? She should be screaming, ordering him to get out. How did she know he wouldn't do something bad to her himself? "You haven't answered my question, Mr. Selby. And you can't deny that it *is* dangerous to be out walking after dark."

"I won't deny it." He sobered slightly. "But there are two sides to every story, Miss Rivers."

Her eyebrows arched. "Ah. So, you remembered my name, too."

He nodded, still smiling softly. "From the supply store." He looked around the small room, then his warm green eyes moved to meet her own. "It is true about walking after dark. When you leave, you don't have to be afraid. You won't see me, but I will be watching you from the shadows. No harm will come to you. I will make sure of it. I know the Comanche." He sobered slightly, straightening with pride. "I *am* Comanche. At least half of me is. And I feel no shame in it—only pride."

She studied the proud specimen of man that he was. "Yes, I can see that. There is nothing wrong with that, Mr. Selby."

His eyes moved over her, and she felt caressed. It was different from the way Jason looked at her. Under Jason's eyes she felt naked, exposed, manhandled. This man did not make her feel that way. She was astonished that she didn't mind his lingering gaze, and she wondered if it was sinful to let such a man as this one be looking at her at all.

He met her eyes again, frowning. "You are an unusual white woman. You show no fear, and you show no contempt for the Comanche. I could tell the other day in the supply store that you are a good woman; you have a good heart."

"My father was very much like you, Mr. Selby," she answered. "He looked very much like you. He was a white man, but he was raised by the Cherokee, and I think his heart was more Indian than white. He used to tell us about there being two sides to every story, as you just mentioned. He told us about the terrible things that happened to the Cherokee, and told us never to judge a man by his blood—to only judge the quality of person that he is."

"Your father spoke wisely. I would like to know him. Does he still live?"

She looked down at the desk, slowly sitting down in the chair behind it. "No. He died not long ago. I didn't even know it until I came home recently. I've been in St. Louis getting an education. I came back here to—" Again she caught herself spilling things out to this near stranger, and for no good reason. She leaned back in her chair. "Mr. Selby, I cannot believe I'm sitting here talking to you so easily like this. I hardly know you, and you have come in here as silently as a shadow with no explanation for your presence. Please do tell me why you're here. I really have to be getting home."

He looked around the room again, his eyes scanning a couple of books that lay on a log bench nearby, then moving to letters she had written on a slate that hung on the wall. He stared at the letters a moment, then stepped closer, lightly touching a book that lay on her desk. He opened it, staring at the print on the page. He moved his eyes then to meet her own again, looking suddenly embarrassed.

"I, uh—" He swallowed before continuing. "I want to learn to read." He swallowed again, closing the book, taking his eyes from hers and looking down at the book. "To read better, I mean. My mother was white. But she hadn't had much schooling when my father captured her. She taught me what little she remembered. But I need to know more if I am to live in the white man's world, which is what I have decided to do. I want to read and I want to know how to write and how to figure numbers."

He had spoken the words quietly, almost bashfully. He met her eyes again then, looking almost like a lost little boy. "I thought maybe you would agree to teach me. After I saw how you were that day in the supply store—how kind and accepting you could be—and knowing you are a teacher—"

He stepped back a little, holding his chin proudly. "It is hard for me to ask," he continued. "You are a woman. It might not be right—a woman doing the teaching. But I want to learn, and I know without asking that no white man around here would teach me. But I also know it could be dangerous for you if people knew. It is probably wrong of me to ask, and foolish of me to think that you would do it." He turned as though to leave.

"Mr. Selby," she called out. He stopped but kept his back to her. "I would be glad to teach you. Everyone has a right to an education. That's the way my mother and father would look at it. They sacrificed hard-earned money to see that I could go to school in St. Louis. If I refused you I would be dishonoring their memory."

He turned to face her. "You will truly do it?"

She rose, pressing her hands on the desktop as she leaned forward. "Yes. But for now it has to be done in secret. I am not personally ashamed to be teaching you, Mr. Selby; but right now I need this job badly. I want to prove a woman can be a good teacher, and I am more or less on my own. There is nothing else I want to do as far as earning money, and the people here have agreed to pay me a fair wage to help bring education to Texas. Needless to say I would lose this job in a minute if they knew I was teaching a half-breed to read and write. I'm speaking for them, not myself, mind you," she added.

Selby nodded, the look of admiration returning to his eyes. "How can we do it?"

She sighed, standing straighter and folding her arms. "Do you live far from here?"

He stepped closer again. "Only about two miles north of town. But you have to leave the main riding path to get to my cabin. It is almost hidden in a small valley behind Bald Hill."

She nodded, turning and pacing a moment, then meeting his eyes again. "In another week we will have to stop teaching altogether. Too many of the children are needed for summer chores. I have been mostly observing these last few weeks, preparing to do my own teaching next autumn. My days will be free soon. I could come out every three days, without telling anyone. All I have to do is tell my landlady that I am going shopping or visiting. I could ride into town where I am seen, then circle around the thick stand of cottonwood on the east side of town and head north. But you would have to be waiting there for me. I can't ride that far alone." The faint smile returned to her own lips then. "I'm afraid of the terrible Comanche."

Now he grinned again. "I am afraid you are right to be afraid. I agree you cannot ride there alone. But I should not be seen regularly that close to town. Someone might suspect something and start following me. If I know the day you will come, I will be watching, even though you do not see me. After you are far enough from town for no one to see, I will come closer and take you the rest of the way."

She stepped a little closer. "How can I be sure you're there? I would hate to get that far from town and find out I really am alone."

"I will be there. You will just have to trust me."

Her eyebrows arched. "Trust you? I hardly know you!" She put a hand to her cheek, frowning and turning slightly away. "I must be losing my mind," she said almost absently.

The air hung silent for a moment. "Please don't change your mind, Miss Rivers. I promise I will be there. I would never let any harm come to you, by anyone else's hand or by my own. I want to learn, Miss Rivers. I will see that you are protected, and you can trust that I would not harm you myself."

She turned, meeting the soft green eyes, feeling the utterly divine warmth surge through her insides again. She was actually agreeing to allow herself to be alone with this man who was not only a stranger, but half Indian! What would Joshua say? Or Lacy? And Jason! He would be furious! Somehow that only made her more eager to do it.

"All right," she said aloud. "Today is Friday the fifth of May. We have already decided that next Friday is the last day we will teach for the summer. The following Monday I will come out to you." She turned and walked to a book that lay on a table nearby. "Come here, Mr. Selby."

The man walked to stand beside her, and his closeness brought again the scent of sage and leather. Rachael wondered if he could smell her soap and perfume, or if he was as curious about how it would feel to touch as she was. She felt suddenly wicked and foolish, and a hot anger at herself made her open the book and turn the pages more eagerly and deliberately than necessary.

"This is an almanac, Mr. Selby. I brought it from St. Louis. It has calendars in it covering several years. Do you know how to read a calendar?"

Brand looked down at her golden hair and the soft flow of her shoulders under the pink dress she wore. She filled out the dress with tempting curves. He almost ached to cup one of the firm, young breasts in his hand, to gently feel of its softness. But he reminded himself he must have no such thoughts about this lovely, trusting woman, who was not only kind but also being very brave. She was risking her reputation and her job in order to teach him.

"I am afraid I know nothing about your calendars," he answered. "I keep track of the days according to the moon and the stars and the way the sun hangs in the sky—the Indian way."

She moved aside a little, showing him the correct calendar. "Right here. This is today." She pointed to the square that showed the day and date. "And this is the month of May." She pointed to the word at the top. "M—A—Y—May. And here the square says Friday, and the number is five. May fifth. Now, here is Monday and the week coming up where Mr. Dreyfuss and I will teach. Here is the Monday after that week—the fifteenth. That is the day I will come out to you. Will you know the day by your own way of keeping track?"

She met his eyes. He stood so close, so overwhelmingly handsome, so tall, so unnerving. "I will know it," he answered, moving his eyes from the calendar to meet her own.

For a moment the room hung silent as their eyes held, each of them thinking things that were forbidden, each of them afraid to voice thoughts they felt were utterly wrong and ridiculous.

"What time will you come?" he asked her.

She noticed how perfectly his full lips were etched into his rugged but beautiful face. His high cheekbones seemed to be the key to his provocative good looks, as well as a straight, finely carved nose and the wide-set green eyes. "How about right after lunch—around one o'clock? Do you keep a watch?"

He grinned then. "Yes. A white man I worked for gave me a pocket watch and taught me how it worked."

She smiled in return. "Good."

Again their eyes held, until Rachael finally looked away, afraid he would see through her, afraid he would sense the disturbing warmth he brought to her blood, and perhaps read in her eyes the faint desires he stirred in her.

"I must leave, Mr. Selby."

"Please, call me Brand. It seems strange to have someone call me by my name, using mister in front of it. Usually it's 'breed' or just 'Selby,' or 'hey, Indian.' At any rate, I appreciate the honor with which you speak my name. But we are fast becoming friends, and I wish you would just call me Brand."

She quickly walked farther away from him, totally annoyed with herself for the feelings he created in her. "I'll have to get used to that. Let's stay with Mr. Selby until I know you just a little better."

He smiled. "All right."

Rachael walked back toward the doorway, almost wishing she could stay and talk longer with him. "A week from Monday then—one o'clock. Make sure you're out there, Mr. Selby, or I might pay a high price for agreeing to teach you." She folded her arms, keeping her shawl wrapped tight. "I trust you can handle yourself." Her eyes dropped to the weapons he wore. "You must speak Comanche—know how to handle them."

He nodded. "You will have nothing to fear. I lived with them for many years. They know me. They would listen to me."

She shook her head, laughing lightly. "As I said earlier, I must be losing my mind." She studied him admiringly. One needed only to look at this man to see how capable he was. No wonder Jason was afraid of him. It made her feel almost giddy at the thought of doing something Jason would be furious about. "You have my mother to thank for this, Mr. Selby. I promised her a long time ago I would teach anyone who needed teaching.

She was very determined to learn herself, and she taught me a lot before I ever went off to St. Louis. Her father—"

Rachael didn't finish the sentence. She heard voices outside, and her smile faded. "Get under the desk!" she said quickly. "Someone is coming—they're probably looking for me, wondering what happened to me!"

Brand hurried over to the desk, ducking under it just as the storekeeper Briggs, Bert Peters, the widower who lived at Lacy's boardinghouse, and the teacher, Leonard Dreyfuss, came inside the little one-room log structure, all three of them brandishing rifles, Dreyfuss holding a lantern in one hand.

"Miss Rivers!" Dreyfuss exclaimed. "What on earth are you still doing here? Mrs. Reed sent Bert to get us to come and find out what happened to you."

"Oh, Mr. Dreyfuss!" she exclaimed, grasping his arm. "I'm so happy to see you. I was reading and I simply lost all track of time. The next thing I knew it was dark. I didn't know what to do. I was just getting ready to leave. I was going to run home as fast as I could."

"Miss Rivers." The man patted her hand. "You must not let this happen again. It's very dangerous to be out alone after dark here in Austin. I've told you that before. It's especially dangerous for a lovely young lady like yourself. You come with us now and we'll get you back to Miss Reed's place as quickly as we can." He led her through the entrance way and outside, while behind them Briggs blew out the lamp inside the school and hurried out after them.

"That was a real foolish thing to do, Miss Rivers," Bert Peters was telling Rachael. "Lacy is beside herself with worry."

"Oh, Lacy fusses like a mother," Rachael answered, hanging on to Dreyfuss's arm. She breathed a sigh of relief that she got them outside quickly. As they walked, Briggs held up the lantern to show the way. Rachael wondered if she should tell Lacy what had happened this night, and tell her she had agreed to teach Brand Selby. She decided she would say nothing until absolutely necessary.

Inside the dark schoolroom Brand Selby came out from

71

under the desk, feelings of hatred and embarrassment raging inside the proud man. He shouldn't have had to hide. He couldn't blame Rachael Rivers. He knew she had made him hide for his own good, not because she was ashamed to be seen with him. For her sake, her reputation alone, he would keep all of this secret. But under no other circumstances would he hide or show shame or cower in front of any white man. He never had and he never would.

He moved to the door, peering out to see Rachael disappearing down the street, busily chattering with the three men and walking as fast as she could. Brand grinned, the pleasant urges grasping at his insides again. Rachael Rivers was more than just beautiful. She was smart—not just in the ways of education, but in the ways of human behavior. How easily she had steered the three men away, without giving one hint that the half-breed Brand Selby was crouched under her desk! She could have given him away, got him in a lot of trouble. But just like at the river, she had said nothing.

Brand moved outside and through the darkness to his horse, mounting up and riding out. He knew that for the next several nights he would not sleep well, for Rachael Rivers would be on his mind. The days would be long and lonely until the day she would come out to him. He would fix up his little cabin as best he could so that she would feel comfortable there. He wished he knew more about how white women liked things to be inside a house.

Brand was more accustomed to the Indian way of life. And he would prefer to continue living that way. But the days of the free Comanche were numbered. And he knew he never wanted to live on a reservation. He would have to try to make it as a white man, and knowledge was the best weapon in the white man's world. He would get that knowledge, from Miss Rachael Rivers, and men like Jason Brown and the storekeeper Briggs would not stop him or rob him of his pride and his rights.

. . .

Rachael took a tiny cookie from the silver tray handed out to her by a young Mexican girl, a servant of Mrs. Harriet Miller. She held the cookie nervously in a cloth napkin, feeling the eyes of all the women upon her. Her manners and knowledge of etiquette were impeccable; but knowing she was being looked at through the judging eyes of the most respected ladies of Austin made her acutely aware of her appearance and actions. It also aroused her anger, an emotion she struggled to keep hidden.

She was the guest of Mrs. Harriet Miller, who had led the original expedition of Austin's upper class to the schoolhouse on Rachael's first day. Her husband, Theodore, owned the biggest mercantile in Austin. As promised, Mrs. Miller had invited Rachael to her house to meet Austin's elite. All the women were anxious to know about all the latest happenings and fashions in St. Louis, and were also curious to meet the new young schoolteacher. Rachael knew that without her St. Louis education these women would not give her the time of day. She was not wealthy, and a few of these very same women had snubbed her mother because Emma Rivers was an uneducated woman from the hills of Tennessee whose husband had been raised by Indians. But most of the women in the room were new to Rachael, new arrivals during the three years she had been gone, for Austin had just recently begun to mushroom in growth.

Rachael patiently answered questions, sipping tea between remarks, while Mrs. Miller and her guests studied her prim, high-necked, lacy blouse, her upswept blond hair, and her captivating blue eyes.

Mrs. Miller moved around the room with all the grace of a horse. She was a big, tall woman, who always overdressed, especially for the wilds of Texas. Her dark hair was drawn up in a tight bun at the top of her head, and the bustle of her dress only accented an already too large rear end. Expensive rings decorated her well-manicured hands and pearls graced the neck of her dark blue taffeta dress. Rachael wondered how anyone could stand taffeta on such a hot day.

The room rang with gossip and chatter once each woman had introduced herself to Rachael and had asked whatever nosy questions she might have for the young schoolteacher. Rachael was nibbling on a cookie when she heard the name Brand Selby.

"The man has actually settled north of town," one woman said. "That's what my Harold told me. And he said there would be trouble. Jason Brown hates the man."

"It gives me the shivers, knowing he's that close," her gossip mate answered. "I've not seen him, and some say he's a fine-looking man—but wild as the mustangs and more untrustworthy than a full-blood Comanche."

"It seems to me like Jason and his men should be able to do something about it."

"He can't. The man has to break the law first, and so far he hasn't. He's a clever one, that half-breed. That's the trouble with them. They're scheming and devilish."

Rachael smiled inwardly, wondering what kind of reaction she would get if she stood up and announced she would be teaching Brand Selby how to read and write—and going to meet him alone to do it! She didn't doubt that half the women in the room would faint dead away.

"Oh, you must miss your Jason, don't you, Miss Rivers?" Harriet Miller approached Rachael, talking in a loud, singsong voice that grated on Rachael's nerves.

"He's not 'my' Jason, Mrs. Miller. He's just a friend."

"Oh, come now!" The woman shook her finger at Rachael and winked. "We all know our Jason has been seeing you regularly since you returned. Oh, what a catch, Miss Rivers! What a catch! He's such a capable man. Everyone in town is so fond of him. And to think he rides out into Indian country and risks his life constantly just to protect us." She clapped her hands together. "Oh, it must be something to be loved by a man like that."

Rachael fought an urge to scream at the woman that she had no love interest at all in Jason Brown, that he was not anywhere near the man everyone here seemed to think he was. But she knew there would be no convincing them.

"I have only been back a short time, Mrs. Miller, hardly long enough to be professing my love for Jason. But he is a good man, and I do hope he'll be all right. And call me Rachael.

I don't mind."

"Oh, well, I must tell you, Rachael, that we all wish only the best for you and Jason. Oh, how we would love to go to a wedding, wouldn't we, ladies?"

Giggles and agreements filled the room. Rachael felt choked, wishing she could just get away and put on something more comfortable. Her mother had never cared for nor understood women like these, and Rachael put up with their scrutiny only because she wanted to keep her job.

More women approached her with questions about a woman teaching: nostalgic questions from women who missed their origins back East. Finally Rachael rose from her chair, walking to the screen door and out onto the veranda of the Miller home. It was a small but immaculately kept home, filled with expensive furnishings. Mrs. Miller carried on over and over about the "grand" house they intended to build in the future, adding, "This little place is just our temporary home," to make sure everyone knew.

Rachael thought how her mother would have loved a house like this, but Mrs. Miller made it sound like a soddy. The house was located at the northwest corner of Austin, and Ted Miller had built a literal stockade around the house for protection against the Indians.

Rachael walked along the veranda, the scent of roses that bloomed all around the house filling her nostrils. She could not see past the stockade fence, but she knew that out there somewhere lived a half-breed called Brand Selby, and she had actually agreed to teach him how to read and write. She could not help but wonder what a foolish decision that might have been, as well as a dangerous one. But she had promised, and she had no way of telling the man she had changed her mind. She was too soft-hearted and too much a woman of her word to just not show up next Monday, which left her with no choice now but to go through with it. The thought of it brought flutters of fear and apprehension to her stomach. But she knew the flutters came from more than that—an odd expectancy, a fascination with the unknown, an unexplainable desire to see the man again.

Inside the house the women carried on about the atrocities of the Comanche, gasping over things it was rumored the Comanche did to women, and again talking about how they wished that half-breed had not settled so close to Austin. Rachael knew she was risking her job and her reputation by helping the man, but the promise she had made to her mother gave her the determination she needed. But for now, somehow, she had to keep what she was doing a secret from these women.

A hawk flew overhead, and she wished she could fly away with it—away from the gossip and questions and scrutiny and talk of Jason Brown. Brand Selby represented everything foreign to these people, and she realized she actually looked forward to their meeting. In just two more days she would see him again, and she would find out if she had made the right decision.

Six

Rachael made her way over the hard ground, watching constantly for snakes amid the rocks and prickly brush. She picked up her skirts as best she could with one hand, while in the other hand she carried books and a slate. She cursed the heat under her breath, suddenly realizing with anger that she cared how she looked.

She told herself she shouldn't mind at all that her hair might wilt and cling to her forehead, or that her dress wouldn't be quite as crisp and clean as when she started out. After all, her duty was to teach, and the way she looked had nothing to do with that. But her anger with herself came from the realization that she must have lost her mind altogether, coming out here all alone this way, literally risking her reputation, and her life, to teach a near stranger how to read.

All night she had pondered not coming at all. The wakeful night had left her eyes slightly puffy, and that upset her, too. She reasoned she should turn back right now and forget this whole thing. If Mr. Selby's feelings were hurt, so be it. Still, she had made a promise, and she didn't like breaking promises. And she could not forget the almost boyish pleading in Brand Selby's eyes. She realized how hard it must have been for such a big, proud man to come to her for help, and she did not doubt his sincerity. The only thing she really feared at the moment was that he would get his days mixed up and she would be a woman alone in this very dangerous land.

A crow flew overhead, cawing loudly. Rachael stopped walking, and turned to see that Austin was completely out of sight. Her heart beat a little harder. She slowly turned back around, gazing out at the distant, barren hills. There was nothing here but total silence. She had known this kind of quiet before, growing up on the Double "R." But then the family had always been around somewhere. This was different. She was totally alone. Did she dare go any farther, or should she turn back?

She walked to a large, flat boulder and sat down, after first walking around it to be sure there were no snakes nearby. She forced herself to sit still and wait. Selby would come. And then she would be perfectly safe, for she was certain of one thing— Brand Selby was a capable man who probably knew his way in this land better than the wild deer. After all, he was half wild himself, had grown up among the Comanche. Who knew this land better than the Comanche? No animal, that was sure.

Comanche! There could be renegades lurking behind the distant rocks or in the very next gully. They could appear and disappear like the wind. And what they were capable of doing to white women.... Her eyes began to tear. If Comanche came and carried her off, no one would have any idea where to look for her or what had happened to her. She had told no one what she was doing, not even Lacy. There would be no help for her, certainly not in time to prevent the horrors of rape and torture and a most certain death. She realized that at the moment even the sight of Jason Brown would be welcome.

Rachael finally heard the sound of a horse coming at a fast trot. But sounds in this land were so tricky that when she turned to look, she saw nothing, and suddenly she lost the sound again.

"Dear God," she whispered, swallowing. "Please let it be Brand Selby, or a friend."

She stood up to wait, turning back again to the direction from which she had first heard the sound.

That's when he appeared, looking almost like some kind of apparition, the heat waves making his image blurred and ghostlike. He was in buckskins, riding a black and gray gelding, big, like its rider. She stared, her racing heart calming somewhat as he came closer and his green eyes held Rachael's reassuringly. She breathed a sigh of relief. It was Selby.

"Why did you stop?" he asked.

"I... I wasn't sure how much farther to go—if you'd

show up."

He dismounted, walking closer with the reins of his horse in his hand. His eyes were surprisingly soft and understanding. "You were afraid. I told you not to be. I have been watching you almost from the moment you were a few yards from town. I said I would be waiting and watching, that I would not let anything happen to you."

She took a deep breath, stepping back a little and angry with herself for letting tears show in her eyes. She blinked rapidly and put on a proud stance. "Well, you must admit I had a right to wonder. After all, I didn't know for certain I could count on you, considering that I hardly know you."

The slow grin made its way across his lips. "You must learn to trust, Rachael Rivers. Right now there are other Comanche out here. Some have seen you."

Her eyes widened, and she looked around. "Are you sure?"

He grinned more. "Yes, I am sure. But no one bothered you, because I told them you belong to me."

She met his eyes then, looking indignant. "What?"

His eyes moved over her, again bringing uncomfortable desires to her insides. "It is the only way I can be sure they will not bother you. Besides, they are my friends. As long as they think you belong to me, you can walk all over these hills if you want. No harm will come to you. But if one of them decided otherwise, he would have to answer to me, and I am a good warrior."

Their eyes held a moment. Warrior! Had he killed whites himself? Maybe that was just what he had in mind for her. And yet here she was, meeting him alone, willing to go all the way to his cabin where they would be even more alone. It irritated her that she almost liked the feeling she got when he mentioned belonging to him. Surely this strong, virile man before her would defend his own woman to the death. It gave her a feeling of warmth and protection. Suddenly she hardly noticed the heat, and all her fear left her.

"Thank you, Mr. Selby, for looking out for me. You can hardly blame me for being a little bit afraid. I realized for a moment that I was all alone out here, and it was so quiet."

"Just remember that I am always watching." He put out a hand. "Come."

She walked a little closer, and he took her arm gently.

"Why did you walk instead of bringing a horse or a buggy?" he asked.

"I decided it would be easier to duck out of town unnoticed if I was on foot," she answered. "Austin is so small that just going shopping doesn't necessitate a horse or a buggy. Lacy would have wondered if I had asked for either, and more people would have noticed me if I tried to get out of town either way."

A sweet warmth moved through her as his strong hands came around her waist and lifted her as though she were a child. He set her up on his horse, then mounted up behind her.

"I am sorry you have to sneak around at all." As he reached around her she could not help but notice the dark skin of his arms where the sleeves of his buckskin shirt were pushed up; nor could she help but notice the powerful forearms, the big hands as he took up the reins. He settled in behind her. Rachael realized with near shame that she liked the feel of his powerful body against her own; liked the wonderful feeling of safety and protection she felt being near him; liked the scent of leather and sage; liked the pleasant urges being near him stirred deep inside. At the same time she was furious with herself for the feelings this man awakened in her being.

"It makes me feel ashamed," he was saying. "I am as good a man as any of those in your town. And yet you dare not be seen with me because half of my blood is Indian. You white people have strange values."

"You needn't include me in the same category as the others," she answered. She wanted to turn and look up at him, but was afraid to meet his face so close. Perhaps he would think her too bold, or perhaps she didn't trust her own feelings. "After all, I'm here, aren't I? I didn't have to come at all."

He turned the horse, moving one arm around her waist. "I didn't mean to include you with the rest," he said then, his voice suddenly softer.

He rode off with her and her heart and mind raced with a mixture of fear and forbidden desires. The feel of his powerful arm around her made her realize how strong he was, what he could do to her if he wanted. For all she knew he was taking her to the Comanche to sell her or to use her for some kind of ransom. And yet there was a wonderfully reassuring feel to that strong arm. Her feelings of safety and protectiveness and trust far outweighed her fears.

She clung to the pommel of his saddle as he rode over small hills and through ravines and gullies, taking her farther and farther from Austin and all things familiar to her. In her own innocence, she little realized the near torture it was for him to have to ride double with her.

Brand Selby felt an intense ache at the feel of Rachael Rivers's voluptuous body pressed close to his own. He could smell the light soapy scent of her hair, which today she wore tied back at the sides but long and loose in the back. He wanted to touch it, kiss it. He wanted to move his arm and gently grasp her breasts with his hand; wanted to lean around and kiss her soft cheek, smell her neck, nibble all the sweet little places such a woman could offer.

Selby had never been this close to a white woman; had never considered how he might feel about one; had never given thought to having sexual desires or emotions for such a woman. But this one was good, understanding. She had risked a great deal to come to him, and he admired her greatly. He could not help wondering if there had ever been a man in her life. She said there had not, and he was inclined to believe it. She had that innocent air about her, which only made him desire her more. How lucky the man would be who took this one first. The thought of it possibly being Jason Brown made his arm tighten around her, bringing forth jealousy and anger. Jason Brown was a cruel man. He would never be kind or patient enough for a woman such as Rachael Rivers.

Rachael felt slight alarm as his arm tightened around her. Was he thinking things he should not be thinking? Was he going to suddenly turn mean? Was he thinking victorious thoughts—

that now he had her and she was his captive?

They came to a rise and he stopped. "That is my ranch below," he told her.

Rachael looked down at a small cabin, a log shed where horses were kept, a building where feed was apparently stored, and several fenced corrals. The entire place looked rather dilapidated.

"It is not much," he told her, heading the horse down then. "But it was all I could have for now. I took it over from a man who gave up and went back East, as so many of them do. People come out here and don't have any idea what this land is like. I think it is very hard for people who have not lived here growing up. This land takes a lot of getting used to. For me it is easy. I will build this place back up."

"I'm sure you will, Mr. Selby. You know the land better than any of us could."

They came closer to the little cabin. "I love this land. It is my home, and it is home to the Comanche. That is why they fight to keep it. You can't blame them, Miss Rivers. It is sad for them."

She said nothing as he rode up to a hitching post and dismounted. He reached up for her and, as he lifted her down, their eyes held. She felt no fear now. She moved away self-consciously as he tied his horse.

"I will tend to my horse later," he said. He came over and led Rachael up two steps to a small porch and through the front door of his one-room cabin. She noticed a few of the boards in the wooden floor curling from the arid climate. There was a window on either end of the cabin and a stone fireplace on the back wall, and the place smelled dusty, although it was apparent the little room had recently been cleaned as best a man can clean.

In one corner lay a pile of what looked to Rachael like skins, perhaps buffalo robes, partially covered by blankets. She realized it must be Brand Selby's bed, remembering just how Indian he was in so many ways. No Indian would sleep in a conventional bed.

The only furnishings were a hand-made table, two chairs,

and an old dresser in another corner. Shelves on either side of the fireplace displayed a few tin plates and heavy iron pots and pans, some canned food and other food stuffed into gunny sacks or crates.

Brand moved to one end of the table, looking nervous. "Welcome to my humble home," he told her. "I must tell you it is not easy getting used to living this way, so if it seems like not much to one such as you, it is only because it is all new to me. I much prefer a tipi, and sleeping under the stars, cooking over an open fire. You whites have a way of confining yourselves, making life more difficult than it has to be. But that is the way you choose to live. This is as far as I have been able to bring myself. I am sorry if you are offended by his small house, which is probably not as pretty and tidy as you would have a home of your own."

Rachael, who had been gazing around the little structure while he spoke, turned her eyes then to meet his. "It's just fine, Mr. Selby. I can tell you cleaned it up as best you could." She smiled warmly. "Back on my father's ranch we lived in a fine, frame house. But you should have seen it when I went back recently after being gone for three years." She set the books on the table. "There were only my father and brothers to take care of it, and my father had died recently." She pulled out a chair. "Whether it's a fine home or a small cabin, when it's men taking care of it, you can't expect much. A home needs a woman's touch."

Their eyes held and she reddened slightly, realizing how the remark sounded. The teasing smile passed over his lips again. "Even among Indians, an Indian man is lost without his woman, whether he is young and it is his mother and sisters, or older and it is his wife and daughters taking care of things. The men think they are so strong and brave, but they know they would be almost helpless without the women taking care of the chores and the cooking and keeping the tipi in order. Is it like that for whites then?"

"Yes. It is very much like that." She pulled out a chair opposite his and sat down. "Tell me something, Mr. Selby. If you actually prefer Indian life, why are you doing this? You must know people will be against you."

He sobered then, leaning forward to rest his elbows on the table. "Half of me is white. I suppose that is part of the reason. But also because I know what kind of future lies ahead for my people. They cannot live that way forever, and for those of us who are able, we might as well start learning to live another way. I want to be ready to help my people however I can. I can help them better by getting myself settled now, learning to live the white man's way, learning their laws, how to read—everything I can learn. I can help better from this side than I can by continuing to live as a Comanche. I am one of them. They listen to me. And to know what we are dealing with from the white man's point of view, I must live this way and learn."

She leaned back in her chair, folding her hands in her lap. "You are a very wise man, Mr. Selby. I must say I am rather surprised at such thinking. Most Indians are so opposed to learning new ways. I can easily see you are a very intelligent man, and a man devoted to his people." She breathed deeply, feeling more relaxed. "I'm very glad I decided to do this. I feel as though it's a move toward peace."

"It is a start." He watched her blue eyes, studied her exquisitely beautiful face. "Where is your father's ranch? Is it a big one?"

She shrugged. "By Texas standards I guess it's small. But it does pretty well. It's northwest of Austin—the Double 'R.' My brother Joshua runs it now, with help from my younger brothers, Luke and Matt. I worry about them. They're all so young. My father was raised among Cherokee, and he had a way with the Indians, plus he knew how to fight the ones he couldn't reason with." She reddened again. "I mean… oh, it's so awkward to sit here talking about fighting Indians to a man who is Indian himself."

Brand grinned. "It is all right. I understand what you are trying to say." He touched a candle holder on the table, absently turning it back and forth then. "Your father must have been quite a man."

"Oh, he was! He was big and strong and such a sure man. I was never afraid when I was around my father. And he and my mother were very much in love. They came here from Tennessee, just before the government began herding the Cherokee into Indian Territory. My mother died about five years ago, and after that Pa was never quite the same, never really happy. It still hurts to think of him being dead, but I know he's happier now, because he's with Mother again."

Again their eyes held in a special understanding, both of them wondering what it must be like to love someone so much that you didn't want to live without them. "Your mother must have been a fine woman to raise such an understanding daughter," he said then. "Did she have your golden hair and blue eyes?"

Rachael looked down, hoping the warmth in her cheeks didn't mean they were red. "Yes." She met his eyes again. "And she was very intent on learning, on making sure all of us had an education and could read and write and all. She's the reason I went to St. Louis to study even more. And she's the reason I'm sitting here now. I couldn't turn you down, Mr. Selby, because of promises I made to her to help anyone who needed help."

Brand smiled warmly. "Then I am very glad your mother made you promise. She and your father must have been very fair. That is hard to find among white people."

Rachael sobered. "Not as hard as you might think, Mr. Selby, I assure you."

"You have not lived on my side of the fence, Miss Rivers. Yes, it is hard—harder than you could ever know. If you are caught doing this, I don't think you would find many people around like your mother and father who would understand. It would be very bad for you."

She leaned back in her chair again. "Well, then, that's just a chance I'll have to take, isn't it?"

He glanced at the door, which he had left open, then moved his eyes back to her. "I am very grateful, Miss Rivers. And we had better get started, before you are missed."

"You mean you aren't going to tell me anything about

yourself? You know something about my family, Mr. Selby. But I don't know very much about you. It might help my teaching if I know how much you already know—you mentioned your mother was white and that she taught you what she knew. Can you tell me more about her?"

He leaned back in his chair, turning sideways and crooking one arm over the back of it. One long leg sprawled forward, and he bent the other leg up to position his foot on top of his knee. His powerful presence seemed to fill the room.

"I was not so sure I should tell you. It might frighten you away."

"Why? Because she was a captive?"

He watched her closely. "Yes. My father stole her from a settlement when she was about fourteen. He wasted no time in making her his wife, if you get my meaning."

She quickly looked at her lap, feeling the hot flush to her cheeks. "I get your meaning, Mr. Selby. It... must have been terrifying."

"I suppose—at first. But by the time I was old enough to know my mother and remember her, all of that was gone. She had come to love my father, and he loved her, if you can believe it is possible for Comanche to love. Some whites don't think so. They don't credit us with any kind of human emotions."

Rachael caught the anger in his voice then. She met his eyes again to see the hurt there.

"We do love, Miss Rivers," he went on. "As passionately as we hate. My mother had a lot to learn when she was captured, but she was a survivor, strong like you. And she decided early on that if she was to live, she had to learn the Comanche way. Her quick acceptance of her new life impressed my father, and he began to be more kind to her. Then the first baby came—" Rachael looked at her lap again. "—and that was the link," he went on. "She told me about my older brother many times, about how she felt when that baby was born, how proud my father was. But he died, and not only was my mother beside herself with grief, she was afraid she would be killed—be blamed for the baby's death. She thought my father would say it was because of her own weak blood. But he came to her and held her, and he wept, too. She told me that was when she realized she loved him. She saw then the human side, and she had already seen it in the others—had seen the Comanche have the same feelings as whites have. They live differently, but love, Miss Rivers, is the same all over the world, with all people. There is no difference in the link between mother and child, husband and wife, father and son. When we lose a loved one, we weep, just like you wept over your father and mother when they died. My mother had chances after that to escape, but she never tried. She wouldn't leave my father."

Rachael looked at him then, curiosity and admiration in her eyes. "What an amazing story, Mr. Selby. Were there more children besides you then?"

He moved his arm from the back of the chair and grasped his ankle, fingering the beads of his moccasins. "None that lived. Among the Comanche there is much more death than among your people. I came along next, and I was strong. I survived. But two more babies died after me. So I have no brothers and sisters. I was twelve when my mother died, but by then she had taught me as much as she knew herself about words and letters and such. I knew your alphabet and could write. My father never kept her from teaching me those things, and she always told me that some day I would have to decide which way to live my own life. Now I have decided. That is why you are here today."

He got up from this chair then, going to the fireplace, where a ladle hung. "You thirsty? There is a good well outside. Hard to believe in this land, but you really can find water in some places. I'm sorry I didn't think until now to ask. It's very hot. Are you comfortable?"

"I'm fine. But I would like a glass of water."

He took a tin cup from a shelf and walked out. She watched his easy gait, watched the dancing fringes of his clothing. Never in her life had she considered with such sincerity the human side of the Comanche. This man made it all so real, so much more clear. She had grown up understanding that Indians had feelings, too, for her father and mother had spoken about their own life among the Cherokee many times.

But somehow the Comanche had always seemed different. There was no doubt they were different—as different from whites as two worlds could be. They lived in a world of spirits and bloodletting and fierce combat. She was well aware of some of the hideous acts they had committed against settlers, but now she wondered about the reasons behind them, wondered about their beliefs. For now Brand Selby had opened up an avenue she had failed to consider—emotions—love. Somehow she had not been able to connect the word love with the Comanche. But this man's white mother had loved his Comanche father, in spite of the brutality under which the man had first taken her. It was surely partly because she had been young enough at the time to still be molded into a new life, and partly out of survival, as Brand had said. But there had to be more after that, for she had apparently gladly borne the man three more children, and there was only one way to get babies.

When Brand returned she quickly opened a book. She could not help thinking—what would it be like getting pregnant by a man like Brand Selby. How did Comanche men make love? The thought made her thumb nervously through the book as Brand set a cup of water in front of her. She glanced at his strong, dark hand.

"Drink some water and we'll get started," he told her, his voice gentle.

She drank the water while he went to get his chair, bringing it around beside her own. He turned it backward and straddled it, leaning against the back of it and peering down at the books.

"Yes, I have ridden against whites and I have attacked settlements," he told her then. "I know you are wondering. But because of my mother I never harmed a white woman."

Rachael drank the water, secretly breathing a sigh of relief. Somehow she wanted very much to know this man had not hurt white women, not because she feared for herself, but because it just made everything easier, teaching him, being his friend.

"Later on I became a scout for the Texas Militia," he continued, "and for a while for the Rangers. Then I worked on a white man's ranch. He's the one who helped me get started here—paid me well, taught me a lot. I settled here so that I can be closer to my people. My father was killed at Plum Creek. I was one of the few who got away. After that I knew there was no future for the Comanche, at least not in the old ways. Those were bad times."

His voice seemed to drift, and she turned to look at him, but he was staring at the books, a terrible sadness in his eyes.

"How sad there is so much misunderstanding," she told him.

He met her eyes, his own moving over her again. She wanted to ask him about Plum Creek, about Jason Brown, about many more things. But she had a feeling he didn't want to talk about those things anymore at the moment. And for her part, she didn't want to talk about Jason Brown.

"What was your mother's name?" she asked quietly.

He looked back at the books. "Mary. Mary Selby. She gave me her own last name to use for my white name. Her parents and a little brother were killed the day she was taken. No other relatives lived here in Texas, and no one ever came looking for her."

Outside his horse whinnied, but inside the room hung silent for several long seconds. Rachael turned back to the books. She turned to a page with the letter "A" on it, in capital form, small print and in longhand.

"Do you know how to print and write in longhand, Mr. Selby?"

"Just printing."

"Can you make words? Read?"

"I can read some, but not some of the bigger words. Same with writing them."

"Good. We have a good start then. First I want you to learn to make your letters in longhand. I'll write the entire alphabet for you on my slate, in both small letters and capital letters. I want you to start by practicing making the same letters yourself. The next time I come we'll do some reading."

"Fine." She picked up the slate and took some chalk from

her handbag. He watched her make the letters, studying her delicate hands and their fair, smooth skin. He wondered what the skin of her breasts was like, certainly even smoother and softer. Surely she was warm and soft everywhere, and he ached to know but knew it was not possible to find out. Even if he had the right to touch her, she was not the type who could be pushed too quickly. This woman was made of fine stuff, strong, independent, proud. If she were captured she would be very much like his own mother had been—a fighter, a survivor. He wondered if he had taken her like his father took his mother, if she would learn to love him eventually.

"There. Now you try it." She handed him the slate. Brand turned his chair around and moved closer to the table. He took the slate and the chalk and started the letters.

"No. Start at this point," she said. She rose and stood behind him, putting her hand over his own then and moving his fingers for him to show him the flow of the letter. The scent of her, the feel of her hand on his distracted him so that it was a struggle to repeat the movement on his own. It made him feel awkward, and he gave out a disgusted sigh.

"It's all right, Brand," she said, hardly aware she had used his first name. "It's only your first try."

He turned and looked up at her. "You called me by my first name."

Her eyebrows arched and she colored slightly. "I did, didn't I?" She pushed a piece of hair behind her ear. "It just slipped out."

He smiled. "Leave it that way then. I told you once to call me Brand."

She smiled in return, feeling more relaxed all the time. "And I guess you might as well call me Rachael."

"You sure?"

"Yes. I'm sure." She folded her arms. "How did your mother come to call you Brand?"

He turned back to the slate. "She told me once that being a half-breed left me branded—a man who would live in two worlds and belong to neither. So she called me Brand. She always worried about what life would be like for me, being a half-breed."

For over an hour they worked together, their friendship already growing; but other feelings were also growing, feelings both of them struggled to ignore.

"I'd better get back," she finally said. "If you like I'll leave the slate here and you can practice. There are more slates at the school."

"That would be good. I'll practice every day. You'll be surprised when you come back."

Rachael smiled, moving around the table to pick up her books. "I don't think I will be. I have no doubt of your abilities, Brand."

"I could never go to a regular school even if one had been available. Whites don't want half-breeds in their schools." He set the slate on the table, his eyes moving over her again. "I just realized I never even tended to my horse. But he should be rested enough to take us back. After I let you off I will watch until I know you are safe."

Their eyes held again, a strange ache growing in Rachael's heart. "I won't be afraid anymore, Brand." She pulled the books to her breast, suddenly aware of her shape, feeling as though he knew exactly how she looked naked. "Do you have an Indian name?" she asked, moving toward the door.

"It is Running Wolf. The wolf is my guiding spirit. I carry the feet of a wolf in my medicine bag, a wolf that came to speak to me and offer its spirit to me after I spent many days fasting and praying as a young boy."

Brand hated to see her go. He had always been a loner and liked it that way. Now, suddenly, he realized he would be lonely after she was gone. When they reached his horse he lifted her with powerful arms, then untied the animal and moved up behind her. Both of them were full of more questions, but strange new feelings prevented further conversation. Suddenly they were each afraid to speak for fear of saying something that should not be said. Brand turned the horse and headed back toward Austin.

They rode silently over sun-blistered rock and clay, through emptiness. This was where Rachael Rivers had grown up, yet suddenly she felt like a foreigner in this land. Brand's arm slipped around her. She wondered what kind of hell she had invited herself to visit by agreeing to come and meet this man alone to teach him. And it seemed that all too soon they were close enough to town that she would have to get off the horse and walk back or be seen with him.

For a moment she was tempted to have him ride her straight into town, in front of everyone. Brand Selby was a good man, struggling to improve his life. Who was there to say that any man in Austin was any better?

He halted his horse and helped her down. Their eyes held. "Thank you, Rachael," he told her.

"It was my pleasure. Come again in three days—same time."

"I will be waiting for you."

She hugged her books to her breast and backed away, smiling at him. "Be careful, Brand. Folks around here carry an awful lot of hatred."

He grinned and shook his head. "You think you need to tell me that?"

Again she wondered about Jason Brown—the story about the old Indian man. "No. I guess it was silly of me to even mention it."

His smile faded. "It wasn't silly. You were just being kind." He turned and moved onto his horse in one swift motion. "Go now before people start wondering."

She nodded, turned, and started walking. It seemed only a moment later that she turned back to wave to him, but already he had disappeared. She looked around, astounded that he could make himself so invisible so quickly. She headed back to town, feeling no fear now. Someone was watching, and now she had no doubt he would come to her rescue in a moment if she needed him.

Seven

When Rachael reached the double front doors to Lacy's boardinghouse she stopped for a moment to stare absently at their frosted windows, breathing deeply to appear calm when she entered. She looked behind her. It did not appear that anyone had noticed her walk out of town. She breathed a little sigh of relief and pushed through the doors to see Lacy coming down the stairs with sheets on her arm.

"Well! You look a mite flushed," the woman commented, glancing at the books in Rachael's arm. "Where are your packages?"

Rachael closed the door, looking down at her books. "Oh, I didn't have much luck today. Nothing I saw interested me," she lied. "I was going to stay at the school for a while but I decided to come back here to work."

"Mmmm." Lacy came the rest of the way down the stairs, her discerning blue eyes studying Rachael so intently it made the young woman nervous. Their eyes held a moment. "It's not that far a walk to the school, Rachael. You look like you've been straggling through the desert or something." She frowned. "You look like you could use a bath. You had better go upstairs and take one, honey."

"Yes, I think I will." Rachael quickly walked past her and up the stairs, anxious to hide the added flush that always came to her cheeks when she was caught in a lie. How she wished sometimes that it was easier for her to be deceitful.

"Just lock the door to the bathing room," Lacy called up to her. "There are already buckets of water up there. Day like today, I don't expect you want anything heated."

"I certainly don't. A cool bath sounds wonderful."

Rachael hurried to her room. Her mind whirled with thoughts of Brand Selby and the unusual afternoon she had just experienced. After she entered she threw the books on her bed and sat down to take off her shoes. Her chest tightened with indecision as she unbuttoned the shoes and pulled them off. Had she done the right thing? Had she completely lost her senses?

She tried to push away all thoughts while she moved to a closet to take out a light cotton dress, then to her dresser for a clean pair of bloomers. She would not bother with slips for the rest of the day. It was simply too warm. She moved to the mirror and pinned up her long hair, studying herself a moment, wondering what Brand Selby thought of blond hair and blue eyes, or if he gave no thought at all to such things. Perhaps he had a special woman waiting for him among the Comanche. She had wanted to ask, but was afraid of how bold it would sound. Perhaps he would have gotten the wrong idea from such a question. And then again, perhaps the idea he got would not have been wrong at all.

That was what confused and angered her the most— the terrible provocativeness of the man, the wonderful but disturbing feeling he stirred in her. It made her feel almost wicked without having done one thing wrong.

She took a towel from another drawer and a tin of powder, then went to the little room with a large tin tub in it that all the boarders shared. She was relieved to see Lacy had already thoroughly cleaned everything. She closed and locked the door, then picked up the buckets of water and poured them into the tub. She peeled off her clothes, then eased herself into the cool water, splashing some over her shoulders and back, around her neck and over her face.

Rachael sighed and leaned back, enjoying the cool water. Brand Selby. Was it bad for a woman to be attracted to a half-breed? She closed her eyes.

"My God," she whispered. "I *am* attracted to him."

She could not deny it, at least not to herself. With her eyes closed, all she could see was his face, so finely chiseled, the high cheekbones, the dark skin, the moving green eyes set wide apart and perfectly outlined with dark lashes and brows. His smile was warm and beautiful, his hands big and strong, his arms...

She straightened, opening her eyes, shaking her head. It was all ridiculous. She had gotten herself into a fix now. She should not go back, and yet she had promised him she would.

She took the soap from its dish attached to the side of the tub and she began scrubbing vigorously, as though with the soap she could wash away the feelings that man gave her. It was not supposed to have turned out that way. She was supposed to teach him and that would be the end of it. It was strictly student and teacher and nothing more. She washed quickly, unable to let herself relax for a while in the tub for fear her thoughts would linger too long on Brand Selby.

She rinsed and got out of the tub, drying off and powdering herself. She looked down at her naked body, realizing how little she knew about being with a man. She knew what was supposed to take place between a man and wife, but she had never done more herself than receive a couple of kisses from young men back in St. Louis, before that unwanted attempt of Jason's. None of those young men, nor Jason Brown, drew from her the wild emotions Brand Selby did.

For the first time in her life she wondered what it would be like to have a man touch her, and to want to do for him, care for him. It certainly must be a different feeling from what she had for her brothers.

Her brothers. Joshua. What would they think of what she was doing? Joshua would probably be furious. And Jason would be even worse. She turned and pulled on her bloomers. What did she care what Jason Brown thought? She didn't answer to the man and vowed she never would. Joshua was the only one she cared about. Somehow she had to find a way to tell him she was teaching Brand Selby how to read and write. She would not mention anything else. It would be absolutely ridiculous, since nothing more was going to come of the situation. She decided her feelings came strictly from childish curiosity. After all, Brand Selby was somewhat of an oddity, someone very different from anyone she had ever known. That surely explained her odd fascination with him.

She slipped on her dress. How she wished her mother were here now to give her advice. As she buttoned the front of the dress, Rachael wondered if the unnerving feelings Brand Selby gave her were anything like the feelings her mother had got when she first met her father. She hoped not, for those feelings had led to something very serious. She could not give any thought to such an outcome with Brand Selby.

She unplugged the tub, letting the water run down a pipe that ran down the outside of the boardinghouse to a ditch behind the house. There were also two outhouses out back, one for the women and one for the men, which Lacy kept painted a bright white, inside and out. Lacy Reed was almost a fanatic when it came to housekeeping, and Rachael picked up another bucket and used some of the water to rinse the tin tub. She did what she could to help, even though Lacy insisted the boarders needn't do any housework.

"It's all part of what you pay for," she told Rachael often.

But Rachael liked to help, especially now that there was no school. She decided that she would do even more now, hoping it would help her keep from thinking about Brand Selby.

She set down the bucket and picked up her belongings. She went back to her room, setting the powder on her dressing table and putting the dirty clothes into a basket. She went to the mirror to take the pins from her hair and brush it.

Again her thoughts turned to Brand. Did he like her blond hair? Did a man tangle his hands in a woman's hair when he...

She threw down the brush and went to her door, opening it briskly. Lacy was right outside the door, preparing to knock, and Rachael gasped in surprise.

"Well, do I look that bad?" the woman joked, coming inside with fresh towels.

"You startled me. That's all," Rachael answered, standing aside.

"You done with that bath already? My goodness, girl, that was fast. I thought you'd want to lay in that cool water for a while." The woman opened a drawer and put away the towels.

"I did, but…" Rachael sighed deeply, closing the door. "Oh, Lacy, I've done a terrible thing and I need your help—your advice."

Lacy frowned, putting her hands on her hips. "I had a suspicion you didn't really go shopping today. You were acting kind of strange when you left, and even stranger when you got back. Go ahead, child. I'm listening."

Rachael walked to a window and looked out. "Promise you won't get terribly angry."

"I can't promise that 'til I've heard. But I've no right to get angry or anything else. You're a grown woman and I've no control over you. But I do care about you, Rachael?"

"I know. I think of you almost as a mother." Rachael closed her eyes and sighed. "I wish my mother were still alive, Lacy. I'm so mixed up. Maybe I should just go back to St. Louis right now before I get myself in trouble."

"What kind of trouble? Where did you go today, Rachael?"

Rachael folded her arms around herself and continued to gaze out the window, which looked south over a land far removed from the shops and theaters and comforts of St. Louis. Here there was little to break the horizon. She watched as a light wind whipped up dust, making tiny tornadolike formations along the ground. Clouds were moving north toward them. It would rain before morning, something that was always welcome.

"I was with Brand Selby today," Rachael finally said.

Lacy's words came in a near whisper. "Dear God." She spoke louder then. "Where? Why?"

Rachael's fingers dug into her own arms nervously. "At his place. I walked out to meet him. I knew that was the only way I could get out of town without anyone really noticing. Jason is the only person who really keeps track of me, and he's gone. I told you I was going shopping so you wouldn't suspect. I'm sorry I lied to you, Lacy, but I was afraid to tell you. Now I need to, not just out of conscience, but because I might need you to cover for me sometime."

Rachael turned, her eyes tearing, a terrible guilt filling her at the sight of the worry in Lacy's eyes. "Oh, Lacy, I shouldn't go back, but I promised him; and I know that wrong as it is, I *will* go back."

Lacy drummed her fingers against her hipbones, shaking her head. "How did all this come about, Rachael?"

Rachael sniffed, moving to sit down on the bed. "He came to the school that night I stayed after dark. I had already spoken to him once, in the supply store. He came in while I was buying your groceries. Mr. Briggs treated him terribly badly, and I felt sorry for him, so I made a point to speak to him so he would know I wasn't like Mr. Briggs."

Lacy shook her head. "You're too softhearted for your own good, Rachael Rivers. So? Why did he come to the school? Do you know how dangerous that was?"

"Oh, Lacy, he isn't dangerous at all. He's a good man who's trying to make a better life for himself." She looked down at the quilt on her bed, picking at a quilt tie. "I was just getting ready to leave, and suddenly there he was, silent as dust. But for some reason I wasn't even afraid, Lacy. Just a little at first. But something about him—his eyes—I don't know. At any rate, he asked me if I would help teach him to read and write."

She looked up at Lacy then. "He looked at me like a little boy pleading for help. I couldn't turn him down, Lacy, not after the promise I made my mother. And everyone is judging him completely wrong just because he's a half-breed. He's really trying to make something of himself. He intends to live like a white man—has a little ranch northeast of town. And he knows that to survive in our world he has to know how to read and write. Oh, he knows some. His mother was white, Lacy, and old enough when she was captured to remember things she could teach him. So he has a head start. And he seemed so sincere. He said nobody else would teach him, but after being kind to him in the store, he thought maybe I would consider it."

"And I don't doubt he thought how pleasant it would be to have a pretty little thing like you sitting beside him giving him lessons, too."

Rachael sighed, looking at her lap again. "I don't know, Lacy. He was so respectful and mannerly. I don't think it's that."

Lacy came over and sat down beside her. "Maybe not all that, but you've got to understand men, Rachael Rivers. And you've got to understand how pretty you are, especially to somebody like Brand Selby." She suddenly put her hands to her head. "Dear God, you actually went off with him alone, clear out there where his ranch is?"

"It wasn't like it sounds, Lacy. If you knew him better—you said yourself there was something about him you liked that day you saw him at the stables."

Lacy rubbed her eyes. "I said he was a good-looking man and very quiet. I didn't say I knew him well enough in those few minutes that I'd ever advise you to go off alone with him. And you—my God, Rachael, you walked all alone out of town?"

"I know it sounds terribly stupid, but Brand promised he'd be nearby, keeping an eye on me. I just—somehow I trusted him, Lacy. And he didn't lie. He was there. He came for me as soon as I was where no one from town would see us. He said he was close enough to any Comanche who might be around to convince them not to harm me. He put me on his horse and rode me the rest of the way to his ranch." She swallowed, hardly able to believe it all herself. "I know the kind of predicament it sounds like I put myself in, but I never felt any danger. We talked, and he told me about his mother—how eventually she learned to love his father, and how he knew some day he would have to decide how he would live; we talked about a lot of things. And I gave him a writing lesson."

She turned and met Lacy's questioning, worried eyes. "Lacy, he's quite intelligent—a quick learner. He wants very much to learn, to improve himself. I can't deny him that, Lacy. My mother would turn over in her grave if I did."

Lacy grasped her wrist and squeezed gently. "Honey, there might be a danger here as great as the danger of something happening to you. Maybe that man didn't frighten you, and maybe his intentions are all perfectly good. But what about the danger of you being seen? What about the danger of you losing your teaching job? Have you thought about what your brothers would think? Let alone Jason Brown."

"Jason Brown!" Rachael pouted, rising from the bed. "What do I care what Jason Brown thinks?"

"Did you ask him about the incident with the old Indian man?"

Rachael turned, leaning against the dresser. "No. I couldn't bring myself to ask him that—not yet. Besides, I didn't feel like bringing up the subject of Jason." She looked at Lacy almost pleadingly. "And I did consider all the things you mentioned. But none of my inner arguments were strong enough to keep me from going."

"Mmmm-hmmm. What about the biggest danger of all?"

Rachael frowned. "What do you mean?"

"I mean what if you find out you have feelings for this man, which I can already see is happening? What if this turns into more than just teaching? You can't tell me Brand Selby wouldn't be attracted to you, young lady; and don't forget, I've seen the man. There isn't a woman alive who wouldn't be attracted to him in return, although most would turn up their noses at him just because he's a half-breed. What are you going to do if the feelings I see in those eyes get stronger?"

Rachael smiled nervously, reddening lightly. "Don't be silly, Lacy. The man is as off-limits as a plague. And he knows there is no future in looking at me as anything other than a teacher."

"Rachael Rivers, you're lying to me again."

Their eyes met, and Rachael's smile faded. She put a hand to her head. "Oh, Lacy, I'm so mixed up. Why do you have to have such good insight?" She turned away, walking back to the window. "All right. I do get the strangest feelings when I'm around him. That's what scares me. My biggest struggle is deciding what's so bad about that. If he were a Jason Brown, there would be nothing wrong with being attracted to him. But I'm supposed to look down on him because he's a half-breed. I can't bring myself to do that. My mother and father never would have stood for that either. But I'm selfish enough, I guess, to worry about what other people would think, just of my teaching him, let alone if... if there were more to it than that."

Lacy rose, going to stand behind her. "Did anything happen,

Rachael? Was anything said between the two of you?"

Rachael shook her head. "No. Nothing like that. He just… he gives me these strange feelings—feelings that make me feel like I've done something wrong when I haven't done anything wrong at all."

Lacy smiled sympathetically. "Honey, I can't help you there. The only thing I can tell you is that if you don't like having those feelings, you'd better cut this off right now and never go back there. That's not an order, mind you, just some friendly advice. You're looking to lose your job, and probably your reputation—and you're heading for pure trouble. I don't want to see that for you. And I don't want you hurt. That's just what will happen if you don't forget this whole thing."

A lump formed in Rachael's throat, as tears of desperation and indecision wanted to surface. "But I promised him. He… he'll be waiting for me in three days—waiting out there all alone. Oh, Lacy—" She sniffed and swallowed. "I can't do that to him. He's so proud. It would be like kicking dirt in his face for me not to show up. He wants so much to learn. People have no right treating him like that. I can't let him down. I just can't."

Lacy put a hand to the young woman's waist. "Then I don't know what to tell you, Rachael, except that I'm here for you, and I'll do whatever I can to help you through this."

Rachael turned, hugging the woman, the tears coming then. "Oh, Lacy, I'm so tired and so mixed up. I feel like I'm digging my own grave."

Lacy patted her back. "I wish you would have told me before you went out there, Rachael. It was a dangerous thing to do."

"Brand would never let anything happen to me," the girl sniffed. The warm, lovely feeling returned to her insides at the words. No. Brand would never let anything happen to her. Brand would fight a hundred men to protect her. Brand Selby was more man than any man she had ever set eyes on. And she knew she would meet him again, just as she had promised.

Again Rachael made her way through the thick stand of trees made up of mostly elm and pine that hid her until most of Austin was out of sight. She moved quickly over the hard ground to just past the one point where someone might see her. Soon the high hill covered with buffalo grass that separated her from town was high enough so that the town was out of sight.

She slowed her walk, not wanting to get hot and sweaty again. It was almost an effort not to hurry, for deep inside she was actually anxious to see Brand Selby again.

She had had a lot of time to sit and think over the past three days. Lacy had been kind enough not to preach at her the whole time. Rachael had felt better ever since telling her what she was doing. At least she had that much off her conscience. But there was still Joshua to think about. She told herself there was really not much to tell him. She had decided any feelings that went beyond her teaching relationship with Mr. Brand Selby were ridiculous and she would get over them. The best way to get over them was to face the man again. No matter how she felt, she could not bring herself to refuse teaching him.

She followed the same path as before, this time feeling no fear. She wore a checked dress of light and dark blue, with a slightly scooped neckline trimmed with lace. This time she carried a parasol, which she opened now against the sun. She looked all around but saw nothing. As she walked to the rock where she had waited before, the thought passed her mind that maybe it would be Brand Selby who would change his mind. But surely if he did he would come this time and watch over her. He would never let her come out here alone. She dispelled the thought, several minutes later reaching the rock and sitting down to wait.

She told herself this time it would be easier. Now she knew Brand, trusted him. She wasn't afraid of her surroundings anymore, and she had told Lacy about what she was doing. That made it all easier; and it seemed since telling Lacy that it was easier to deal with the feelings Brand had stirred in her. She was more sure than ever that those feelings were out of silly curiosity and the fact that she had never known anyone like him before.

He was a figure of mystery and she had allowed that mystery to overwhelm her better sense. Three days away from the man had helped her see things more clearly. This time it would be easier to look at him as a student and perhaps a friend, but nothing more.

Again there came the silence. There was not a sound, not a bird, not even a breeze. It was easy to see why people from the East thought this land desolate. In the midst of the trees she had heard a wind gently humming through the pine, as well as the calls of a few birds. But here, only several hundred feet from the small cluster of trees, it seemed to Rachael that the wind had stopped, and all life had stopped, too. In this land life seemed clustered in bunches, a little town here and there, where people moved and talked and there was some form of civilization; and surrounding those spots of life was nothingness.

She hoped Joshua and Luke and Matthew were all right. She was getting worried since she had not heard from them, and now Jason was gone and unable to check on them. She owed the man a thank you for that much at least, but she almost wished that she didn't. She didn't want to owe him anything. And she decided that this time she was going to ask Brand what he knew about Jason Brown.

It was then she heard the call that sounded like some kind of bird or wild animal. It came from a gully to her right. She looked in that direction and saw nothing. Her heart quickened. Was it Comanche? She heard what sounded like a reply signal to her left, where another hill rose, dotted with huge boulders. Intuition told her it was not animals. It had been too silent. And animals were not very active in these parts in the middle of the day. Was she being watched?

She told herself to remain calm. Brand had promised he would be here, promised she would be in no danger. Was she a fool after all to trust him? In the next moment her pounding heart eased when she heard a horse coming. She stood up, watching the distant horizon, where the ground rose and fell to such depths that a man could not be seen when at a low point. He appeared then, coming closer, a big man on a big horse. He wore buckskins, and the horse was the same one as before. It was Brand.

Eight

The moment she set eyes on Brand, Rachael realized with an almost sinking heart that this surely must be the special feeling her mother had always told her about; that excited, wonderful but almost frightening feeling, as though fate were in total control of her life. She felt as though she was in the Garden of Eden, and Brand Selby was the forbidden fruit. Were these feelings sinful? Or was it something beautiful and right? Either way, she had no right experiencing them, for they could lead nowhere. She didn't even know if Brand shared them. But then there was something in those soft green eyes as they moved over her.

"Would you be offended if I told you you look especially beautiful today?" he asked.

She felt a warmth in her cheeks. "No. No woman minds hearing that." She wondered where she had found her voice, for she was all but stunned by the way he looked. His dark brown hair hung in one braid, beautiful beads wound into it and a beaded leather hair ornament tied at its base close to his head. He wore only a vest today, rather than the long-sleeved buckskin shirt. The vest was beaded with incredible intricacy, in beautiful colors, and its sleeveless design gave full view to his arms— hard, powerful, dark. He wore a bone and shell necklace around his throat, and a longer necklace of turquoise and silver hung over his chest, part of which was exposed where his vest hung open. His buckskin pants were beaded in a stripe down each side of the legs, and his moccasins were also beaded. Copper arm bands decorated his powerful biceps, and when his horse shifted nervously, little bells tied into the fringes of his buckskin pants tinkled. Rachael wondered if a more perfect specimen of man existed.

He was dismounting. "I am glad you came again," he was saying. "I was afraid you would change your mind."

She hugged her books close. "I was afraid of the same thing."

He smiled softly. "If I had, I would not have let you come out here alone. I would have come to tell you. But as it is, I have come to take you back to the cabin again, if you are still willing."

"Yes. You see I have my books."

He nodded. Their eyes held for a moment. He reached out to take the parasol from her hand, his fingers lightly touching her own. As the wonderful warmth ripped through her insides again, she tore her eyes from his and turned to pet his horse's neck.

"I heard sounds," she told him, "like animals calling. But I don't think it was animals. Was it Comanche?"

"It was," he answered matter-of-factly, closing her parasol and sticking it into a parfleche that hung on his gear. "This umbrella thing—it was a good idea. One with such fair skin should not get too much of this Texas sun."

She looked at the contrast of their skin. His was dark, with a shining look to it. "I don't suppose the Texas sun does you much harm."

He laughed lightly then. "Not much." He turned to see her gazing around in different directions. "You are worried about the Comanche?"

She crossed her arms, hugging herself. "A little."

"I told you not to be. I thought you trusted me."

She turned and looked at him again. "I do. It's just… I mean, what if there were perhaps twenty of them? You could never fight them all off."

He grinned broadly then, a handsome, provocative smile that made her legs feel weak. "You might be surprised," he told her. He grabbed her about the waist and lifted her easily. "I am a great warrior," he told her, deliberately making his voice more gruff. He laughed again. "But you are right. That might be a few too many. Still, it is as I told you the first time. They think you are my woman."

He eased up behind her, feeling his own near painful desires as he settled in against her.

I wouldn't mind being your woman, she felt like saying as a strong arm came around her again.

I would love for you to be my woman, he was thinking. *I want to smell your hair, taste your lips, feel your naked breasts against my skin, move inside your body and be one with you. But one so beautiful and so fair is forbidden to one such as I.*

"You will be proud of me," he said aloud. "I know all my letters in longhand."

"Already? I can see this is going to be an easy task for me."

He turned his horse, and Rachael gasped as four Comanche men suddenly appeared, seemingly out of nowhere. She cringed back against Brand's chest. His arm tightened reassuringly around her and he rode slowly forward to meet them.

Rachael felt as though the blood were suddenly drained from her body. She wondered if any animal could look wilder than the men who watched her this moment. Their faces were painted, their bodies naked except for loincloths. Their torsos were also painted and bedecked with necklaces. Their hair was jet black, blowing free in the wind and decorated with feathers and beads. One of them wore bells tied into the tops of his moccasins that were bigger and tinkled louder than Brand's. Their eyes were dark and menacing, and their skin even darker than Brand's. Three of them were young, and quite handsome. The fourth was much older and carried a fierce, threatening look about him.

It was the older one who rode close, his eyes boring into Rachael's, then moving slowly to meet Brand's eyes. He spat something out in the Comanche tongue, apparently referring to Rachael. Brand answered the man with equal authority. The Comanche man sniffed, looking her over again. Then a slow grin moved across his oiled lips, and his smile revealed bad teeth. He said something more in the Comanche tongue, then reached out to touch Rachael's golden hair.

A quick, powerful hand grabbed the older man's wrist. Brand squeezed, saying something more in a growling voice. He squeezed until the old man's hand started to shake violently, then he shoved hard, nearly knocking the Comanche man from his horse. The Comanche man took a moment to reposition himself on the back of his horse, while the three younger men snickered. The older man glared at Brand a moment longer, then tossed his head, and turned his horse to ride off. The other three Comanche said something to Brand in a friendlier fashion. Brand replied, and they rode off with the older man.

Rachael closed her eyes, hugging her books tighter and still cringing against Brand. "What was that all about?"

Brand sighed, watching them ride off. "The old man was Rotten Mouth. He is one of the stubborn ones. He thought he could convince me of your value to the Comancheros, rather than keeping you for myself."

"Comancheros! Surely you don't deal with them, Brand!"

"No. And I have advised Rotten Mouth and others who do that it's a bad thing for them. Dealing with outlaws won't help their cause. It will only make things harder for them once they are all on reservations, and force them to be starving fugitives when not on the reservation. At any rate, you don't have to be afraid of them. It is as I told you. They think you belong to me. Rotten Mouth just thought he could convince me to do other things with you—let them trade you for guns and food."

Rachael shivered at the thought of being at the hands of someone like Rotten Mouth. She felt Brand's arm tighten again, as though he read her thoughts. "You're safe as long as they think you belong to me," he told her, his voice gentle now. He rode at a gentle lope toward his ranch.

"I've heard about Comancheros—the horrible things they do."

"Some of them are worse than the worst renegade Comanche," Brand answered. "They keep the Comanche at war and hurt all efforts at any kind of peace. They convince them to raid settlements, steal everything in sight, including women. Then the Comancheros trade guns and ammunition to the Comanche in return for the stolen goods, then sell everything down in Mexico, including the women, for pure gold. They get rich, and all the Comanche get is deeper in trouble, making themselves more and more hated. I have tried to make them understand that, but to those who are determined to continue the fight to keep their land, new rifles and the ammunition to use them are a treasure. But I know where it will end eventually. That is why I do what I am doing. If I can get established, learn to do business and communicate the white man's way, there might be something I can do to help the Comanche. What the outlaws do only hurts them, but I can't make some of them see that."

"Jason Brown says the outlaws out here are as much a problem as the Indians." She felt his mood change at the words.

"Jason Brown," he muttered. "He is no better than the outlaws he chases after. You should not be friends with Jason Brown. He has a bad heart."

Rachael frowned. She had not even meant to bring up Jason. "A bad heart?" she asked curiously.

"Bad. Evil, you know? We call it a bad heart. You should not be around him at all."

She felt her curiosity growing. Now that she had brought it up, she might as well find out what this man knew about Jason. "Why don't you like him, Brand? What do you know about him?"

"It is not my place to say. Let's just say he's no good."

They rode on silently for a few minutes. Finally the little ranch house came into view.

"I wish you would tell me, Brand," she pressed. "The man thinks he's in love with me. He wants to marry me. I'm supposed to be considering his offer while he's gone and give him an answer when he returns."

He slowed his horse, then stopped the animal completely. "Don't marry him," he said then, surprising her by the urgency in his voice. "I know it is not my place to tell you such things. I have no business telling you what to do with your life. But in this case I cannot help saying it. Don't marry Jason Brown, Rachael. You are too good-hearted for him. He would not appreciate a good woman. He would be cruel to you."

He got his horse into motion again. Rachael said nothing until they reached the cabin and Brand dismounted, tying the horse. He reached up for her and she held his eyes.

"You can't leave it like that, Brand. You have to tell me what you know about Jason. Then I can decide for myself."

His big hands closed around her waist and he lifted her down, slowly, holding her eyes as he put her on her feet, wanting to grab her close, tell her it was Brand Selby to whom she should belong. He would be kind to her, gentle with her; he would appreciate all the beautiful things about her. He would all but worship her golden beauty, her sky blue eyes.

"There are certain things I am pledged not to tell."

"Is that why Jason is afraid of you? Are there things you know about him he knows could ruin him?"

He took his hands from her waist. "You are a very wise woman." He took her arm and led her through the door of the cabin. "What you say is partly true. Jason also knows he could never take me, in a fight or with a gun. He would like to, but he knows better than to try."

Rachael could feel the hatred in the air and almost wished she had never brought up the subject at all. Brand pulled out a chair for her. "Are you thirsty?"

"A little."

He went and got the ladle and a tin cup again, going outside to the well. Rachael noticed a beautiful carving sitting on the table. It was a wolf. She picked it up and carefully studied it. The carving was amazingly intricate, with tiny lines dug in to create the look of fur. The face was true, the lines of the body near perfect. When Brand came back inside he hesitated at the doorway.

"Do you like it?" he asked.

"It's beautiful. Surely you didn't make this yourself."

He smiled almost shyly. "I did. I like to make things from wood. But I don't have much time for it." He came closer and set the water in front of her. "I sat up late at night carving that one special—for you. I'm glad you like it. I will do a horse for you next."

Her eyes widened in surprise, and she continued to finger and study the carving. "Oh, Brand, you didn't need to do that. But I truly appreciate it. It's absolutely beautiful!"

He sat down in a chair just around the corner of the table

from her. "I carved a wolf first because the wolf spirit is a part of me. The wolf spirit gives me power, makes me wise and quick."

She carefully set down the carving. "You told me last time I was here that you carry the wolf's paws in your medicine bag. What is a medicine bag? Is it something religious?"

He studied her inquisitive blue eyes. "A medicine bag is something all Indian men carry close, filled with things that bring them luck, or give them power." He was sober now, his green eyes holding her blue ones. He felt a need to try to make her understand the side of him that was so different from her world. "It is the way. To be one with the animal spirits, the land, is to be wise and powerful. Every man must find his spirit within himself, and find the animal spirit that will guide him through life. Mine is the wolf."

She saw the sincerity in his eyes, wondering at the power the spirit world played in an Indian's life. Her own father had tried to teach her some of that same spirit, had taught her about the Cherokee. But she had never really lived among them, and she had been brought up a Christian. Her parents had both taught her that there was really very little difference between Christianity and the way Indians worshiped, but it had always seemed the Comanche were different.

"Is anyone else allowed to see your medicine bag?" she asked Brand.

Their eyes continued to hold. "No. It is sacred."

She looked around the room. "Where is it? Where do you keep it?"

The faint smile began to move over his lips. "It is small. A man wears it on his person, at the place most sacred to him, the place that makes him a man."

She frowned for a moment, then began to redden deeply. "Oh!" She looked away, picking up the tin cup of water and eagerly drinking, hoping the swallows would help dispel her total embarrassment.

"I did not mean to make you uncomfortable," he told her. Her innocence brought even more painful desires to his being. "You asked me. You are teaching me white man's ways. So I teach you Indian ways. There are some beautiful things about Indian life, Rachael. The Indian is not inhibited by all the rules and stiff clothing and social niceties of the whites. You people strangle your spirit, keep it locked away. You do not know your inner power. You only know the power of weapons, numbers, money, rules, but not the power within yourselves. I think you must have a very beautiful spirit. I would think your kindred animal would be a bluebird—light, beautiful, happy, free…"

He suddenly rose, seeming himself embarrassed. "I'm sorry. I didn't mean to go into all of that. You are here to teach." He walked over to get his slate, while Rachael breathed deeply to make the red in her cheeks go away. She felt as though she had somehow invaded this man's privacy, had stepped too far into his life. And all it had done was make her want to know more, make her wonder more about what it would be like to be loved by such a man.

"It's all right. I want to learn, just like you do," she answered, picking up the carving once more.

"Who told you Jason Brown was afraid of me?" he asked, setting down the slate.

She put down the carving again. "A man who boards at the rooming house where I live. He didn't tell me directly. He told my landlady, Lacy Reed." She met his eyes then. "He had been in a tavern, where a Ranger who rides with Jason got drunk and started saying things, something about…" She watched his eyes. "About Jason whipping some old Indian man." She saw his eyes darken with remembered anger and knew immediately the story must be true. "He said you came along and stopped him, and that Jason acted as if he was afraid of you." Her eyes teared slightly. "Is it true, Brand? Did Jason really whip an old man?"

He slowly nodded. "It is true." His green eyes glittered with bitterness. "Jason hates the Comanche—the worst kind of hate, Rachael, for he hates them for no good reason. He simply thinks the white man is superior, and he is a man who likes the power of his job. He has done other things—worse things. That is why I tell you to stay away from him. He might act kind and good in front of you and your people, but I know what kind of man he really is. And I know things about him that could destroy him. I once rode with him, Rachael, when I scouted for the Militia and then for the Rangers. But I quit, after a certain incident involving Jason Brown. He is no good, and if I ever get the chance to prove beyond any doubt that he is still up to no good, I will do it. I would like to see his badge taken from him. He is a disgrace to the Rangers, but they gave him a second chance. If he continues in his wrongdoings, he will lose his job."

"But why didn't you tell them about the old Indian man?"

Bitterness still showed in his eyes as he leaned back. "I would have to come to them with something more important to them than one old Indian man. I am a half-breed myself, remember? Atrocities against the Comanche are not enough, not unless they are more openly evil. The old man had stolen a calf. That is enough to keep the Rangers from coming down hard on Jason Brown, even though it was a terrible thing he did." His jaw flexed in anger. "The old man died in my arms. I took him back to his village." The last sentences were spoken more softly, and he moved his eyes to the slate, as though he was afraid to let her see there might be tears in them.

"I'm sorry," she told him gently. "And I thank you for telling me at least that much. It's all I need to know."

He kept his eyes on the slate. "Do you love him?"

She reddened a little and looked down at her lap. "No. I never felt I loved him. I felt a little bit obligated. He's been so adamant about marrying me. The man won't leave me alone, but then I've never given him a firm no either. I can see now that I will have to when he comes back from this latest duty."

Brand shifted and she could feel his tension. He leaned closer to her. "Be sure you tell him while you are at the boardinghouse, or someplace where there are other people around."

She frowned, meeting his eyes. "Why?"

"Just do as I say, Rachael. If you anger him, it is hard to say what he might do. Jason Brown doesn't like to be crossed or insulted, certainly not by a woman. Make sure you are someplace where he can't hurt you for fear of others being nearby."

Her eyes widened. "Hurt me? Oh, Jason would never—"

"Don't underestimate him, Rachael. He puts on a good show when he needs to."

She blinked in confusion. "But he watches after me—and after my brothers—checks on them all the time to make sure they're all right."

"Damn it, woman, will you listen to me? You've only seen one side of him! I've seen the other side!"

She jumped slightly at the curse, spoken in a louder voice. Their eyes held and his softened.

"I'm sorry, Rachael." He closed his eyes then and sighed deeply. "You are a fine woman, good and kind. I just don't like the thought of you in the hands of someone like Jason Brown. You must believe me when I tell you he can be dangerous."

She swallowed, blinking back tears of disappointment at finding out things were much worse than she thought. "I believe you," she answered quietly, looking at her lap again. "I just... I guess I just don't *want* to believe you. But down deep inside, there has always been something about Jason that frightened me. Lacy doesn't like him at all, and she's a woman of keen intuition; and she's older. She knows people better than I do. Lacy is like a second mother to me, since my own mother is dead." She met his eyes. "I told Lacy about coming out here to meet you."

He looked surprised, leaning back again. "You did? Didn't she tell you to stop?"

Rachael smiled then. "She tried. But it wasn't anything to do with you. She's just afraid for me to be walking alone, and afraid of what people will do and say if they find out." *She's also afraid I'll fall in love with you*, she felt like saying. But she kept the words to herself. "Anyway, she always tells me to do what I think is right, and she'll support me."

He smiled himself then. "She must be a good woman."

"She is. She has seen you. She said she was at the blacksmith's once getting a horse shod, and you were there. You didn't speak, but she saw you."

He grinned and nodded. "I think I know who she is now. I smiled at her, and she gave me a kind smile. She seemed like a spirited white woman who fears no one."

113

Rachael laughed lightly. "That's Lacy, all right."

Their eyes held again. "You will remember what I told you about Jason Brown?" he asked then, sobering again.

She nodded. "I'll remember." She wanted to know more, to know what else this man knew about Jason. But he apparently could not or would not tell her. It was enough to know what he had done to the old man. It was all she needed to know to make her want nothing to do with Jason.

Brand picked up the slate and began writing. "We had better get to the lesson," he said. "I am anxious to show you." He was writing the alphabet in longhand without hesitation. Rachael quickly moved him into connecting the letters to write words that he knew, then taught him some new ones, as well as going through a primary reader with him. She dove into teaching, hoping it would help quell the deep feelings that were growing in her heart for him.

The lesson seemed finished too soon. "What do you know about numbers?" she asked him then.

"I can add and subtract."

"How about bookkeeping? If you're to deal with white men you should learn bookkeeping. It will help you keep your financial situation in order, help you see where you stand, how much money you're making."

He grinned and shook his head. "I don't know about this thing called bookkeeping. It sounds like more of the white man's rules that pen a man up."

She smiled. "I suppose that's just what it is. But who is to say you can't learn these things, and still be Brand Selby in spirit? You don't have to stop believing what you believe about life, Brand, or stop worshipping however you please. Maybe that's what the Comanche and other Indians need to learn—how to live in the white man's world and still be Indian. Do you think that's possible?"

"I suppose it could be. But it would not be very easy."

"No, I suppose it wouldn't. But I'll bet if anyone can do it, you can." She rose from her chair. "At any rate, I'll bring some ledger paper the next time I come, and I'll show you a little bit about bookkeeping. And I'll leave that reading book here so you can practice. You make note of the words you don't know or understand. Next time I come I'll bring a more difficult reader. I think the one I brought is too simple. You know more than I thought you did. Your mother taught you well."

"She was a good woman, like you."

She blushed a little. "Well, considering her circumstances, she must have been very strong, very remarkable."

He rose, coming a little closer, holding her eyes. "The circumstances were not so bad. My father was kind to her. Some captives are not treated so kindly."

She folded her arms, looking down. "I'm sorry, but I can't understand some of the things the Comanche do, nor can I ever accept it."

"It is easy to understand when you look at it from the other side, Rachael. The Comanche cannot understand or accept some of the things the white men do. And their own women have been abused—raped, murdered, sold into prostitution."

"Don't," she almost whispered, turning around.

"I just want you to know that some acts are pure revenge for the terrible hurts we ourselves have suffered. We love our women, too, and our children and our old ones. White men come through our villages and murder, slaughter babies and helpless children; do terrible things to the women and then kill them; kill defenseless old people. Why should we not feel the same hatred, Rachael, the same bitterness, the same need for revenge?"

She swallowed back a lump in her throat. "I know what you're saying. But it's still hard to accept—the cruelty, the torture." She turned to face him, her eyes full of tears. "You've never taken captives, tortured anyone, have you?"

His eyes remained gentle and understanding. "No white women. But I did live and ride with the Comanche, Rachael. I was a warrior. Do you understand what I am telling you?"

He read the doubt in her eyes. "You've killed white men?"

"Of course I have killed white men. But those days are over for me now." He stepped a little closer, noticing she stiffened slightly when he took hold of her arms. She kept her head down as he spoke.

"Rachael, I can't stand here and explain the Comanche ways in five minutes. You could try and try for months, years, and never truly understand why they do some of the things they do—how they believe that to torture a brave man makes their own spirits stronger—how they honor bravery even though they might kill the person—how blood and warfare have been a way of life for them for centuries. How can I explain that to a softhearted white woman who has never known that kind of life? I wish I could make you understand, but I know in my own soul it's impossible. But remember one thing. There are white captives living among the Comanche who don't *want* to go back to their own world. They have learned to love their new way of life, learned to love the Comanche, have become a part of their way of life. Doesn't that tell you something?"

She raised her eyes to meet his then. "I guess it tells me the way they live is just... just another way of life... and just because it's different from how we live doesn't mean it's wrong or terrible."

He smiled a little. "That's good for starters. It also tells you love is the same everywhere; that it's possible for whites to love the Comanche, and for the Comanche to love a white person."

His eyes held hers like magnets, and for a brief moment she wondered if he was thinking about kissing her. She had no idea how much he wanted to do just that, and more. But he kept his composure and let go of her arms.

"I didn't mean to go into all that," he told her. He moved to the fireplace where he took down the ladle again. "Here. I'll get you another drink before we go back." He picked up her cup and went out.

Rachael picked up the second book she had brought along, and the carving, and followed him out, watching the broad shoulders and the strong arms as he lifted a bucket of water from the well. How would it feel to be held in those arms, to be kissed by that perfectly shaped mouth? She wanted to ask him again about having a woman of his own, but again she was afraid it was too bold a question. He approached her with the cup of water. "Here you go."

"Thank you." She took the cup, drinking most of it down. When she handed it back to him, he drank down the rest.

"Can't waste a precious thing like water," he told her. He walked over to his horse, untying it and leading it to the well. He poured water from the bucket into a trough near the well and let the animal drink. He turned while the gelding guzzled, pointing to a nearby corral where several horses roamed lazily. "That's part of my herd, my best horses. They're on feed right now. I'm giving the grass in my best grazing pasture time to get a little higher before I turn them out. What do you think?"

Rachael watched them, walking a little closer. "They're beautiful. Are they all broken?"

"No. Only a couple of them. I have my work cut out for me, but I won't let it interfere with my lessons."

She kept watching the horses, several sizes and colors, most of them looking strong and healthy. "Mustangs?"

"Mostly. I bought a few from the man I used to work for. Then I went out and chased down a few more, weeded out the weaker ones. Some mustangs aren't in very good shape. And I traded some supplies to Comanche friends for those two big Appaloosas."

She looked at him. "You aren't afraid they'll be stolen whenever you're gone?"

He grinned. "Most horse stealing around here is done by Comanche. They won't steal mine, so I'm pretty safe. I do pay two young Comanche boys in candy and supplies to watch the ones I keep out on the grazing land where I can't see them. They stay out there most of the time. They don't like being inside a building—scares them."

Rachael frowned. "Scares them?"

He nodded. "Bothers me a little, I have to admit. I sleep outside more than inside." He went and got his horse, leading it over to where Rachael stood. "There is something about being enclosed that gives an Indian the jitters, for the spirits of the land and animals can't get to him, maybe not even his own spirit. Inside you're separated from nature, the sky, the sun." He looked down at her. "I don't suppose you can understand that."

She looked up at the sky, watching puffy clouds float by, seeming whiter than white against the brilliant blue. "Oh, I think I can, to some extent. It must be a form of what we call cabin fever."

"Cabin fever?"

She laughed lightly. "Yes. When we're confined inside for too long because of bad weather, we get sick of looking at the same four walls and feel a little crazy. We call it cabin fever, a kind of depression and craziness that sets in because we feel a need to get out."

He grinned. "Well, maybe there is more Indian in you than I thought."

She frowned in thought, looking up at him. "Maybe it doesn't matter what color our skin is, or what nationality we are or whatever, Brand. Maybe it's simply a matter of how we're raised. And if that's the case, then down deep inside we are all of the same spirit. My father was white, but deep inside he had the spirit of an Indian."

He sobered, studying her with admiration in his eyes. "You are beginning to understand, Rachael Rivers. But most whites don't understand that at all. We are all brothers here." He put a hand to his heart. "Inside. But we live differently, and each thinks his way of living is the only right way. The only difference is the whites try to force their way of living on everyone around them. The Comanche don't ask the whites to live as they live. They only ask that the white men leave them alone and respect their way of life and let them live the way they choose, the way that they are happiest."

He reached around her waist and lifted her onto the horse. "I have said far more than I intended to say. What is it about you that makes you so easy to talk to? I am usually a very quiet man." He eased up behind her.

"Maybe I just ask too many questions," she told him.

"No. It's more than that. You are easy to be with. And you are a good listener. You care. You want to learn."

"Yes, I truly do want to learn, Brand." She watched the

strong arm come around her, astounded that she felt safe alone with this man who had once ridden with the Comanche on raids against her own people.

Brand rode off with her, wishing with all his heart that she did not have to leave, wishing she could stay forever, share his nights as well as his days. Rachael Rivers would make a good companion; and he knew instinctively that here was a woman who would go to great lengths to please the man she truly loved. The thought of Jason Brown pestering her made him want to kill the man, and he suddenly realized how dangerous it would be for her if the man found out she was coming out to see him.

"Maybe you should stop coming," he said aloud. "That Lacy Reed was right to warn you to stop. It would be bad for you if anyone found out, especially Jason Brown."

Rachael pouted. "I don't care what Jason Brown thinks of anything I do. I never have. My life is my business. He can't tell me what to do. He doesn't own me."

He grinned at the words. "You just remember what I told you. Don't let yourself be alone with him, not if he finds out about this, not even when you tell him you will not marry him and you no longer want to see him."

"I'll remember."

They rode for a few minutes in silence, Rachael in turn wishing she didn't have to leave. She cradled the beautiful carving close to her breast, knowing that no matter what happened, she would treasure it forever.

"There must be many men in Austin besides Jason Brown who have their eyes on one so beautiful as you," he said then.

She laughed lightly. "Thank you. But I'm not sure. No one has bothered coming around since I've been back because the whole town thinks I belong to Jason—not because of anything I've done but because that's what he tells everyone."

Again they rode in silence, finally reaching the flat rock. He halted his horse but stayed on it a moment, his arm firm around her. "I will miss you, Rachael Rivers," he said softly. "You brighten my day, and you are proof that there are some whites who are kind and accepting."

She felt a terrible urge to turn and hug him. "There are more of us than you think, Brand. I hope you'll find that out some day. Maybe... maybe the two of us together can make people understand."

"Maybe. For now it is best we continue this way. But the moment you sense danger, do not come. I will understand if I come here and you don't show up."

She put a hand on his powerful forearm, wondering at her own boldness as she squeezed it gently. "I'll be here. Every three days, just as we planned."

Brand dismounted. "Just the same," he told her, lifting her down. "Don't risk too much, Rachael. I will be here in three days. You do what is best for you."

She met his eyes, her pride and stubbornness showing. "I said I would be here, and I will." She looked down at the carving. "Thank you so much for this, Brand. I will treasure it always and I'll..." She looked up at him again. "I'll think of you every time I look at it." She quickly turned and started walking back toward the small spot of woods that would hide her until she was on the outskirts of town. "Don't you let old Rotten Mouth get me," she called out, afraid to look at him again for fear he would see the desire in her eyes.

Brand grinned, watching her lovely form, the sway of her hips, wondering if she meant what it seemed like she meant when she said looking at the carving would make her think of him. Would such a woman consider loving a half-breed? It seemed hopeless, but the ache in his own soul grew bigger every time he saw her. Still, even if she could have those feelings for him, it would be bad for her, and wrong for him to allow it. For people would be cruel to her. Then again, somehow he sensed she was strong enough for that.

He watched until she was well out of sight. She had turned once, appearing as just a tiny, lovely blue dot in the distance. She waved, and he waved back, knowing already that the next three days were going to be much too long a wait.

Nine

Lacy greeted Rachael at the door. "Your brother is here," the woman said quietly. "He's in the parlor."

Rachael paled slightly. "How long has he been here?"

"Quite awhile. He came earlier and when I told him I thought you were at the school, he went looking for you. Now he's all upset because he couldn't find you. I told him you must have been shopping, but he said he looked all over town."

Rachael closed her eyes and sighed. "Thanks for your efforts," she whispered.

"Are you going to tell him?"

"I don't know. Here, take these things for me. How do I look?"

"A little better than the first time. At least today it wasn't so hot. Are you all right?"

Rachael smiled wearily. "Yes. I could use something to drink, though."

"You go in to Josh. I'll bring something." She patted Rachael's arm. "We can talk after he leaves." The woman looked down at the carved wolf. "What is this?"

"He made it for me. It's a wolf."

"I can see mat, but why—" Lacy looked back up at her sternly. "Rachael, you shouldn't have accepted it."

"Oh, Lacy, please let's talk about it later. Just take it up to my room for now, would you, please?"

The older woman sighed, shaking her head. "You'd better tell Joshua what's going on, and soon."

While Lacy turned and went up the stairs, Rachael looked at herself in a mirror that hung between coat hooks in the hallway. She took a handkerchief from a pocket of her skirt and pressed it to her face to absorb the perspiration, then toyed with her hair a moment, shaking it out behind her back. She took a deep breath, then walked down the hallway and into the parlor.

Joshua looked up from a love seat, where he had been sitting looking at some books Lacy kept lying on a nearby table. "Rachael! Where in hell have you been? I looked all over for you."

"Oh, Josh, I'm sorry." She approached him, her arms out, and he rose, moving to embrace her. She thought it would be easy to tell him, but suddenly all courage left her. He was already upset that he had not been able to find her, so he wouldn't be in the best of moods; and their opinion of the Comanche differed drastically. "You must have missed me wherever you went. I was just feeling so bored lately, what with no school and all. I've been all over town."

"Austin isn't that big. I can't believe I could have missed you."

"Well, here I am. You can see I'm perspiring and a little tired. I walked all over town, visiting here and there." She moved away from him and sat down on the love seat. "Joshua, sometimes living in Austin is like living in a prison. No one can go out of town alone without risking life and limb. It gets so frustrating sometimes. I have such urges to just get in a buggy and go riding."

"Well, don't you do it." He came and sat back down beside her. "You stay right in town. Maybe some day Jason and his men will clean things up enough to make it safer, but until then don't you even think of going out alone."

She looked away at the mention of Jason. "Sometimes I think Jason Brown creates more trouble than he helps."

Joshua frowned. "What are you talking about?"

Rachael leaned back, folding her arms. "Oh, it's just a rumor we heard—that Jason used that bullwhip of his on an old Indian man." She looked at her brother. "Remember when he told us back at the ranch that they had a little trouble with an old Indian man? All he said was that he 'took care' of it. But a boarder of Lacy's was around one of Jason's men one night when he was drunk, and the man said Jason used his whip on the old man. I don't call that a very good way of taking care of things, not if we're trying to make peace with the Comanche."

Joshua shrugged. "What did the old Indian do?"

"Josh!" She met his eyes then. "Would anything warrant whipping an old man? I can't believe you would go along with such a thing."

He sighed and leaned back, running a hand through his hair. "No, I wouldn't. But you ought to ask Jase about it. It might not even be true."

She watched him, tempted to tell him she knew for certain it was true—to tell him how she knew it was true.

"Well, I think it is. Father always said a man usually speaks the truth when he's drunk. And I still say there's a mean streak in Jason. That's why I don't like him. And when he comes home next time, I'm going to tell him to please leave me alone. He asked me to marry him, but I won't do it."

Joshua turned a little, bending a knee and moving that leg onto the love seat so he could face her. "I think you're wrong there, Rachael. But I want you to be happy. If Jason Brown doesn't make you happy, I can't force you to marry him. I just don't think you've given him a fair chance."

She held his eyes. "I know what I feel, way deep inside, Joshua. And way deep inside I'm afraid of Jason Brown."

He's cruel and vicious and a disgrace to the Rangers, she wanted to continue. *Brand Selby is ten times the man Jason is.*

"Oh, let's not talk about Jason," she said aloud. She put a hand on his arm. "It's good to see you, Josh. I've been so worried. I've lost track of how many weeks it's been since I came home."

"Well, you know how it is in spring around the ranch—planting, branding, mending fences. It never ends. I came to town to order some lumber and seed. I'll be coming back in another week or so, so I'll get to see you again. Luke and Matt send their love."

"Oh, give them mine in return. Try to bring one of them with you next time you come, Josh."

"Well, I don't like leaving one of them there alone. I almost sent Matt this time, but I was afraid he'd get the wrong kind of lumber. I reckon they're all right. Things have been pretty quiet most of the winter and this spring. I think the Indians know Jason checks up on us pretty often. Of course he hasn't been around much himself lately. He's out on some patrol."

"I know. He said he'd be gone a month or more."

Lacy came into the room then, carrying a tray with two glasses of lemonade. "Here you go. Drink up, children."

"Oh, thank you, Lacy." Rachael took her glass quickly, gulping down the refreshing drink.

Joshua watched her, uneasy about her explanation of why he couldn't find her. He reached for his lemonade. "I still can't figure out how I could have missed you, sis," he said after gulping down some of his drink.

Rachael looked up at Lacy, then back at Joshua. "I can't either. I'm sorry you had to run all over town."

"Well, I got some supplies ordered at least, and it was kind of nice to be around people again. Gets pretty lonesome back at the ranch."

"You staying the night, Joshua?" Lacy asked him.

"I think I'd better. I'll leave real early in the morning so I can get home by tomorrow night."

"Will your brothers be safe overnight?"

Josh ran a hand through his thick, sandy hair. "I can only pray they will be. We haven't had any trouble in a long time."

Rachael thought about old Rotten Mouth being so close to town, a man who traded with outlaws. She felt torn between a desire to tell her brother she had seen renegades close to town, and a fear of telling him just yet about Brand Selby. "Well, you be extra careful, Josh," she said aloud. "You've said yourself Comanche can be around without being seen at all." She looked at Lacy, who frowned and nodded.

"Mmmm-hmmm," was all the woman said in reply. She moved her eyes to Joshua. "I have an extra cot in the storage closet under the stairs. I'll take it out and you can sleep on it in the hallway tonight if you like."

"Well, that's real nice of you, Lacy."

The woman smiled. "Anything for the children of Joe and Emma Rivers. I'll go drag it out and get it ready." She turned and left, and Rachael met her brother's eyes.

"You remember what I said, Josh. Please be careful."

"Oh, you know me. I'm as good as Pa with a gun. And Pa made friends with some of the closest Comanche. They've been leaving us alone."

"I know. But what about outlaws?" She wanted to tell him what she knew about the Comancheros from Brand, but she used Jason's name instead. "Jason says they do as much dirty work as the Comanche, and sometimes the Comanche get blamed for it."

"Well, no outlaws have come around our way. And I expect the Comanche deserve the blame for most of the violence that takes place around here. You're too quick to defend them, Rachael. You know yourself some of the things those animals have done."

Rachael set her glass back on the tray. "Don't call them animals, Josh. Pa would never have called them that."

"Pa leaned a little too much toward the Indians because of how he was brought up. But I told you before, the Comanche are different. Jason has told me stories—"

"Jason!" She got up from the love seat. "You act like you think the man is God, Joshua. And how do you know he always tells the truth?" She walked to a window, folding her arms.

Joshua frowned. "What's with you, Rachael?" He leaned forward, resting his elbows on his knees. "You act like you hate Jason, like you know something I don't. Do you? Did he try something with you?"

She reddened, but he couldn't see her face. "No," she answered quietly. "Oh, he kissed me before he left—a kiss I didn't want. He didn't really do anything offensive. It was just … the way he kissed me." She shivered. "I didn't like it and I don't like Jason. I think you are making him out to be a better man than he is, Josh, that's all. I've been more sure of it ever since hearing about him whipping that old man."

Joshua studied his sister, wondering if there was a prettier young woman in all of Texas. He liked and trusted Jason Brown, but he didn't like to see his sister unhappy, nor did he like the idea of anybody touching her.

"You do what you think is right about Jason," he told her. "I think he's a good man, but if he tries to force a kiss out of you again or keeps bothering you after you tell him you don't want to see him anymore, you tell me, Rachael."

She smiled, turning to face him, her cheeks still crimson. "Thank you, dear brother. But I can take care of it. I don't want to ruin your friendship. But I do wish you would look at Jason with a little more objectivity. I'm sorry if I disappoint you by not wanting to marry him."

Joshua rose. "Hey, Rachael, I just wanted the nice feeling of knowing you've got a husband and are being taken care of, that's all. I hate you being here all alone. I feel like I should be doing something to take better care of you."

Rachael turned, moving toward him and putting an arm around his waist. "Josh, you don't have to take care of me. And I am not going to marry a man just for that reason. I'm perfectly happy here in Austin, and Lacy is so good to me. It's just like having a mother again." They sat back down on the love seat. "Maybe I should come and stay with you and Luke and Matt for a while before school starts again."

Josh frowned. "I don't know. We're away a lot, mending fences, rounding up young stock and such. It's probably best you stay here. Just because we haven't had any trouble from the Comanche doesn't mean it will stay that way."

But all I have to do is tell Brand, and he'll make sure no one bothers us, she wanted to tell him. What would he say? Would her own brother hate her if he knew? Somehow she couldn't bear the thought of his disapproval.

"Whatever you say," she answered. "But you must need the house cleaned again."

Josh grinned. "We're getting better. And I'm not such a bad cook."

Rachael grinned, putting her arm up on the back of the love seat and turning to face him. "I think *you're* the one who needs to be married, Joshua Rivers. It wouldn't hurt to have a woman around to take care of the three of you."

Joshua shrugged. "We've got along for a long time without that. But I have to admit things were a bit easier when Ma was alive, that's for sure. Trouble is, I don't have much time to go running around meeting girls. The only kind of women I have time for are the kind a man doesn't have to woo first, and they aren't the kind a man marries."

"Joshua Rivers!" Rachael reddened. "Such talk." She looked at her lap and Joshua laughed lightly.

"Rachael, I'm twenty years old."

"Well, you shouldn't be around women like that, not my brother." She faced him again. "There is going to be a dance here in town the last Saturday of May, a kind of pre-celebration of Austin becoming the capital of Texas. The Millers are holding it. I think they're being a little premature, but I expect it's more an excuse to get the town together and have a party. Why don't you come to it? Maybe you could hire some men to watch the ranch for a couple of days and you could bring Luke and Matt with you. You might meet someone at the dance—someone *nice*, someone *worth* wooing. It's time you did some serious looking."

He laughed again. "You're as bad as I am."

Rachael smiled in return. "All right," she answered. "When we find the right person, we'll tell each other."

Again she was tempted to tell him. *I've met someone, Josh. He's strong and brave but gentle and good.*

Joshua sobered. "The way things are going with Mexico, maybe I shouldn't get too serious about anybody yet. I might be fighting Mexicans."

"Oh, Josh, do you think it would get that bad?"

He shook his head. "I like to hope not. But Mexico refuses to recognize Texas as a Republic, insists she still owns us. It looks like statehood is a sure thing now. The minute we're annexed to the United States, Mexico is going to let loose, mark my words. There is even a rumor that Santa Anna might be called back to lead Mexican soldiers. Nobody is going to fight harder than somebody with a bone to pick, and he's got one. He'll never live down that defeat at San Jacinto."

"Well he didn't win the first time, and he won't win this time," she answered, sitting up straighter on the love seat. "We have a bone to pick, too. Just thinking about the Alamo is all our men will need to win another round." She met his eyes. "But I would hate to see you go to war, Josh. I hope it never comes to that."

"So do I. I'd lose the ranch for sure if I had to leave it. I'm having trouble making a go of it as it is."

She frowned. "Is there anything I can do?"

"Not really. The best thing you can do is stay here where it's safe so I'll have less to worry about."

"Well, I hope you're making Luke and Matt practice their reading and writing. That's so important. I wish they were close enough to come to school."

"Ma taught me good and I've taught them. They'll do okay."

"Well, I have a couple of books to give you to take back to them. Make sure they practice reading them."

He bowed slightly. "Yes, ma'am."

Her eyes teared a little. "Things were a lot easier when we were young, weren't they, Josh? I mean, life was hard, but Father and Mother, they were always there and everything was okay as long as they were there."

He sobered, taking her hand. "Yeah. I miss Pa an awful lot. Nothing to do with needing his help. It's just that it was nice having him around. Seemed like he always had all the answers."

She looked down. "It was that way with Mother, too." How she wished she could tell Emma Rivers about Brand Selby. Her mother would understand better than anyone.

Joshua squeezed her hand. "Everything okay, Rachael? Is there anything you want to tell me?"

She shook her head. "No."

"If you want to go back to St. Louis, I'd understand, Rachael."

"No. I want to be as close to my brothers as possible, at least for now. I promised Father I'd come back, and I promised Mother I'd help children learn, children who had little opportunity. There are plenty of schools back in Missouri, but out here…" She sighed deeply. Everything would be fine if it weren't for her feelings for Brand Selby. Why had she allowed herself to agree to teach him? Why hadn't she asked Mr. Dreyfuss about another way to teach the man? Yes, it was true there was probably no one in Austin who would agree to it, but maybe she should have tried.

Rachael knew the feelings she had for Brand had been there from the moment she saw him at the river. That was the real reason she had agreed to teach him—just to get to know him better. Rachael had walked right into this mess with her eyes wide open, and today she realized things were not going to get better unless she stopped seeing Brand.

She looked at her brother again. Would he understand? "Out here there is such little opportunity for learning," she finished aloud. "Mr. Dreyfuss really needs my help. Austin is growing more, now that it's a sure thing this town will be the capital when Texas becomes a state."

Joshua searched her eyes. "Well, if there's anything you need to tell me, don't be afraid to," he answered, letting go of her hand. " 'Course if it's about a man, I don't know how much help I'd be. Apparently I'm not too good at picking the right one for you. But you can talk to Lacy."

She nodded. "Yes. Lacy is wonderful." She sighed deeply. "But it isn't that," she lied. "I'm just still adjusting to being back, I guess. I would do a little more socializing with women my age, but most of them are married and even have children already."

Joshua laughed lightly. "There, you see? A husband and kids would keep you plenty busy. It's probably what you need."

"Oh, Josh!" She rose from her seat. "It's almost time for supper. You'll eat with us, won't you?"

"Sounds good to me." He rose, coming to put his arm around her shoulders. "You go upstairs and change. You probably want to freshen up."

"Yes, I do. There is a smoking room if you want to smoke a pipe. One or both of the men boarding here might be in there. Lacy can bring you something a little stronger than lemonade if you want. Just don't overdo it, big brother."

Joshua grinned. "Something stronger sounds real good." He watched her as she ascended the stairs. Something was wrong, but she was apparently not about to tell him. He felt sorry for Rachael, realizing how difficult it must be for her here in Austin after living in St. Louis for three years. She was so beautiful, and now so educated and sophisticated. He couldn't blame her if she wanted to go back East.

Rachael reached her room and closed the door. She picked up the carved wolf from the dresser where Lacy had put it. She studied it closely, admiring the intricate detail. Brand Selby seemed to be an intelligent man with many talents. Perhaps a man from two worlds was the best kind of man there was, a man who truly understood life to the fullest. Her eyes teared as she realized the feelings that were building for him were becoming much too strong for her own good.

Was this love? Was this how it felt? She had just left him and already she missed him. Was love what made a person do something so foolish as to risk everything—career, reputation, maybe even her brother's love? She felt suddenly miserable, wondering how she would ever be able to eat anything at the supper table. Did love do that to a person, too, take away their appetite, bring this tight feeling to the stomach?

"My God," she whispered, setting down the wolf. It was impossible! Wrong! Not with a half-breed! She opened a drawer and put the wolf inside it. Maybe it would help to keep it out of sight. Besides, Joshua might come up to her room and ask about it. Joshua. How was she ever going to explain this to Joshua, let alone Jason Brown?

Rachael merely picked at her food, while Joshua, the widower Bert Peters, and the banker, Stewart Glass, ate heartily.

"Mr. Peters told me his story about Jason," Joshua said to Rachael and Lacy. "I think the man must have exaggerated. He even said Jason backed down from that half-breed, Brand Selby, said the breed stopped the whole thing."

Rachael felt a knot forming in her stomach.

"I can't imagine Jason being afraid of anybody, least of all a half-breed," he added. "Remember him mentioning that man back at the ranch, Rachael?"

Rachael looked at her brother. "Yes, I remember," she said quietly.

Lacy came over to the table, setting a platter of biscuits down with more force than necessary.

"Well, Jason didn't have much good to say about him. I'd like to see that man myself."

Bert Peters spoke up. "I've seen him around town once or twice. He never stays long, doesn't cause any trouble. But he makes people nervous, nonetheless. They say he's more Indian than white."

"Wonder why a man like that decided to settle around here? He ought to know he's not welcome," Joshua added.

Rachael stared at him, wanting to get up and scream at him. "Why shouldn't he be welcome?" she asked, trying to keep her voice as calm and casual as possible. "Did you ever stop to think that he's probably just a man, like you? He *is* half white, Joshua. He has a right to try to settle like any other man. After all, what he's doing is what we wish all the Comanche would do—settle down and live like white men. Isn't that true?"

Joshua met her eyes, seeing the challenge there. He wondered at her rather bold defense of a man she didn't even know. He frowned. "Yeah, I guess that much is right. But if he wants to settle like a white man, seems like he'd cut his hair and dress like one."

Rachael returned to fussing with her stew, staring at her bowl again. "What difference does it make how a man dresses? Father always dressed in buckskins, and he let his hair get pretty long sometimes. To the Indians long hair is important to a man. Maybe cutting his hair is as bad to him as you wearing a dress."

The other two men at the table laughed lightly, but when Rachael looked at her brother she colored slightly at the discerning look in his eyes. "I know you're a softhearted girl, Rachael, but you be careful defending a man like that. It's okay here, but don't do too much of it out in public."

She felt her temper rising. "Why not? The Christian thing is to help people who want to help themselves, and not to wrongly judge a man. You already make Jason Brown out to be better than he is; maybe you're making Brand Selby out to be *worse* than he is. You can't judge someone you don't even know."

Joshua just stared at her, then looked away, reaching for a biscuit. "All I know is I've never heard anybody who had anything good to say about a half-breed."

"I'm inclined to agree," Peters put in. "I've seen that man. He's big and he's mean looking, and I wouldn't turn my back on him for one second. As far as Jason Brown being afraid of him, hell, I'd be afraid of him, too."

"We don't use profanity at this table, Mr. Peters," Lacy reminded him, walking around and pouring coffee. "And I think Rachael has a point. We shouldn't judge a man we don't even know. If Mr. Selby is trying to settle like a white man, we should give him the benefit of the doubt. There are certainly a good share of white men in this town I wouldn't trust any more than I would trust a half-breed."

"Well, Austin will soon be rid of its riffraff," Glass put in. "After all, we're going to be the state capital once Texas joins the United States. Thanks to people like Rachael here, our children will be educated. We have just about every kind of shop necessary, and plans are already in the making for a hospital. We're working hard to get some eastern doctors to come here. I attended the last town meeting, and Ted Miller had all kinds of plans for Austin. 'Course Miller owns half the businesses in town, so it's to his benefit to see it grow, but it's to our benefit, too."

"That reminds me, Rachael," Lacy spoke up, setting the coffeepot down on a hot plate on the buffet behind her. "Harriet Miller was here today. She wanted to know if you and I would help at the punch table at the dance. It's nearly three weeks away, but she's planning quite a spring party. She feels that if you help at the punch table, more people would see you and get to know you before the next school season starts."

Rachael met her eyes, feeling like crying. "Yes, I remember.

I'd be glad to help." She wondered what Harriet Miller, with her big bustles and fancy hats and expensive parasols would think of a man like Brand Selby.

"Good." Lacy sat down beside her, reaching over and patting her hand. "I'll tell her."

"Rachael, you feel okay?" Joshua asked.

Rachael put a hand to her stomach. "I just have a little upset stomach," she answered. "I'll be all right." She looked around the table at the others. "Excuse me. I think I'll go to my room."

All three men partially rose from their chairs as Rachael left. She hurriedly climbed the stairs to her room and lay down on her bed, curling up and hugging a pillow. Brand. How could she get anyone to understand? How could she tell Joshua? She had never felt so alone. Nothing had ever hurt this much.

Moments later she heard a knock at the door. "Rachael? Are you all right?" It was Joshua.

"I'll be fine. You can come in."

The young man came inside and sat down on the edge of the bed. "You've been acting funny ever since you got home, sis. I wish you'd tell me what's the matter."

"Nothing, really, Josh. It's just … just a bad time of the month for me. I'm a real crank, and I'm sorry." She felt her cheeks coloring.

Josh rubbed her shoulder. "You want me to get Lacy?"

"No. She's busy. She'll come up later."

Joshua sighed. "I'm sorry if things I said upset you."

"Same here, Josh."

He moved his hand down to take hold of hers, squeezing it lightly. "Well, I'll let you rest. If you feel better later, I reckon I'll be up late. Otherwise, I'll see you in the morning."

She sat up then, hugging him. "Thank you, Josh. I'm so glad you came, really. I'm sorry you had to wait and all."

He patted her back. "It's okay. You rest now."

She lay back down and Joshua left. Minutes later Lacy came quietly into the room. She moved to the side of the bed, reaching down and smoothing back Rachael's hair. "It's getting to be more than you thought, isn't it, honey?"

Rachael looked up at her, then sat up. She burst into tears. "Oh, Lacy, I don't know what to do. Josh would never understand."

"Don't underestimate your brother, honey. But first you'd better know your own heart. I told you not to go back. I could see by your eyes it was the worst thing you could have done. Now you've gone, and you'll go again, and Lord help me there isn't a thing I can do to stop you, short of tying you to this bed. But God knows I understand that terrible ache, that powerful tug at a woman's heart when a man has found a way to crawl into it. You have to make your own decisions, Rachael. I can't do it for you, and neither can Joshua. But you're not alone, honey. I'm right here."

Rachael gulped in a sob. "I just feel like I'm ... like I'm headed for disaster, but I'm running full speed, welcoming it with open arms."

"Well, that's a pretty good description, I'd say." The woman gave her a squeeze. "But things always have a way of working out in the end, Rachael. Things will look better in the morning."

Rachael sniffed and let go of the woman, blowing her nose. "He's a good man, Lacy, and very smart, and so creative. He's kind and respectful—and it kills me to hear people judging him to be bad simply because he's half Comanche. He isn't bad at all. And he's helping me to understand both sides a little better." She wiped at her eyes. "And I have to see him again, for Joshua's sake. I want to ask him to do what he can to make sure the Comanche leave Joshua and Luke and Matt alone. He'd do it, I know he would. Today four Comanche men actually came right up to us."

"Rachael! What you're doing is very dangerous!"

"That's just the point. They won't touch me because they think ... they think I belong to Brand." She blew her nose again. "He told them that and they leave me alone." She met Lacy's questioning eyes. "Don't you see, Lacy? They respect Brand. I mean, they don't obey his every order or anything like that. But he's part of them, and because of that they won't touch anything he asks them not to touch. He doesn't have to worry about his stock. He even has two Comanche boys who help him guard it. If I ask him to talk to them about Josh and the ranch, my brothers will be safer. And Josh doesn't have to know anything about it."

Lacy took her hand. "Well he *does* have to know eventually, Rachael. If you keep this up, you can't get around it. Even if there is nothing more than friendship involved, you can't keep meeting this man alone to teach him without someone finding out eventually. You'd better come out with it yourself before someone finds out the wrong way. Either that, or stop this whole thing right now—nip it in the bud, Rachael." She frowned. "Unless the bud has opened to full bloom. Has it?"

Rachael sighed and lay back against her pillow. "No. It's just me—inside. When I'm with Brand it's just teacher-student, that's all."

"Mmmm-hmmm. Then it should be easy to end it."

"But he's learning so fast, Lacy. And he's so eager. I just can't bring myself to stop now. It isn't fair to him. I made a deal with him, and I have to keep my end of the bargain."

"Not at the expense of your emotions, honey."

"I'll find a way to deal with that."

Lacy sniffed. "Easier said than done. Look at you. Already you're crying at the drop of a hat and can hardly eat." She got up from the bed. "You get out of that dress and get some sleep. We'll have a nice breakfast in the morning before Joshua leaves, and I expect it will have to be early. I'll come and get you when it's time."

"Yes, do. Give me plenty of time to visit with Josh a little more. I wish I had known he was coming. I'd have gotten something for the three of them for Josh to take back."

"Well he's coming back in a week or so. We'll be ready for him. I'm putting up some strawberry jam. We'll give him some of that to take back for starters."

"Oh, that's nice of you, Lacy."

The woman patted her hair again. "Whether the advice is right or wrong, Rachael, the only way I can tell you to go is to follow your heart. In your case your heart might be a little too soft. There's nothing anybody can do about that. But to go against your gut feelings, against your heart, is to live a life more miserable than whatever might happen if you do what your heart tells you to do. I'm only saying that this is all still new, still preventable. All you have to do is stop seeing the man while this whole thing is still nothing more than it appears now. You pray on it, Rachael. Pray real good on it."

"Thanks, Lacy."

The woman left, and Rachael hugged her pillow again. "Brand," she whispered. Somehow she was sure that if he were here, holding her this very moment, everything would be all right. New as their friendship might be, she realized the feelings she was experiencing were not preventable at all. She had gone too far the moment she set eyes on Brand Selby.

Ten

Rachael's head ached as she took her usual path toward the meeting place. She was determined to tell him this time, determined that this would be the last meeting.

It was already the third week of May, and this was her fourth meeting with Brand Selby. Her feelings for him were far too intense now for her to ignore them. The last time she had come to this place, she had been determined to think of some excuse to end the meetings for once and for all.

But she couldn't come up with an excuse that time, nor one for today. It seemed hideous enough that she had to sneak around this way. It wasn't right. She hated it, hated the people of Austin for creating this problem, hated prejudice. There was no reason why Brand Selby shouldn't be able to come to Lacy's boardinghouse for his lessons. And being around other people would make her own predicament so much easier. It was being alone with him that intensified her feelings.

What bothered her most was that apart from the passion that was growing in her heart for Brand Selby, she also thought of him as a friend. He was so easy to talk to and she had learned so much about the Comanche. He was such an interesting man, so surprisingly gentle and genuine. To end the meetings would be to end a wonderful relationship, a friendship that she would miss very much.

She walked briskly to the flat rock, no longer concerned about the possibility of Indians lurking behind the hills. Today she wore a bright green cotton dress. She hoped it would not be too noticeable that she had not worn all her slips. It was simply too warm. She wore gloves and carried a parasol, all to protect her from the cruel Texas sun. She sat there thinking how amazing it was the way God made people so different. She wondered if someone like Brand ever got sunburned. The thought made her laugh lightly.

She heard a horse, and turned to see him approaching. He was again wearing the buckskin pants and moccassins, but with a blue calico shirt. His hair was tied at the base of his neck, and a round hair ornament of silver and beaded leather decorated one side of his head. He smiled as he approached, and already her courage was slipping. He looked so happy, so eager... and so handsome.

"You are a woman of your word," he commented, dismounting.

Why was it so much easier to find excuses to keep coming than to find excuses to stop coming? Rachael wondered.

"I know most whites don't keep their promises, Mr. Selby, but this one does," she replied, smiling.

"You are helping me have more faith in the white man," he teased back, grasping her around the waist. He lifted her, noticing he could feel her hipbones through her skirt.

Rachael closed her parasol and he shoved it into the parfleche before they rode off. Neither said much on the way.

They arrived at his cabin and he lifted her down. "Come. I made you something to eat this time," he told her, after tying his horse near a watering trough.

"Brand, you didn't have to do that."

"It is not much, but I never offer you anything when you are here."

He took her inside, pulling out a chair for her. Rachael laid down the ledger paper she had brought along and sat down. There was a wonderful aroma in the little cabin, and he had put a checked tablecloth on the rugged, homemade table. He brought over a basket with a cloth over it, and a jar of honey.

"Indian bread," he told her. "Indian women make this often. It is hard for me to do all these things for myself. Indian men are not raised to do these things. It is woman's work. But now that I am alone, I have no choice."

He opened the cloth, and several hunks of bread were

inside, still warm. He had apparently made them just before coming to get her.

"I cooked it outside over a fire. It is too hot to cook inside. The bread is really nothing more than sweetened dough that is fried."

"Oh! Kind of like the sweet bread my mother used to make," she replied, picking one up. "Sometimes she would roll them in sugar."

"I suppose it would be good that way. We put honey on ours." He set a tin plate in front of her and gave her a spoon. "I made coffee. It is out back over the fire. I will go and get you some."

He left, taking two tin cups with him. Rachael wondered at his statement, "now that I am alone." Did that mean he had once been married? Moments later he was back with the coffee, setting the cups down and going to get his slate.

"Look. I wrote a whole sentence by myself. Did I spell it all right? Connect the letters right?"

Rachael spooned some honey over her bread roll, then studied the slate. "My name is Brand Selby and I own a ranch near Austin, Texas," she read aloud. She smiled and met his eyes. "Brand, it's perfect."

"I did some of that bookkeeping, too. I will show you later and you can tell me if it is right." His eyes glittered with pride, and she knew she would not tell him she wanted to stop. She was determined to teach this man until outside forces prevented it.

"Today I will read a whole story to you," he told her. "I have been practicing with the reader you left me."

She laughed lightly. "I wish I could get this much enthusiasm out of the children, especially the boys. Children get so restless in school." She took a bite of the bread, surprised at how soft and delicious it was.

"That is because their spirits want to be free, to explore," he answered. "While they are children, whites and Indians are very much alike. If we could all remain like children, the world would be a happier place."

She swallowed the bite of bread and looked at him

thoughtfully. "Brand, that's a beautiful statement. Do you know it's very much like what we learn as Christians? Our own Christ taught that we can only enter the kingdom of heaven if we have the spirits of little children."

He grinned. "You see? It is the spirit that matters, not social custom or dress or the color of a man's skin." He picked up a piece of bread and poured some honey over it, holding it over his own tin plate. "How do you like the bread?"

"Oh, it's wonderful. Who taught you to cook it? Did you have a wife?" She asked the question as casually as possible, taking another bite of bread.

"No wife. I used to watch my mother and other women make it. After my mother died, my father's brother and his wife took us in and she did the woman's work. Then my father and uncle were both killed at Plum Creek. By then the sons of my aunt and uncle were big enough to take care of my aunt, hunt for food and such. I had already started scouting for the Militia and then the Rangers. But when I go back to visit, my aunt always makes bread for me. I love it."

Rachael breathed a secret sigh of relief that he had had no wife. "Brand, I was wondering if you could do something for me."

He swallowed his bread. "I would do anything for you. By the way, I intend to pay you for these lessons. I guess I never mentioned it. I am surprised you didn't ask."

"Oh, it isn't necessary. I never even thought about taking money for it."

"But you should. It is only fair." He drank some coffee. "What is it you want me to do?"

"Well, I was just wondering if there was any way you could insure my brothers' safety. They run my father's ranch northwest of Austin. It's about a day's ride. I thought maybe you could say something to your people, or whoever the renegades are who keep raiding the settlers—maybe get them to promise not to raid the Double 'R' or harm it or my brothers. I worry so much about them."

He frowned. "I can make no promises. I can talk to them,

but I am no chief or leader or anything like that, Rachael. But I have convinced them you are my woman, and since they are part of my woman's family, I might be able to keep the Comanche from bothering them."

She kept her eyes averted, not wanting him to see the longing there at the way he said "my woman." "I would appreciate anything you can do. I know you can't make any promises, but just knowing you will talk to them helps. Do you see them often?"

"Not so much. Those left are the most stubborn, the most determined. The tribe with which my aunt lives moves around a lot. Whenever I go to see them it becomes a scouting exibition—tracking them all over the plains. But I usually find them. The ones you see around here, like Rotten Mouth, they are just scattered renegades, hitting where they can, dealing with outlaws. The whites have done a good job of breaking us up. To be apart and to disagree on what to do only weakens us."

He finished eating his bread.

"Brand, anything you can do would help me sleep better at night. My brothers are good people, and they're all the family I have left. They're the main reason I came back to Texas, but Josh won't let me live at the ranch for fear of an attack."

Brand drank some coffee. "It is more likely an attack would come from outlaws, Comancheros, than from the Comanche renegades. But I know there has been trouble from the Comanche, too. I wish I could stop it, but they still think they can defeat the whites and drive them out of Texas. They think that eventually they will frighten all the whites away."

She sighed. "I'm afraid there are few whites more stubborn than Texans," she replied. "Lamar already showed most of the Indians how the settlers feel. He just about sent us into financial ruin with all the money he spent getting rid of the Indians. I'm glad he isn't president of the Republic any longer. I remember my father saying how he hated that man."

She sensed an anger rising in him at the mention of ex-President Lamar. "A lot of people hated him," he answered.

Rachael finished her bread in silence, realizing she had

unwittingly struck a raw spot. She didn't want to talk about anything sad today, or anything that brought out his bitterness.

"We had better get on with the lesson," she said then, drinking down some more coffee. "Thank you for the bread. It was so good."

"I will give you some to take back with you. Let your landlady taste it."

"Brand, you don't have to—"

"I want to," he interrupted, meeting her eyes. Their eyes held for a moment, and she began to redden at the hint of desire she saw in his green eyes. "You make me happy, Rachael. You are kind and helpful and you look at a man for what he is. The man I used to work for was very much like that. He was a German man, Oscar Kruger. You are the only other white person I have met who was truly good, who truly accepted me. When I scouted for the Militia, they paid me well. But the prejudice was always there, lying just beneath their skin, just behind the eyes they pretended were kind. Some people are true and some are not. Mr. Kruger was true, and so are you. The only difficult part is that you are a woman." *And a very beautiful woman*, he wanted to add.

"Difficult?" she asked.

Her eyes were glued to his until he rose, picking up their plates. He took the reader down from a shelf where he had laid it and brought his chair closer, opening the book to begin reading.

Rachael managed to maintain a cool but friendly disposition as Brand read to her. She corrected him here and there. When he finished reading she spread out the ledger paper, and he took down a quill pen and a glass container of ink. Rachael ran through a few pointers in bookkeeping.

"This is very complicated," he commented. "With the Indians, one simply trades a few robes for some beads, tobacco, whatever. No one needs to keep books. Why do whites make everything so confusing, have so many rules, so much book work?"

Rachael smiled. "I wish I could answer that. I sometimes wonder myself."

Rachael felt removed from herself when she was with him,

as though the Rachael Rivers who was educated and should have common sense and self-control left her completely whenever she set eyes on Brand Selby. She had read books about forbidden love. Now that same kind of love had become a reality for her. She could think of no other description for her feelings.

Again the lessons ended, and again he rode her back to their meeting place. Rachael had lost her desire to tell him she would not be back. She clutched the extra bread he had given her, wrapped in a cloth, and turned to tell him goodbye. A flood of passion moved through her at the desire she saw now in his eyes. Could it be he did feel the same as she? Were they both just too afraid to admit to it? She turned and left, walking as fast as she could, determined to get away before she said something she shouldn't. When she reached the trees she looked back, and he was gone.

"I thought that fourth meeting was your last," Lacy said, as Rachael made ready to leave again. "This has been going on nearly three weeks, Rachael."

"But he's doing so well, Lacy," Rachael replied. "I just don't have the heart to stop the lessons. He's so eager, so intelligent."

"And you're so much in love," the woman added for her.

They sat in the kitchen again. Rachael drank some lemonade before leaving. She reddened at the words, left momentarily speechless.

"I see how you're dressed. That's one of the prettiest dresses you own. You don't dress like that to teach children, all pink and pretty and lacy. And I've seen you struggle, Rachael, watched your eyes, heard all your arguments in the man's defense. But the real reason you won't stop the lessons is because you don't *want* to stop them, not down deep inside. You don't like the idea of not seeing Brand Selby anymore. Right?"

Rachael closed her eyes and sighed. "What should I do, Lacy?"

The woman came and sat down across from her. "You can't keep it bottled up forever, Rachael. You might as well tell the man."

"Tell him!" Rachael looked up at her. "Oh, Lacy, I'd make a fool of myself. What if I told him my feelings, and found out he has no such feelings for me at all! I'd be devastated! Shamed! I would just want to die!"

Lacy smiled, shaking her head. "Rachael, you're the easiest person in the world to love. My guess is if you stopped those lessons, Brand Selby would be disappointed for more reasons than his inability to get an education. So what if you *do* tell him and you *do* find out he doesn't have the same feelings? At least it's a kinder reason to stop the lessons than having to say you're afraid you'll get caught with a half-breed, isn't it? At least the excuse that you love him and find continuing with the lessons too difficult emotionally is a flattering letdown for him. I'm sure he would feel honored no matter how it turns out. And you'd feel a whole lot better and maybe sleep better at night."

She reached out and took the girl's hand. "And another thing. Joshua is coming back any day now. In fact he should already have shown up. I think this time you had better tell him, too. Get it off your chest, Rachael, no matter what the consequences. Whatever happens after that, I'll be behind you. At least this Brand Selby has apparently shown he's an honorable man. You aren't a bad woman for thinking you love him, Rachael. Every woman falls in love at some point in her life. I think like you. Brand Selby is just a man, capable of loving and being loved like any other. It's only the outside hurts I worry about—how you'd be treated. But you can't go on like this. You've got to do something about it. You're losing weight and losing sleep."

"I know." Rachael rose. "I'd better go, Lacy."

"There's one other thing to remember."

"What's that?"

"Jason Brown. He'll be back soon. You'd be better to tell Josh first and have him on your side before you tell Jason."

Rachael shivered. "I don't know if I can tell Jason. I'll tell him I don't want to marry him. But I'm afraid to tell him about Brand. He hates Brand, and Brand hates Jason. And Jason has so much power, through the Rangers. I'm afraid he'd try to hurt Brand."

"Honey, I've seen Brand Selby, remember? I don't have any doubts that one can take care of himself."

Rachael smiled softly. "Yes, I suppose you're right there." She picked up her parasol.

"By the way, tell him he's a good cook," Lacy told her teasingly. "That was darned good bread." She came around the table and hugged the girl. "God be with you, Rachael."

"Thanks."

Rachael went out, and Lacy watched from the back door, thinking how powerful and passionate young love was. Rachael Rivers was a strong, determined young woman. Once she made that final decision, she would be steadfast. She would not break easily.

Rachael had not even made it yet to the flat rock when Brand came riding toward her at a hard gallop. She gasped when he circled her, reaching down and scooping her up with one strong arm, plopping her on the horse in front of him.

"Men are coming from the direction in which we usually ride. We have to go another way," he told her, heading east. They rode into a gully, following it for at least a half mile before climbing out of it and heading over a hill and down the other side of it.

"I don't know who they were," he said louder then. "Good or bad, I didn't want them to see us together."

"Could it have been Jason coming back?"

"I don't think so. I can spot that man a mile away. It was probably just settlers coming into town." He moved into a dried-up arroyo, following it awhile, then heading for a stand of cypress trees. "Now that we are this far east, I know of a different place where we can go."

"But we don't have the slate or the book."

"I will just practice writing and spelling today. You can give me some bigger words. There is a stream where I am taking you, and sand. I will write in the sand with a stick." He kept a firm arm around her, and she let herself lean against him. She realized then that perhaps this terrible burden she carried would at least be lighter if she told him, especially if she discovered Brand Selby felt the same way about her. Lacy was right. She couldn't go on this way much longer.

Brand caught the soapy scent of her hair, feeling the urge to nuzzle it. He was surprised at the way she leaned into him, but pleased. He wondered how much longer this aching need for her could go on. Perhaps he should convince her not to come anymore, that it was too dangerous and he had been wrong to ask her. If he had known his feelings would be this strong, he never would have asked her in the first place, for now he couldn't bear the thought of her being hurt on his account. He had done a terrible thing to this precious, beautiful woman, for she had too soft a heart to have sense enough to turn him down; and he had been too infatuated with her beauty to have sense enough to not ask in the first place. He chided himself for being so weak in her presence. His whole world had changed since getting to know Rachael Rivers.

He rode into the stand of trees, and to Rachael it was like being suddenly in another world. It was instantly cooler, and there was soft green grass on the ground, as well as an array of wildflowers. Brand rode up to a stream, where tufts of grass dotted nearly white sand.

"This will be a pleasant change," he told her, dismounting.

He lifted her down, their eyes holding for a moment. Was that something special he read in her eyes? He dared not believe it. He let go of her reluctantly, thinking that she seemed thinner, hoping she was all right. He untied a blanket from his gear and tied his horse to a branch, then carried the blanket toward the stream.

"Come," he told her. "We will sit by the stream." He took her arm and led her toward the water.

Rachael felt led by forces beyond her control. It was as though this man had some kind of power over her. How quickly she had learned to trust him.

"I like this place," he was saying. "It's like a secret retreat."

He spread out the blanket and sat down on it, looking up at her.

"It is beautiful," she told him, walking to stand by the stream. "You don't see many places on the plains where water runs freely like this, unless you're right beside the river. There is a small tributary from the Colorado that brings water to my brother's ranch. It seems like in Texas there is green beside the water, and then when you ride a little away from it, everything is barren again. I don't understand how the buffalo grass grows." She turned to face him. "Back in Missouri it's green everywhere."

"Tell me about it. I have never really seen a city like St. Louis."

She walked closer, hesitant about sitting down on the blanket beside him. He leaned back, resting on one elbow. He wore only a vest again, his arms glistening dark and strong in the sun. When he leaned back more of his chest and some of his flat stomach showed. Rachael walked past him, suddenly terrified of her own feelings. She rattled on about St. Louis, doing her best to describe brick streets and theaters where people acted and sang on stage; about the Missouri River, the Mississippi River, the huge shipping business that kept St. Louis alive; how St. Louis seemed to be the focal point for all settlers headed West.

"They have a beautiful courthouse," she told him. "It's several stories high, and magnificent murals are painted on each circular wall of the dome, at each level, and on the dome itself. In the spring it's a real outing just to go there and see all the wagons lined up. Hundreds, sometimes thousands, all of them headed West." She walked nervously between the blanket and the stream.

"There must be a lot of people in the East."

She laughed lightly. "Oh yes. I'm afraid western settlement has just begun, Brand. In the East people are crowded, overtaxed, a lot of the land spent from farming it for too long. People think they can come out here and get land cheap and start over. Some come for other reasons, dreaming big dreams. Most of them go all the way to California or Oregon Territory. You talk about spirit. There is a spirit in the white man that makes him want to explore, to go places he's never been, to conquer new lands."

She turned to face him and their eyes held.

"Is that spirit in you?" he asked.

"I guess it is, to some extent."

He saw her trembling. "What is wrong, Rachael? You act as though you are upset. Is it that I saw those men, or that I brought you here?"

She wanted desperately to tell him, and yet she could not make the words come. What if she made a grand fool of herself? What if he laughed at her? There was so much more she needed to know about him—things he still had not told her.

"It's just... I can't help wondering what it is about Jason Brown that you haven't told me, Brand. I don't feel like having a lesson today. I want to talk." She put a hand to her forehead. "I'm so confused about... things."

He sat up, frowning. "It is a bad thing I would have to tell you."

"But I have to know. Jason will be back before long."

She saw the contempt for Jason Brown in his eyes. "I would not tell you if I was not concerned for your own happiness."

I love you, Rachael Rivers. He wanted to shout it. *I can't bear the thought of Jason Brown touching you.*

"Come and sit down," he told her. "If you are so determined to know, I will tell you."

She moved to the blanket, cautiously sitting down as close to the edge as she could. Brand watched her curiously, smiling to himself. She seemed to be struggling to remain reserved and proper. He thought about the look in her eyes earlier. But he told himself he dared not do anything to find out if some kind of passion smoldered beneath her proud chin and the lovely dress she wore.

"I will tell you what you want to know," he said. He turned around, moving closer to her and facing her. "We are good friends now, so I will tell you about Brand Selby and Jason Brown."

She could feel his tension growing. He bent his knees and crossed his ankles, resting his elbows on his knees.

"I am glad you would rather talk. It is best you know everything about Jason." He looked over at a cluster of bluebonnets. "After the massacre at Plum Creek I knew that the old way of life was ending for the Comanche. My father was killed there. That's when I decided I had to learn the white man's way. I thought if I could do that, maybe somehow I could help my Comanche friends. I turned to scouting because it was all I knew at the time, and because I could help find renegade Comanche and maybe convince them to go to where they would be safe.

"I met Jason when I started scouting for the Rangers. From the very beginning I didn't like him. He considered me Comanche, and he didn't want anything to do with me, even after I saved his life once. He got himself into a knife fight with a Comanche man—Pawing Horse. He thought he could handle the man, but I knew Pawing Horse. Few men could go up against him with a knife and live to tell about it. And Jason had no real experience in that kind of fighting. I jumped in on it and ended up killing Pawing Horse myself."

She looked at him then—the powerful arms, the wild look about him. She reminded herself that this man had killed other men, that he could probably be as vicious as the wildest Comanche if the situation called for it. A knife fight! How gruesome. And yet he had risked his own life to save Jason's.

He met her eyes, his own very determined. "Yes, Rachael, I have killed men. I told you that. A man does what he has to do." He looked away again. "But I have since wished I had let Jason fight Pawing Horse," he said then. "Then Jason Brown would have died and would not have been around to do some of the other things he has done." He met her eyes again. "He is afraid of me, all right, because he knows I would like nothing better than to kill him and he knows that I can do it, with ease. I know the kind of man he really is. That scares him, too."

He got up and walked a few feet away from her. "Jason only got angry after I saved him that day. Apparently he thought I made him look bad. Whenever I was assigned to scout for him, he complained that he wanted an all-white scout, not me. He told them I shouldn't be allowed to scout for them at all—that I couldn't be trusted because of my Indian blood. But I was good at what I did and the Rangers wanted me and trusted me.

"I knew that Jason was raiding peaceful Comanche villages, killing women and little children. He never did those things when I was with him, but I heard about them, usually firsthand accounts from the Comanche. He had certain men he rode with who were as bad as he and who would not talk about what he did. And I knew that unless I could prove certain things beyond any doubt, it was useless to say anything. Jason Brown would just deny it and say the Comanche were lying. I think the man was deliberately doing things to keep the Indians stirred up."

"But why would he do that?"

He turned to face her. "It is something I have thought about for a long time. I have an idea, but I could probably never prove it. I think he deals with the Comancheros for a share of the money they get from the Mexicans."

"Oh, Brand, surely not!"

"You don't know him as I do. I think he uses his position for both sides. But who is going to listen to a half-breed, especially one that his superiors know hates Jason Brown."

She frowned in confusion, looking down at her lap. "It's so hard to believe," she said.

"Believe it." He came closer, kneeling in front of her. "He has a bad heart, Rachael. Once when I was out riding alone, I saw buzzards circling, and when I went to see what it was, I found two dead Comanche, a man and a woman, both of them shot in the head. I buried them, and then I followed tracks that moved away from the spot, curious to see if I could find out what had happened. The tracks led me by nightfall to a campfire, where two men sat talking. I recognized them as those who ride with Jason. They did not see me in the shadows. I moved in closer, and suddenly Jason himself came out of a tent, pushing a naked Comanche girl in front of him. She could not have been more than twelve."

Rachael shivered and put a hand to her head, her eyes tearing.

"The girl tried to run," Brand continued. "Jason grabbed his bullwhip and started beating her with it. In the firelight I could see how quickly he drew blood. 'You little animal,' Jason was saying. 'I'll teach you to bite me.' He was naked, too, so I knew what he had already done to her. The two men by the fire just laughed while the girl screamed and cried. I hurried in then, ordering him to stop. I pulled my gun on him, but Jason stopped only for a moment, saying I wouldn't dare shoot him, that I would hang for it. I knew he was probably right. They would say it was worse for me to shoot him than for him to whip the little Indian girl. A white man can torture and kill Indians, but Indians dare not raise a hand against a white man. I am a half-breed. And the two men with Jason would never testify on my behalf."

He rose again, and she could see him outwardly trembling. "Never in my life have I wanted to kill a man more than I wanted to kill him that night. I ran to the girl and started to pick her up, and Jason lit into me then with the whip. I grabbed the whip and yanked it out of his hand, and he charged at me. I beat him about the head with the handle of the whip until he went down. The other two men just stared at me. They were not sure what to do because I was a valued scout, not just another Comanche. They knew I was very angry, and that I was a good fighter. They were afraid to rise up against me. It was all I could do to keep from killing Jason. I told him that I was going to his superiors and take my chances, and that the next time I caught him at something like that, I *would* kill him. I came close to it the day I discovered him whipping the old Indian man. But I decided that day that I had to catch him at something even worse, something involving dealing with white outlaws. Abuse of an Indian is not quite enough to get him kicked out of the Rangers. But if I could prove he is deliberately stirring up more trouble, that would anger the whites against him and get him out of that position. Either way, I knew he was capable of raping and beating little girls."

She blinked back tears. "Did you go to his superiors?"

"Oh yes," he answered in a near sneer. "They listened, and they even believed me. But all they did was give their precious Ranger a slap on the hand. 'He's done many good things,' they said. 'He's a damn good Ranger. We have to give him the benefit of the doubt.' I will never forget the look of victory in his eyes.

After that I could not bring myself to have anything to do with the Rangers. I quit scouting and went to work for Oscar Kruger, the rancher I told you about. His ranch is far from here, and I stayed away a long time. But I know that to this day it worries Jason that I know what I know. He would never want any of the people he knows in Austin to know that he raped a mere child, even though she was Indian; or even that he whipped that old man. And I am sure he has done other things no one even knows about. But like I say, I need proof. I am not sure how I will get it, but I thought about it a lot while I worked for Mr. Kruger. I dreamed of coming back here and making Jason Brown a very nervous man."

Rachael rose, looking up at him. "So, that's why you came back here. There's more to it than just settling and going into ranching."

He watched her closely. "Yes. I cannot erase from my mind the things he has done."

She stepped closer, touching his arm. "Brand, what you're thinking is dangerous."

His eyes glittered with hatred. "Dangerous for Jason Brown. Not for me." He grasped her arms then. "Stay away from him, Rachael. I asked you once before. Now you know just how vicious the man can be. And I can't bear…" He swallowed, his jaw flexing with repressed emotions, a new look coming into his eyes, an almost pleading look. "If you want to know the truth, I cannot bear the thought of Jason Brown touching you." His voice changed to a gruff whisper. "I can't stand the thought of *any* man touching you. You're the most beautiful creature I have ever set eyes on, Rachael Rivers, and the kindest, bravest white woman I have ever known."

He let go of her, backing away slightly. "I think perhaps we should stop meeting. I will find another way to learn."

Her eyes teared, and she stood trembling. "I… don't want to stop meeting."

Their eyes held, each afraid to believe what they saw there.

"It's too hard, Rachael," he said. He swallowed again, looking suddenly like a nervous little boy. "My feelings for you… are too strong. I have never desired a woman the way I desire you, and I can no longer trust myself around you. But you are too good for me, and too precious to—"

"Brand!" She stepped closer, one tear slipping down her cheek. "Are you saying you love me?"

His eyes were watery, and he stood rigid, fists clenched. "More than my own life," he said in a near whisper.

She sniffed, wiping away the tear, but more kept coming. "Oh, Brand, I love you, too. Surely you know that. I've… needed to say it for so long."

He watched her in surprise, his heart pounding with joy and desire. He stepped closer, daring to reach out for her, and she seemed to nearly collapse against him, breaking into a torrent of tears.

"Hold me, please, just hold me," she sobbed, wrapping her arms around his waist.

He moved his powerful arms around her, and Rachael clung to him, glorying in the feel of Brand's arms around her, at last!

"Rachael," he whispered.

Eleven

Now that he held her, it felt so right, so very right.

Rachael felt one of his hands move up her back and under her hair. He gently tangled her golden tresses in his fingers, gripping her hair lightly so that her head tilted back. She felt his lips trace their way over her forehead, down to kiss her eyes, then to kiss the tears on her cheeks.

"I love you, Rachael Rivers," he said softly. "Please don't cry."

The touch of his lips to her face sent fire through her body, and new, wonderful sensations began to sweep over her, pushing away the tears. She knew his lips would find her mouth, knew it would be bold of her to let their lips meet. Yet she could not bring herself to stop him. She didn't want to stop him. She had wondered too long what this would be like; wondered what a kiss from Brand Selby would be like compared to Jason Brown; wondered if she would feel the same passion her mother had felt for her father; if she would know, as her mother had known, that this was the man meant for her.

She kept her eyes closed as his lips traced their way to her mouth. Aching passion surged through her insides when their lips finally met. She felt like a wanton woman for letting him part her mouth, for delighting in utter ecstasy at the feel of his tongue lightly tasting the inside of her lips. Her feelings turned from curiosity and innocent delight to heated desire as the kiss lingered and grew more demanding.

Brand Selby was in full command of her body, her heart, all senses of reason. Surely the proper thing to do would be to pull away and not let this continue, but the kiss was so utterly sweet, so very gentle and yet commanding. It was as though they were

154

both suddenly unable to satisfy their appetites.

Yes! Surely this was what her mother had been talking about. It was all so natural, as though she had known him forever, as though he belonged to her, and she to him. Both of them were trembling as he left her lips. He pressed her tight against himself, and she knew he was pleased with the feel of her breasts against his chest. She felt a hardness against her belly as he kept hold of her hair, holding her head against his shoulder, kissing her hair. She knew what she felt, and her mind raced with a mixture of fear and curiosity, apprehension and excitement. She did not know all the intricacies of mating, but she knew what it was, what men and women in love did together to get children. The thought made her gasp and hold him tighter, for she knew that in spite of her fears she wanted no other man to do such a thing to her. With someone like Jason it would be humiliating and painful. But she knew already that with Brand Selby, it would be beautiful.

He moved an arm from around her and shifted it under her hips, lifting her in his arms. She opened her eyes to meet his, seeing there watery tears mixed with intense desire. "Now you truly will be my woman," he told her. Their eyes held as he stood there with her in his arms.

An aching need swelled deep inside her at the meaning of his words. "It's... not right," she said in a near whisper. "It's too soon."

"Not by Indian custom," he answered. "When such a need comes, it is done, and the man and woman are husband and wife. The piece of paper your people insist on having makes no sense. The spirits brought us together. If the spirits say it is good, nothing can make us be apart."

"But you'll think less of me," she whispered, tears welling in her eyes.

A soft smile moved over his mouth. "I could never think of you as anything but the most wonderful woman I have ever known." He pressed her closer. "Tell me you don't love me. Tell me you don't want me as much as I want you."

Their eyes remained locked as she sniffed in another sob.

"You know I do," she answered, her voice tiny from crying.

He did not let her continue. He met her mouth again in a harder, more demanding kiss. His tongue moved deeper, searching, teasing, taking command. When he left her lips she felt weak, defeated. This had all built up in her for too long. It felt so good to let go of her feelings, so good to let someone else be in control.

Her heart pounded as he carried her back to the blanket and lay her on it. She made no protest as he rose to his knees and removed the vest he wore. His chest and shoulders were magnificent, and as he bent closer he hovered over her like some powerful, wild being, his long hair touching her shoulders. He rested on his elbows above her, moving one leg over her thighs. Every muscle in her body seemed to tighten as a fear of the unknown began to creep through her.

He placed a big, dark hand against the side of her face. "Rachael," he said softly. "Don't be afraid. This is the happiest day of my life, for I have loved you from the moment I first set eyes on you from across the river. I have dreamed of tangling my fingers in your golden hair as I do now, dreamed of tasting your mouth…" He began kissing her lightly about the face. "Dreamed of seeing you lying naked beneath me, offering your breasts like sweet fruit…" He nibbled at her lips. "Dreamed of being one with you, putting my life inside you, giving you pleasure in return."

He met her lips then in another hungry kiss. All fear, all common sense, all thoughts of what was proper left her in that moment. She had never wanted anything so badly in her whole life as she wanted Brand Selby to make a woman of her. She closed her eyes and let him unbutton her dress. He pushed it open, his lips moving lightly over her chest as he untied her undergarment.

She gasped as a big, rough hand moved inside the undergarment and pushed it to one side to gently caress her breast. She whispered his name as he lightly rubbed over her nipple until it peaked in aching response. He whispered something in the Comanche tongue, and in the next moment her breathing came quicker as his warm, moist lips settled over her nipple. She still wondered at how easy it all was, how natural. She wondered if she would faint from sheer ecstasy.

He whispered beautiful words of love, sometimes speaking softly in the Comanche tongue, as he pulled the dress and undergarment all the way off her shoulders and to her waist. He tossed the stiff undergarment aside, and she shivered with tense apprehension and overwhelming excitement as she let him slip the dress down over her hips.

She lay there naked to the waist, still wearing her lacy bloomers. He ran a hand along her leg and thigh, then came down close again. "So many clothes you white women wear," he whispered before meeting her lips in a savage kiss. His big hand pressed firmly at her flat belly, then slipped inside the bloomers. She groaned into the kiss as his fingers touched places no man had ever touched before. She had no idea it could be this wonderful. She felt removed from the real world, alive, on fire.

Brand Selby had never known such ecstasy as he experienced now. Rachael Rivers lay nearly naked beneath him, responding to his kisses, his touch. He felt the satiny moistness of her love nest, and fire ripped through his blood. Rachael Rivers would belong to him! How he loved her! He had never in his life felt this way about anyone, never wanted so badly to possess something the way he wanted to possess this woman. He shuddered as he explored private places he knew he was the first to touch. He moved his lips over her face, her eyes, kissing, licking, tasting, while he could tell his fingers were drawing out all her womanly desires, awaking her to the pleasures of being with a man for the first time.

Rachael felt the unbelievably delightful climax. She cried out, gasping for breath, wrapping her arms around his neck and kissing him wildly. She felt his hand move around to her hips, and he pulled at the bloomers. She raised up, letting him slip them down to her ankles. She kept her eyes closed as he moved to pull them off, over her shoes. This was all so new. She couldn't bring herself to look as she sensed he was unlacing his buckskin pants. She was sure her whole body was pink with embarrassment, and yet she didn't want to cover up. She hoped he liked what he saw, little realizing just how pleased Brand was at the sight of her.

She felt him come closer. He drew her close, moving his bare chest over her breasts lightly, pushing one knee against her left leg so that it parted enough for him to settle between her legs. She felt the hardness against her thigh, and her fingers dug into his powerful shoulders.

"You are the most beautiful creature ever born," he told her softly, nibbling at her lips again. "Your legs are firm and milky white, your bottom soft, your belly flat, your breasts full and pink. Everywhere you are pink and white, like a delicate desert flower."

She breathed deeply as his lips moved over her neck. He bent his head, tasting her breasts again. He rubbed his manhood against the soft hair of her love nest as his lips moved back to her mouth.

"The pain only lasts a moment, my sweet Rachael," he almost groaned. "I am sorry for it. After this time it will be beautiful."

She felt the sudden penetration, and her first thought was that perhaps she should have looked first. The pain was more than she had expected. It made her cry out with surprise. It was as though something was tearing inside of her, and she dug her fingers deep into his dark skin, her eyes coming wide open as she screamed his name.

He moved one hand down under her hips to support her, while he slid the other arm under her shoulders. She raised up, burying her face in his shoulder, as he groaned words of desire in the Comanche tongue, his own breathing now labored. He pressed his face against her hair and pushed deep inside her.

He was lost in her, hardly aware of how deeply her nails dug into his skin. He wondered if any man had known this much pleasure. But he knew how much he had hurt her, too, and he allowed the ecstasy of the moment to come full force so that quickly his life spilled into her. He could not bring himself to prolong her pain. He cried out at his own throbbing release, then he held still a moment, breathing deeply, taking a moment to come down from his mountain of ecstasy and meet reality again.

He gently released his hold on her, and Rachael lay back against the blanket, shaking and crying. His heart went out to her. He did not like bringing her pain, and never had he loved anything as much as he loved Rachael Rivers this moment. The woman he was sure he could never have had just let him mate with her. He wondered if he was just dreaming and would wake up soon to discover this was not real.

He gently stroked her damp hair back from her flushed face. "Don't cry, Rachael. It was only your first time. Soon this part of it will feel as wonderful as all the rest. This I promise." He bent closer and kissed the tears on her cheeks. "Don't cry, little one. The pain will go away. Tell me you still love me, Rachael, for I could never love anyone as much as I love you. I didn't mean to hurt you."

"It isn't... just the pain," she whimpered. She wiped at her tears with a shaking hand. "Oh, Brand, what have I done!"

He enveloped her in his arms, pulling her close and kissing her hair. "You have done nothing wrong, if that is what you mean."

"We aren't even married!"

"Aren't we? What did I tell you about that piece of paper? It means nothing. Would it be more right if you had married a white man before one of your Christian preachers, signed that piece of paper, but did not love him? Would your God smile upon such a marriage, one where there is no passion, no desire?"

She sniffed, clinging to him. "I never thought of it that way."

"I am not so sure your God is any different from mine, Rachael. But I know that the spirits have willed this, that it is as right as it can be. Whether we go before a white man of God or not, I have already made you my wife. You belong to me now, and I belong to you. And somehow our love will make all of this work out right, for we are meant to be together."

She felt calmer, realizing that her brief fear that he had used her was silly. Brand Selby loved her. He thought no less of her.

He would never use her. "I need a handkerchief," she told him, releasing her hold. "There is one in the pocket of my dress."

"I will get it." He gently released her, laying her back on the blanket. Their eyes held for a moment, and her face began to redden at the realization of what this man had just done to her. Brand Selby, the half-breed. She had let him invade her body as though it was as natural as breathing.

He smiled softly, as though sensing her thoughts. "You are so good and so beautiful," he told her. "If I had any sense I would have told you I do not love you; should have taken you back right away. But you make me weak, Rachael. When I am with you, you are the one with all the power."

She closed her eyes, grasping his hand. "I didn't feel very powerful. I'm sure it was the other way around, Brand. And right now I feel totally spent, so tired."

He squeezed her hand and rose, and she allowed herself a glimpse at his naked splendor. It was as she had imagined. He seemed a perfect specimen of manhood. She noticed a small strip of rawhide about his waist that led to a pouch tied to the inside of his thigh, another piece of rawhide tied around his leg to secure the pouch. She realized it must be the medicine bag he had told her about. She had not noticed it when he made love to her and it apparently had not gotten in the way.

He walked to his horse and got down the canteen and took a cloth out of his parfleche, then untied a second blanket. Rachael noticed white stripes on his back, scar tissue. She realized with horror that they must be from Jason Brown's bullwhip, from the night Brand had tried to grab the little girl. She shuddered at the thought of it, and dread moved through her blood at the realization of the danger Brand would be in once Jason discovered she loved the man.

Brand came back to her, setting down the cloth, canteen, and blanket and picking up her dress. He rummaged for the the handkerchief and handed it to her.

"We will go to the stream and wash," he told her as she blew her nose. "I would like nothing more than to make love to you again and again. But I have hurt you. You need a couple of days to heal before we do this again."

Before we do this again. The words swam in her head. He had said it as though there was no doubt about it. But already she was wondering what she was going to tell Lacy, and worse, what she should say to Joshua. How would she explain this? Should she tell him how far it had gone? She had given no thought to things getting so out of hand. She had planned simply to tell him her feelings and then ask him to take her back to town. None of his had turned out as she had thought it would, and she felt a mixture of wonderful happiness and relief, combined with a terrible dread of what the consequences could be. Her heart tightened when she realized it could be worse for Brand than for herself.

Brand untied his medicine bag and laid it carefully aside. He picked up the cloth he had brought over, then reached down and picked Rachael up in his arms. "We will go and wash."

She hugged him around the neck. "Tell me again that you love me," she whispered. "I love you so much, Brand, and I'm so scared."

"I love you more than my own life," he answered. "And why are you afraid?"

"I'm afraid for you. People are so terribly prejudiced. When I tell Joshua that it's you I love—"

"Hush, Rachael," he interrupted. "Wait until we wash. Do not let your mind fill with too many things at once. It is enough that we have told each other, and now we have sealed that love. That is all that matters for the moment."

He walked into the water with her and she squealed at the feel of the cold stream against her feet when he stood her in it. Brand grinned as he bent down and wet the cloth. He wrung it out and rose to gently wash her hot, flushed face with its cool dampness. She wondered at how easy it was to stand there naked before him, letting him move the rag over her body, her neck, her chest, under her breasts.

He moved the cool rag to her belly, noticing a little blood on her thigh. It tore at his heart. He felt like a cruel man to have hurt her that way, and yet it could not be helped. At least after this time each time would be more enjoyable for her. He washed off the blood, then dipped the rag again and held it against her belly. He looked up at her, seeing tears in her eyes. He rose, touching her face gently. "Are you in a lot of pain?"

She reddened. "It isn't that." She looked down. "Oh, God, Brand, I'm afraid for you. When Jason finds out, he'll surely try to kill you."

Brand sighed, grasping her chin and making her meet his eyes. "Do I look afraid?"

"Oh, Brand, you shouldn't take it so lightly."

"How else can I take it? It is right, Rachael, you and me. If the spirits have willed it, things will turn out right, even though we might go through some hell for a while. Here." He handed her the cloth. "Hold the cold cloth between your legs for a moment. It might even be better if you sat down in the water. It will help ease the pain and stop the bleeding."

She blinked and looked down at herself. "Bleeding?"

"It's all right. It is natural. Sit down in the water for a moment and I will bring over the extra blanket to wrap around you when you come out so you don't get chilled."

He took a moment to splash water on himself, while Rachael eased herself into the cold water.

"Don't be worrying about anything else today," he told her. "You have been through much this day. Today you became my bride, the Comanche way." He turned and gave her a reassuring smile, moving out of the stream to get the other blanket. He brought it to the edge of the stream.

"Sit there a moment. I'm going to put my clothes on and take a look around, make sure we're still alone. I took a chance letting you undress out here." He grinned. "But I didn't have much common sense at the moment."

She watched him walk back to tie on the medicine pouch and then his loincloth. She studied the scars on his back. Jason Brown! So, the man was even worse than she had imagined. The thought of letting Jason do what Brand had just done to her made her feel sick.

She watched Brand pull on his buckskin pants, then pick up

his rifle and walk farther away. He disappeared into the trees and rocks for a moment, but she was not afraid. The only thing that worried her now was how much Jason Brown and Brand Selby must hate each other.

Moments later Brand returned. "Everything looks quiet," he told her. He set the rifle aside and picked up the blanket, holding it open. "Come on out. I'll wrap you up."

Rachael smiled, standing up and walking toward the blanket. She stood there a moment, feeling the fire of desire begin to move through her all over again as his green eyes drank in her beauty. She stepped into the blanket and he folded it around her, keeping his arms around her, meeting her lips again. They kissed, a long, sweet kiss that seemed to seal what they had just done. His breath was sweet, and his hair smelled clean as it brushed against her face. And she knew he was right. They would make love again, many times, for the rest of their lives. Surely this was what her mother had meant about that special feeling, about knowing without a doubt the right man had come along.

She wondered if it had happened this way for Emma Rivers, if Joe Rivers had come along and swept her off her feet, perhaps taking her the Indian way as Brand had done today with her. Her mother had hinted it had happened that way, but she had never come right out and said so, perhaps thinking Rachael wouldn't understand at her young age.

Brand picked her up in her arms then, carrying her back to the blanket on the ground and setting her on it. Rachael realized how much the man resembled her own father. Surely that was partly what she loved about him.

"Brand, I don't even know how old you are," she said then.

He sat down beside her. "I am twenty-nine summers. How many are you?"

She kept the blanket wrapped tightly around her. "I'm nineteen."

His eyebrows arched. "Nineteen, and you have taken your first man. You do not find nineteen-year-old Indian women who are not already married and have children."

She smiled softly, reddening at the remark. She met his eyes then. "I never had the right feelings for a man before now."

He grinned in return. "And I am glad for that, or you would already belong to someone else, and I could never know the joy I know today." He moved closer, laying her back and cradling her in his arm. He gently touched her face, and she wondered how such a big man could be so gentle. "I have complicated your life this day, Rachael Rivers. I am sorry."

She shook her head, turning to kiss the palm of his hand. "I brought it on myself." Her eyes teared a little as she turned her head, holding his hand against her face. "And you didn't hear me telling you to stop." Their eyes held. "I never thought I could love anyone this much, Brand. It almost hurts."

He nodded. "I know what you mean. It is the same for me."

She closed her eyes, keeping his hand against her face. "I never knew love could be so wonderful and so scary and hurt so much but bring so much joy, all at the same time," she said wearily.

He pulled her close, running his fingers through her hair. "Soon it will be time to take you back. Let's just lie here together. I want to hold you a while and think only of how much I love you, and to know that you love me."

"I don't want to go back—ever."

"I know. Nor do I want to let you go. But that is what we must do, for today, at least. Hush now. Just rest."

She closed her eyes and nestled against him. The strain of the past weeks combined with the intense emotions she had experienced this day quickly brought on an exhausted sleep.

Brand watched her, studying the beautiful face, the golden hair, gently opening the blanket just enough to gaze upon her full breasts. She belonged to him now! Rachael Rivers was his woman. It made his heart swell with great pride and overwhelming love. But he also worried that he had been wrong to take her, not for the act itself, but because now they were committed, and that could mean tragedy for his precious Rachael. He vowed he would never let anything or anyone hurt her, least of all Jason Brown.

He let her sleep until the sun told him she must go back.

How he hated to wake her. She looked like an innocent child lying there, but she was no longer a child. She was a woman. He had made sure of that. He gently roused her and she blinked awake, looking confused at first.

"It is time to go," he told her, kissing her nose.

She watched him, her eyes widening as she realized where she was, what had happened. She hugged him tightly. "Brand, it was real then, wasn't it? We made love."

"Oh yes, it was real." He kissed her ear. "Let's not wait three days this time. Come again tomorrow, and we will go to the cabin. We will have some time to think, and we can talk more about all of this, and we can make love again."

He met her mouth and she gloried in her newfound love, relishing the waves of ecstasy that rippled through her body at his touch. This big, strong, handsome, wild man loved her, Rachael Rivers! His hand moved inside the blanket and over a breast ever so lightly, bringing the terrible, wonderful desire to her body again. How strange it seemed to have slept in the Texas wilds in the arms of this man who was as wild as the land—to wake up and know she had not dreamed what had happened earlier. Brand Selby had made love to her.

He pulled away from her mouth, his jaw flexing with his own desires, his eyes looking glazed. He looked down where the blanket had fallen open, drinking in the sight of her full, white breasts.

"I want nothing more than to be one with you again," he told her. "But it is best to wait until tomorrow."

She ran a hand over his chest, then traced her fingers along his neck and up over his lips. "Let me stay, Brand. I want to sleep with you tonight. I'm scared to leave you, scared something will happen that will keep me from being able to come back."

He smiled, love shining in his eyes. "Nothing will happen. I told you, the spirits have willed our union. I will not allow anything to keep us apart. For a little while yet we must be careful. Soon I will have some horses ready to sell. I will have some money to buy even better stock and to be a good providor for you. Then we will try to find a preacher who will agree to marry us your way. I do not believe it is necessary, but I know it means something to you, so I will sign your silly piece of paper, Rachael Rivers. Then you will legally be Mrs. Brand Selby."

Her eyes glittered with love in return, but tears came into them. "You truly don't think I'm bad, Brand?"

He grinned. "If you were a bad girl, I would have known it when I took you." He leaned forward and kissed her eyes. "I was your first man. And you took me in sweet love," he said softly. "There is nothing bad in that, Rachael." He grabbed her close again, breathing deeply. "This is the happiest day of my life. It is right. I know it is right."

"I've never been so scared and so excited both at the same time."

"Do not ever be afraid, Rachael, not of anything. I am here, and soon we will be together every hour of every day."

She met his eyes. "My father used to tell my mother to never be afraid of anything. You remind me of him in so many ways. He was so strong, and he held many of your beliefs. He was so solid and dependable." She sighed deeply, pulling away from him reluctantly then and sitting up. She reached for her bloomers. "Somehow I've got to find a way to tell Joshua about us. I'm not quite sure how he'll react, but I've got to try to get him on my side. That will help me through whatever lies ahead for us."

"And if he is against it?"

She met his eyes. "If he is against it, then so be it. It won't change my mind, not now, Brand. It wouldn't have even before we made love. But now there is no going back, not for me."

He sat up and touched her hair again. "Nor for me. I am only sorry I am a half-breed and that it will cause trouble and pain for you."

"Don't ever be sorry for your blood." She stood up and pulled on her bloomers. "And I am not the only one who will have problems with this. Like I said, my problems will be social, emotional. You are the one who might be in physical danger."

"It is worth the danger," he answered. He watched her finish dressing, again marveling at the layers of clothes white women wore. He pictured Jason Brown touching her, and rage swept through him at the mere thought of it. It was tempting to keep her with him from this moment on. "Rachael," he said, rising and standing behind her. "Even now, if you changed your mind, I would never hold it against you."

She turned in surprise, watching his eyes. "Why do you say that?"

He took her hand, holding it up beside his own, displaying in the sun the contrast of their skin. "Do you see the difference? That is why I say it, and because I love you as I love my own life. To see you get hurt would be like tearing out my heart."

Their eyes held. "We've said how we feel, Brand, and we've sealed it today. I gave myself to you because I love you. I don't intend for any other man to touch me that way." She breathed deeply. "I'm not going to let myself be afraid, Brand. You told me not to be, and I know my mother would tell me the same. She would approve of this, and so would my father. I know they both would. I don't care what anybody else thinks, including my own brother."

He grinned softly. "Then it is done." He leaned down, meeting her lips again, tantalizing her with light flicks of his tongue.

Rachael knew that if there was time, she would let him make love to her again, in spite of the fierce ache that plagued her insides. How was she going to stand being away from him, even for one night?

"Oh, Brand, Brand," she whispered as his lips left her mouth. "I'll come back tomorrow. But let me come earlier—ten o'clock instead of one. Then we will have longer to be together."

How he wanted to take her again, this very moment. "Yes. Come at ten. I will make sure the Comanche boys who watch my horses will take care of things. We can have the whole day alone." He kissed her neck, "But there will be no lessons, at least not from you. It is I who will do the teaching and you will do the learning."

The splendid warmth moved through her body at the realization of what he meant. Yes, he would be the teacher. And she would enjoy the lessons immensely. What woman could ask for more than to be held in the arms of Brand Selby!

Brand gathered up their things and retied the blankets onto the horse. He picked up his rifle and shoved it into its boot, then lifted her onto the horse. "Are you all right to ride?"

She reddened again, finding it difficult to believe Brand Selby had seen her naked this day, had invaded her body. Already he knew her intimately. It embarrassed her, but he seemed to understand. Somehow she suspected Jason would have laughed about it.

"I think so," she answered.

He mounted behind her, moving away from the stream. She felt like crying again. Would she ever come back to this place? Her whole life had changed beside this stream.

There was so much to talk about. Tomorrow. They would talk tomorrow. How had the afternoon slipped by so quickly? She looked down at her arms, touching them, feeling almost as though none of this was real. Suddenly she was not the same Rachael Rivers. She was a woman now. She had taken a man. She would have to be brave now, brave like her mother had been when she first married Joe Rivers, who was hated because he was raised by Cherokee Indians. But this would be worse than it was for her mother. Brand was half Comanche. And few whites hated Indians worse than the Texans hated the Comanche. She prayed she would have the strength to face whatever lay ahead.

Brand's arm tightened around her, as though he sensed her thoughts. She leaned against him, and she knew that whatever strength she lacked, Brand would make up for it. He would never desert her, never let anything happen to her. They had each other. Surely that was all they would need.

Twelve

Rachael reached the trees, looking back to see Brand still sitting on his horse, watching after her. How she hated going back to town! There he was, far in the distance, sitting alone. She didn't want him to be alone. If he had too much time to think he might decide what they had done was a great folly and that things must end. Maybe he would even pull up stakes and go away.

She raised her hand to wave, and he waved back. If only she could go back to him, lie in his arms this night. If only they could be together right now, this very day. But Joshua would be furious enough when she told him gently and slowly. And she was committed to her teaching job. A lump rose in her throat. She didn't really care what anyone, including Joshua, thought; nor did she care now if she lost her teaching position, although it meant very much to her. She knew no one in Austin would marry them, and she couldn't bring herself to shame her brothers by living with a man without marrying him the Christian way.

Brand was right. They were already married, in heart and body. She felt the same way. And his reasoning about a piece of paper seemed practical. But no one in her family and none of her friends would see it that way, and she was determined they should be allowed to properly marry and live as husband and wife. Somehow she had to make that happen, without endangering Brand's life.

It took all her strength to turn away again and head into the trees. She was hot and tired, and she was anxious to talk to Lacy. The woman would probably be shocked at first, but today had been a traumatic one for Rachael. She had to share this first experience with someone, someone older who might understand. Lacy was the only white woman in town who had at least a little sympathy for Brand's situation, who didn't totally judge him by his blood.

She hurried through the trees, anxious now just to get home and take a cool bath; anxious for the day and night to pass so that she could come back tomorrow and be with Brand again. That was all that mattered now, her time with the man she loved.

"Oh, Mama, you'd like him so much. I just know you would," she said softly, looking up at the clouds as she came out of the trees. She wished her mother's grave was closer so that she could stand by it; still, she was sure that her mother was with her, watching her, guiding her. And so was her father.

She hurried to the back of the buildings on the east side of town, then through an alley between two buildings. She stepped over rocks and weeds and two whiskey bottles, then opened her parasol and took a deep breath before emerging onto the boardwalk in front of one of the buildings.

"Afternoon, Miss Rivers," came a voice to her immediate left.

Rachael gasped. Her mind had been so preoccupied she was not even looking; and she was so worried about being caught it made her jumpy. She stepped aside, turning to see Jules Webber standing against the building, one foot bent behind him and braced against the gray wood. A thin cigar hung from his mouth.

"Jules!" She swallowed. "Didn't you go with Jason?"

"Had a stomach problem. Stayed behind."

His eyes moved over her as though he knew something, and she struggled to keep her composure. Not only did she dislike this man more than she disliked Jason but also he actually frightened her. Surely Jules was one of those who had been along when Jason raped the little Indian girl, and when he did whatever other dastardly deeds he might be up to. She stepped back more.

"Well, I hope you're feeling better."

He nodded, then looked around the building into the alley. His eyes shifted back to hers. They were dark, discerning eyes. Rachael noticed he needed a shave, and his shirt was stained. It seemed the only time Jules Webber dressed decently was when he was on duty for the Rangers.

"You always go skulkin' around in alleys?" he asked, his eyes moving over her again. "Doesn't seem very ladylike for somebody like you. It could also be dangerous."

"What I do is none of your business, Jules," she answered, remembering her promise to Brand not to be afraid. "If you must know, I just felt a need to get away from people. I took a little walk."

"Alone? Outside of town?" He shook his head. "Bad idea. Jason wouldn't like that very much."

"Jason has no say in what I do."

The man's eyebrows arched. "That so? Not according to Jason."

Rachael lowered her parasol, closing it. "Good day, Jules." She turned and strutted away.

Jules Webber watched after her, thinking what a fool Jason was for not selling her to the Comancheros. She would bring a fortune.

Rachael hurried now, feeling Jules Webber's eyes on her back. Did he suspect something? What would he tell Jason? She decided she would have to be very careful tomorrow—make sure Jules Webber was not in sight when she left. She hurried toward Lacy's, then spotted Harriet Miller coming down the street toward her.

The last person Rachael wanted to see today was Harriet Miller. She stepped off the boardwalk and readied to cross the street, but Harriet called out to her then. Rachael had no choice but to turn and acknowledge the woman's greeting, and Harriet waved her over.

It seemed that everything ached as Rachael moved toward Harriet, who stood by a buggy that she was preparing to board. A driver waited to take her back to her well-guarded home.

"Oh, Rachael, I've been wanting to talk to you," Harriet cawed. Her voice reminded Rachael of a crow. "I was at the boardinghouse earlier to see you, but Mrs. Reed said you were doing some shopping." The woman patted her damp face with a lacy handkerchief. "Oh, it's so warm, isn't it? I liked it much better near the coast, but Mr. Miller insisted this was the place to open more businesses, since we're soon to be the capital of Texas."

Rachael wondered at how the woman could so cleverly manage to get something immediately into the conversation that involved announcing that her husband was an area businessman.

"Well, I suppose he was right," the woman continued. "Austin just seems to keep growing and growing, and so does business." She laughed lightly, and two other women walked by, nodding to Harriet Miller and giving their greetings.

"Yes, we certainly are growing," Rachael answered, trying to sound enthused. "What was it you wanted, Mrs. Miller? I'm not feeling too well, and I'm anxious to get home."

"Oh!" Harriet looked her over. "Yes, I see you haven't purchased anything." She chuckled and leaned closer. "When a woman goes shopping and doesn't purchase anything, she certainly *must* be sick!" She laughed again and patted Rachael's arm. "I hope it's nothing serious, dear. It's so nice having young ladies like yourself come to Austin. You add so much to our town. You're so pretty and intelligent—and we need teachers so badly. How wonderful of you to leave St. Louis and come back to Austin."

Rachael struggled to remain in good spirits. She had heard all of this before, and she didn't feel like standing here babbling on about nothing. "Thank you, Mrs. Miller. You said you had been by to see me?"

"Oh yes! I just want to make sure you will be available to help with the punch the night of the dance. It's next Saturday, you know—only seven more days."

"Yes, of course," Rachael said absently. The dance! She didn't want to go at all. She wanted to be with Brand.

"Will your Jason Brown be back by then?"

"My what?" Rachael blinked at the way the woman put it.

"Jason Brown. Will he be back in time for the dance?"

Rachael put on a smile. "Mrs. Miller, he is not 'my' Jason Brown. I am not sure I will be going with Jason to the dance. I think I prefer to go unescorted, which I am sure is better anyway if I am to work at the punch table."

"Oh!" The woman looked surprised and a little bit offended. "Well, I just assumed—"

"Everybody in town is assuming the same thing," Rachael interrupted. "But no one ever asks me how *I* feel about Jason. I have no interest in any particular young man, Mrs. Miller." She checked herself, realizing her temper was rising a little too high. She closed her eyes and sighed deeply. "I'm sorry, Mrs. Miller. It's just that Jason tells people these things, but it isn't serious at all, truly. And if I go to the dance unescorted, I will be able to meet all the other available young men in town. Won't that be more exciting?"

The woman blushed and tittered. "Oh, well, of course! If that's what you prefer, it would be delightful. Oh, I love matchmaking! Why, I remember the day you left Austin. We hadn't been in town too long and I didn't know your family too well then. We never believed you'd come back after being in St. Louis. We're all so thrilled to have you here. We want to fill Austin with the best. Oh, will your brothers be coming to the dance?"

Rachael fingered her parasol nervously, wanting nothing more than to get away. "I don't know. I hope so—at least I hope my oldest brother can come. If you want to do some matchmaking, do it with my brother, would you? He needs a mate much worse than I do. He and the younger boys are so alone out there on the ranch. And the house really needs a woman's touch."

"Oh yes, yes. I can imagine!" She patted Rachael's shoulder. "You really do look peaked, child. Are you eating right?"

"I'm fine, Mrs. Miller."

"Well, you look as though you had better go home and get some rest. I wouldn't want you to miss the dance. You be there at six o'clock, can you? Ted and I are holding it at the big barn next to the house. We'll have it all cleaned out. Oh, how I wish we had the grand home we had back East, with a ballroom and all. But it will come. It will come."

"I'll be there, Mrs. Miller."

"Oh, good. I'm so delighted. I've planned this event for so

long. It's a kind of celebration over Austin being chosen for the capital. Statehood is only three or four months away, you know."

"Yes, I know. I really must be going, Mrs. Miller."

"Oh, of course. You get some rest now, like I told you."

"I will."

"Good-bye, dear."

Rachael nodded and quickly left. Harriet Miller could be friendly and helpful in her own way, but only if she liked someone. Rachael knew the woman was a snob at heart, and supposed she would faint dead on the spot if she knew that Rachael had made love that very day with the half-breed, Brand Selby. The thought of telling Mrs. Miller flat out what she had just been up to brought a little smile to her lips. It would almost be fun watching the look on her face.

Rachael walked fast, looking straight ahead, praying no one else would call her over. Never in her life had she been so anxious to get to the privacy of her room. A buggy clattered by spraying dust over her dress and into her hair. She coughed and waved it away, wondering when Austin would have brick and paved streets like St. Louis. She stepped over horse dung and realized that her nostrils were getting so used to the smell that she hardly noticed it anymore. That was Texas—dust and horse droppings and wild growth; Indians, Mexicans, Germans—people of every race and life-style, from the most destitute farmer to people like Harriet Miller.

And Texas was Brand Selby—dark, wild, rugged, hard to put down. She had come back to Texas, and Texas had folded her into its arms.

At last Lacy's boardinghouse was in sight. There had been no more interruptions. She walked faster. Brand seemed so far away now. She felt as though she had left him a thousand miles back. To be one mile from him was to be too far away. Would he be waiting for her tomorrow, or had he just used her because he knew Jason Brown loved her? Was it only for spite? No! Not Brand. She simply could not believe that was all it had been. It was too beautiful, his eyes too sincere.

She finally reached the door and went inside, where it was

cooler. She closed the door, leaning against it, feeling almost too weak to climb the stairs. She moved to the stairway, grasping the top of the large oak post at the bottom of the railing.

"Rachael?" Lacy was calling from the kitchen.

"Yes," she answered with what strength she had. "I'm going to my room."

She started up the stairs but could not reach the top before Lacy was standing at the bottom of the steps. "How did it go? Did you tell him, child?"

Rachael turned to look at her, and Lacy's eyes widened.

"Rachael, you look terrible!"

Rachael put a hand to her face, wondering if that was how she had looked to Harriet Miller. "I... I shouldn't look terrible," she answered. "I mean, when a girl is in love she's supposed to look beautiful."

Lacy frowned, lifting her skirt and coming up the stairs. Rachael looked away and went the rest of the way up, and Lacy followed her to her room, closing the door behind them. "What happened, Rachael? Did he say he loves you, too?"

Rachael smiled in spite of the tears that welled in her eyes. She moved to her bed and sat down wearily. "Yes, he loves me," she said softly. "And I love him. And we—" She looked away, toying with the fringe of her parasol. "We made love, Lacy."

She sat waiting, sure there would be a torrent of protest and reprimands from Lacy. But the room hung silent. She was afraid to look at the woman before finishing what had to be said. "Please don't yell at me, Lacy. I'm tired and I... hurt. We couldn't help what happened. The moment was too beautiful, and I wouldn't take it back for all the money in the world. I love Brand Selby and we're going to be married, as soon as he's more on his feet and as soon as I can tell Josh and get his approval."

She heard a long sigh from Lacy Reed. "It's a little late to worry about approvals, isn't it?"

Rachael swallowed back a painful lump in her throat. "I suppose. But it just... happened... and we belong to each other now. I don't care what anybody else thinks."

She choked back a sob. Lacy sat down beside her and began

rubbing her back. "I know you don't care, honey, but when this comes out this is going to be about the worst thing you've ever had to handle. It might be worse for Brand Selby."

"I know," Rachael whimpered. "But Brand... told me not to be afraid. Somehow we'll make it work, Lacy. We might have to move to another town, but we'll make it work. I just... wish we could make it work right here. I don't want to leave Josh and Luke and Matt."

"I know."

"Don't think that I'm bad, Lacy."

The woman patted her back. "Honey, I could never in my life think that of you. But you're so sweet and innocent and trusting. I just pray to God that Brand Selby hasn't just used you. Are you real sure he loves you, Rachael?"

"Of course I'm sure." She sniffed and faced Lacy. "Oh, Lacy, if you could have seen his face when he told me—his eyes. It's right, I know it's right. When he kissed me, it was nothing like Jason. It was so beautiful. I love him so much." Her face twisted into more tears and Lacy put her arms around the girl.

"You must be so confused, and hurting. I'll fix a tub of water for you."

Rachael hugged the woman tighter, the trauma of the day seizing her. "Oh, I miss him so already. I hate leaving him. I'm going back tomorrow—in the morning this time."

Lacy closed her eyes and sighed. "Well, there's not much I can do to stop it now, is there? My, oh my, oh my. I didn't suspect something like this to happen, not this quickly. And not to Rachael Rivers."

Rachael pulled away, taking the used handkerchief from her pocket. "It was so natural and it seemed so right." She blew her nose. "In Brand's eyes we're already married, Lacy, in heart and body."

Lacy reached out and took her hand. "Love can do strange things to people, child; makes them totally irrational. I'm not saying it's wrong because nothing is more right than loving someone. It's just the consequences that worry me. And if you're going to keep meeting Brand Selby, you'd better come out with it quick and find a preacher, or you're going to be carrying a baby with no legal father."

Rachael reddened, her eyes widening. She absently put a hand to her stomach. "A baby!"

Lacy leaned closer, a wry grin on her face. "A baby. That's how they're made, you know."

Rachael blinked, looking down at her lap. "I never even gave it a thought."

"I'm sure you didn't. Most young lovers in your situation *don't* think about it. You've got yourself in deep, Rachael, and there's not much I can do but be here for you when you need me."

Rachael sniffed again, meeting the woman's eyes. "Thank you for understanding, Lacy." Her eyes began to glitter with her newfound love. "Oh, Lacy, he's so kind and gentle, and he loves me so. I know in my heart it's right. I'm going to tell Josh when he comes back for the seeds. I can only pray he'll understand."

"And Jason Brown?"

Rachael stiffened, rising from the bed. "Brand told me all about Jason." She faced the woman. "He's done some terrible things, Lacy. Brand warned me to stay away from him all together; and after what he told me Jason did, I'll have no trouble doing that. Brand thinks he's even mixed up with Comancheros."

"Comancheros! Is he sure?"

"No. He just suspects. But he says he'll prove it somehow. And when he does this town will learn what a good man Brand Selby is, and what a vicious animal Jason Brown can be!"

Lacy rose then herself, grasping Rachael's arms. "I hope he can do it, Rachael. You know how I feel about Jason. In the meantime, this has been a trying day for you, to say the least. We have a lot to talk about, but right now I want you to take that bath. I'll bring up something for you to eat, and then you sleep as long as you want." She studied the girl's eyes. "You're really in love, aren't you?"

Rachael smiled through tears. "I've never felt so wonderful in my whole life, except that I'm so scared for Brand."

"Well, try not to think about that for now." Lacy smiled reassuringly. "I have a feeling he's a man who can take care of things right proper. And if he truly loves you, he'll not let anything happen to you. He'll make this work. I expect maybe you're made for each other. Both of you are strong and have lots of courage. And I suspect he's a little bit like your pa. Am I right?"

Rachael smiled with relief. How good it felt to share this with another woman. "Oh yes, Lacy, very much like my father."

"Mmmm, well, then, you've got no worries. Your pa had a way of taking care of trouble, and I expect Brand Selby does, too. If that man wants to marry you, he'll make sure it happens. You just look on the bright side of things and get a good sleep tonight." She squeezed Rachael's arms before letting go of her. "I'll go draw your bath."

"Thank you, Lacy, for understanding."

The woman walked toward the door. "Well, there's no stopping young love. I went through it myself, and I've seen it happen to others. God be with you, honey."

The woman turned and left, and Rachael walked to the drawer where she had put the carved wolf. She opened the drawer and took out the carving, holding it up and studying again the intricate designing. Brand's gentle spirit showed through. She caressed it softly, then set it on top of her dresser.

She loved him so much that her chest hurt. She looked in the mirror, surprised herself at how she looked—haggard, too thin, her face stained from tears. What had Jules Webber thought of how she looked? Would he tell Jason he had seen her coming out of an alley looking worn and flustered? If he did, Jason would ask questions.

She looked at the wolf again. "Let him ask," she murmured. "Brand told me not to be afraid, and I won't be!"

She breathed deeply, putting a hand to her belly. She was still sore. She wondered if she was still bleeding. But she knew that whether she was or not, she would go to Brand again tomorrow, and he would make love to her again and she would let him. She belonged to him now and nothing could change that—not Joshua, not Mrs. Miller, and certainly not Jason Brown. For now, the night could not pass fast enough for her, for tomorrow she would be in Brand's arms again.

Thirteen

Rachael made her way toward the schoolhouse. She decided she must keep changing her schedule and direction now, in case certain people had noticed her head in one direction at the same time every few days. Today would be different. It would help to have people see her go to the school. It was a natural thing for her to do. And this was the very next day from yesterday's outing, which would break the pattern of her being gone.

She felt much better today, her outlook brightening with the rising sun. Finally the next day had come! She would see Brand again! Her step was lighter, and her heart swelled with love. She had eaten a bigger breakfast than she had eaten in days, and she felt relieved that at least Lacy understood her love for Brand.

She wore her hair tied into a bun at the base of her neck, but with the removal of a few pins she would shake it out long and loose for Brand, for she knew he liked it that way. Her dress was a soft blue, and her parasol matched it. She decided she would get a couple of more books from the school to take with her this time. If she and Brand didn't have time for regular lessons, she would leave them with him to read. She smiled and shivered with anticipation, realizing that indeed, there would probably be no schooling today, at least not book learning.

She passed a livery, and moments later she sensed the footsteps of someone coming up quickly behind her. She stopped and turned, paling slightly at the sight of Jules Webber. The man approached her, tipping his hat.

"Morning, Miss Rivers." He was clean shaven this time, and wore a clean shirt. Webber was a wiry man, with a sharp nose and dark eyes that always seemed to be looking through her instead of at her.

"Good morning, Jules." Rachael turned to keep walking.

"Where you headed?"

"None of your business."

He kept up with her pace. "Why are you so uppity with me, lady?"

Rachael stopped and turned to face him. "Because I don't like people spying on me."

"That what you think I'm doing?"

Rachael hugged her books close. "Ever since I've come back home I've had Jason Brown hanging over me. Now he's gone and you seem to have decided to appoint yourself to keep an eye on me. Did Jason tell you to watch me?"

The man grinned. "Why no, ma'am. But he's my friend, and I just figured I'd do it as kind of a favor—you know—watch over his woman and all."

Rachael stiffened, reddening with anger. "For once and for all, I am not his 'woman'! Now stay away from me!"

She turned and started walking again, and Webber caught her arm. Rachael faced him again, jerking her arm away. "Don't you ever grab me like that again, Jules Webber!" She felt a creeping fear at the sudden look in his eyes. It reminded her of the look in old Rotten Mouth's eyes, and she remembered what Brand had said about the possible dealings of Jason and these friends of his.

"Look, lady, I only warned you last night for your own good," he almost growled. "I just thought maybe you was headin' to go outside of town again. You got any idea what the Comanche do to women?"

She turned away and started walking again. "Get away from me!"

Webber stayed up with her. "They rape them, lady, sometimes ten, twenty men all taking turns. The lucky ones are the ones who get killed, only they die slow from torture—insides cut out, hot coal held against their privates. Women captives are always stripped, sometimes beat 'til they can't do more than crawl. Some are made into slaves, constantly raped and tortured, dragged behind their captors' horses, used like animals. Them that gets rescued is plum crazy."

"Stop it!" Rachael almost screamed the words, whirling and facing him. "Why are you doing this!"

Jules grinned, enjoying upsetting the proper Miss Rachael Rivers. How he would love to see her in the hands of Comancheros. He put on an innocent look. "Ma'am, I'm just tryin' to make you see how careful you've got to be. Women like you, you got no idea what it's like out there."

"I was raised on a ranch under the constant threat of Comanche raids," she spat back at him. "I know exactly what it's like!"

"Not until you've seen it with your own eyes, like me and some of the other Rangers have. Why, I seen a man once that they cut the bottom skin right off his feet, then they made him walk for miles before he gave out and died. And I've seen men with their privates ripped right off—not cut off, mind you, but ripped off and then the rest of them cut up and scalped—and all before he's finally killed outright."

Rachael had closed her parasol by then. Her ears rang hot with the horror stories, and in the next moment she whacked Jules Webber across the side of the head with the umbrella, making him stumble sideways.

"Why you—" The man had instantly whirled back around, raising a fist. Rachael's eyes widened in surprise. Brand's stories were beginning to make sense.

"Go ahead, Jules Webber," she hissed. "A couple of men just came out of the livery over there. Show them the kind of man the illustrious Ranger Webber is!" Her eyes drilled into him as he slowly lowered his fist. A white welt was beginning to form on his left cheekbone. "If you bother me again I'll go to your superiors. And Jason won't be too pleased either!"

The man glowered at her. "Jason don't know how much he's losin' by keepin' you for himself," he snarled. The man stomped away, a little worried that he had let his temper get the better of him. He had said too much, shown a side of himself he was not supposed to show around the citizens of Austin. But the uppity Miss Rachael Rivers had brought it on. He hoped

Jason taught her a good lesson when he returned. If she married the man, Jason would break her quick enough in their bed. If she refused to marry, maybe then he could convince a hurt and insulted Jason Brown to kidnap the girl and sell her. It would serve her right.

Rachael watched Jules walk off, keeping her composure until he was farther down the street. She headed quickly then for the school, completely shaken by the incident. He had spoiled the beautiful morning with his ugly words, and she shivered at his last statement. "Jason don't know what he's losin' by keepin' you for himself." What could the man possibly mean by it? She really barely knew Jules Webber, only that he was a friend of Jason's and that she always felt uncomfortable around him. Now that she knew some of the things he and Jason and the others had done, the man frightened her.

She hurried to the school and went inside, then waited a half hour, keeping an eye out the window to see if Jules Webber was watching. She saw nothing. She grabbed the extra books then and went to the back of the little one-room building. She opened the door and peered out, seeing no one.

She closed the door behind her then moved down the back steps. Several pine trees dotted the landscape behind the school. She darted through them and into a cornfield. The corn was an early variety and just barely tall enough to give her some cover. The rows ran in the same direction she needed to go, and she ran through it, breaking into the open at a different place from where she had come through before. She saw the stand of trees far ahead of her and to her right, and she realized that if she walked straight ahead, she would reach the approximate position of the flat rock where Brand always picked her up.

She walked as fast as she could, her head reeling with Webber's stories of torture. But then there had been torture and humiliation and rape and murder on both sides. But those who would eventually find out about her and Brand would not consider the Comanche side to the stories. Their hatred was too deeply embedded, and she would be considered a "white squaw." Most white women were terrified of any Comanche;

yet here she was, rushing to meet a man with Comanche blood. Brand Selby had not only stolen her heart and body, but also he had stolen all her abilities of reason. She was almost surprised herself at the powerful feelings she had for the man, feelings that drove her to do the unthinkable, to risk everything to be in Brand Selby's arms.

She lifted her skirt, climbing a small, rocky hill. The other side became softer with buffalo grass as she descended. As she headed toward the flat rock, the cornfield, the town of Austin, and the little school disappeared on the other side of the hill.

Now she was free again, free of the rules and social amenities of her own class of people. Out here her spirit could soar; her passion could be released without judgment; her love could be expressed. She saw him already, riding toward her from the left, disappearing into a gully, reappearing, coming closer, looking grand in buckskin pants and a red shirt and red headband. Yes, he did love her. He had not used her. He had come like he promised, and there was the beautiful, provocative smile on his handsome face. His green eyes glittered with love as he came closer and scooped her up onto the horse.

"Brand!" she said with great relief. She sat in front of him now, staying sideways for a moment to hug him around the neck. He held her close and without another word their lips met in a sweet, lingering kiss. Already she was on fire for him, and she wondered if perhaps she was a captive after all. He had kidnapped her heart and soul, and her only torture now would be if she had to live without him.

They rode in near silence to the cabin. Rachael noticed a black kettle hanging from a tripod over an open fire outside, and a delicious aroma filled the air.

"What smells so good?" she asked.

"My stew." He kissed her hair. "That's for later, after we have worked up an appetite."

Rachael's skin tingled at the words. Brand dismounted and lifted her down, holding her against himself and off her feet for a moment. Their eyes held. He crushed her close, meeting her mouth in a more hungry kiss. She felt him trembling as he slowly released the kiss, and his lips moved to her neck.

"Are you all right?" he asked her. "Did you sleep well?"

"I'm fine. And I wish I could have slept with you," she whispered.

He set her on her feet, and she turned at the sound of a horse. A young Indian boy rode up close to them. Rachael guessed him to be only about fourteen, a dark, wild-looking boy who looked at her with curiosity and a hint of contempt. Rachael had heard stories of boys as young as this one committing depredations against settlers, and this boy looked strong and capable in spite of his age. He said something to Brand in the Comanche tongue, and Brand answered, handing the reins of his horse to the young man. The Indian boy turned and rode off with Brand's horse.

"That was Standing Horse. He is one of the young men who helps me." He put an arm around her waist and led her into the cabin. "I just never know when I can depend on Standing Horse or his friend. They're young and looking for excitement. Sometimes they just go riding off after buffalo or to follow a raid into Mexico. That's what is so hard for whites to understand about them—that natural instinct that makes them want to break out, gives them a need to show their bravery, their ability to defeat the enemy. Putting them on reservations is like trying to keep a buffalo herd inside fences."

He closed the door, and the inside of the cabin was lit only by sunlight that came through a small front window, and by a lantern Brand had lit and set in the center of the crude table. Rachael noticed he had tidied up the cabin again, and bowls were set out on the table. The slate also lay on the table, with the entire alphabet written on it. A vase full of wildflowers sat at the center of the table. This seemed such a stark contrast to Jules Webber's ugly words of only an hour or so ago. But seeing the young Comanche boy reminded her that Brand Selby was also called Running Wolf. He had been raised among them and had an Indian name.

Brand set aside his rifle and bolted the door, turning to face her. "We can eat now, if you're hungry."

She shook her head. "No. I had a big breakfast." She studied him, standing there so dark, so Indian, so powerful. She realized that in full Indian dress, with paint on his face, he would look like the rest of them, in spite of the green eyes and lighter-colored hair. "Brand…"

She hesitated, and he watched the agony in her eyes. "What is it?"

"When you… lived among the Comanche… did you ever… ever torture anyone?"

She saw the anger come into the green eyes. "Someone has been telling you things."

Her eyes teared and she turned around. "Jules Webber—a friend of Jason's. He didn't ride out with Jason this time. He… stopped me yesterday when I emerged from an alley. I think he suspected something, but I don't think he really knows. He warned me not to be walking alone. Then this morning he followed me when I was walking to the school. He began… telling me about some of the ways the Comanche have of torturing people… what they do to women." She swallowed. "Did you ever witness such things?"

There was a moment of silence, followed by a quiet sigh from Brand. "When I was an Indian, Rachael, I lived as they did. It's part of a way of life I told you would be hard for you to accept or understand. I don't ask you to do either one. I can only tell you I never touched a white woman myself because of my mother; and that it was a long time ago. I have lived more like a white man for many years now. If I was still Comanche, you would have been taken away and sold off to Comancheros the day I saw you at the river. Even then I saw trust in your eyes when you looked at me. And yesterday I made love to you. Did you fear me then? I felt no doubt in your heart. This Jules Webber must have told you some terrible things."

She turned to face him, tears in her eyes. "But they were true, Brand. I just… hadn't given much thought to it, because of you. But also because of you I wish I could understand better.

Why do they do those terrible things, Brand?"

He straightened more, the Indian pride in him showing. "To them it is not terrible. It is simply their way—warfare, taking captives and looting, getting strength from torturing the brave ones. Part of defeating the enemy is to humiliate them, to show superiority, to flaunt their conquests. The white man is their greatest enemy. When they make war against the white man, they humiliate him in the worst ways possible—and that's by stealing his children and raping and humiliating his women. They did the same thing to enemy Indian tribes and to Mexicans for centuries. It's a way of life, Rachael—as ingrained as breathing. If you were raised in that life you would think nothing of it. And many captured whites have chosen to stay with the Comanche after awhile, like my mother did."

Rachael stepped closer. "I remember when I was only about ten years old, a girl just about my age was captured by Comanche—Cynthia Parker. Everybody talked about the Parker massacre, how horrible it would be for those taken captive, the awful things done to those at Parker's Fort who were killed. I remember being scared for a while that something like that would happen to me. And now, here I am, in love with a man with Comanche blood. It's all so strange." She searched his eyes. "Have you ever seen Cynthia Parker?"

"Once—several years ago. Most of the surviving captives had been ransomed by then. But she had married a Comanche man and had no desire to go back to her own people. She was taken by the Quohadi Comanche, who ride far north and west from here. Her husband is Peta Nawkohnee, and she is now called Naduah, meaning Keeps Warm With Us. The Comanche are her people now, Rachael. I haven't seen her for years. The Comanche live spread out over the whole western half of Texas territory. They don't ride in huge single tribes, and for most it is every man for himself. Peta Nawkohnee claimed the white girl Cynthia Parker, and now she is happy and even has a child, maybe more than one, I don't know."

She frowned. "If rape and murder are a way of life for the Comanche, then why did you think it was so terrible of Jason

Brown to do what he did to that little Indian girl? It sickens me to think that he did that; but the way you were raised, it doesn't seem like it would seem so terrible to you."

He grasped the back of a chair. "Think how you felt when I told you. *That* is why it was terrible—simply because such actions are not a way of life for the average white man. For the Indian to do such things *is* a way of life—almost a religion. But to the white man it is unforgivable. There is the difference, Rachael— custom, a way of life. That is what makes Jason Brown bad— because he goes against the ways of his own people. For the Indian it is not evil at all. It is his way, a necessary thing; it is all that he knows. But for the white man, such acts are evil. I have listened to some of your Christian priests and missionaries. And I believe that for people to stop dying, we must live a new way. I do not kill men, Rachael, unless they need killing, unless I must defend myself. Jason Brown kills for the thrill of it, rapes for the same reason. He is no more civilized than the Comanche, perhaps less, because for the Comanche it is the way. But it is no longer *my* way, Rachael. I can't stand here and explain in five minutes or five years the spirit and reasoning of the Comanche because their way of life is so totally foreign to someone like you that there are some things you could probably never accept. All I can do is tell you how *I* feel, and that is that I love you, more than my own life, and I have more reason than ever now to settle and be a successful rancher."

He stepped closer, reaching out and touching her face. He half expected her to jump back. But she stood still, watching him, looking as curious as a child. "I told you yesterday that if you wanted to stop seeing me, I would understand. Perhaps it is all more than you can understand after all. But you have seen how I am trying to change my life." He swallowed, running a thumb over her cheek. "Rachael, what Jules Webber told you is probably true. But that's just the way things are. It is a fact of life that cannot be changed. Don't let it destroy your love for me."

She reached up and grasped his wrist, turning her face to kiss his palm. "Nothing could make me stop loving you," she said softly. "I guess I'm just trying to understand my own emotions, how I came to love a man with Comanche blood." She met his eyes again. "It isn't that I look down on that blood, Brand. You know better by now. It's just that I know how others feel about the Comanche; how I'm *supposed* to feel. But now I can only look at you as a man, not an Indian or a white man, just a man. But Jules Webber awakened me to all the hatred that is out there, and the reasons for it, and it frightened me. I promised I wouldn't be afraid, but it's hard to keep a promise like that."

He moved an arm around her, and his large, warm hand pressed into the small of her back. "Then let me make it easier." He moved his other hand from her face and around her shoulders. "You can depend on me, Rachael. I will not desert you, and I will never hurt you. I know the Comanche side of me is hard for you to accept; but this is the side you know—the side called Brand Selby. And Brand Selby loves you more than any man will love you. I have already made you my woman the Indian way; and when the way is clear, we will be married the white man's way. You make my heart sing like the wind across the Plains, and you make my dreams soar like the eagle. I want you and only you to be my companion for life."

She rested her head against his chest, and her breath caught in her throat as he began pulling the hairpins from the bun at the base of her neck. Her hair spilled down over her back, and he kissed the top of her head. "Don't let others spoil what we have found, Rachael," he groaned. "All I do is think of you, every waking moment, every aching hour that it takes me to go to sleep at night."

She tilted back her head and eagerly met his lips as they pressed against her mouth. She reached around his neck, her nails digging into the skin there as a light teasing of his tongue brought out all the wonderful warmth and excited pleasure she had felt the day before. He gathered her up in his arms and carried her to the bed of robes, carefully laying her down.

He moved on top of her, his red shirt and red headband becoming a blur against his utterly handsome face and gentle green eyes. She was quickly lost in him. She realized he was right. They must not let his past, or the words of someone like Jules

Webber come between them. She realized she was much more afraid of men like Webber and Jason Brown than she had ever been afraid of Brand Selby. How ironic it all seemed.

Their kisses grew wild and hungry. She cried out as the bare, damp skin of his chest came in contact with her taut nipples.

It was all so right. She could come up with no more arguments against loving Brand Selby. She had no choice but to face the consequences, for it brought her pain to even think about being apart from this man. Anything that happened to her because of loving him was better than being away from him.

He left her mouth and she gasped for breath, her heart pounding wildly as he worked his lips down over her neck, her creamy shoulders, moving down to taste the delicious sweetness of her breasts, lingering there to tease her, to draw forth the almost agonizing desire from the depths of her belly.

Clothes lay strewn here and there as their naked bodies lay tangled together.

He moved on top of her, gently settling between her legs. "It will hurt again, but not as much as before," he said softly. "I love you, Rachael. I would die for you."

The words rang in her ears as he entered her. She could only pray that loving her would not bring his death after all. She gasped at the pain, at first wanting to cry at its stinging hurt. But moments later it diminished, and this time she began to experience the breathtaking pleasure of feeling him move inside of her with much less pain. There was a rhythm to his gentle thrusts, and she began to respond to it, arching up to him in sequence.

"Rachael, Rachael," he whispered, grasping her under the hips and pushing hard, their bodies meeting in perfect timing. Everything in the room seemed dim and blurred. She arched her head back, wanting to give and give and give, realizing she was boldly flaunting her nakedness in sheer ecstasy now, in an intense desire to give him pleasure while she took her own.

Rachael felt an exquisite climax that made her cry out. There was no pain anymore.

Brand could see she was truly enjoying him and he moved

in rhythmic thrusts. He drank in her naked beauty as he held out as long as possible before his own pleasure consumed him. He spilled his life into her. Afterward, he relaxed, settling beside her and holding her close.

"Rachael, my Rachael," he whispered. "Just love me for who I am now."

The morning and afternoon passed much too quickly, spent talking and making love. Their bodies ached, but it was a nice ache. Their passion remained intense, and they relished every movement, every touch, every kiss, every intimate moment, knowing they must soon part.

"Oh, Brand, I don't want to go."

He kissed her hair. "And I don't want to let you go. Each time I let you out of my sight I fear I will never see you again."

"I feel the same about you."

He raised up on one elbow and looked down at her. "Maybe I should just ride back with you right now—today. I am not afraid, Rachael."

She reached up and touched his face. "Josh is coming back to town any day now. Let me tell him first. And in only six days there is a dance in town I'm expected to attend. Emotions are running high right now in Austin, Brand, what with statehood coming and all. This is a bad time to get people stirred up if we can help it. Wait until I tell Josh, and until this stupid dance is over with. I don't like the waiting any more than you do, but with this dance and all the talk about statehood—people are more against the Comanche than ever. And I have a feeling that Jules Webber is spying on me."

She raised up and hugged him around the neck. "Oh, Brand, I don't want to be away from you. But I think I should wait until after Saturday to come back. I'll know a lot of things by then. I'll talk to Josh, and I'll go to church Sunday. Josh might come for the dance, so he'll probably stay over Saturday night. To keep everything calm I'm going to have to wait until Monday, especially since I know that Jules Webber will tell Jason I've been seen out walking a lot. I've got to try to win over Joshua first. Maybe he and I can come out together. He can meet you and get to know you better."

He got up, reaching for his loincloth. "I don't like you going through all of that alone." He tied on the loincloth. "We have nothing to be ashamed of, and I am not afraid."

"Please, Brand, let me try it my way first. Just wait 'til after the dance. That's all I ask."

He sighed deeply. "I am going out to get some water so you can wash."

Her heart ached at the look of defeat on his face. This was destroying his natural pride, and she despised the ugly prejudice that prevented them from being together with everyone's blessing. They would get curses rather than blessings, she was sure. Brand was strangely quiet when he returned. He pulled on his soft, doeskin pants, then left to let Rachael wash. Her heart weighed heavy in her chest as she dressed, and she could not shake the black dread that plagued her.

Brand returned, bringing her some water. She drank deeply of its cool refreshment, while Brand leaned against a wall and watched her.

"Monday," he said then. "I will wait no longer to come and claim you. If we have to leave Austin to find a preacher, then we will leave. Somehow I will find a way to start over someplace else. I came here to go after Jason Brown, Rachael, and to learn and to build a new life. But now this little ranch and Jason Brown don't matter anymore. Nothing matters but being with you." He sighed deeply. "Monday is eight more days. I don't know if I can go that long without seeing you. And how will I know if you are all right?"

"I'll be right in town with Lacy. I'll be all right."

"What about your brother? What if he is furious when you tell him? Would he hurt you?"

"Josh?" She smiled softly. "No. He might yell a lot, but Josh would never hurt me. I love my brothers very much, Brand. I hope somehow you can be friends. You would like Josh as a person. He's a fine man—strong and courageous, a lot like our father." Her eyes teared. "Oh, Brand, eight days sounds like so long to me, too. I could hardly stand one night without you. But if this is found out before I can tell Josh and before the dance, it will just be all the harder. Maybe after a few days we can just go away quietly and travel until we find a priest who will marry us. If we settle in some other town as husband and wife, it will be more easily accepted."

A sneer passed over his lips. "Accepted? When I come into Austin people look at me as though I was a walking plague. And I know how they will label you—the dirty white squaw, that's what they'll call you. The bastards!" He hissed the words, opening the door.

"Brand, I don't want to leave with you feeling like this."

He walked closer, grasping her arms, his eyes growing softer. "I can't help the anger, Rachael. I don't want to be away from you for so long. Maybe you will change your mind and never come back."

"Oh, Brand, you know I won't." She reached around his neck and he swept her into his arms. "I *will* come back. And we'll be together from then on, Brand. When I come back next Monday I'll bring a carpetbag of clothes, and I'll come with Joshua's blessing. We'll find someone to marry us, and maybe we'll go to the Double 'R' first. It would be safer for us if we were all together. You could even herd your horses over there for the time being, until the town got used to our being together and things calmed down. Then we could come back here and have our own place." She leaned back and kissed his cheek. "Or we could go someplace entirely new—if we had to."

"What I think is best is that we stay together right now." He kissed her passionately, his whole body trembling.

Tears filled Rachael's eyes. "I know, Brand," she whispered as he moved his lips over her cheek. "But that would only make people even more outraged. And I have an obligation to my brother to at least try to make him understand before we go off together. I can't hurt him by just running off without an explanation, Brand."

He kissed her hair. "You white people and your 'obligations.'

You are always finding ways to keep from being free and happy."

She met his eyes. "Don't be upset with me, Brand."

A tear slipped down her cheek and he kissed it. "I am not upset with you. I am upset with your people who impose such stupid rules on you that keep you from being happy. I will give you your time, Rachael, but every day I will wait around our usual meeting place at one o'clock, like always. If you are having bad troubles, you come there and you tell me. I should be with you. And remember what I told you about Jason Brown. Stay away from him."

"I will."

They hugged tightly, neither of them wanting to let go.

"Remember, every day I will be there waiting. Do not hesitate to come to me."

Reluctantly he led her outside to where Standing Horse had brought back his horse saddled and ready to go. Rachael left the books behind. Brand lifted her into the saddle and eased up behind her. "Someday we will get back to the reading and writing," he told her, taking the reins.

"Someday we'll have time for those things," she answered. "You'll work the ranch and I'll do the woman's work by day; and at night we'll sit and study. We'll be Mr. and Mrs. Brand Selby, and life will be good."

The strong arm moved around her, pressing her close. "Yes. It will be very good."

She clung to his arm as he turned the horse, and her eyes stung with tears at having to leave the little cabin where she would rather stay forever. The afternoon had been filled with ecstasy, love, and passion. She wasn't even sure how many times they had made love, and she didn't care. She could go back and do it again this very moment. A delicious ache caressed her insides, and she had never felt more loved, more beautiful.

If only Josh would accept this now, she could bear the ridicule of any others. She knew that waiting a few days was best—to tell Josh and to keep the town calm; and especially to throw Jules Webber off her scent. She had to do this, for Brand's sake. But the pain of being apart would be close to unbearable.

They rode off, while farther north more riders were headed for Austin—Jason Brown and his men. Jason rode them hard, hoping to get home in time for the Saturday dance, where he hoped to announce his engagement to Miss Rachael Rivers.

Fourteen

Rachael sat on her bed studying the carved wolf and wondering how she was going to bear the next seven days. Waiting seemed the only answer, and she wished Josh would come soon so she could get it over with. She set aside the wolf, rose, and walked to the window. Pulling aside a lace curtain, Rachael looked into the darkness. She knew the landscape without being able to see it. The hills behind Lacy's house rolled away in a sea of buffalo grass. Here and there an elm tree or pine tree dotted the landscape; but she knew that far to the north and west the land was much more barren, a hot, wild land where renegade Comanche still lived. Texas would not give up to civilized settlement any easier than would the remaining Comanche.

Poor Brand was a man stuck in the middle of it all. Surely in spite of his strength and bravery, inside there was a man terribly confused and hurt. Because of his Indian blood, whites thought him incapable of loving, literally denied him the right to love whomever he chose. But she would prove otherwise. No matter what the cost, she would show people that Brand Selby was just a man.

She turned when someone knocked at the door. "Lacy?"

"Yes. Let me in quick, honey."

Rachael went to the door and Lacy slipped inside. "He's here."

"Who?" Rachael's heart tightened at the thought of Joshua or Jason having come.

"Brand Selby."

"Brand!" Rachael whispered the name.

"He came to my backdoor—said for you to meet him at the woodshed out back—he needs to talk to you."

Rachael quickly moved to the mirror, fussing with her hair a moment.

"You'd better take a shawl. It's cool outside," Lacy told her. She put a hand to her chest. "I forgot just how handsome that man is," she added. "He looks mighty fine tonight."

Rachael smiled, reaching for her shawl. "Did he seem all right? Was he upset?"

"Who can tell with that one? You be careful now. And don't go riding off without telling me."

"I won't, Lacy."

Rachael hurried out, watching to be sure neither of the two boarders saw her. But no one was about, and she remembered that only Bert Peters was there at the moment, and he was in his room. She hurried through the kitchen and out the backdoor, walking through the moonlight to the woodshed. "Brand?"

"Here." He stepped out of the woodshed, and she realized that if she didn't know who it was, she would be terrified. In the moonlight he looked like some mighty warrior anyone in his right mind would be afraid of.

"Brand!" In an instant she was in his arms. They had been apart only a little over twenty-four hours, but she felt as though it had been weeks.

"I couldn't stay away," he told her softly.

"Oh, Brand, hold me. It's dangerous for you, but I'm still glad you came."

They took a moment just to enjoy holding each other. She turned her face to his, and their lips met in a hungry, urgent kiss. The kiss lingered, their breathing coming in desperate gasps, their bodies pressed hard against each other.

"I wasn't sure what your landlady would do," he told her, moving his lips to her soft cheek.

"Lacy is wonderful. She understands, Brand. I told her everything."

He kissed her forehead. "I decided we should see your brother together, and not in town. I have come to take you to his ranch. I cannot let you do all these things alone, Rachael. It isn't right. I am not afraid to face anyone with this and I will not let you do it alone. If we leave tonight, perhaps we can get to your ranch before your brother even leaves for Austin. We can go quite far in this moonlight, and then we can sleep together under the stars."

He met her lips again, and she whimpered with great joy and passion. How good it felt to be in his arms.

"What if someone comes looking for me?" she asked. "What would Lacy tell them?"

"She can tell them you went to visit your brothers—that Joshua came and got you. I brought a packhorse with everything we need. All you need is a change of clothes. We will come back in a couple of days."

"Oh, Brand, what about all the work you need to do at your ranch?"

"This is more important. Standing Horse and Gray Bear know what to do. If outlaws come through and rob me clean, so be it. You will not shoulder all of this alone. I am your husband, Rachael, whether it's on paper or not."

She smiled through tears, resting her head against his chest. "I'm so glad you came. I've been so worried about how I would tell Josh, what he would say. It will be so much easier if we're together."

"I should never have even considered letting you tell him alone. Go back inside now and tell Lacy. I will wait here for you."

She kissed him lightly. "I'll be right back," she whispered. She hurried back to the house, feeling greatly relieved. Yes, they would tell Josh together! Of course! Why hadn't she thought of that? And surely Josh would accept her love for Brand once he met the man.

Jason rode into Austin with Sam Greene and three new Rangers—men Sam and Jason had picked up in San Antonio, men no better than outlaws. Jason needed more Rangers on his side to help him open up new connections with marauding outlaws.

They brought with them two horse thieves who were to be jailed in Austin and were awaiting a traveling judge. Bringing back criminals always made an impression on the people of this town, Jason knew, many of whom were now shouting out to him in greeting.

"Good job, Brown," someone yelled.

Jason gave him a nod, sitting proud and straight in his saddle. Other than the outlaws with whom he dealt, he always made a point to "do his duty" in other ways when he went out on patrol. After all, people expected him and his men to help keep the peace and rid Texas of its trash. The worst trash was the Indians; next to that came runaway slaves from the South; and, of course, the men who came to Texas just to raid and rob and rustle.

Two women whispered and pointed at the horse thieves as Jason rode by with them. It was so easy to play both sides. His cut from the Comancheros had been hefty this time, just for letting them through his territory to turn over their loot to men who had come up from Mexico. That loot had included a young girl from a wealthy Mexican family who had been stolen away by Comanche then handed over to the Comancheros to be ransomed back to her family for a great deal of gold. The Comanche renegades received new rifles for the girl, and the Comancheros received the gold from the Mexicans who came to get her.

Jason patted his money belt. When he married Rachael, he intended to build her the finest house in Austin and dress her the way a girl that beautiful ought to be dressed. If she said yes this time, he would set the date right away. He was not about to wait any longer to make Rachael Rivers his wife. The thought of getting inside her drove him crazy in the night. She was a little uppity, but he would break her spirit quick enough and show her what it was like to be with a real man. She would learn to like it soon enough, and that would be that. Pretty clothes and a fine house would keep her satisfied in every other way, and Jason Brown would be married to the prettiest girl in all of Texas.

More people greeted them as they rode up to the small prison house where the thieves would be kept until the judge came. Jules Webber came out of the jail and nodded to Jason as

Jason dismounted. Jason gave him a dark look.

"You been staying away from the liquor while I was gone?" he asked warily.

Jules nodded. "Sure have. You'll be glad for the way I kept my eyes open while you were away, boss." He grinned as Jason tied his horse. "You're back just in time for the big dance. It's only four days away. You takin' that fancy teacher lady?"

Jason removed his hat, ordering Sam Greene to herd in the thieves and lock them up. "After that, everybody go to the saloon of your choice and wet your whistle," he told the other three. "You'll like Austin, boys."

The three men grinned and tied their mounts. "We'll tend to these horses in time. I'm itching for a drink," one of them said in reply.

"Explore the town some, boys. And don't forget, you're Texas Rangers. Don't give the Rangers a bad reputation." He winked at them and turned to Jules. "Jules, this is Dan, Hank, and Wendel. They'll be riding with us from now on."

Jules nodded to the three men. "Jules Webber."

"Glad to meet a fellow Ranger," the one called Hank answered. Jules noticed one of Hank's eyes wandered as though it wasn't really seeing anything. He grinned knowingly. Hank and Dan were big men, well armed and perhaps in their thirties. The one called Wendel was more slender, a young man of perhaps twenty with a cocky look about him, the look of a young man who enjoyed trouble. All three of them rode sturdy horses and struck Jules as men who could take very good care of themselves.

"See you boys around," Jules told them before following Jason inside headquarters. Sam Greene followed with the prisoners.

"They on our side?" Jules asked Jason of the three new men.

Jason remained silent until Sam herded the thieves into a cell. Then he nodded to Jules. "Found them in San Antonio— spruced them up and saw the head man there and got them approved. They're good men, all three of them." He patted his money belt again. "We did good this time. There's more in my saddlebags."

Jules grinned as Jason sat down behind a desk. "What do you think of me running for some kind of office, Jules? Think I'm popular enough around here?"

Jules rubbed at a stubbled chin. "I reckon you are, Jason."

Jason leaned back, putting his hands behind his head. Sam Greene came from the room where thick adobe walls and iron bars made by the local blacksmith now held the prisoners. He closed a door that separated the cells from the outer room.

"Well, I've been thinking," Jason was saying. "If I marry Rachael Rivers, I don't want to be gone so much. And besides, she ought to have a husband with some status. If I could get into politics, I might be able to enhance our profits. You boys could keep things going out there while I drum up even more business. There's a lot of money to be made just getting involved with the slavery issue, making deals with the Indians, you name it."

Sam laughed lightly, folding his arms and shaking his head. "You think of just about everything, Jason."

"That's how a man gets ahead." He sat up straighter, opening a desk drawer and taking out a cigar. "By the way, Jules, Lobo and his men are camped not too far north of here."

"The Comancheros? Kind of close to Austin for them, isn't it?"

"It is. But who's going to stop them if they do any raiding? Besides, I have a job for them."

Jules looked at a grinning Sam while Jason lit the cigar and puffed on it for a moment. "The Comancheros are going to raid Joshua Rivers's place—burn everything down and steal everything they can get their hands on. They'll hit him the day after tomorrow and make sure all of those boys die."

Jules sobered in surprise. "Rachael Rivers's brothers? I don't get it. You always kept an eye on them."

"Only to impress Rachael." Jason chewed on the end of the cigar, holding his chin up haughtily. "But I've been thinking about that. And I decided that I'll make sure Rachael has no reason to turn me down when I ask her to marry me this time. Once her brothers are dead and the ranch destroyed, she won't have anything left. She'll need me. She'll turn to me for comfort.

And, of course, I'll go after the renegades who murdered her brothers, and she'll admire me for that. Lobo and his men will do the raiding—make it look like Indians. And we'll go out and come back with a few stray renegades to blame it on. The bastards will hang for it before they know what hit them, and Rachael will be grateful to me for finding them." He took the cigar from his mouth. "In fact, it might be real easy to put some blame on Brand Selby."

Jules chuckled and shook his head. "You'd do anything to get under that Rivers girl's skirts, wouldn't you?"

Jason's eyes were cool and calculating. "You bet I would. I would also do anything to get rid of Brand Selby. That sonuvabitch doesn't fool me for a minute. He settled around here to give me trouble. He knows too much. I thought when he left this area he was gone for good. He's going to regret coming back here."

"Well, you won't have much trouble putting the blame on the breed," Jules told him. "He's been in town a time or two, and it makes folks right nervous. It would be easy to make people believe he's behind any raiding that might take place."

"Exactly. Lobo and his men will hit a couple of other settlements, too, not just Joshua Rivers's place. I don't want Joshua to seem singled out. That might make Rachael suspicious. I'm sure she'd never think I could be behind something like that, but I want to make damned sure. Getting Brand Selby hanged for all of it will just be the icing on the cake."

"Pretty good plan, don't you think, Jules?" Sam Greene put in. The man had pulled up a chair and turned it backward, straddling the seat as he sat down.

Jules rubbed his chin. "Yeah, I reckon it will work." He met Jason's dark eyes. "Long as we can catch Brand Selby. That won't be easy."

"Lobo can help us there," Jason answered. "You know how ruthless he can be. And he has nine other men with him. That ought to be enough to take down Brand Selby, don't you think?"

Jules grinned. "Well it will definitely even the odds."

"You bet it will," Jason told them. "And we'll be along to

help them. All we have to do right now is wait until the news begins trickling into Austin that some of the outlying settlers are being raided. In four or five days Rachael will find out her own brother's place has been destroyed and her brothers are dead. Then we move out—bring in a few strays—and Brand Selby. They all get hanged. I've captured the killers of Rachael's brothers, and she turns to me for comfort and out of gratitude." He grinned, the cigar still in his teeth. "And she's mine."

Jules and Sam both chuckled, and Jules leaned against a wall, taking a pouch of tobacco from his pants pocket and opening the little leather bag. He pinched some of the sweet-smelling tobacco between thumb and forefinger and shoved it into his mouth between gum and cheek.

"By the way, Jason," he said slowly. "You probably ought to know your bride-to-be goes trottin' around town alone an awful lot. She's takin' a chance wandering around like that. One day I caught her comin' through an alley—said she'd been for a walk alone away from town."

The man felt a personal satisfaction at the way Jason's face darkened. "Rachael? Walking alone?"

Jules nodded. "I told her she'd better be careful—laid it down about the kinds of things the Comanche do to women. She's lucky that half-breed Selby didn't spot her and drag her off to his place. You know how men like that think about white women as pretty as Rachael Rivers."

Jason puffed on the cigar, his dark eyes showing their anger. "Why in hell would she do a thing like that?" Fire came into his eyes. "She isn't seeing someone, is she?"

Jules shrugged. "Don't think so. I think she was just bored and wanted the exercise." He rubbed the back of his neck. "Course it wasn't that I cared what happened to her. I only cared because of you. Far as I'm concerned, I still say you'd be better off sellin' her to the Comancheros. That woman is worth a fortune."

Jason glowered at him. "I don't want anymore of that kind of talk. That one belongs to me. I've known Rachael since she was fourteen years old. I've waited years for her to be ready to marry."

Jules snickered. "Good luck on your wedding night. She's an uppity bitch, far as I'm concerned."

Jason took the cigar from his mouth and studied it a moment. "I'll take care of that my own way."

Sam and Jules both grinned.

"Jules, Sam's trail weary," Jason said. "Let him go to the bathhouse and get a drink and some rest. You watch the prisoners this afternoon. I'm going to get cleaned up myself and go see Rachael. And I think at the dance Saturday I'll talk to Ted Miller—kind of feel him out about running for some kind of office. Maybe he can help me." He rose then, the cigar between his teeth. "Oh, and look at this." He reached into his pocket and pulled out a tiny box. "Lobo stole this for me down in Mexico City."

"I thought Lobo was quitting the Comancheros. Last time I talked to him, he was going to settle down in Mexico with all his loot."

"He always says that," Jason answered. "But he can't resist the excitement. Men like Lobo enjoy the killing and pillaging more than the money they get from all of it." He opened the small box, displaying a set of rings. A huge diamond decorated one gold band, and the other band was set with several sparkling diamonds that fit around the engagement diamond in a swirling design. Jules whistled.

"Lobo knows how to pick out rings, doesn't he?"

"I just hope it fits. It fits the end of my little finger, and I think that's just about the size of Rachael's ring finger. Think this will help her make up her mind?"

"I don't know any woman who'd turn that down," Jules answered.

Jason stared at the ring, puffing on the cigar a moment. "Me either. She won't say no this time. I won't let her." He closed the box and put it back in his pocket. "If she does, she'll change her mind once she finds out about Joshua."

Jules grinned wryly, remembering Rachael's furious words about Jason Brown. Jason was in for a surprise. Rachael Rivers would turn him down again in spite of the ring, and he doubted the death of her brothers would change anything. But he was not about to tell Jason how Rachael talked about him. Let the man find out for himself. Maybe once Jason found out what a bitch she really was, he would finally agree to sell her to Lobo and his men. Jason was getting his hopes up way too high, and that was just fine with Jules Webber. The next few days were going to be interesting. And with the Comancheros so close by, Rachael Rivers could be swept away before people had a chance to blink.

"Well, Sam, let's go get that bath and a couple of drinks," Jason said, rising from his chair. "The next few days will be the best of my life. I'm going to see Rachael and give her the ring; and Saturday I'll announce our engagement at the dance. If all goes right, Rachael and I will be married by Sunday. At the least, Rachael will be weeping in my arms in a few days, begging me to go after her brothers' killers." He faced them both with a big grin. "And once the prim and proper Miss Rivers is my wife, I'll kill anybody who bothers me for the next forty-eight hours while I'm holed up at the hotel with my new bride."

They all laughed as Jason and Sam left to visit the bathhouse.

Rachael laughed and ran naked out of the waters of the Colorado River. She was soon caught up by Brand. She screamed as he grabbed her and carried her to the blanket, where he fell with her, both of them laughing.

"Now you are my captive," he told her, rolling on top of her. Rachael's eyes sparkled with love and passion.

"Please don't kill me."

He grinned. "You will die from making love too much. It will be more than you can stand."

She ran her fingers along the powerful arms. "When will you start the torture?"

He sobered a little, meeting her lips lightly. "Right now." He teased her mouth with light little bites, then moved over her neck, lightly licking with his tongue, removing drops of water from her skin here and there until his lips reached the sweetness of her breasts.

Rachael had never known such happiness as the past night she had spent sleeping under the stars with Brand; making love twice and then lying in his arms in the wilds of Texas with only the moon for light. Any other time it would have been a terrifying situation for a young white woman, being alone so far from people, in country where renegade Comanche rode. But she felt not one moment of fear, for she was with Running Wolf.

They had risen early this morning and had already ridden far. In only another hour or so they would be at the Double "R." They had stopped for one last moment of lovemaking and to cool off in the Colorado River before going on. Rachael had no idea what kind of reaction to expect from Joshua, and she fully realized the next several days might be trying indeed. She wanted to make love once more; to feel Brand Selby inside of her and to remember the ecstasy of it; for after they confronted her brother, it might be awhile before they had another chance to do this.

Her breath caught in her throat as he entered her. He magically brought forth her silken moisture, and she shuddered with ecstasy as her insides pulled at him in glorious climax. She was sure this was the most beautiful feeling a woman could experience. Brand grasped her hips with strong hands, pushing deep, branding her as his own.

She felt his life flowing into her, and she whispered his name. He lay down beside her, breathing deeply from his own spent passion.

They lay there quietly for several minutes before he spoke. "We'd better bathe once more."

"Yes."

He drew her close. "I love you, Rachael. Everything is going to be all right."

She kissed his chest. "I hope so," she whispered.

Lacy answered the knock at the front door, and was startled when she saw Jason Brown standing there. She struggled to quickly regain her composure while he removed his hat.

"Hello, Lacy. I've come to see Rachael."

He stood there in a neat suit, holding a bouquet of flowers. His hair was freshly cut and his face was clean shaven. There was no question that Jason Brown was a handsome man, but now that Lacy knew what she knew about the man, she could see only evil.

Lacy swallowed before answering. "Rachael... isn't here, Jason."

Jason frowned, looking past her as though he didn't believe her. "Isn't here? Where is she?"

"She's gone to see her brothers."

His dark eyes moved back to Lacy's. "Her brothers? How did she get there?"

Lacy folded her arms, finding her courage through anger, as she reminded herself the kind of man Jason Brown was, and what he would do to Brand Selby if he found out about Brand and Rachael.

"Joshua came visiting and Rachael went back with him. It's just for a day, Jason. She'll be back late tomorrow—in plenty of time for the dance."

"Tomorrow!" His jaw flexed in anger and worry. "Are you sure? Are you sure she'll be back tomorrow night?"

"Yes," Lacy answered, curious at his anxiety.

"Will Joshua go right back?"

"Well, I... I suppose." She frowned. "It isn't the end of the world, Jason. Besides, she had no idea when you would return. The poor girl was feeling low and getting restless, so she went to see her brothers."

His face actually brightened a little. "Feeling low? Was it because she missed me?"

"You would have to ask her that."

He looked past her again. "Well, didn't she talk about me at all, give you any idea about marrying me?"

"Not really. Rachael is a pretty independent girl, Jason, you know that. Sometimes she doesn't say what she's feeling. You'll have to discuss it with her."

The hope left his eyes. They bore into Lacy's. "You wouldn't lie to me about her not being here, would you?"

Lacy stepped aside. "Come in and see for yourself."

A sneer moved across his lips. "Never mind! You're sure she'll be here tomorrow night?"

"That was her plan. If you come by Thursday morning, she'll probably be here."

Lacy could see the man was struggling with some kind of indecision before he put on a smile, handing her the bouquet of flowers.

"Then I'll give these to you, Mrs. Reed."

Lacy took the flowers hesitantly, hardly fooled by the smile and the flowers. She did not envy Rachael having to tell this man she was not going to marry him. And if Rachael was smart, she would leave town with Brand Selby without mentioning their relationship until they were both safely away.

"Thank you, Mr. Brown," she quipped.

"I'll be here bright and early Thursday morning to see her," Jason told her. "And you tell her I came to see her as soon as I got back and that I brought her those flowers, will you? Oh, and tell her I'm taking her to the dance. I hope she didn't promise anyone else."

Lacy faced him squarely. "I'm sure she didn't."

Jason bowed slightly, putting his hat back on. "After Saturday there will be no doubt whose girl Rachael Rivers is," he told her with a grin.

He turned and left, and Lacy closed the door, then leaned against it, breathing deeply. "Oh, Rachael, Rachael, God help you and Brand both," she murmured.

Jason quickly left, heading for the bathhouse. He charged inside and ordered two prostitutes who were bathing Sam Greene to leave.

"Hey! What's goin' on?" Greene protested.

Jason quickly closed the curtains and bent close to Greene. "Get the hell out of that tub and start riding! You can make time yet tonight. I want you to go to Lobo's camp right away!"

"But we just got here! My ass is sore as hell, boss. I've been ridin' every day for a month!"

"Do as I say!" Jason barked. "Tell Lobo to wait 'til Friday for that raid, understand? Rachael is out there at the ranch! She's supposed to come back Wednesday night, but just in case she doesn't, I don't want Lobo raiding the Double 'R' Thursday. That will give her an extra day. Joshua will probably bring her back. That means he won't be at the ranch."

"But then he won't be killed!"

"I'll just have to make other arrangements for that—maybe when he does go back you or Jules can follow him and shoot him down after he gets there. Then we'll just add him to the casualties of the raid. No one will know the difference."

"Why don't you just wait a few more days, Jason?"

"I don't *want* to wait! Lobo is already getting itchy to move on. He's staying on to do this as a favor for me. Now get the hell out there and make sure he understands he's to wait an extra day. And you tell that Mexican that if by chance a white woman is at the Double 'R,' he'd better not lay a hand on her. She is to be left alive and untouched, understand?"

"Sure. But what should they do with her?"

"Leave her. Abandon camp. Then I'll ride in and 'rescue' her."

Sam laughed. "Maybe you should go ahead and let it happen that way."

"No." He stood up and grabbed Sam's arm. "Come on. Get out of there and get going."

"Okay! Okay! You sure know how to spoil a man's fun. You gonna pay me extra for this?"

"Don't worry. You'll be rewarded."

Jason turned and left, irritated with Rachael for creating this new problem for him. Now he had to find a way to kill Joshua. "Stupid woman," he grumbled.

Fifteen

Rachael's heart pounded as she rode in front of Brand toward the Rivers ranch house.

"I think that's Josh riding toward us," she told Brand as someone approached on horseback.

Brand slowed his horse, coming nearly to a halt as Josh came closer, brandishing a rifle.

"Josh, it's all right. It's just me," Rachael called out.

Joshua rode up close, total confusion moving through his brown eyes, followed by stubborn challenge. "What the hell is going on here!" He glared at Brand. "You put my sister down from that horse this minute, or I'll blow your head off, Indian!"

"Josh, it's all right. This is Brand Selby, and I came here with him willingly. We need to talk to you."

Brand kept his composure, reminding himself this was Rachael's brother, expecting the reaction he was sure would come at first. Joshua's horse turned in a restless circle, and Joshua kept a grip on his rifle.

"What do you mean, you need to talk to me?" Joshua asked, anger replacing the bold, challenging look.

"Joshua, can we go to the house?"

The young man kept looking from Rachael to Brand and back to Rachael. "Brand Selby? He's the half-breed who's been living north of Austin—the one Jason talked about—the troublemaker."

"He's not a troublemaker," Rachael answered anxiously. "Please, Joshua, let's go to the house. And keep Luke and Matt outside while we talk, will you?"

Joshua hesitated, looking past them as though he suspected some kind of trick. He looked back at his sister. "Is he forcing you to say that? He got friends out there?"

Rachael closed her eyes and sighed. "No, Josh, it's just me and Brand."

Joshua still held the rifle as though ready to fire it. "I don't get it. This man is a half-breed, Rachael. What are you doing riding on the same horse with him, sitting right against him like that? What the hell is going on?"

"If you'll ride to the house with us, I'll explain."

Joshua's eyes moved to Brand's. He could not help realizing what a handsome and powerfully built man Brand Selby was, nor could he ignore the proud and honest look about him. But the man was half Comanche, and the sight of his sister sitting close to him on the same horse infuriated him.

"I would have preferred a friendly introduction," Rachael told her brother. "This is not the kind of hospitality Father would have offered." She looked back at Brand. "Brand, this is obviously my brother, Joshua Rivers."

Brand nodded to the young man. "Obviously." He held Joshua's eyes challengingly. "I have come in friendship, Joshua. No one is with us, and I look upon you with honor because you are Rachael's brother. Take us to the house and hear us out, if you will."

Rachael could see the hurt and anger building in her brother's eyes as he began to realize there was apparently something more than friendship between her and Brand. Friendship would have been bad enough, but something more would be shocking for poor Joshua. The young man rammed his rifle into its boot, red blotches forming on his cheeks.

"Come to the house then," he almost hissed. He yanked on the reins of his horse and turned it, heading in a near gallop to the ranch house. Brand and Rachael followed, their packhorse tied to the tail of Brand's horse.

Far out in one of the corrals Luke whistled to his brother. "Anything wrong, Josh?"

Joshua removed his hat and waved it, their signal that everything was all right. When Luke noticed his sister he ran out of the corral toward her. As he came closer, his smile faded.

Brand slowed his horse. "Hi, Rachael." Luke looked up at her with questioning eyes.

"Luke," Rachael said softly, reaching out and touching his dark hair. "It's only been a few weeks, and look how you've grown."

Brand dismounted and lifted Rachael down. He walked around the other side of the horse with her, where Luke stood. Brand kept hold of his horse's reins as Rachael hugged her brother. Luke looked past her and stared at Brand, who looked huge to the thirteen-year-old boy. He pulled away from his sister but kept hold of her.

"You all right, Rachael? Who's this big Indian man? How come you're with him?"

"Luke, this is Brand Selby. He's only half Indian, and he owns a ranch northeast of Austin." She took hold of her brother's hand and turned to Brand. "Brand, this is my youngest brother, Luke. Luke, Brand and I are... we're very good friends. I'll tell you more about it after we go in the house and talk to Josh."

Luke studied Brand with curiosity rather than hatred. He put out his hand hesitantly. "Hello," he said. Brand smiled, shaking his hand. "Hello, Luke. I'm glad to know you."

They let go of each other's hands and Luke looked over at Rachael. She was smiling. He turned back to Brand. "Glad to know you, too, I guess."

"Luke, where is Matthew?" Rachael asked.

"He's farther out—a couple of cows strayed off this morning. He went after them." He scratched his head. "What are you doing here, Rachael? I mean, I'm glad to see you, but Josh was coming into town in a couple more days. You know it's dangerous to be riding out here."

"We had a special reason for coming," she answered. "And I'm in no danger when I'm with Brand. He has lived among the Comanche—knows their language and knows many of them personally. They won't bother me as long as I'm with him."

Luke looked up at Brand again. "You look kind of like my pa with them buckskin pants and all. Did you know my pa?"

"No," Brand answered, smiling softly. "But from the way

Rachael has talked about him, I wish I had. I'm sorry your pa died, Luke."

The boy sobered. "Yeah. He was a real good man. It's kind of hard around here without him."

"I expect so. My place is a lot smaller than this one, but it takes a lot of work to keep it going." He looked around at tidy corrals and neat sheds. The horses in a nearby pen looked sturdy and well cared for. Green hills rolled out toward open plains to the north and west, and to the northeast he could see stands of elm and cypress trees that ran in a row along the Colorado River. "This is a fine place you have here, Luke."

"Thanks, Mr. Selby. My brother, Josh, he's the one who really keeps it going. We all three own it now, but Josh, he makes all the big decisions right now."

"That's how it should be. You should listen to your big brother."

Rachael gave Luke another squeeze. "You go ahead with your chores. We'll be inside with Joshua for a while. If Matt comes back, tell him to stay outside awhile, will you?"

"Sure, sis. Is something the matter?"

Rachael released her hold and smiled for him. "No. I'll explain later, Luke."

The boy shrugged. "Okay." He looked up at Brand. "Nice to meet you, Mr. Selby."

Brand felt some hope in Luke's friendly attitude. But then Luke was only thirteen. He wished Joshua would have had the same friendly greetings for him. He nodded to Luke. "Thank you, Luke."

Luke quickly kissed his sister's cheek, and turned to leave. Brand could already see through Rachael and Luke the love this family must have shared, and the kind of people their parents must have been. He prepared for the worst with Joshua, telling himself as he took his horse's reins and they walked to the house that he must stay calm. Joshua was obviously prejudiced, although under other circumstances he would probably be at least friendly, although cool, to Brand. But because his sister was involved, it would be another story. Joshua's love and concern for his sister was going to come far above any other feelings, perhaps even above Rachael's own feelings and wishes. Joshua was reacting like any big brother, and now that their father was dead, the young man would feel even more responsible for his sister's welfare, let alone the fact that he had been listening too much to Jason Brown.

Joshua stood on the front porch glaring as Brand and Rachael came closer and Brand tied his horse. Josh turned and said nothing as he went through the door, leaving it open for them. Rachael looked up at Brand, her eyes tearing with apology.

"It's all right," he told her softly. "I had a pretty good idea how he'd react. He's your brother, Rachael. I don't blame him. Let's just go inside and get this over with."

Rachael shook her head. "Don't hate him, Brand. Josh is a good man. Once he gets used to the idea, I know you can be good friends."

"Let's just take one thing at a time." He looked over at Luke, who was walking back to the corral. "At least I have one person on my side." He looked back at Rachael, giving her a smile. "Of course, he doesn't know I want to marry his sister."

She took his hand and squeezed it. "Luke would understand. He's a very open, loving boy." She turned and led Brand onto the porch and through the front door of the modest frame house. Inside Joshua was hurriedly picking up dishes from the table and setting them on the counter next to a bucket of water and a wash pan.

Brand looked around the Rivers home, with lace curtains at the windows and braided rugs on the hardwood floor. There was one main room, with a cast-iron cooking stove that he was sure also served as a heating stove. At the back of the room two doors led to two bedrooms. He noticed penciled drawings hanging on one wall, and he was startled at how much the woman resembled Rachael. The man had long hair and was quite handsome.

"Your parents?" he asked Rachael.

"Yes. A Cherokee friend of my father's drew those for them when they were first married, just before they came to Texas.

Josh and I were very small then. We don't remember when my folks lived in Tennessee."

"I'm afraid we've been too busy to keep up the house again, Rachael," Joshua muttered. He stood with his back to them as he stacked the dishes.

"It's all right," she answered. "I'll clean up a little for you before I leave. Are you keeping your clothes washed?"

"Luke does that." The young man turned, his face alive with animosity. Brand seemed to fill the room with his size, his long hair and Indian features making him look even bigger and more fierce.

Brand faced him squarely, deciding the handsome young Joshua Rivers must be a grand mixture of his mother and father. He didn't really look like either one of them in particular, and yet he held many of their features—his father's brown eyes, his hair a very light brown with almost a blond cast to it from being in the sun. He had his father's firm, squared jawline, and he appeared to be a strong, hard man, not quite six feet in height but with strong arms and shoulders.

"All right," Josh said. "What the hell is going on?"

"Brand and I are—"

Rachael's words were cut off when Brand gently but firmly grasped her arm. "I'll say it myself, Rachael." He kept his eyes on Josh. "Rachael and I are in love, Joshua. We intend to be married. But Rachael loves you very much and was hoping to get your approval first. She's not likely to get approval from anybody else, but no one else matters to her the way you do."

Joshua stood there blinking, staring at them with near shock in his eyes. "Married!" he muttered. He stepped closer, fists clenched. "Have you gone clean crazy!" he all but growled at Rachael.

"I'm in love with him, Josh. I met Brand in town, and then he came to the school and asked me if I would teach him to read and write better. You know the promise I made to Mother and you know how she would feel about my refusing to teach someone because of his race. So I said I would do it, and we started meeting at his ranch. Before long we knew we were in love."

Joshua put up his hand, motioning for her to slow down. "Just a minute." He looked at her with anger and disgust. "A stranger comes to you—a half-breed, no less, and asks you to teach him. And you go running off to meet him alone at his ranch? What the hell is the matter with you?" he hissed. "How did you know he wouldn't rape you—or hand you over to his Comanche friends? What in God's name were you thinking!"

She held his eyes challengingly. "I trusted him, the same as you know how to trust a man by watching his eyes, Joshua Rivers. I did what I know Mother would have wanted me to do, and what I knew no one else in town would do. Brand wants to settle, Josh, like any man. He has a ranch, which he bought with money he earned working for another rancher over on the Brazos. He's trying very hard to lead the life of a white man, and he knows that to do that well he needs to be able to read and write. His mother was white, and she taught him some writing, but he needs to know more. I admired his courage in coming to ask for help; and his determination to make a better life for himself. He's a good man, Joshua, as good as you or any other honest settler."

He stared at her, then snickered nervously, turning away and walking back to the counter where he had set the dishes. "You're really serious!"

"Yes, I am," Rachael answered. "Brand and I are in love and I want to be his wife."

Joshua's eyes burned with hatred as they moved to look at Brand. He scanned the man quickly, realizing that to get to the ranch at this time of day they would have had to leave the day before. That meant they had spent a night alone on the plains. The thought of the big half-breed before him touching his sister made his blood boil. He turned fiery eyes back to Rachael.

"I sent you to Austin to protect you from the Comanche," he said. "And now you come prancing in here telling me you want to *marry* one! What in God's name is wrong with you, Rachael! Do you know what people will call you when they find out? They'll call my sister a whore—a dirty white squaw! The list is a mile long of names people have for white women who marry Indians!" Rachael covered her face and turned away. "People don't even want anything to do with white women who have been captives against their will, let alone one who would *willingly* let an Indian—"

"That's enough!" Brand shouted. "She is your sister, and she is a good woman, a woman with a kind heart that is full of love for everyone—a woman who does not judge a man by his race. Rachael cared enough about you to come here and tell you first. This will be hard for her. You could make it much easier by accepting it and letting her know that at least one person besides myself is on her side. She needs your support, Joshua, not your insults."

"They aren't *my* insults, Selby. They're the brand *others* will put on her, and you know it. I'm sorry to put it so bluntly, but you ought to know better than anybody what they'll say about her! How dare you put your heathen hands on my sister!"

"Stop it!" Rachael shouted. "Brand has even helped keep you out of danger, telling his Comanche friends to leave this ranch alone."

"I'd rather be attacked by Indians than to see my sister *marry* one!"

"He might be half Indian, but he's also half *white*," Rachael answered, tears on her cheeks. "What about that side of him? You don't even know him, Josh! Talk to him. He's a wonderful man, and he wants peace, not strife." Rachael stepped closer to her brother. "Look at me, Josh. You know me. You know I would never fall in love with a man who wasn't honorable and kind and hardworking and honest. He's so much like Father, Josh."

"Like Pa? He's nothing like Pa. Pa was a *white* man!"

Rachael jerked back as though someone had struck her. Terrible disappointment filled her eyes, making Joshua feel a shame that he refused to show. "Oh, Joshua," Rachael said, the hurt evident in her voice. "I'm glad our mother and father aren't alive to hear you say that."

She turned away. And Brand, standing there, felt torn, his heart aching for Rachael, and his fists clenching in a strong desire to hit Joshua Rivers.

Joshua kept his eyes on Rachael. "It's different here in Texas than it was in Tennessee, Rachael, and you know it. The Comanche are nothing like the Cherokee. You know what they've done to some settlers, what they do to women and little babies."

Rachael whirled. "And I suppose no white man has ever committed such acts against the Indians and even against their own kind! Men are men, Josh. Some are good and some are evil. There are white men I wouldn't dream of being caught alone with. You judge each man by his personal worth and accomplishments, Josh. That's what Father always taught you. When did you become so prejudiced? We've never had any real trouble from the Comanche."

"I don't need personal trouble with them to know. Everybody knows what happened to the Parkers."

"And from then on every Comanche has been judged the same, even the peaceful ones. When do we reach the point of forgive and forget, Josh? It has to end somewhere. We can start by at least accepting the ones who are peaceful and trying to make a better life like Brand."

Joshua's eyes moved back to Brand, and he stepped away from Rachael and closer to Brand. "What did you do to her? You two came all the way out here alone, spent last night alone. What have you done to my sister, you bastard?"

"Joshua!" Rachael grasped the back of a chair while the two men glared at each other challengingly.

"I love your sister more than my own life," Brand answered calmly. "I would gladly kill any man who would call her a bad name for doing nothing but loving someone. I have done nothing bad to her. I have only loved her. And she is already my wife—the Indian way."

Joshua's eyes widened in rage, and he lunged at Brand, cursing him. As Rachael watched in horror he shoved Brand up against a wall and began to land his fist hard into Brand's belly. Brand grabbed Joshua's wrists, shoving hard. Joshua flew backward across the table. Then Joshua leapt up and came at him again, ready for a fight that would surely be close to an equal match. But Rachael screamed his name and moved up to grab him. Joshua shoved her, and she fell. Startled, he backed away, looking at her apologetically, going to her to help her up.

"I'm sorry, Rachael."

She broke into tears and walked over to Brand. Joshua looked at her helplessly, then turned hate-filled eyes to Brand. "Damn you! Look what you've made me do!"

"If you would stay calm and not resort to fists right away, it wouldn't happen," Brand answered, standing in a defensive pose. "If you want to fight, then we will fight, but to do so would only hurt Rachael more. Don't make me fight you, Joshua."

"Why? Would you stick a knife in me? I've always heard the Comanche are good at that!"

Brand straightened, watching him sadly. "No. I would not stick a knife in you. If you were truly my enemy, I would cut you from head to belly. But you are *not* my enemy. You are Rachael's brother and you can call me your enemy, but I will not call you mine."

Joshua breathed deeply for control as Brand put his arm around Rachael. "I am just a man," Brand said calmly. "I love your sister very much. We have come to you hoping you would understand and give your sister your blessing. Soon Rachael and I will go away to find a white preacher who will marry us your way, so we'll have that damned piece of paper you whites insist on having signed when two people marry. But we are just as married right now as we would be with a piece of paper! Rachael is everything to me—*everything!*"

Joshua turned away. "Don't you love your sister, Joshua?" Brand continued. "Do you think she would fall in love with just any man? She has a gentle heart, and much more capacity to love apparently than her brother! She is educated and intelligent. Does that not say something for my worth? And what about the fact that I came here willingly, hoping to gain your friendship and acceptance? We did not have to do this, Joshua. We could have run off together and told you about it later. But it meant very much to Rachael that you know about it and accept it. You have hurt her deeply today. I do not care for myself. I have heard the kind of words you speak many times over. I can stand the insults and the words of those who are ignorant of the Comanche people and their ways. But I cannot stand to hear you insult your sister! Surely you know the kind of person she is."

Rachael sank down in a chair next to her. She put her face in her hands and wept. Brand walked over to her and put his hands on her shoulders. Joshua watched Rachael with an aching heart, torn between absolute shock and disappointment and the great love he had for his sister. She was so much like their mother. Because their own parents had gone through hell back in Tennessee when Emma Rivers married a man called the "white Indian," Joshua and Rachael had been taught tolerance of all races. But he had never been faced with this kind of challenge, and his love for his sister made him feel sick at the thought of what others would think of her—the labels that would be put on her if she married this half-breed.

He walked to a window and breathed deeply to gather his thoughts before saying another word. He watched Luke at his chores. Joshua would have liked nothing better than to shoot Brand Selby, but then his sister would hate him for the rest of his life, and he didn't want that, either. Joshua turned back in time to see Rachael wiping her eyes with a handkerchief. She reached up and grasped one of Brand's hands at her shoulder, and Brand squeezed her hand lovingly.

"How long has this been going on?" he asked Rachael. "Is this why you were late that day I came to see you? Does Lacy know about it?"

Rachael turned watery eyes to her brother. "Yes, she knows about it. She understood it right away, perhaps because she's been in love herself. Maybe if you were in love, you'd understand it, too, Josh." She sniffed. "Yes, the day I was late I had been with Brand."

"Why didn't you tell me then?"

She swallowed, wiping at her eyes again. "Because I wanted to be sure myself first. I struggled with it for a long time, not because Brand is a half-breed. I loved him almost from the moment I set eyes on him. It was only that I knew how you would probably feel, how others would react."

"What about Jason? He loves you, too."

She rose, still clinging to Brand's hand. "Jason Brown doesn't know the first thing about love. He only wants to own me. Brand knows Jason well—scouted for him in the Rangers. Anything Jason has told you about Brand Selby is because he hates Brand. He hates Brand because Brand knows the kind of man Jason *really* is."

Joshua folded his arms. "How do you know you can believe anything this man says about Jason? He probably hates Jason in return."

Rachael let go of Brand's hand and stepped closer. "I know because I know how I feel when I'm near Jason—afraid. This man is bigger and stronger and half Indian, yet I have never once felt the fear in his presence that I have felt when I'm around Jason. And once Brand caught Jason and two of his men raping a young Indian girl no more than twelve. Jason whipped her with that bullwhip of his. Brand has scars still on his own back from trying to protect her. And that old man Jason told us about when he came here after that last patrol—Brand was there, all right. He stopped Jason. But it was too late. After Jason left them, the old man died. Jason Brown killed him!"

Rachael saw a hint of understanding begin to move into Joshua's eyes. "I know most people have plenty of reason to hate the Comanche, Joshua. But it's no excuse to rape and whip a little girl or to whip an old man to death. It doesn't take a very brave man to do that. That's the kind of man your Jason Brown is. The things he does only perpetuate the raids and the killings and the hatred. And Brand suspects Jason has dealings with Comancheros!"

Joshua's surprised eyes darted to Brand. "That's impossible. Jason Brown would never—"

"Oh, Joshua, use your head!" Rachael interrupted. "It would be easy for him, riding out there with a Ranger badge on. Why fight them when you can make money off of them?"

"But Jason's done a lot of good things. He almost never comes back without a horse thief or outlaws or somebody along with him. And he always takes time to come out here and check on me and Luke and Matt."

"He only does that to get on your good side because of me," Rachael answered.

He waved her off. "You've got me all confused." He paced for a moment, then turned to face Rachael. "What am I supposed to do now? Give you my blessing?"

She breathed deeply to soothe her aching heart. "It would be nice."

He looked darkly at Brand again, then back at Rachael. "Well, I can't." He watched the hope in her eyes dwindle, and he looked over at Brand. "And if you really loved my sister, you wouldn't have let this happen. You of all people should know what it will mean for her, even if she leaves Austin. She wouldn't be able to settle with you any place in Texas."

"Then we will go somewhere else."

Joshua let out a long, disgusted sigh and turned away again.

"I knew what it would mean for her," Brand told him. "That is why both of us fought our feelings at first, denied them. But when two people are truly in love, those feelings cannot long be controlled. I have not shamed your sister, Joshua. I have not used her, and I have no intentions of deserting her now. I love her as my own life. I am not even sure I would want to go on living if it means living without Rachael. She came here hoping against hope that at least her brother would be on her side, to help give her the strength she needs to get through this. She has never known abusive words and hateful stares and evil gossip. And as her brother, you should be outraged at what people would say about her, rather than saying those things to her yourself."

Joshua ran a hand through his hair, turning to face them. "I didn't say them myself."

"But you thought them." Brand held the young man's eyes challengingly. Joshua turned his gaze to Rachael. "I didn't think them myself, Rachael, I swear. I was just... so surprised." He moved his eyes over her, realizing with full clarity that she was a grown woman. "I always think of you as a little girl, I guess, even though you're only a year younger. You were always so small, and you always came to me with everything. Now you've gone and done this without saying a word about it. I'd have been upset even if it was just some other man in town that I didn't know—a white man. But you bring home a half-breed and tell me you've already slept with him and you want to marry him, and I'm just supposed to say it's wonderful and good luck." He shook his head. "I can't do that. I need some time to think about this."

Their eyes held. "Then take the time." She sniffed.

She stepped closer, holding his eyes. "Josh, you know how Father would feel about this. He would question Brand, talk to him, get to know him. He might not have accepted it at first either, but it wouldn't have been because Brand has Indian blood. It would have been for the same reason any other father is cautious about the man his daughter will marry. And Mother went through this same thing, Josh. You know that. Her love for Father held them together. You know what they went through. But you also know how much they loved each other. That's how it is with me and Brand."

Joshua sighed. "Sometimes I think you've been away too long, Rachael. You have forgotten just how deeply most folks around here hate the Comanche. I'm not near as bad as most, because of Pa, I suppose." He frowned, studying Brand. "And how do you know this man is going to stay this way? Maybe someday that wild side of him will take over and he'll abuse you, maybe even get tired of you and sell you, maybe start drinking, decide to take a second wife. Comanche men usually have more than one wife, you know."

Rachael closed her eyes and turned away. "Comanche men take more than one wife for survival," Brand spoke up. "If a woman is widowed, she usually goes to her sister's husband because she could never survive on her own. Most babies born to the Comanche die very young, so a man takes more than one wife in order to have enough surviving children to make sure the race does not die out. There are many reasons for taking more than one wife. But I am Comanche by blood and in my spiritual beliefs only. I have not lived as a Comanche for a long time—long enough to show that that life is over for me. I do not drink the firewater and I never have. And because of my white mother, even when I lived among them I never harmed a white woman."

Joshua faced him. "So, it was your mother who was white. A captive?"

Brand held his eyes. "At first. But she loved my father. When she had a chance to escape, she chose to remain with him."

"She still alive?"

"No. Both my mother and my father are dead. My father was killed at Plum Creek."

Joshua nodded. "I was only fifteen then, but I heard about Plum Creek. That was the last really big battle."

"Massacre."

Joshua watched his eyes, seeing something there that he liked but not wanting to admit to it. "Yes, I suppose it was. At any rate, that chased out most of the Indians except for the renegades who roam the borders now. You probably know who they all are."

"I know them. I tried to convince them to stop, but men like Jason Brown keep the hatred alive. After he raped the little Indian girl and his superiors did nothing about it, I quit scouting and left this area for a long time."

"Why did you bother coming back here?"

"To be in Jason Brown's territory again. I intend to prove he deals with Comancheros—at least was my plan. Then I met Rachael. Now it doesn't matter to me anymore. I just want to be able to marry her and be at peace."

The words were spoken in quiet passion. And Joshua knew that half-breed or not, if this man truly loved his sister, he would be a wildly protective husband. Surely he was a gentle man in spite of his size and appearance, for he had stolen Rachael's virginity and she was certainly not upset by it. A girl as innocent and trusting as Rachael would not still love a man who had been brutal with her. But it still ate at Joshua's pride that it had happened at all, and he actually struggled with jealousy. Rachael Rivers was his sister. No man should have touched her without Joshua Rivers's permission. Who else was there to look after her best interests now?

"Well, there sure isn't much I can do about it now, is there?" He shook his head again, confused by all he had just heard, especially by the stories about Jason Brown, who he had always felt would marry Rachael. "I can't give you my blessing, Rachael, not yet. I've got some thinking to do. I'll be coming to Austin next Monday or Tuesday. I was going to come earlier and go to the dance Saturday, but there's too much to do around here. Besides—" Disgust came back into his eyes. "I'm not exactly in the mood for a dance now." His jaw flexed in repressed anger. "Can you do one thing for me and hold off on things 'til I come? Will you wait for me at Lacy's before you two go riding off?"

Rachael looked over at Brand, not sure how to answer her brother.

"You can have the time," Brand answered. "We owe you that much. Rachael and I will marry just the same, but we will not leave until you come to Austin and see her once more. If you approve of this and accept it, it will help our own decision on whether to stay in Austin or leave. There is strength in numbers, Joshua, but if we must do this alone, we will do it."

Joshua moved hurt eyes to Rachael. "You staying the night?"

"Yes. We will leave early in the morning and try to make Austin by nightfall. I don't want to be gone too long and arouse suspicion. Lacy will tell anyone who asks that you came for me and I came out for a short visit."

"I must get back as soon as I can myself," Brand put in. "One of my prized horses was very sick when I left. And I have only two young Comanche boys to watch my place. They do not have the experience of you and your brothers. I want to be back by tomorrow night."

"I intend to go to the dance, Joshua. I don't want this to come out until afterward. People are all wound up for Saturday and I'm afraid an ugly mob would form if people learned about me and Brand beforehand. I don't want Brand to be hurt. We'll wait until after the dance and then quietly leave. I pray it will be with your best wishes. My biggest hope was that Brand could sell everything he has and pool the money into the Double 'R' and work together with you and Matt and Luke. Together we could have an even bigger ranch, Josh—more horses and cattle. We could all be together, and I'd be here to keep the house and cook for you and—"

"Stop it, Rachael!" The disappointment on her face tore at his heart, but he could not bring himself to listen to such an outlandish idea.

Rachael blinked back tears. "I'll make some supper and clean things up a bit before we go," Rachael told him. She looked pleadingly at Brand. "We can at least all eat a meal together, and I want to see Matt and Luke."

Brand nodded. "We will eat together and I will meet Matthew," he told her. "We will tell both your other brothers about us." Rachael was grateful for the strength and determination Brand showed. He folded his arms and turned his eyes to meet Joshua's. "We will talk about horses," he continued. "That is one thing we both know about. Perhaps if I tell you how my sick horse is acting, you will have some idea what is wrong with him."

Their eyes held, and Joshua realized the effort Brand Selby was making to befriend him. He was indeed more civilized than the average Comanche. If Brand Selby was the vicious Indian others made him out to be, Brand would have gladly continued their fight and would probably have done a fine job of carving him up.

Still, the man was a half-breed, worse than a full-blood in most peoples' eyes. Anger and disappointment still boiled in his gut that his sister would not only marry such a man, but also that she had already given herself to him. Surely Brand Selby had used some kind of trick to seduce poor Rachael. He told himself he must not trust a half-breed. How did he know what Brand said about Jason was true? He had known Jason Brown a lot longer than he had known this man standing before him.

"All right," he said aloud. He looked at Rachael. "We'll eat supper together. I appreciate your offer to make it. There's some deer meat in the smokehouse and a few potatoes down there in the bin where Ma always kept them. I hope to God you know what you're doing, Rachael."

She straightened more, lifting her chin. "It's God who

means for us to be together, Josh. I know it in my heart. Some day you'll know also."

Joshua stepped closer. "You just think about what you're doing. *Think* about it, damn it, Rachael!"

"I *have* thought about it."

Joshua sighed and headed for the door, turning to face them both before going out. "We'll have supper together, and I'll try to keep it pleasant. Matt and Luke can make up their own minds, but I don't think a few days of mulling it over is going to change my mind at all." He turned his eyes to Brand. "You might love my sister and be a good man and all of that, but you're still a half-breed; and I can't stomach the thought of my sister marrying you. It's wrong, Selby—she's going to be hurt and hurt bad."

"The only people who can truly hurt her are those she loves," Brand answered, anger in his own voice. "The others do not matter to her. If you love your sister you will help her through this by accepting it. And I see behind those angry eyes the goodness that is in Rachael."

Joshua's nostrils flared with indignation. "You see a man who loves his sister and wants the best for her; a man whose right to decide what is best for her has been stolen away without a word!" He looked over at Rachael. "I don't know if I can ever forgive you for this," he growled. "I love you, Rachael, because you're my sister. But I'll never understand what you've done."

He walked out, slamming the door behind him. Rachael turned to Brand. "I never thought it would be this bad," she said brokenly.

"I was afraid it would be. That is why I wanted to be with you."

"Now what do I do, Brand?"

"You go back with me and we will wait as we promised. After he has had time to think about this, he will know the right thing to do is to come and tell you it is all right with him."

"I don't think he will. I just lost my father to death, and now it's like... like Joshua has died, too. I've lost him."

Brand came closer, taking her into his arms. "You have not

lost him, Rachael. You share the same blood. He will not turn away forever."

Outside Joshua walked straight to the graves of his parents. He stared at the stone markers as a hot Texas wind ruffled his thick hair. "Jesus, Pa, what should I do?" He closed his eyes and lowered his head, wishing with all his heart that Joe Rivers was still alive. It was so hard suddenly being the one in charge. "Rachael. My God, Rachael," he wept.

Sixteen

"Are you a *real* Indian?" Luke asked Brand.

"Finish chewing before you speak, Luke," Rachael said quietly. She glanced at Joshua, who was glowering at his little brother.

Brand swallowed a piece of venison, keeping his patience with the question. He detected only innocent curiosity in Luke's dark eyes.

"I am only half Indian, Luke," he answered.

Matthew turned blue eyes to look at Brand Selby again. He was undecided on the whole subject of his sister marrying this half-breed. It didn't seem right, a sister of his marrying a man who was half Indian; yet there was something about Brand that he liked, and both he and Luke admired Brand's powerful build and obvious abilities, but Matthew was not so sure he was the right man for his sister.

It gladdened Rachael's heart to realize that both younger boys at least seemed more tolerant of the whole idea than did Joshua. If she could win them over, perhaps they could eventually win over Joshua.

"Did you live with them?" Luke was asking.

"When I was young."

Luke rattled off more questions—about Brand's parentage, his scouting experiences.

"Luke, your stew is going to get cold," Rachael reminded him. She turned to Brand. "You have hardly had a chance to eat for all the questions."

"I don't mind. Your brothers should know all they want to know about me."

"Like whether you have connections with the Comancheros?"

228

Joshua put in sarcastically. "And like what your real plans are for our sister?"

"Joshua, please stop it," Rachael told him, her cheeks turning pink.

"I have no connections with the Comancheros," he told Joshua. "It is Jason Brown who deals with them, and some day I will prove it."

"Jason would never deal with men like that," Matthew put in. "He's a Texas Ranger."

Brand moved his eyes to meet Matthew's. "There are bad men in all walks of life, Matthew. There are good and bad white men, and good and bad Indians. Most Rangers try to do good, to keep law and order. I have worked for them myself, remember? But just because Jason is a Ranger, it does not mean he is a good man."

"I bet you're real good with guns and knives and things like that, aren't you, Mr. Selby?" Luke asked, unperturbed by the rest of the conversation.

"As good as most," Brand answered.

"You ever been in a knife fight? I always heard Indians were real good in knife fights."

"Luke, finish your stew," Rachael told him.

The boy grudgingly dipped his spoon back into the mixture of potatoes, vegetables, and venison.

"Yeah, I reckon he's real good with a knife," Joshua answered for Brand. "You ever lift any pretty blond scalps, Selby?"

Rachael closed her eyes and bowed her head, still clinging to Brand's hand. "Oh, Joshua," she whispered.

"I have never touched a white woman," Brand answered.

"Not till you touched my sister. Maybe she's stupid enough to trust in you, but I'm not, Selby."

"Joshua, why are you talking like this in front of Matt and Luke?" Rachael asked sadly.

Brand stood up and turned to Rachael. "I am going to check on the horses. I think we had better leave yet tonight. We can make a few miles even in the dark."

He walked out and Rachael rose from the table. "I never

thought I could be so ashamed of my own brother, Joshua."

Joshua threw down his spoon. "Damn it, Rachael, I only want what's best for you."

"Then be happy for me! I love him, Joshua. Don't you understand?"

"No! He's half *Indian*. My God, Rachael, what is wrong with you?"

She stiffened, facing him squarely. "I am our mother's daughter. Emma Simms Rivers would have acted no differently." She swallowed back tears. "I'm going outside with Brand. I'm sorry for how you feel, Josh. I guess we needn't bother waiting for you to come to town. We'll be leaving Monday, whether you show up or not. I'm really sorry you can't understand, sorry I have to go. I had hoped we could live right here and be a family, because I love you." She looked at Matt and Luke. "All of you."

"I like him, Rachael," Luke spoke up. "Don't go away forever."

Rachael smiled sadly. "That's up to your brothers, Luke." She looked challengingly at Joshua. "I'm glad Mother and Father aren't here to see you acting like this."

After she turned and walked out, Matthew turned a pouting face to Joshua. "Why don't you hold a gun on him and make him leave Rachael here and ride out?" he asked.

Joshua leaned back in his chair. "That wouldn't work," he said. "She'd call my bluff and go with him anyway. I can't shoot him down in front of Rachael."

Matthew shrugged. "Why don't you tell Jason then? He'd stop it. Jason loves Rachael anyway—wants to marry her."

Joshua stared at the table, trying to decide if Jason Brown could possibly be as bad as Brand Selby claimed. "I don't know. Trouble with that is Jason probably won't even want her for himself after this." He leaned forward, his elbows on the table. "But at least I bet he could stop it. Maybe I *will* go to that dance and have a little talk with Jason."

"I like him, Josh," Luke said, a scowl on his face. "You shouldn't be mean to Rachael like that. She likes him, too."

"You're too young to know what's best for our sister, Luke.

The man is a half-breed. He could turn on her at anytime—go back to his Indian ways."

"Pa didn't have anything against the Indians."

"Comanches are different from the Indians Pa knew best. I bet Pa wouldn't approve of this either."

"I bet he would."

"Shut up and eat your stew, Luke," Matt put in. "What do you know?"

"Just as much as you. You're only two years older. What makes you think you know so much?"

"Both of you be quiet," Joshua said, rising. "This is up to me." He walked to a window, looking out to see Rachael and Brand standing out under the elm tree, at the graves of Joe and Emma Rivers. The two of them embraced, and he could see Rachael was crying. Joshua felt torn inside. He wanted his sister to be happy, but marrying someone like Brand Selby was only going to bring her heartache. He couldn't let it happen, no matter how much she might hate him for a while. He decided he had no choice but to tell Jason Brown. Jason would know what to do.

They made their way by the light of the moon, through a night of breathless quiet. Rachael held no fear, for she was with a man who knew this land like the back of his hand, knew every rock, every stand of trees, every turn of the river. In the moonlight the rock formations looked to her like grotesque beings guarding the night, and distant trees were just jagged, dark lines. Alone, this land would be one of wrenching isolation, and Rachael realized that was how she felt about Joshua—isolated now from his love.

Brand pressed her close against him. "We'll sleep soon," he told her. "I know you're tired." He kissed her hair. "You can still change you mind, Rachael."

"No. You're as good as any man in Austin. I'm just… so ashamed of the way Joshua talked to you."

"I wasn't completely surprised."

She couldn't help the sob that jerked at her body. "Oh,

Brand, I don't want my brothers to hate me."

He halted the horse, getting off and lifting her down. "Rachael, they don't hate you. They're just disappointed and confused right now." He kissed her forehead. "Behind all the yelling and insults I saw a lot of love down deep inside Joshua Rivers. That's all it is. He loves you and he isn't sure I'm the best man for you. What we have to do is prove that I am—prove to him how much we love each other. If he's anything like you, was raised the way you were, he'll come around." He gave her a hug. "Besides, I've got at least one of them on my side. Luke likes me."

She smiled through tears, hugging him tightly. "I love you, Brand. I can bear anything others say and do, as long as I can be with you."

He watched her quietly for a moment, but she could not read his eyes well in the moonlight. He bent close, putting his face close to hers and lifting her off her feet. It was then she felt his tears.

"What am I doing to you?" he said, his words choked.

She hugged him tightly around the neck, realizing just how deeply wounded he was. The sad and confused child in him was suddenly exposed.

"You're loving me, that's all," she whispered. "You're making me feel alive and loved and happy. You've made a woman out of me and I belong to you, Brand Selby. It's gone too far now. Don't make me have to live without you. Please, Brand." She broke into tears herself. "Oh, we should never have come out here."

They hugged tightly for several long seconds until he moved his lips to her cheek. She turned to meet his mouth with her own, and they tasted each other's tears. The desperate feeling of outside factors possibly tearing them apart brought an urgency to the kiss, as though they must enhance the memory by bringing forth their wildest passions.

It was all understood as he slowly lowered her and walked with his arm around her, leading his horse and the packhorse down into a gulley Rachael didn't even know was ahead of them. But she knew Brand had spotted it with the keen eyes of a scout, a man who seemed to see even in the night. He quietly unloaded the riding horse, then untied the packhorse from the lead animal's tail and hobbled both horses.

"We'll have to go another night without a fire," he told her. "I'm not worried about the Comanche, but you never know about outlaws. Out here a fire can be seen for miles. One look at you and Comancheros would kill each other trying to get to you."

Rachael shivered at the thought of Jason Brown possibly dealing with such men. If only she could change Joshua's mind about Jason.

Brand spread out a blanket, then turned to her, stroking her lustrous hair. "This might be our last chance for a while. Once I take you back I'll wait until after Saturday. We'll be back by tomorrow night. You go ahead to the dance Saturday, but stay with a crowd. And don't even hint to Jason about us, understand? I'd take you away right now, but Jason Brown is probably back. Next thing you know he'll be riding out here to ask Joshua about you, and then he'll know. If Lacy can put him off a couple of days, we can get far enough away that by the time Jason gets in touch with Joshua and finds out, they'll never find us."

"Oh, Brand, it isn't fair to you. You have your ranch and—"

"It's the only way now. Standing Horse and Gray Bear can run my horses up the Colorado to the nearest Comanche camp. Nothing will happen to them. I can find a way to come for them later. Besides, when Jason Brown finds out about this, I have a feeling I won't have a ranch to come back to."

Their eyes held in the moonlight, each of them feeling the weight of what was ahead of them. He rubbed a thumb over her cheek. "It's probably selfish of me, but I don't want to be without you, Rachael." He swallowed, his last words sounding strained again. Her heart ached for him. "I guess this ends our lessons for a while, doesn't it?" he tried to joke.

"I guess it does," she whispered.

He leaned down and met her mouth, and she parted her lips willingly. He began unbuttoning the back of her dress, and the kiss lingered as he slid it down over her shoulders. Her skin almost glowed a milky white in the moonlight as he left her mouth and pulled the dress to her waist.

"You are so beautiful, like a small, soft doe," he told her, running his hands over soft skin. She stood still as he moved his hands down to her chest and began unlacing the undergarment. "You are everywhere, Rachael, in my mind, my heart, my blood. You have become my strength, my reason for being."

He cast the undergarment aside, moving his big hands over her ribs, nearly able to reach all the way around her waist. He moved them up over her breasts, massaging gently. Rachael closed her eyes as his hands moved back down and he pulled her dress and bloomers down to her ankles. She stepped out of them and he moved his hands back up over the calves of her legs, the back of her thighs, bringing his head up with them. She sucked in her breath when he gently massaged her bottom, kissing her gently. Wild desire shot through her with a force that made her groan, and he moved upward and tasted her breasts, her neck.

He picked her up in his arms and lay her down on the blanket, then stood and undressed. She watched him in the moonlight, a grand specimen of man, looking huge and wild in the moonlight. He threw his weapons and clothes aside to kneel down over her.

She grasped his arms and raised up, kissing his chest.

She moved her arms around his powerful shoulders, leaning up to kiss his neck. He whispered her name and moved his hands under her hips to lay her back down. He pushed deep, relishing the tender moment, reminding himself by her reaction of obvious pleasure that this woman really did love him and wanted to share that love forever.

Never had he known this kind of love, this kind of pleasure. He vowed this creature of gold and pink and sweetness would be his mate for life, would bear his children, would sleep next to him at night for the rest of his life. He would let nothing and no one stop it from being so.

"My sweet Rachael," he whispered, as his life surged into her. He gathered her into his arms then, kissing her over and over. "I knew the day I saw you at the river that I wanted you for my own. It is a force stronger than I, a force that keeps me from doing what I know is best for you, and that is to leave now and never come back."

"No!" she whispered. "Please don't ever leave me, Brand. Together we can face them all. We can do it, Brand."

He pulled a blanket over them and enveloped her in his arms. "I'm a fool, but I won't leave you. Life wouldn't be worth living without you."

The night hung in a breathless quiet as they lay there together, small creatures compared to the powerful landscape that surrounded them in the dark of night. And Rachael realized she was not fighting just Joshua and Jason Brown. She was fighting Texas. Such a big land it was; yet there might not be enough room there for a white woman and the half-breed man she loved.

Lacy answered the back door and Rachael hurried inside. "Back so soon?" Lacy exclaimed. "I didn't expect you 'til tomorrow night."

"Oh, Lacy." Rachael sighed deeply, setting down her carpetbag and hugging her. "It was terrible. Joshua was so abusive we just couldn't stay. I never thought he would be that ugly and stubborn. Poor Brand. Joshua said terrible things to him."

"I was afraid of that," Lacy told her. "What are you going to do now, honey?"

Rachael walked to the kitchen table and sat down wearily. "We can't stay here, that's certain. We'll wait 'til after the dance, when things are calmer and more quiet. We'll leave Monday." She met Lacy's eyes apologetically. "I'm sorry, but you'll have to lie for me for a couple of days if Jason or anyone asks about me. Tell them I'm sick in my room. Brand and I will need a couple of days to get some miles between us and Austin, especially once Jason finds out."

"Well, the man is back and he's already been here looking for you."

Rachael closed her eyes and shuddered at the thought of having to face him. "I was half hoping he wouldn't even get back until Brand and I were gone." She looked back at Lacy. "What did you tell him?"

"Just what you told me to tell him—that you had gone to Joshua's for a couple of days. How are you going to explain that you came back so quick?"

Rachael ran a hand through her hair. "I don't know. I'll think of something." Her eyes teared. "We don't know what else to do but just get out of Austin, Lacy. I don't want to leave you, and I sure don't want to leave my brothers. But between Jason and Joshua, we have no choice."

"Oh, I understand. I just think it's a shame it has to be this way for you, but I warned you, Rachael."

"I know." She closed her eyes and put her head in her hands. "Josh and I were always so close. It hurts so bad to think of having hard feelings between us now, Lacy. But I love Brand too much to change things just for Joshua."

Lacy patted her arm. "He'll come around eventually, Rachael. After a while, after you and Brand are married and are doing fine on your own, he'll miss his sister and he'll want to patch things up. You'll see. He's stubborn, and I expect you've hurt his pride some, seeing as how he probably felt like it was his place to look after you. But he's a Rivers, and with folks like those you had, he'll accept it after a while because he's got his mother's good heart and his father's ability to accept a man for his worth."

"Brand thinks like you do. But how long is it going to take? I hate being at odds with Joshua." Her eyes teared. "My heart feels as heavy as a stone. Sometimes I wish I never would have come back to Texas. I wonder how things would have turned out for me if I would just have stayed in St. Louis."

"Oh, I expect you would have met some dandy gentleman who could have given you all the finest things a woman could want—except that he could never please you in the really important ways, never set you on fire and make you breathless the way I'll bet Brand Selby does."

Rachael looked at her in surprise and Lacy chuckled. "Oh yes, I remember how it was. I'm not that old, Rachael Rivers."

Rachael reddened and pulled out a handkerchief, wiping her eyes.

"Real love, the kind you and Brand share, is not easy to find, Rachael. It's worth fighting for. Don't you fret over Joshua. He'll get over it. You go ahead and leave with Brand and you be happy."

Rachael smiled through tears. "Thank you, Lacy. I don't think I could have managed through all of this without you."

Lacy smiled and rose to make some tea. "You just go on up to your room and relax and I'll bring up some tea. How does that sound?"

"It sounds wonderful." Rachael rose, picking up her carpetbag and heading for the stairs, her feet feeling like lead. How she hated leaving Brand again. What if he really did decide it was best to go away? He was on his way back to his ranch right now, alone and lonely, probably full of doubts as to whether he should allow Rachael to face what she would surely face by running off with him. The next four days were going to be miserable, wondering how Brand was, if he would really come for her on Monday. With Jason back, there was no way she could go to Brand. Jason would be watching her every move. The thought of having to face him now, knowing what she knew about him, loving Brand the way she did, made her shiver with dread.

Seventeen

Rachael put the last pin in her hair and studied herself in the mirror. The last thing she wanted to do was go downstairs and face Jason. Luckily he had not even come around until this evening. She had had all day to rest and prepare for the unwanted visit.

The thought of seeing Jason Brown again repulsed her. She knew too much now. Moreover, she was determined to make sure Jason knew she wanted nothing more to do with him. Monday night Brand would come for her and they would quietly leave together, whether Joshua showed up or not. She had once hoped Joshua would come to the dance, for his own sake. But now she hoped that he didn't. She was afraid he would say something to Jason before she and Brand could leave. Surely he wouldn't do that to her, in spite of how he felt about her love for Brand.

She swallowed back tears and picked up a cameo pin she had purchased when she lived in St. Louis. She pinned it to the neckline of the high-necked dress, thinking how far away St. Louis seemed now, and how long ago it seemed that she had been there. Yet she had only been back in Texas for seven weeks. So much had happened in that short time. Her whole life had been turned upside down. She longed for a mother and father to talk to, was sure that if Joe and Emma Rivers were still alive, they would have backed her all the way. But her parents were gone, and she knew she had to rely on her own strength and make her own choices. That choice was Brand, even if it meant losing her brothers' love and respect.

Her heart tightened when she heard Jason raise his voice downstairs. She had better hurry up and get down there or he would think she was primping especially for him.

"Is Joshua around?" she heard Jason ask as she went to the door. "I wouldn't mind having a talk with him."

"He went right back," Lacy lied for Rachael.

"After that long ride here? He'll be riding after dark."

"He was having trouble with some sick cattle or something. Didn't want to stay. He'll be back in a few days to pick up some feed and lumber he's got ordered. The supplies hadn't arrived yet."

"He won't be at the dance?"

"I don't think so."

Rachael hated the sound of his voice. Little did she know why Jason was asking about Joshua.

"I'll go up and see if she's ready," Lacy was saying. The woman came up the stairs and Rachael let her into her room.

"Oh, thank you, Lacy, for that excuse for Joshua."

Lacy closed the door. "He's dressed fit to kill. I expect you know why he's here. I'll stay close by, Rachael."

Rachael hugged the woman tightly. "Thank you for everything, Lacy."

"You just be careful around that man, Rachael."

Rachael took a deep breath and went to the door. She dreaded even setting eyes on Jason again. Having him gone had been a wonderful relief. She had practiced over and over in her mind what to tell him, but now that the moment had come she could feel her mind going blank. She told herself to think of Brand, to be strong for this moment, because in just a few more days she would leave with Brand and be with him forever. She left the room and descended the stairs, moving on rubbery legs to the parlor. She breathed deeply to control her pounding heart as she entered the tidy room where Jason Brown stood beside the fireplace, holding something in his hand.

Jason was dressed in a dark suit of clothes. His open suit jacket revealed a ruffled shirt and a gray satin vest, and a black tie was tied into a bow at his throat. It amazed Rachael how a man whose appearance was so handsome and friendly on the surface could be capable of doing the things she was sure Jason Brown had done. All she could see when she studied the dark eyes was a man who had raped a twelve-year-old girl and then whipped her bloody.

"Rachael!" he said softly, walking quickly to stand in front of her. He took one of her hands before she could offer it. "It's good to see you again." As his dark eyes moved over her, she shivered at the thought of letting this man do to her what Brand had done to her.

"Hello, Jason. I'm glad you've returned unharmed," she lied.

"You look more beautiful than ever," he answered, bending down and kissing her cheek with cold lips. "How was your trip back?"

"Tiring. I couldn't stay. Josh was having some kind of trouble with the stock and he didn't want me out there alone while he and the boys were so involved with their problems. I'll just have to pick a better time to visit, I guess."

"Well, I'm so glad you're here. I've been back since Tuesday. You can imagine how disappointed I was to find out you weren't here."

She pulled her hand away, and noticed a hint of anger in his eyes when she did so. She knew he was already struggling to remain calm and friendly. He took a deep breath, looking her over again. "Well, I'm glad you'll be here for the dance. I had a hell of a time getting back in time myself, but I wanted to be here, for you."

She turned away, rubbing her hands together nervously and moving to a window. "You didn't have to do that, Jason."

"Of course I did." He walked over to where she stood. "Rachael, all I thought about the whole time I was out there was you. Ever since you came back to Texas I've been going crazy with the thought of being with you again, making you my wife." He put a hand on her arm and pressed gently, turning her to face him. "Rachael, let's dispense with the formalities. You know why I'm here. You know what I asked you to think about while I was away."

"Jason—"

"Wait! Don't answer me yet." He held out the box. "Take a

look at this first."

She looked at the little box, already knowing what was inside. "Jason, please. You asked me to think about it, and I told you before you even left that I didn't feel ready to marry. I'm sorry, but I still feel that way. I just don't want to marry you, and for now I don't even want to see just you."

She felt a chill at the look that came into his eyes, and wondered if he was going to hit her. He squeezed her arm tighter.

"Why!" he hissed. "I'm not bragging, Rachael, but I do have a mirror. Other women have told me I'm handsome. I have a steady income, and I'm even considering running for some kind of government office, what with Austin becoming the capital of Texas and all. I know a lot of people, Rachael, have a lot of influence. I can offer you so much, and I... I love you."

He seemed to struggle with the word love, as though he had only said it to win her affection. Rachael closed her eyes and turned her head away.

"Jason, I can't explain why. I'm not blind. I agree you're very handsome, and I know your accomplishments. But I have to love you in return, for more reasons than your looks or your attributes. There has to be a special feeling there, if I am to be your wife. And it just isn't there. I'm sorry, but I can't force it to be there just because it's what you want."

He squeezed her arm tighter. "It would be there if you would let me... if you would just marry me and let me make a woman of you. You would learn to love me, Rachael, I promise. You must have *some* feeling for me!"

She faced him squarely. "You're hurting my arm," she said, her own anger rising at the way he held her. She jerked her arm away. "To tell you the truth, Jason, I have always been afraid of you. I can't marry a man who frightens me. There is a coldness about you, a look in your eyes that tells me to stay away from you. I might as well tell you exactly how I feel, Jason. Maybe then you will give this up. As you said, you're a handsome man. There are plenty of other women who would probably marry you."

His jaw flexed in an effort to stay in control. "Rachael! Why in God's name should you be afraid of me?"

She rubbed her arm. "I don't know. There is just... something about you... like the way you held my arm just now. And I can't forget that story about you whipping an old Indian man."

"Oh, for God's sake!" He turned and started pacing. "The hell with that story! You want to know the truth about that? The old man stole cattle from a settler. He resisted arrest. So I whipped him. So what? He was just an old Indian, one foot in the grave already."

Her eyes widened at the crude statement. "Just an old Indian? In other words you considered him of no more worth than a dying animal."

"There's not much difference!" he snapped, his dark eyes glittering now with anger. "What the hell do you care about Indians. You got any idea what they would do to you if they got hold of you?"

"Your kind friend Jules Webber already spelled that out for me once, Jason!" she answered, equally angry now. "I don't care to hear it again. But they aren't all that way, Jason. I was raised to be tolerant, to try to understand both sides of a situation."

"There is no room for tolerance when it comes to the Comanche!" he growled. "Jesus!" he hissed, turning away from her for a moment and pacing again. "I don't believe this," he grumbled. "I come over here to ask you to marry me, and we end up arguing over an old Indian man. This is ridiculous!"

"It isn't ridiculous at all, Jason," she said in a calmer voice. "It's just an example of why I could never marry you. The woman you marry will have to be just as prejudiced against the Indians as you are. I can't live with that. And I simply don't feel the passion a woman should feel for the man she marries. I truly am sorry if that hurts you, but I don't love you, Jason, and I don't think I ever could."

He let out a disgusted snicker, turning then to face her. "Passion? What the hell would you know about passion? You've never even been with a man!" He stepped closer. "Marry me, Rachael, and I'll bring out the kind of passion you're talking about."

She reddened slightly, and she realized the incredible danger Brand would be in if this man knew the truth. She swallowed before answering. "The passion has to be there first, Jason, not afterward."

He searched her eyes, actually breaking into a sweat with the want of her. "What are you trying to tell me, that you have already felt that passion? That you love someone else?"

"No," she said, quickly turning away.

Jason grabbed her arm painfully again. "Who is it?" he growled. "There's someone else, isn't there!"

"No!" she answered in a louder voice. She faced him boldly. "Ask anyone in town. I've been with no one. It isn't someone else, Jason. It's just that I don't love you. Why can't you accept that and let it go? I've told you I'm sorry. I truly am. I just don't want to marry you."

He let go of her arm but immediately grabbed her wrist. He turned her hand up, slamming the little box into her palm. "Look at that!"

"Jason, I don't—"

"*Look* at it!" he growled.

Rachael swallowed back her fear and opened the box with a shaking hand. Her eyes widened at the sight of the magnificent ring inside. "Oh, Jason, you shouldn't have gotten this before talking to me again first." She closed the box and handed it to him. "It's the most beautiful ring I've ever seen. Some other woman will be overjoyed to wear this ring some day."

He clenched his fists. "I don't *want* some other woman to wear it! I want *you* to wear it. I'm going to be an important man someday, and I want you at my side—the most beautiful woman in Texas."

She gasped when he suddenly hit out at her hand, knocking the ring to the floor. Rachael stepped back.

"I'm sorry, Rachael," he said quickly.

"Please leave, Jason."

He stepped closer again. "Don't you understand? I have to have you, Rachael. I love you and I want to marry you."

She shook her head.

She watched him tremble as he glared at her. "Keep the goddamned ring," he said, his voice low and gruff. "I'll find a way to change your mind, Rachael, you'll see. Everybody in town expects me to announce our engagement at that dance Saturday, and that is exactly what I intend to do."

"Then I would have to turn you down in public. Is *that* what you want?"

"You wouldn't dare!"

"Try me!"

His breathing came heavily as he watched her for a moment. He walked past her and picked up the ring, then turned to face her. "You *will* belong to me someday, Rachael Rivers, one way or another!"

"If you really loved me, Jason, you wouldn't threaten me. That's just an example of why I'm afraid of you. You had better leave."

He stepped closer, struggling to bring himself under control and keep the bitter hatred from showing in his dark eyes. "Forgive me, Rachael. Just give me a chance, will you? I haven't had that much time to see you since you got back from St. Louis. Let's... let's just start over. We'll talk. Let me keep seeing you."

"Please just let it go, Jason."

He put the ring in his pocket, then grasped her arms. "Give it a chance!" he hissed. He jerked her close, and she kept her mouth closed tightly as he bent down with an uninvited kiss, pressing at her lips so hard that he forced them apart. His cold tongue slated over her clenched teeth and she twisted away from him.

"It's time to leave, Jason," they both heard Lacy say.

Jason turned, shoving Rachael away at the sight of her standing in the doorway to the parlor.

"You've got no business butting in," he growled.

"This is my house. Anything that goes on here is my business. I believe Rachael asked you to leave her, and I expect you'll honor her request."

"This is none of your business, Lacy Reed!"

"Rachael is like a daughter to me. Now you get out of here.

Rachael has made it clear what she wants, so just leave."

Jason breathed deeply, looking from Lacy to Rachael. "Some welcome!"

"I'm sorry, Jason. I tried to keep it friendly, but you're the one who won't let it be that way."

"Somehow you've got the wrong idea about me. I'd be good to you, Rachael."

"I'm afraid I can't believe that."

"Joshua knows me. He would be in full agreement. He knows how much I love you."

"Joshua has never been in love himself. He doesn't understand how I feel. Right now I have far too many questions about you. I am sorry this ruins your homecoming, but I can't give myself to a man in the hopes that I'll love him someday. I have to love him first, not afterward."

A sneer formed on his lips as his dark eyes raked her body. She felt totally naked under his gaze. "Someday I'll show you what you've been missing, Rachael Rivers," he told her. He turned and walked through the door, giving Lacy a threatening look before going out, slamming the front door as he left.

Rachael withered into a love seat, putting her head in her hands. "Oh, Lacy, I almost told him. It was so tempting to tell him I know more about him than he thinks—to throw it in his face that I love Brand."

Lacy walked up to her, kneeling in front of her. "You don't dare. He'd have every man he can get riding out to Brand's place to kill him. Just hang on a couple more days, Rachael, and you and Brand can leave and be free. Waiting until after the dance is a good idea. It will give Jason a chance to cool down some. He'll be watching you close the next day or two."

Rachael nodded. "Oh, Lacy, I hope we can get away without his knowing it. I've never seen Jason this angry. Now I know more than ever the kind of man he is. He'll try to kill Brand if he finds out!"

"Well, it would take a lot of men to bring down Brand Selby."

"He can round up all the men he needs."

Lacy took her hands. "Just stay calm, Rachael. Go to that

dance Saturday and act like everything is just fine. You smile, and you dance with a few other young men and serve punch and act just as normal as you can. Everything will work out, honey, you'll see. In a couple of days you'll be off with Brand Selby, and by the time Jason Brown finds out about it, you'll be too far away for him to find you. You go off and be with the man you love."

Rachael met her eyes. "I'm not so sure anymore that any place would be far enough, Lacy. You saw Jason today. He'll come looking for us. Brand won't be safe anywhere."

Lacy squeezed her hands. "Brand knows how to keep from being found. You just let him take care of that part of it and enjoy being his wife."

A tear slipped down Rachael's cheek. "I wish he was here right now," she said longingly. "When I'm with Brand I'm not afraid of anything. But when we're apart—"

"You're a strong, brave girl all on your own. You don't need Brand Selby for that. And you *will* be with him, soon enough. Come into the kitchen now and have a cup of strong coffee, and we'll talk some more."

Lacy rose and patted her cheek. She left the room, and Rachael stood up and walked on shaky legs to the window, looking out to see Jason storming up the street. His last words haunted her—"You will belong to me someday, Rachael Rivers, one way or another. Someday I'll show you what you've been missing."

Joshua's saddle squeaked and his horse snorted rhythmically as he worked his way around the four mares and two colts that had strayed too far from the north pasture.

"Come on now, girls, I don't want you chomping on this grass yet. Save this section for later." He worked his horse first in one direction, then back in another, pleased with how the new gelding he had been training was progressing. The horse was obedient and seemed eager to please as hooves dug into the soft earth with each quick turn.

Joshua had kept busy all morning, not wanting to think about Rachael. It had been two days since she had been there and left. He had thought about riding into Austin and telling Jason, but he decided to wait. He was beginning to wonder if he had been too quick to judge, too cruel to poor Rachael. She had always been intelligent and reasonable, and she was a good-hearted, gentle woman.

He reasoned there must be some good qualities about Brand Selby. How else could Rachael have fallen in love with him? Joshua didn't mind being friends with and dealing with Indians or half-breeds, but having his sister marry one was a far different matter. He wished he could make her understand it wasn't so much prejudice on his part as it was concern over what such a marriage would do to Rachael. He had to put her welfare above all else, and marrying a half-breed was certainly not to her benefit.

"Git up there! Come on! Get going!" he shouted, grasping looped rope in his hand and swinging it in the air in a motion to startle the horses and keep them moving. All four mares and the two colts ran faster, headed in the right direction. Joshua followed, slowing his own horse a moment and looping the rope back around his saddle horn. "Damn," he muttered.

It was Friday. If he was to make the dance, he should be leaving. But he was in no mood now for a dance. There was too much to think about. He knew Rachael would be labeled with every filthy name a man could think up once this came out in the open. Only Joshua realized how much she loved Selby to have given herself to him already.

"She's a grown woman, you idiot," he told himself. What right did he have telling her who to love? She was well educated, and surely she had met her share of accomplished young men back in St. Louis. Yet it was a half-breed who had won her heart. It all seemed so impossible and he knew it would take awhile to recover from the shock of it. Maybe then, maybe in a few weeks or months, he could accept it. Apparently he would have to, for Rachael intended to go through with marrying the man, with or without her brother's approval.

Joshua sighed deeply, looking up at puffed white clouds hanging lazily in a deep blue sky.

A hawk flew overhead, and Joshua watched it drift away. He knew what Joe Rivers would have done. He would have been able to accept a man like Brand Selby, would have judged him on his abilities and his desire to succeed, and would have understood how much his daughter loved the man. Joe Rivers would have stood behind his daughter, protected her at all costs, given her the strength she needed to get through what lay ahead for her. Joshua wanted to feel those same feelings, but his hurt pride kept getting in the way. It wasn't right. It just wasn't right.

Maybe Rachael would think about what he had said; would break things off because she couldn't stand losing her brother's love and respect. He urged his horse into motion again, realizing he had both love and respect for his sister. He just wanted her to think he didn't. It seemed like that was the only edge he had in saving her from a life of hardship and insults.

He headed up a gently sloped hill, still a good mile from the ranch house where Matt and Luke were doing their chores. As he crested the hill, he heard shooting and war whoops. His heart quickened. Indians? They had not had trouble with the Comanche for a long time. And Rachael had said Brand Selby had given the word to his Comanche friends to stay away from the Double "R."

"Bastard!" Joshua hissed. "I'll bet this is his doing! He sent them out of spite."

He kicked his horse into motion, moving into a hard gallop toward the ranch house, which he still could not see. The gunshots grew louder. Yes, they were coming from the direction of the ranch house. Luke! Matt! Both boys were good shots, but had they had time to get to their guns? He pulled his rifle from its boot as he crested another hill.

"Oh, my God!" he groaned, spotting the house. It was in flames. He rode straight toward it, slowing his horse when he got within shooting range. He raised the rifle and took careful aim, then fired. One of the circling Indians went down. He saw Matt running out of the flaming house then, knew it was him because of the blond hair. Joshua rode closer and fired again as four Indians circled Matt. Joshua heard the boy scream out as a hatchet came down. Joshua aimed and shot down another of the men, but more rode up and shot several arrows into Matthew.

It was then Joshua felt the tearing pain at his side. The force of the arrow knocked him from his horse, and he flew off sideways, his rifle knocked from his hand as he hit the ground. His left foot remained caught in the stirrup, and his horse took off at a gallop. Joshua screamed with pain as his body was dragged over rocks and the spearing needles of ground cacti. He felt his clothes ripping away and gravel scraping away his flesh, some of it becoming embedded in the skin. His foot finally came loose and he tumbled against a toolshed, hitting his head hard.

He lay still for a moment, trying to clear his mind against the pain. He pulled at the arrow that remained embedded in his right side, but it would not budge, and the pain brought him close to fainting.

"Damn!" he groaned. "Sons of bitches!" Tears came to his eyes at the realization that Matthew had surely been killed by now. And they were sure to come for him. He lay helpless, looking around for his rifle, for anything he could use as a weapon. But there was nothing nearby. Smoke rolled black and ugly into the air.

Joshua heard the screaming and cursing then. Luke! He was fighting someone. Joshua was in too much pain to realize he heard someone speak in English.

"Come on, boy. A good, strong, young man like you will bring a good price."

"Tie him to that horse," someone else said. "Let's get out of here."

Someone was speaking in English. One of them had a Mexican accent. But the English. Brand? Sure. Brand spoke good English. Any Comanche friends he had had probably learned it from him. He hadn't seen any of them up close, but there was no doubt in his mind they were Comanche. He had seen their long hair and painted horses. He had heard their war whoops. He tried again to get up. He had to help Luke. But nothing would move, and he was unaware that he was wedged in a washout at the side of the shed, in such a way that his body was hardly noticeable.

His mind reeled with helpless fury. Someone was stealing poor Luke away, probably to sell to Comancheros, to be sold again into slavery in Mexico. He heard whistles and shouts as the Indians rounded up horses, and Joshua knew his best steeds were being stolen. There would be nothing left. Nothing. He would lose everything his mother and father had worked so hard to build. Vomit rose in his throat—his parents dead, now Matthew—Luke stolen away—and his sister in love with the man who probably planned all of this out of spite.

Now Rachael would know the kind of man Brand Selby was! He wasn't sure he could ever love his sister after this, or even look at her. This was Rachael's fault. He tried again to crawl out of the washout, but the hard blow to his head made him lose consciousness and he collapsed into the hole, one hand still grasping at loose rock at the edge of the washout.

In the distance Comancheros rode off with Luke, as well as stealing away tools, saddles, meat from the smokehouse, horses, and cattle.

"Jason was right," one of them said. "This was a good haul."

"Did you get the oldest one?" someone else said in Spanish.

"*Sí*," another replied. "My arrow went deep, and then his horse dragged him."

"Jason wants him dead."

"No man lives long when he is dragged halfway across Texas," came the reply. There was a round of laughter. "The last I saw of him, the horse was still running with him bouncing over the ground like a ball, the arrow still in his side. You want me to go looking for him, Lobo?"

"No, we had better get going. Others have seen the smoke from the house by now. We cannot let ourselves be seen too close or they will see we are not Comanche."

"The Comanche, they have done a bad thing today, no?" someone else said.

There came another round of laughter.

"Be sure to pick up our dead so no one finds out they are not Comanche," the one called Lobo said then. Lobo was a big man with skin so dark that it made his teeth seem whiter than they really were. His almost black eyes danced with the excitement of the raid, and his thick, black hair hung past his shoulders, grown long so that he looked from the distance like an Indian. He wore buckskin pants and no shirt, but weapons belts were crisscrossed over his chest, and he had painted his face. "Did someone pick up Enrico? He was wounded."

"Sanchez has him."

Lobo took a moment to gaze around at the broken fences and burning house. "Set fire to the barn, too," he said. His keen eyes scanned the remains of the ranch, but he saw no movement. "We lost two men today. That oldest one, he is a good shot. But he will shoot no more, hey?"

They all laughed again. Some of the other men picked up the two dead men and gathered the remaining horses, while another set fire to the barn. They rode off, quickly disappearing beyond the next rise.

The air hung silent, interrupted only by the crackling of the fire that lapped at what remained of the house and barn. Matthew's dead and mutilated body lay near the steps of the crumbled Rivers ranch house, waiting for someone to come and bury him beside his mother and father.

In the distance Joshua Rivers moved again, consciousness returning. He groaned as he again struggled to get out of the hole. He told himself he had to get up. He had to help Luke. Someone had to pay for this! And it would be Brand Selby! He had to survive, had to somehow get to Austin and get help. He would find Jason. Jason would help him. Together they would go after Brand Selby. Selby would hang for this! He dug his fingers into the loose gravel, straining to rise.

Eighteen

The sun hung high and hot in the azure sky, beating down on Joshua Rivers as he made his way toward Austin. Loss of blood and the blow to his head made him dizzy at times, but he continued on, with a stubborn determination to get to help and to Jason Brown, even if he had to ride all night.

Joshua was not sure how long he had lain in the washout beside the toolshed, but the realization that Matthew lay exposed to the sun and animals gave him the strength he needed to finally climb out of the hole. He knew he had to get to his brother and somehow bury him. Inside the toolshed he had found a hatchet, a shovel, and a spare bridle. The bridle had been hung where it didn't belong, probably by Luke, but now Joshua was grateful, as the barn, where all gear for the horses was usually kept, had been burned down.

Now, as he rode on in spite of his pain, he wept again over Matthew and Luke; wondering if he would ever be able to close his eyes again without seeing Matthew's body, chopped up beyond recognition; or if he would be able to get out of his mind the memory of the Indians riding off with Luke. Had they killed him, too, or would they torture him just for the fun of it? The Comanche were good at that. The thought made him grasp his stomach.

"Luke," he groaned.

He sat up straighter on his mount and winced at the intense pain in his right side where an arrowhead was still lodged. With the hatchet from the toolshed, he had managed to chop off most of the shaft of the arrow. The rest of his body felt on fire from deep scrapes and cuts, but he had ignored the pain and had taken the shovel from the toolshed and managed to start digging a hole. When he realized pain and weakness would prohibit him from ever digging a hole large and deep enough to protect Matthew, he had been forced to give up the idea. Instead, through tears and pain, he had dragged Matthew's body over to the toolshed and put it inside, then had the grim task of going back with a crate and putting into it the pieces of the body that had come loose as he dragged it. He put everything into the shed and closed and hooked the door.

He continued to pray that the shed would protect his brother from scavenging animals. There was nothing more he could do until he could send someone out to give the boy a proper burial. He wasn't sure how many times he had vomited from the memory of the sight, and the vomiting had left him even more drained. A few horses had been left behind by the raiders, and Joshua had managed to coax one to him, slipping the bridle he had found in the toolshed over the horse's neck and managing to climb up onto the animal's bare back. He headed first to the area where he had been hit with the arrow, and to his relief he spotted his rifle still lying on the ground. He had dismounted and picked it up, wondering what other few things he would end up being able to salvage.

He clung to the rifle now, heading again for the river. He had stopped beside the river several times before to dismount and lay in the cool water for relief from his many superficial wounds. He had removed what was left of his torn shirt and had tied it around the arrow wound, but as he looked down at it he could see the wound was still bleeding slowly. He dismounted again, stumbling into the water, taking a good, long drink. Then he just sat in the water for a while, the tears coming again. Gone! Everything his mother and father had worked for was gone. Things had been peaceful for so long that he had become careless, and it had cost Matthew's life, and probably Luke's by now. And if he couldn't get back his cattle and horses, he was ruined; but then it didn't matter if both his brothers were dead. And Rachael might as well be dead, too, for she was dead to Joshua Rivers as long as she stayed with the bastard half-breed who was responsible for this. Even if Rachael saw the light and realized Brand Selby had destroyed her family, Joshua was not sure he could ever feel the same about his sister, could ever love her or give her shelter again.

He climbed out of the river and picked up his rifle, crying out with the pain in his side when he again mounted the horse. Stubborn pride, the strength of youth, and a dogged determination to get revenge were all that kept him going. He rode out again toward Austin, determined to get there by Saturday night. He would go straight to the dance. Everyone would be there, including Rachael. He would show her in front of the whole town of Austin the kind of man Brand Selby really was!

Rachael dipped a ladle into the punch bowl, and poured a drink into Harriet Miller's glass. It seemed the whole town had turned out for the dance. Flowers decorated refreshment tables and were tied to barn posts; paper decorations hung everywhere; and a sign hung overhead that read: "AUSTIN! PERMANENT CAPITAL OF THE GREAT REPUBLIC OF TEXAS—SOON TO BE THE BIGGEST STATE IN THE UNION!"

Rachael handed the drink to Mrs. Miller, hardly aware of what she was doing. She wanted nothing more than to be with Brand, to have this dance over with and to get through the next two days until finally she and Brand would be together, never to be apart again. Her whole body felt tight with tension from the memory of her encounter with Jason. She worried that somehow he would find out about Brand before they could get away.

"Isn't it terrible about the raids?" Mrs. Miller was asking Rachael.

Rachael turned her attention to the woman. "What?"

"The raiding that's been going on in outlying areas. Isn't it terrible?"

"Raids?" Rachael's heart quickened.

"Why, yes. Haven't you heard?"

"No. I was gone for a couple of days, visiting my brothers. I've been at the boardinghouse ever since, resting."

"Why, I'm surprised your Jason didn't tell you about it."

Rachael glanced over at Jason Brown, who stood talking and drinking with some of the more prominent men of Austin. Local musicians began playing a waltz with a piano that had been hauled from the church to the Miller barn by several men, two fiddles, a banjo, and a guitar. Jason looked over at Rachael, his eyes hard and threatening. She knew he would ask her to dance, and she also knew that for just this night she would have to oblige him to appease the curious public. Her threat to publicly deny their relationship would have to be just that—a threat. She realized that to actually humiliate Jason Brown in front of others would not only make Jason more suspicious, but also would start tongues wagging and cause her to be watched more closely than she cared to be watched.

"Jason didn't tell me," Rachael answered Mrs. Miller. She poured a glass of punch for another woman. "There has been raiding close to Austin?"

"Yes. Why, it frightens me to death. Two different families came in today, or at least what was left of them. Their homes were burned, crops destroyed and stock stolen, all by those horrible Comanche. And in one case a woman was stolen away!" Mrs. Miller waved a handkerchief in front of her face as though she might faint. "Oh, dear heaven, I dread to think what they will do to that poor soul. And the worst part is even if she survives and is brought back, she will be shunned by her own kind. After all, who can be seen in the company of a woman who has been with Indian men?" She leaned closer. "If you know what I mean," she added in a near whisper.

Rachael felt sick with anger. So, such would be her own treatment if people knew about her and Brand.

"She would need her family and friends more than ever," Rachael answered. "Why shouldn't others be seen with her? It isn't her fault what might happen to her. She should have sympathy and kindness, not be shunned."

Mrs. Miller sipped her punch. "Well, I suppose. But surely you know what I mean. It would be very difficult to befriend such a woman."

"Not for me." Rachael poured herself some punch, struggling to keep her temper in check.

"Oh, but you're too young and innocent to understand, dear," the woman told her. "At any rate, Jason Brown has promised the raiding will end soon. He's quite convinced that the man behind it is that half-breed living north of town—Brand Selby I believe they call him."

Rachael felt herself paling as she slowly set down her punch. "Brand Selby?"

"Yes. Jason says since all the raiding started just recently, he thinks Mr. Selby came here to scout things out for his Comanche friends. Jason says ever since Mr. Selby left the Rangers he's had a grudge he's wanted to settle. Jason thinks this is all Selby's doing, and he intends to go after the man."

Rachael breathed deeply, forcing herself to remain calm, but her hand shook as she filled another glass with punch and set it on the table. Although she was tempted to run out this very moment and warn Brand, she knew she didn't dare do it. Jason would follow, wondering why she was leaving so quickly. "When will he go after Mr. Selby?" she asked, trying to appear casual.

"Who knows? Jason says he's going to do some scouting around first—try to catch the half-breed in the act, so to speak. But he says either way, he'll bring him in very soon. The whole town is buzzing about it, asking to see Brand Selby hanged right now, proof or no proof. That man has made this whole town nervous, skulking around here, pretending to need supplies. I say Jason is right. The man is just scouting us out and sending messages back to his people. Oh, it's dreadful what those poor settlers beyond our help are suffering."

Rachael moved her eyes to Jason again. "Yes, isn't it?"

"I do hope your brothers will be safe, Rachael, dear."

Rachael looked back at the pompous woman. "Yes. So do I." Rachael didn't doubt Joshua would be just fine. After all, Brand had asked the Comanche to leave the Double "R" alone. She looked over at Jason again, wondering at the man's sudden accusations of Brand. Was it really Comanche who were committing the crimes against the settlers? It seemed so convenient—the sudden raids, the quickness with which Jason blamed Brand.

More people came to the punch table, and suddenly Rachael found herself being introduced to some of them, exchanging niceties with them while all the time her mind whirled with worry over Brand's safety. She knew how much Jason hated Brand and would like nothing better than to see him dead. Was it possible Jason himself was behind the raiding? After all, he had friends among the Comancheros, and Brand had already told her how good Jason was at deliberately keeping the fires of hatred stirred. Brand! As soon as this dance was over, she decided she must find a way to warn him of the talk going around town. Whether it was really Comanche, or men hired by Jason to do the raiding, Jason was making sure Brand Selby got the blame.

It seemed everyone standing around Rachael then was talking about the raids, voicing their anger at the hated Comanche. Rachael didn't want to believe Jason could truly go so far as to deliberately allow outlaws to raid the very people he was supposed to be protecting, but she did not underestimate the lengths to which he would go to get rid of Brand. Still, he surely wouldn't let any harm come to her brothers.

"I say Jason is right," one man nearby said. "I think the breed is behind some of it, maybe all of it. The sooner Jason goes after that troublemaker the better."

Rachael faced the man, handing him some punch. It was the storekeeper, Mr. Briggs. "Does anyone have any proof Mr. Selby is the culprit?" she asked now. "From what I know, he's been quite peaceful. Has he ever actually started any trouble around town?"

"Well, no," he answered. "But everybody knows how breeds are. You should be glad yourself to see the man disposed of, Miss Rivers. I remember how he looked at you the day he saw you in my supply store. And you should remember how belligerent he was that day."

"What I remember is how belligerent *you* were, Mr. Briggs. And I believe we are taught in church not to cast the first stone."

"Miss Rivers, can I have this dance?" The question came

from a young man to whom she had been introduced during the buzzing talk over Comanche. Rachael moved her attention from the frowning Briggs to the young man, who appeared to be perhaps no more than Joshua's age. But Joshua was built much bigger than the slight young man before her, who seemed like a mere boy compared to her brother and Brand.

"Of course," she told him, wanting nothing more for the moment than to get away from talk of raids. As they walked together into the middle of the dance floor, Rachael realized how incredibly different the young man with her was from a man like Brand. Now that she had been in Brand's arms, no one else could compare; and it seemed ironic that not long ago back in St. Louis she had dated young men like this one. But she was a girl then herself, not the woman Brand had made out of her.

"The name is Lester Rogers," he was telling her, "in case you forgot."

"Oh yes." She took his thin hands and they whirled around with the other dancers. Rachael was glad the tune had turned to a rapid square dance so that there was little opportunity to talk. She had to think about how she could warn Brand to get away. Perhaps if she went to him tonight, they could go away together right away.

The dance soon ended, and Lester started to lead her back to the punch table. "Uh-oh," he commented. "I hope I didn't do anything wrong," he told her. "Here comes Jason Brown."

She deliberately gave the young man a kind smile. "You didn't do anything wrong, Lester. There is nothing serious between myself and Mr. Brown. Thank you for the dance. Maybe later we can dance again."

By the time she got the last words out Jason was within hearing distance. Lester Rogers paled at the look on Jason's face and he quickly left without saying another word. Rachael could feel people watching as Jason put a hand to her waist and took her hand as a slower dance began.

"I don't care to dance, Jason," she told him.

She felt an angry power as he began sweeping her around the straw-covered floor. "Oblige me this much, Rachael. At least let's end this gracefully. Don't put the final closing on it right here at the dance."

Their eyes held as he whirled her around, and she tried to see into his dark gaze.

"Mrs. Miller tells me there has been a lot of raiding going on," she told him, watching those eyes. "You didn't mention it when you came to see me."

"I had more important things on my mind, if you will recall." His eyes fell to the milky skin of her breasts where the bodice of her dress was cut gracefully and bordered with lace. Rachael felt a shiver go down her spine. "My men and I will rustle up the renegades who are doing it, don't worry about that," he continued, moving his eyes back to meet her own again. "I have a good idea who is behind it all."

"Brand Selby?"

He frowned. "What made you mention him?"

"The others already said you've been blaming him. But one of Lacy's boarders mentioned once that you and this Mr. Selby had a personal hatred going. You shouldn't blame the man just because you don't like him, Jason."

"The man is a half-breed who couldn't even cut it as a scout. I never trusted him then, and I don't trust him now. My men and I will ride out to his place tomorrow and have a little talk with the breed."

Rachael didn't need to ask what he meant by "a little talk." And she didn't dare say anything more for now without stirring suspicions in Jason's mind. Either way she knew she could not wait until Monday. Brand had to be warned, and she vowed she would risk darkness and danger to get to him and warn him yet tonight. How she wished she could boldly tell Jason Brown right now that she was Brand Selby's woman! She struggled against tears of terror for Brand, wondering how she would get through the rest of the evening. She didn't dare leave early. She would have to endure the entire dance.

"I don't suppose you've given second thoughts to my proposal?" Jason asked her.

"Not really."

"Rachael, let me apologize for my behavior. I'm really not the mean person you think I am. I could never hurt you, Rachael."

There was a gentleness to his voice that Rachael told herself was an act. But she realized that if she gave Jason Brown the tiniest ray of hope, he would forget about plans for going after Brand, at least for the night.

"But you did hurt me. I have a bruise on my arm. That's why I wore this long-sleeved dress."

He frowned, squeezing her hand. "I'm sorry, Rachael. Truly I am. It's just that you frustrate me so. I've wanted to marry you since before you went to St. Louis."

She sighed deeply. "Jason, you know it would never work. We're just too different."

They continued to whirl around the dance floor, Rachael's blue dress sweeping away pieces of straw.

"Just say you'll forgive me for the other day," Jason asked her. "Do that much for me, will you, Rachael?"

She decided that above all things she must keep Jason's black temper from coming to the surface again. "All right," she answered. "I accept your apology. I'll even dance with you for the rest of the night so that everyone thinks things are just fine between us. You're itching to run for some kind of office, so I won't embarrass you in public."

He grinned. "Well, then, this will be more enjoyable than I thought. Give me another chance, will you, Rachael?"

"Jason, give me a few days. You won't—you won't be riding out after this Brand Selby right away, will you?"

His eyes brightened with hope. "Not if it means I can see more of you."

"Only as a friend," she told him. "It can never be anything more than that, Jason; unless through a lot of talking we can come to terms on some things."

"I'll do whatever you ask."

She found it ironic that this man could be so handsome and well liked by others, but that she could feel so repulsed by his touch. All she could think of was the little girl, and the vicious whip. But if she could buy Brand some time by making Jason stay in Austin, she would do whatever she had to do.

"Give me tomorrow to be alone," she told him. "You can come and see me Monday, after I've thought over some of the things we said to each other. I suppose I should apologize myself."

"You just don't know me well enough, Rachael. You'll find out I'm not so bad."

They continued dancing, and Rachael breathed easier. She could go to Brand tonight and they could leave together. Jason wouldn't know the difference until he came to see her on Monday. Even then he wouldn't know. She would have Lacy tell him she went back to Joshua's. By the time Jason rode out there and found out the truth, she and Brand would be long gone.

"The rest of the night you'll dance only with me," Jason told her. "Promise me?"

She started to answer when their conversation was interrupted by gasps, and the orchestra quieted as people parted to let someone enter.

"Jason! I need to see Jason Brown," came a man's weak voice.

Rachael felt as though someone were draining the blood from her body. It sounded like Joshua's voice, but she couldn't be sure until the man, whose torn and bloody shirt was wrapped around his middle, stumbled into the center of the crowd, holding his side. His body was covered with scabbing scrapes and cuts. His face was so bruised and cut that at first no one recognized him, no one but the person closest to him.

"Joshua!" Rachel gasped.

"You!" Joshua hissed through gritted teeth. "This is partly your fault, Rachael!"

Her eyes widened and she stepped away from Jason, who looked at both of them in shock. Jason's first shock came from seeing Joshua alive. Lobo and his men were supposed to have killed him. But to have Joshua come to Austin and blame what had happened on Rachael left him totally confused.

"Joshua, don't," Rachael was saying, begging him with her eyes not to say anything about Brand. Her eyes moved over his sorry condition in worry and concern, as well as dread. "Joshua, what happened to you?"

He stumbled closer, moving his eyes to Jason Brown. "I came here for your help," he said to Jason, his voice growing weaker.

Rachael walked toward him. "Joshua—"

"Get away from me!"

"Josh, you're hurt."

His brown eyes drilled into her. "Thanks to your Brand Selby!"

A ripple of mumbles moved through the quieted crowd of people, and Rachael's face reddened.

"Josh, what are you talking about?" Rachael asked in a near whisper.

Joshua moved his eyes back to Jason's. "My ranch was attacked yesterday by Comanche," he said. His whole body shook, and he put a hand to his side. "Matthew is dead—all chopped up."

"Oh, my God," Rachael gasped, covering her mouth. Her eyes teared. "Where is Luke?" she whimpered.

Joshua kept his eyes on Jason. "They took him away with them," he almost growled.

Rachael choked back a sob, but Joshua showed no emotion. "I came to you for help, Jason. We have to get Luke back."

Jason blinked in temporary confusion. He had not expected this turn of events and he struggled to think quickly. "You're hurt, Josh. You go see a doctor and get yourself healed up. Leave this to me and my men."

Jules Webber stood in the background, trying not to grin. He realized Lobo must have decided young Luke would be worth something in Mexico. He watched Jason. The Comancheros had failed to kill Joshua Rivers.

"I have to go with you," Joshua was saying.

"No. You're wounded. We can take care of it." Jason looked from Joshua to Rachael and back to Joshua. "What did you mean—that this was thanks to Rachael and Brand Selby?"

Joshua moved his eyes back to Rachael, seeing the pleading in her own eyes. But he had been through too much to feel sorry for her. He looked back at Jason.

"My sister has been seeing Brand Selby. They came to my

place Wednesday to get my approval to get married."

More gasps moved through the crowd, and Rachael could feel all eyes on her; but she saw no one but Joshua, standing there and exposing her love as though it were a public disgrace. Tears ran down her cheeks as he continued to talk, while Jason Brown's dark eyes widened with rage. Jason began to visibly tremble, turning his hate-filled eyes to Rachael as Joshua continued.

"I didn't go along with it, for obvious reasons," Joshua told them. He winced with pain, beginning to break out in a sweat. "And I think Brand Selby told them to raid our place, to get me out of the way."

"Brand wouldn't have done that!" Rachael cried out. "How can you think he—" She hesitated, feeling Jason's eyes on her. She faced him, forcing back the terror his look brought to her blood. Lacy Reed moved through the crowd to stand closer to Rachael.

"I say it *was* Brand," Joshua insisted.

The mumbles among the crowd grew louder. "Let's go get the bastard," someone grumbled.

"He ought to hang," came another voice.

"Goddamn half-breed scum!"

"He must have raped her," Rachael heard a woman behind her. "She agreed to marry him out of shame. It's the only logical reason I can think of that she would be with a half-breed."

Rachael sucked in a sob, turning to face the woman. "I love him!" she said boldly. "I love Brand Selby!" She turned to face Jason while Mrs. Miller fanned herself frantically, sure she was going to faint. "Brand didn't do this," Rachael said pleadingly to Jason. "He hasn't done one thing to warrant all the things people are saying about him. He's settled and trying to make a good life for himself. He… he came to me and asked me to teach him how to write and read better. He has never caused any trouble since he came to Austin. Joshua just wants to believe it because he's angry over my wanting to marry Brand."

Jason's hands balled into fists, and his face was a deep red with rage. "You dare to stand there and say you're in love with a goddamn half-breed?" he hissed. "You rode to your brother's place with him? Spent your nights on the trail with him?'"

"Oh, dear, oh, dear," Harriet Miller fussed.

Jules Webber watched with great amusement, his mind already racing with what this could mean. Maybe now Jason would see Rachael Rivers for what she was. Maybe now he would finally sell her to the Comancheros. Jules looked forward to seeing her suffer at the hands of Lobo and his men.

"Poor Jason," someone whispered.

"The little slut," came a man's voice.

"And to think I wanted to marry you," Jason sneered in front of them all. "You acting so pious and good—as though you were too good for the likes of me! I patiently wait for you, while all the time you're laying under that half-breed bastard like a filthy white squaw!"

Rachael jerked back as though she had been hit. Lacy was immediately at her side, grasping her arm.

"That's enough of that talk!" Lacy barked. "Rachael has done nothing wrong! It's all you peoples' prejudices that's wrong! Brand Selby is a good man. What other kind of man would a lady like Rachael Rivers fall in love with?" Her eyes drilled into Joshua. "How can you stand there, the brother she was counting on to help her and protect her—and let Jason call your sister names in front of the whole town? You know her better than that, Joshua Rivers!"

"All I know is that after she and Brand Selby left my place I got raided. I've lost everything! Everything! All my cattle, my horses—the house and barn are burned down." He looked at Rachael. "Nothing is left, Rachael. Everything Ma and Pa worked for is gone! And it's all because of that half-breed you claim is such a good man!"

"It isn't so! It isn't so!" Rachael wept.

Jason's mind reeled with the reality of what he was hearing. Rachael and Brand Selby! Never had he known such hatred as he felt now! Brand Selby seemed to always outdo him; now the man had stolen Rachael right from under his nose! The irony of it made him feel as though he might explode any minute. He struggled to keep his senses. Joshua had conveniently blamed

Brand, which only made his job easier.

"Joshua, please," Rachael weeped. "Why are you doing this?"

"Because I know I'm right," he growled.

"You don't know what you're doing." Rachael stepped closer. "Please come back to Lacy's with me. We'll help clean your wounds. We'll talk about this."

Joshua turned his head away. "Get away from me, Rachael."

"Josh—"

"You didn't have to pick up Matthew in pieces with a shovel!" he shouted, turning back to face her. "You didn't have to watch everything you've worked for burn to the ground! You didn't have to watch those bastards riding off with Luke! You come here from St. Louis with all your education and refinement, and you forget what it's like here in Texas, Rachael! You talk about trying to understand—having some compassion for the Comanche! I've got no compassion or understanding for a people who destroy my family and my possessions! And I've got no use for a half-breed bastard who tricks my sister into laying with him! I never dreamed you could be that stupid… that gullible!"

"Oh, Josh, I can't believe you're saying these things," Rachael wept.

"Yeah? Well, I couldn't believe it when you came to me wanting to marry that half-breed, either!"

"Come on, Rachael, let's get out of here," Lacy told her quietly. "There's no reasoning with him right now."

"That's right. Get her out of here," someone in the crowd spoke up.

That set the rest of them off, and Lacy led Rachael out amid shouted dirty names, mingled with outcries of revenge against Brand Selby.

"Go get him, Jason! Hang him high!" the men began to shout.

Jason watched Rachael leave, his eyes red-rimmed with rage. Rachael Rivers had made a total fool of him, had publicly chosen a half-breed over Jason Brown, the very man Jason hated most on top of it! And surely, from the way she and Joshua talked, she had already slept with the man! Never in his life had he had to struggle this hard to stay in control of his vicious temper.

"I'll get Selby," he promised Joshua. He looked over at some men standing nearby. "Take Joshua to a doctor and get him some help."

Joshua started to protest, but he was too weak to pull away from the men who took his arms and led him out the door. Jason moved his eyes around the crowd. "Any of you men who want to go with me, be ready in two hours," he told them. "We're going after Brand Selby. His neck will be stretched by morning!"

Fists went up and men shouted their approval while women whispered and gossiped and fanned themselves.

"I don't think we need anymore proof than this," Jason added. "All of you know how I felt about Rachael Rivers, so my need for vengeance is doubled. But Brand Selby is a hard man to bring down, so I need all the help I can get."

Jules Webber watched, grinning.

"We're with you, Jason," men shouted.

"Go on home now and get ready. Meet me in front of the Ranger office in two hours. We'll go tonight, attack his place while he's sleeping," Jason told them. "Tomorrow's sun will rise on the body of Brand Selby hanging from a nice high branch of the big elm tree near the schoolhouse. He wanted an education! The schoolhouse is a fitting place for him to breathe his last breath!"

More shouts went up and Jason stormed over to Jules Webber, signaling Webber to follow him out. People slapped both men on the back as they went outside, and Jason quickly led Jules away from the barn and the crowd, then stopped and turned.

"Get over to Lacy's place. If my guess is right that little slut I almost married will try to get to Brand Selby to warn him. The minute she leaves and is far enough away, grab her."

Jules grinned. "What do I do with her then?"

Jules could feel Jason's rage through the dark night air. "Take her to Lobo and the Comancheros. Wait for me there. This other thing will take until tomorrow. Then I'll be out."

Jules snickered. "You finally going to sell that bitch?"

"I'll sell her, all right," Jason hissed. "You just make sure neither you nor Lobo or any of his men touch her. You save that little whore for *me!* I'll teach her to act so innocent and pious around me! And I'll show Brand Selby what happens to a man who takes what belongs to Jason Brown! Now get over to Lacy's and stay out of sight! She could leave anytime!"

Jules spit out some tobacco juice. "My pleasure."

Jules walked away and Jason stood in the darkness shivering with hatred. He couldn't think of enough things to do to Rachael to pay her back for this horrible disgrace! He would do everything he could to shame her, humiliate her, hurt her. There would be no holding back now. He would show Rachael Rivers the grave mistake she had made turning him away! Fire ripped through him at the thought of it—Rachael Rivers lying naked and begging beneath him, helpless to stop him. He would enjoy every move, every curve of her body, every protest, every tear!

Shouting men began exiting the barn now, and Jason headed for his office. He would be sure to tell Brand Selby in private what he had planned for Rachael Rivers before he put a noose around his neck. Brand Selby's last thoughts would be of what Jason would be doing with his pretty white squaw once Selby was dead.

Nineteen

Rachael hurried to her room, breathless from running practically all the way back to Lacy's. Lacy came up the stairs behind her, panting even harder, putting a hand to her chest.

"Rachael, don't go!" she pleaded.

Rachael was already taking off her fancy dress. Lacy came inside her room and closed the door.

"I have to! I'll be lucky to get to him first as it is, Lacy!"

"It's suicide! You already know that someone is out there raiding, either the Comanche or outlaws; and even if you reach Brand, the man is going to have to run for his life. Having you along would only slow him down. If he leaves you behind, you'll be caught all alone out there with Jason and those men. God only knows what they would do in their anger. If you go with Brand, you'll be in danger from the confrontation that is bound to take place when Jason and his men catch up with him. And they will, if Jason thinks you're with Brand. He'll never stop looking for you, Rachael."

Rachael already had on her heavier riding dress. She pulled on a fitted jacket. Nights in open Texas land were cold. She sat down to remove her dress shoes and began pulling on boots.

"I don't care what happens to me, Lacy. I have to warn Brand. Jason will ride in there and kill poor Brand in his sleep!" She hesitated a moment, staring at one of the boots. "Oh, Lacy, Matthew is dead! What a horrible way to die!" She could not stop the sudden sob that welled up from deep in her soul. "I can't believe… this is happening! I can't believe Josh would really think… Brand would deliberately let that happen. I'm so mixed up, Lacy. I don't know who to cry over the most—losing Joshua's love and respect—or what happened to poor Matthew and Luke—or what's going to happen to Brand if I don't warn him. Oh, God, Lacy, I'll lose him now. I'll lose Brand. He'll have to go away and never come back!"

Lacy's eyes teared and she stroked the girl's hair. "I feel like part of this is my fault. Maybe I should have tried harder to discourage you from seeing Brand Selby in the first place."

"You tried your best, Lacy." Rachael wiped her eyes and pulled on the boots, which were just a blur at the moment. "It wouldn't have mattered. I would have found a way to go to him. I love him, Lacy. I know he didn't have anything to do with these raids. I just know it!"

"Of course he didn't. But now you're up against ruthless men, Rachael. You can't go out there alone. Brand is an experienced, capable man. You have to trust in his instincts to save himself."

"No. I have to try to warn him, Lacy. I won't be in that much danger. Jason will be riding out there with men from town. He'd never harm me in front of them, no matter what I've done. I'm white. And Jason wants to look good in front of all of them. He might insult me, but he won't harm me physically. I can take all the insults all of them want to hand out as long as I know Brand is safe."

She rose from the bed, taking a handkerchief from a dresser drawer and blowing her nose. "I need to borrow a horse and saddle, Lacy."

"No. I won't let you. I want you to stay right here."

Rachael faced her. "Lacy, don't make me a horse thief on top of everything else."

Lacy faced her squarely, and sighed deeply. "Why do I always have trouble setting my foot down with you, girl?"

Rachael wiped more tears away. "Because you know I'm right; and you know my mother would have done the same thing for my father. I'm so glad Mother isn't here to know what happened to Matthew—and to the Double 'R.' Father, too. Thank God they're both gone."

Lacy put a hand on her arm. "Matthew is with them now, Rachael. You just remember that. And maybe if Brand gets away, he'll find a way to rescue Luke. Maybe he can even prove it's Jason who's behind all this."

Rachael studied the woman, hope in her eyes. "You think so, too?"

"Of course I do. It was the first thing I thought of when I heard about the raids at the dance and heard Brand was being blamed."

"I thought of it, too. But I can't believe even Jason would have allowed a raid on the Double 'R.' He's always been so protective of my brothers."

"For a reason, Rachael. He wanted to impress you. But maybe he thought that without your brothers around, you'd be a little more dependent on him. Who knows how a man like that thinks? I think he's every bit as bad as Brand Selby says he is. He proved that this morning."

Rachael closed her eyes and breathed deeply for control. "I have to go right away, Lacy. I'll pack a carpetbag with a few necessities while you saddle a horse for me. Would you?"

"If you are determined to go, then I'll saddle the horse— only because I want to help you get out of town fast, before Jason musters up his own men." The woman blinked back tears and left, and Rachael hurriedly packed a bag, pulling open drawers and throwing in some underwear, a couple of blouses, and two skirts. Her riding boots would have to do for a while. She noticed the carved wolf when she started to close a drawer, and she picked it up, her eyes tearing again as she studied it.

"Brand," she whispered. She could not imagine a life without him now. She forced back the tears and put the wolf back in her drawer, realizing that after tonight the wolf might be all she had left of Brand Selby. She wanted nothing more than to fling herself on a bed and cry and cry until there were no more tears left. But the tears would have to come later. She grabbed two spare blankets that lay folded on a footstool at the end of the bed and tucked them under her arm. She would tie them to her gear.

She hurried down to the kitchen, glad that neither Bert Peters nor Stewart Glass had come back to the house yet. She set down the blankets and carpetbag and took a small flour sack from under Lacy's cupboard where she knew they were kept. She stuffed it with a few potatoes, a loaf of bread, and a small jar of homemade jam. She had to be prepared in case she was able to ride out with Brand. She hurried outside then to the horse shed, where Lacy had a lantern lit so she could see to saddle a horse.

Rachael left her things there and took a canteen from a hook in the shed, hurrying to the well to fill it. She looked around at the shadows beyond the dim light of the house windows, feeling a shiver at the thought that someone could be watching. But she was sure she had acted quickly enough that she could get away before anyone knew. Surely Jason wouldn't think her capable of riding out into the night alone. But she had some experience at these things now. She had gone for all those rides with Brand, had walked out all alone to meet him, had ridden with him during the night right through hostile country. She felt proud of herself for what she was doing now.

She carried the canteen back to the shed, and Lacy had the horse saddled and ready. "I only have the two horses," Lacy said, "and neither one is much good for anything but pulling a light buggy at a slow pace. But Gray Legs here, she'll get you where you want to go, and she doesn't spook easy."

Rachael petted the horse, a black mare with gray legs. "You'll do just fine, Gray Legs," she soothed the horse. She turned to Lacy. "I don't know if I'll see you again, Lacy. I don't know what will happen."

Lacy's eyes teared. "I know, honey. I'll be… praying for you." The woman's voice broke and the two of them hugged tightly for a few seconds. Rachael forced herself to let go and she climbed up into the saddle.

"Thank you, Lacy—for everything. I'll find a way to come back someday and let you know we're all right—or I'll get a letter to you." She swallowed back a painful lump in her throat.

Their eyes held a moment longer. Then Rachael turned the horse and rode out into the night.

The night air was quiet, crisp, and cold. Once Rachael's eyes adjusted, she was surprised at how well she could see in the bright moonlight. She headed Gray Legs through the now familiar woods, telling herself not to be afraid of the dark shadows and night creatures. Brand had taught her not to be afraid. She had to be brave and strong now, for his sake.

She saw no sign of a gang of men headed out of town yet. It would take awhile for men to get changed and head out, and she was sure she had gotten a good head start on Jason and his men. Even from Lacy's house she could at first hear the continued shouting, and she shivered at the realization that all those men would be going after Brand.

At least now that she was beyond the first hill that hid the town from outlying areas, she no longer heard any sounds at all, other than night insects. After living in Missouri for three years, the total silence in western lands amazed her. She had forgotten how utterly lonely and quiet this land could be. And never had she felt this lonely. Her precious big brother hated her. Another brother and both her parents were dead. And Luke might be dead, too. All she had was Brand, and if she didn't get to him in time, he also might be dead by morning. She would have nothing then. Nothing.

She slowly made her way through the trees, praying Gray Legs would not stumble over some fallen branch or log that she could not see. They broke into open country, and Rachael headed for the familiar rock where she used to meet Brand. How well she knew the way now, even by moonlight. She was sure she could find her way all the way to Brand's cabin. She moved Gray Legs into a faster trot, her heart growing lighter at having gotten away before Jason knew about it. Soon she would be with Brand. Brand would know what to do. He would never let anything happen to her.

She rode for several more yards before she heard the faint sound of a galloping horse. Her chest tightened, and fear shimmied down her spine. Who would be out here riding hard and alone this time of night? Brand? Did he already know? She slowed her horse and listened, then turned when she realized a horse was galloping up from behind her. Instinct told her it was not Brand Selby. Joshua? Joshua was too wounded to ride that hard.

She was left with no choice but to try to outrun whoever was following her, to get to Brand before the stranger got to her. Maybe it was a Comanchero! Or maybe it was old Rotten Mouth, the Comanche who had tried to buy her once! She kicked Gray Legs into motion, and she knew already that Lacy was right. The horse was capable of no more than a loping gallop that any healthier, younger horse could meet and exceed. She rode the mare as hard as the animal could muster, but she could hear and feel the rider behind her getting closer and closer.

"Brand! Brand!" she whimpered. Someone rode right up beside her. She screamed as a strong arm came around her and jerked her from her horse. She began fighting wildly while the man slowed his horse, then threw her to the ground.

At first Rachael could do nothing. She lost her breath completely when her back hit the ground hard, and she opened her mouth, trying desperately to scream. A man came to stand over her, straddling her and looking down at her.

"Well, well. If it ain't the pretty white whore who likes to sleep with big bucks. You maybe thinking of riding out to your lover and warning him he's gonna be hanged tonight?"

Rachael recognized Jules Webber's voice. She continued to gasp for breath as she tried to wiggle out from under him, but he sat down on top of her, taking a bandanna from around his neck.

"I expect I'd better take advantage of you not being able to scream, bitch. Sounds carry mighty far on the plains at night."

He quickly tied the smelly bandanna tight around her mouth, shoving her over on her stomach to make a tight knot behind her head. Rachael tried to get up, but he shoved her face into the dirt and put a knee in her back, pulling her arms behind her. He pulled a piece of rawhide from his pocket and began tying her wrists so tightly that she wondered if she would lose her hands from lack of blood.

"I'm gonna enjoy watching Lobo and his men have a good time with you, little missy. You, trottin' around town like Miss Prim and Proper, and all the while you were spreading yourself for that half-breed scum Selby." He ran his hands over her bottom, squeezing painfully and making her whimper. "Yes, ma'am, after tonight Selby will be dead. Then Jason Brown will come to Lobo's camp and have himself one hell of a time with you. Then it's our turn." He moved a hand under her skirt and groped at her between the legs. "You're gonna be wishing you would have accepted Jason's offer of marriage, bitch! It would have been a lot easier on you than what's gonna happen to you now. Ain't none of us gonna worry about goin' easy with an Indian-loving whore."

He laughed, yanking her to her feet and holding her around the chest with one hand, making sure to use his hand over her breast to support her. He whistled for his horse and reached out to grab its reins when it trotted up to him. Rachael regained most of her breath, and she began struggling, kicking at him wildly and trying to get loose from the gag so that she could scream, even though it was not likely anyone was about to hear her. But there was always the possibility Brand was out there somewhere.

Jules jerked her around and backhanded her so that she whirled around and hit the ground hard, for she was unable to put out her hands to help stop the fall. She felt tiny bits of gravel bite into the side of her face, then felt herself jerked up again.

"Don't be trying to fight it, slut! Besides, there ain't a man in Austin who would come to your aid right now. There was a time when Jason Brown might have defended you, but he's the one who sent me out here. Jason figured you'd try to ride out and warn the breed. But Jason, he's got other plans for you, little missy. Ever been to Mexico? Hmm?"

He laughed again, and Rachael tasted vomit in her throat. Jules half dragged her to his horse, then threw her over the saddle.

"Now where's that damned horse of yours?" he muttered. "Goddamn old mare took off on me."

Rachael was glad for the tiny bit of hope. Maybe Gray

Legs would go back home. Lacy would find the horse and know Rachael never reached Brand.

Jules mounted, and his knee hit her in the face. She struggled not to think about what might lay ahead for her, and she tried not to think about the filthy bandanna in her mouth and the ugly words and touches of Jules Webber. She wondered if anything more terrible than this night could happen to anyone; poor Matthew dead, Joshua wounded and hating her, Luke gone, Brand might be hanged. No! She must not think of those things. Brand had said God meant for them to be together. She had to believe she and Brand would somehow survive this.

Brand stirred awake, realizing the lantern he had hung in the stall had gone out and that he had fallen asleep. The sick horse he had been watching over whinnied and stirred slightly, but still lay on its side. Brand started to relight the lantern when his keen ears heard the distant approach of horses. He realized then that it was not the lamp going out that had subconsciously alerted him. Danger approached.

He moved in darkness to the stall entrance where his rifle sat propped. His handgun was in the house, but he wore his hunting knife, and he kept spare ammunition in the barn. He moved to the barn door, peeking out and listening. Several horses were coming, but they seemed to be riding quietly. He realized that whoever was coming this time of night would expect him to be inside the cabin, not out in the barn.

For the moment, he was glad for a sick horse. Being in the barn instead of the house could be to his advantage. He moved through the darkness to his own horse, setting the rifle aside and feeling for the small, stuffed buffalo hide saddle he used. He took a blanket that hung over the wall dividing the stalls and threw it over Shadow, then quickly put on the saddle, tying it underneath the horse. Long years of doing this day after day left him little need for light. He threw another blanket over the top of the saddle, then took the bridle from where he always hung it and slipped the bit into Shadow's mouth.

"You've got to be real quiet, boy," he told the gelding. He petted its nose and finished slipping on the bridle. He had no supplies, but he suspected that would be the least of his worries tonight. He had survived the Indian way too much of his life to be concerned over such things. He turned Shadow, leading him out of the stall, picking up his rifle again and walking over to the barn door that faced the cabin.

He could hear the horses clearly now, and saw torches. His chest tightened at the realization that they were white men, some of them looking like average settlers and townspeople. Surely they were from Austin.

Rachael! Had something gone wrong? Why were these men here? They quickly and quietly surrounded the cabin.

"Come on out, Selby," someone shouted. Brand recognized Jason Brown's voice, and a chill swept through him. He knew! Surely he knew! What had happened to Rachael?

"Come out now, or we'll burn you out, you half-breed scum," Jason yelled. "We know you're behind the raids, and we know about you and Rachael Rivers! Come out of there, you filthy rapist!"

Brand stood stock-still, knowing he should ride out but wanting to hear all he could. He had to know what had happened to Rachael.

"Maybe he ain't in there, Jason," one of the other men said.

"This time of night? He's in there. Indians don't like the dark. Think the night spirits are going to get them."

They all laughed, and Jason raised his rifle, firing a shot through a window of the cabin. "Come out of there, breed!" he growled. "You're going to hang tonight, Selby! Hang—for giving information to the Comanche so they could raid settlers! Why'd you let them raid Joshua's place, Selby, huh? Just because you were disappointed that Joshua Rivers didn't want you marrying his sister? Well, you sure as hell won't be marrying her, because we're going to stretch your thieving, traitorous neck tonight!"

Shouts went up from the men who surrounded the cabin solidly so that no one inside could possibly get out without being seen.

"Let's burn him out of there!" someone shouted.

Jason nodded. "Go ahead. But not everybody. We need the torches for light. I don't want that snake slithering out under our feet."

A few of the men let out war whoops, throwing torches onto the roof of the cabin, a couple more throwing torches through the windows.

"Keep a good watch now, boys," Jason warned them. "He's a clever bastard. When he comes out, just shoot to wound him. I want to see him hanging high in Austin tomorrow morning."

Guns were pulled and men shouted, their horses prancing about restlessly as flames began to show at the windows and on the roof of the cabin. The crackling sound penetrated Brand's heart. He knew that he was going to lose everything he had worked and saved so hard to have.

"Soon as we have the breed, shoot down all his horses," Jason ordered. "Then we'll burn everything else."

Brand moved away from the barn door, hurrying to the stall where the sick horse lay. He bent close, petting its nose. "I'm sorry, boy." Tears stung his eyes. He knew this horse he had been trying to save would be shot tonight. There was nothing he could do to save anything, and he had to think of Rachael. Something had happened he didn't know about. If there had been raiding, he had a strong suspicion it was not Comanche men doing it, not if they had raided Joshua's place. This had something to do with Jason Brown, and if he could get away, this might be his chance to prove a connection between Jason Brown and Comancheros.

The first thing he had to do was find out if Rachael was all right. If Jason Brown knew about Rachael and him, God only knew what the man would do. The shouts outside grew louder.

"Where the hell is he?"

"No man can keep from running out of a burning house."

"Maybe he ain't even in there!"

"Yeah. Maybe he rode into town to sleep with Rachael Rivers."

Brand tried to put things together in his mind. Jason had just gotten back from a tour of his territory. If it was Comancheros doing the raiding, maybe Jason had brought them back with him for that very purpose. But why? And why would he risk bringing them so close to Austin?

He had to find out about Rachael and then find the Comancheros. He had a good idea where Comancheros would hide if they wanted to be relatively close to Austin, but he couldn't find them or help Rachael if he got himself hanged. The first thing he had to do was save himself from Jason Brown and the men with him outside.

He moved away from the sick horse and led Shadow to the rear door of the barn. He reached for a leather strap that hung on the wall, which bore loops on it through which he could shove his rifle while he was riding, and to which he could tie supplies. He quickly strapped the belt around Shadow in front of the saddle, then eased the rifle into the loops. He took a parfleche down from the wall that held more bullets for the rifle, tying the rawhide straps of the parfleche through another loop. Then he took down a belt that held more bullets and slung it over his shoulder. He opened the barn door quietly, then eased up onto Shadow.

He petted the horse's neck, whispering in its ear. "You'll have to run hard, boy, like the good Indian mount you are. Running Wolf needs you to be swift tonight."

He headed out, quietly at first, then breaking into a hard gallop northward.

"Hey!" he heard someone shout. "Somebody's riding out!"

"Goddamn sonuvabitch!" someone cursed.

"Get after him!"

Brand heard more shouting and war whoops. He kicked Shadow's flanks with moccasined feet, tearing into the darkness. The surefooted animal charged over rock and buffalo grass, feeling its master's tenseness, sensing that the life of the man who rode him depended on his swiftness. Mane and tail flew outward as Shadow put his heart into the ride, his eyes wide, the whites of them showing in the moonlight.

Brand heard at first the thunder of many horses coming

after him, but Shadow soon left them behind. Shadow dashed down an escarpment, loose gravel sliding with him. The horse whinnied and stumbled slightly, but Brand Selby rode a horse with as much ease as he breathed; he hung on, easing Shadow the rest of the way down, then charged through the center of the gulley below. He knew he was near the peaceful stream where he had made love to Rachael for the first time. Now he prayed there would be more beautiful moments for them like that one. What had happened to poor Rachael?

Far in the distance he could see the long, dark shadow, and he knew it was the red-rock wall of a butte that meandered northward, breaking up the open plains. There were any number of caves and holes and crevices along that butte wall in which a man could hide. He did not let up on Shadow, realizing that Jason and his men might be too far behind to catch up, but that they might keep coming anyway. He headed Shadow up the other side of the escarpment, slowing the animal then for just a moment to look back. He could see the orange flames, now far behind him, and his heart ached at the sight of his cabin and barn burning. He wondered if they had killed his horses yet.

Shadow snorted and tossed his head, and Brand could feel lather on the horse's skin when he petted its neck.

"Just a little farther, boy. We'll hide out for a few hours, then I'll find a way to get back to Austin and find out if Rachael is all right."

He knew the danger of trying to sneak to Lacy Reed's boardinghouse, but he had no choice. Besides, Austin would be the last place Jason Brown would even look for him. It was more likely the man would form a new posse in the morning and come hunting for him in the hills. Already Brand had his own plans. It was Jason Brown who would be hunted, not Brand Selby. And Brand would do the hunting.

He kicked Shadow into motion again, riding out across open land then toward the butte. He knew every crack and crevice of that rocky bastion. He would wait until morning light, then head back to Austin. Jason Brown was going to pay for trying to get him hanged. If Rachael was all right, he intended to head out and do some scouting. He had little doubt he would come across Comancheros who were being paid by none other than Jason Brown.

Shadow charged into a dried-up arroyo, his hooves spraying mud but no water. The horse thundered on at his master's command, disappearing into the night.

"Hold up! Hold up!" Jason shouted to the others.

Saddles squeaked and horses shuffled and snorted as the men slowed their mounts and gathered around him. "We'll never catch him after dark like this," Jason announced.

"What should we do, Jason? We can't let him go."

"He won't get away. You men from town don't need to go galavanting into Indian country and risking your lives. We'll head back to town and me and my boys will hunt down Brand Selby ourselves."

"The man ought to hang," one of the townspeople grumbled.

"And he *will* hang," Jason promised. "My men and I are experienced at this. No need for all of you to endanger yourselves. Selby could be heading for the Comanche for help."

"Let's go shoot down the rest of his stock," someone yelled. "And burn down all his outbuildings—tear down his fences."

Several others responded in the affirmative.

"We're depending on you to get him for us, Jason," said another.

"Don't worry about that. You just get the rope ready. It might take a few days, but we'll be back with Brand Selby."

There was a low mumble among those who had come from town as they turned their horses and headed back. Jason waited until they were out of hearing range, then turned to his own men. All of them had come with him—Sam Greene, and the three new men—Dan, Hank, and Wendel. Jules was not with them, and Jason was glad none of the townsmen seemed to notice. The night had been one of confusion and heated emotions.

"What do we do now, Jason?" Sam asked.

Jason's horse turned in a circle, sensing its master's frustration. "Damn!" Jason muttered. "I didn't want Selby to get away. The bastard!" He turned and faced Sam. "We have to go back to town for tonight. I have to make an appearance in town tonight so I'm not linked in any way to Rachael's disappearing. We'll head out in the morning—just before sunup. In the meantime, Jules should be on his way to Lobo's camp. We should get there just a few hours after Jules gets there with Rachael. I just hope to hell he caught her and she'll be there!" His burning jealousy and hatred could be felt by the others through the darkness. "That bitch will regret the day she set eyes on Brand Selby!"

"You gonna strip her down and use that whip on her, boss?" Greene asked with a grin. "Hope we get to watch."

"Oh, you can watch, all right. And I'll be doing more than that to her! After that, anybody can have at her that wants to. I'll sell her off to Lobo and we'll find Brand Selby and shoot him on sight. Nobody will give a damn now if we kill him. Everybody thinks he's guilty anyway. Lobo will leave and the raiding will stop. With Brand dead, it will all make sense."

"We'll be cleanin' up a lot of problems all at once, won't we, Jase?" Greene put in. "We make a bundle off the Comancheros for the woman and we get rid of Brand Selby."

Jason turned and watched the house burn. "And I'll finally get my hands on Rachael Rivers!"

"What about her brother?"

Jason enjoyed the smell of the smoke in his nostrils. "We'll just tell Joshua we found Rachael dead when we were hunting down Selby—that Selby turned on her and gunned her down. If Jules has her, it will be because she rode out to warn Selby. That makes our own explanation easy. Rachael rode out to warn Brand Selby, then rode off with him and he killed her. Joshua Rivers will never know his sister is living in hell down in Mexico. Serves her right—the whoring little bitch!"

"What if she never left Lacy's place after all, boss?" one of the others asked.

"I'll worry about that later. There are other ways of getting to her. In the meantime, she can witness us bringing back Brand Selby's dead body!"

"We have to catch him first, Jase," Greene put in. "That ain't gonna be easy. You know Selby. He's part Comanche, and nobody knows these parts like the Comanche."

"We'll get him. We've hunted down Comanche before. He's a wanted man now. If we don't get him, some citizen will. I don't doubt he'll come sneaking back to Austin to try to find out what happened to his precious white squaw, but he doesn't dare show his face around here! He's a dead man, any way you look at it, and once he's out of the way, there will be nothing left to stop us from continued business with the Comancheros. We will be rich men."

There were snickers and nods from the others. "It's all a piece of cake once we get rid of Selby," Greene laughed.

"Yes," Jason answered. "I had hoped once I could share my success with Rachael Rivers at my side. But that can never be now, and that woman is going to suffer, Sam, suffer dearly for what she's done to me!"

They headed back to Austin.

Twenty

Lacy rubbed her puffy eyes, downing yet another cup of coffee. The sun was already rising, and she had not slept all night. Gray Legs had come back, without Rachael.

Lacy was frantic with worry, her mind full of questions. If Rachael had reached Brand, perhaps Brand had decided to leave Gray Legs behind because the horse was too slow. But it didn't make sense that all of Rachael's supplies had been left tied to the horse. The only other answer was that Rachael had somehow taken a spill from Gray Legs and was lying out in the wilds somewhere hurt; or worse, that she had been taken by outlaws or Comanche—perhaps a band of Comancheros.

Tears came to her eyes again as she sipped the coffee. She should be starting breakfast, but she was not in the mood. She had to decide what to do about Rachael. Should she ride out herself and try to find her? She had no idea which way to go, and for a woman to ride out alone was very dangerous, especially now.

Lacy knew she couldn't even go to Jason Brown for help. It was too late, anyway. Jason and his men had probably already ridden out to search for Brand Selby. But by now Jason couldn't care less what happened to Rachael Rivers, and Lacy suspected he might even have something to do with Rachael's disappearance. That's what worried her the most. As far as going to any of the other men in town, their attitude would be the same as Jason's. Lacy could still hear the names whispered behind Rachael's back at the dance. There was not a soul in Austin who would be willing to try to find the poor girl. Lacy's only hope was that Rachael had reached Brand and they had gone off together. But again, why would they leave behind Rachael's carpetbag and blankets?

Lacy put her head down on the table. With dread she realized Rachael couldn't have reached Brand. Bert Peters had ridden with the mob that had gone out to Brand's place, and he said Brand had still been there—that he rode off alone and got away.

"There was no woman with him?" Lacy had asked anxiously.

"No, ma'am."

When Lacy told the man Rachael was missing, he had just shrugged and shook his head.

"A woman goes out into that country alone, she risks the consequences," was all he had said. "She should have known better than to be messing with a half-breed. Maybe she reached him and he killed her and left her to burn up in the fires. That would explain why the horse came back." Peters shook his head. "I'm sorry, Mrs. Reed, but it seems like a proper ending for a girl who's done what she did."

Lacy had ordered him out of the house for his remark, and the man was upstairs packing right now. Lacy sipped some more coffee, wondering where Brand had gone, how she could get word to him that Rachael was gone. If anyone could find and help her, Brand Selby could.

The sleepless night began to catch up with her then, and her eyes closed, but her light sleep lasted only a few minutes before someone knocked at the front door. She jumped awake, thinking for a moment before realizing what she had heard. Rachael? She got up from the kitchen chair and walked on aching legs to the front door, opening it to see Joshua Rivers standing there. Immediately Lacy's eyes showed her contempt.

"What do you want?" Lacy snapped.

Joshua noticed the woman's disheveled look, the dark circles under her eyes.

"I want to know if Rachael is here. We might as well have our last say."

Fire came into Lacy's eyes. She could see that Joshua was still in a great deal of pain. He was pale, and he stood slightly hunched over, but she could feel no sympathy for him.

"No. Rachael is not here," she answered coolly. "By now

she's probably either dead or perhaps being raked over by Comancheros who will send her off to Mexico."

Joshua frowned. "What are you talking about?"

Lacy was so angry that her eyes teared. "You're a damned fool, Joshua Rivers! I hope some day you love someone as passionately as your sister loved Brand Selby. And I hope something happens to take the woman away from you! Maybe then you'll understand what you've done to Rachael! Your own sister! You should have known just by the kind of person she is that—"

"Where is she!" Joshua interrupted.

Lacy blinked back tears and stepped aside. "I don't know." She motioned him inside.

Joshua limped through the door and Lacy closed it. She led the young man to the kitchen, then pulled out a chair. "Sit," she told him.

Joshua sat down gladly. Everything hurt and stung. The doctor had removed the arrowhead, which had been thwarted by a rib from doing any dangerous inner damage. But the rib in which the arrow had lodged was cracked and extremely painful. The wound had been stitched, and his midsection was tightly wrapped. The rest of his body was scabbed and badly bruised, and every movement seemed an effort.

But Joshua couldn't bring himself to just lie around waiting to see what had happened to Brand and Rachael. He bought a change of clothes with money he still had in his pocket from the day of the raid, then went and got his horse from the livery where other men had taken it. Stu Bates at the livery had loaned him a saddle, and Briggs, the supply store owner, had let him take a repeating rifle on credit. Because it was Sunday, Joshua could not get to his bank savings, although what he had would be far from enough to buy a whole new herd of cattle and all the material he would need to rebuild. That was something he would probably not be able to do for a long time to come, but for now it didn't matter. All that mattered was to find the strength to ride out and find Jason and the others and have a hand in bringing down Brand Selby.

Lacy turned from the stove where she had poured Joshua a cup of coffee. "I suppose you know they didn't catch Brand Selby last night," the woman told him, setting down the cup of coffee in front of him. "And I'll tell you right now I'm glad of it!"

"Well, I'm not!" Joshua answered. "I just came to check on Rachael before I go after Jason and help him find Luke and bring Selby in. And at least they burned down Selby's place and killed his stock, just like what his Comanche friends did to me! He's got nothing left to come back to now."

"Doesn't he? You think anything Jason and the men around here have done will stop him from coming for Rachael? He *loves* her, you stupid fool! You're blaming the wrong man, Josh. You mark my words. I'll tell you who's behind the raids— the man who *wants* Brand Selby blamed so he can get Brand out of the way for once and for all. Jason Brown."

"Don't be ridiculous!" Joshua almost yelled.

Lacy put her hands on her hips. "*You're* the one being ridiculous, Joshua Rivers!"

Joshua looked away. Lacy sat down near him. "Drink some of that coffee," she told him. "You look terrible. You probably shouldn't even be up walking around."

"I've got no choice," Joshua said in a calmer voice. "Luke is out there somewhere. I'm going to ride out and find Jason and his men and help find Luke. Luke comes first, then Selby." He took a sip of coffee.

"You go riding out to help Jason Brown and the man will find a way to do you in, Joshua. My guess is that wherever Luke is, Rachael is with him by now."

Joshua set down his cup. "What do you mean? What's happened to Rachael?"

"Do you really care?"

"I do if she's in trouble."

"You didn't act much like you cared last night."

Joshua looked down at his coffee. "She deserved that. If it weren't for her loving that half-breed—"

"Oh, Joshua, use your head, boy! You've behaved like a child instead of the man you're supposed to be, and I hope your parents don't know what you've done. If they do, they're sorely ashamed of their eldest son!"

She got up and poured herself more coffee while Joshua stared at his own cup. "Where's Rachael?" Joshua asked again.

"It's like I told you. I don't even know for sure. Can't you see by this ugly old face that I've been up all night?"

Joshua looked at her. "How can you not know where she is?"

Lacy rubbed her eyes. "She rode out last night, as soon as we hurried home from the dance. She was determined to go and warn Brand that Jason and the others were coming after him—that he'd been blamed for those raids."

Joshua gripped the tin coffee cup tighter. "She rode out alone?"

"She knows the way to Brand's place. But she's never gone after dark, Josh; and a couple of hours later my horse showed up back here—with all her supplies still on it." Her eyes teared again. "Something has happened to her, Josh. And I don't know who to turn to. Nobody in this town is going to go looking for her. They don't care now. If she went off with Brand on a faster horse, she would have taken her supplies with her."

Joshua frowned, fingering his coffee cup. "She didn't go with Brand—not the way the men who came back from there tell it. They said they surrounded the house, but Brand wasn't inside it. He was in the barn. He went tearing out of there like a bat out of hell, and none of them could catch up with him. A man can't ride that fast if he's got the weight of an extra person riding with him. Not only could the horse never gain that speed, but it would be way too dangerous after dark like that. Those that saw him say he was alone, and there was just the one horse." He met Lacy's eyes. "And you're right—even if Rachael did go with him, she wouldn't have left her supplies behind. It wouldn't make sense."

"Oh, Josh, she's either lying out there somewhere hurt, or Comanche or outlaws got her. My God, Josh, you're her brother! Won't *you* at least go out there and try to find out what happened to her?"

Joshua sighed deeply, running a hand through his thick, sandy hair. "Damn," he muttered. "I've never been so mixed up in my whole life. I haven't even had time to mourn my own brother. My ranch is ruined, and I've got another brother out there with the Comanche. Now my sister is missing. What the hell is going on, Lacy? I don't know which way to turn."

"Well, my advice is *not* to turn to Jason Brown. It's time you opened your eyes and saw Jason for what he really is. Don't you think it's quite a coincidence that all this raiding started as soon as Jason got back from his last outing? And you know the man hates Brand Selby. Brand knows things about Jason he probably never even told you. Isn't it convenient that Jason blames the raids on Brand? He wants the man dead, Joshua. And now that he knows about Brand and Rachael, he wants him dead even worse. But more than that, he'll want revenge against your sister."

Joshua looked at her in disbelief. "Jason would never hurt Rachael."

"Wouldn't he? You didn't see him yesterday morning when he came here to get her final answer on marrying him. You didn't see the look in his eyes when she turned him down again, Josh. You didn't see how he grabbed her—the bruise he left on her arm. You didn't see how his fist was clenched like he wanted to strike her. She's always been afraid of him and you know it. Just think about it, Josh. Maybe she saw things you didn't simply because Rachael is a woman, and Jason's attentions to her were different from the friendship he shared with you. A woman knows, Joshua. She senses the danger in men like Jason."

Lacy reached out and pressed his arm. "Josh, I think she's in a great deal of trouble. And I think Jason is behind it. If he can't have her the right way, he'll have her any way he can get her, and he'll make sure she suffers. He threatened her yesterday morning—said that one way or another she would belong to him. Can't you imagine what went through his mind when you blurted out in front of the whole town last night that Rachael was in love with Brand Selby?"

Joshua rubbed his eyes. "It's so hard to believe Jason would do anything to hurt her. He loves her."

"He loves her beauty. And he *wants* her, Joshua. Wanting and truly loving can be two different things. He would have used her like a harlot—a thing to get his pleasure from, not the gentle, sweet woman that she is. Jason Brown would have destroyed her sweet nature."

Joshua quickly drank down his coffee and rose. "I don't know what to think about anybody any more. What the hell do I do now? I've got a sister and a brother to find. Which one do I go after first? God only knows where poor Luke is by now."

"Josh, I don't think Comanche raided your place. If they did, then it was renegades hired by Jason Brown himself."

Joshua shook his head. "I just can't believe that."

"You think hard on it and you'll know I'm right. Whatever you do, don't go to Jason, Josh. Go get some other Rangers, if you have to—men who don't work with Jason. Tell them what has happened. Get some help and then try to find Luke and Rachael. I think they were taken by the same men. Surely you don't hate your sister so much that you don't care if she's with Comancheros! You know what they're like, Joshua. Surely you don't wish that kind of thing on poor Rachael. No woman as sweet as she is should suffer at the hands of those men!"

Joshua felt a lump rise in his throat. He wanted to go and bury Matthew. He wished he could go back and see the house still standing, Matthew, Luke, and Rachael waiting for him on the steps. But reality stabbed at his heart like a long, cruel blade. Luke! Such a young and trusting boy. And Rachael! Was she really in the hands of outlaws! Maybe she was lying hurt somewhere. Either way, he had caused it himself.

He rubbed his neck, wondering how he was even going to manage to put in a full day on a horse. "I'll ride out and look for her. Selby's place was northeast of here, wasn't it?"

"I think so."

"I'll ride in that general direction and see what I can find. I guess then I'll have no choice but to go to the next closest Ranger headquarters and find some men who will help me look for Luke and Rachael."

Lacy closed her eyes. "Thank God," she said quietly.

Josh looked at her. "What about Selby? If he loved her so much, won't he come back here looking for her?"

"I have no doubt that he will."

"The fool will get himself hanged."

"I think he knows how to be seen only when he wants to be seen."

"Well if he never shows up again, it will prove I was right after all. He just wanted her because she was a pretty white girl. My bet is he'll keep right on going and never come back."

Lacy rose from her chair. "He'll be back, all right. If he shows up here, I'll tell him what has happened, where you've gone. I expect Brand will do some searching of his own. Men like him know this land like the back of their hands. I just hope either he or you can catch Jason Brown red-handed. Has Jason already ridden out?"

"Yes. He and his men are going after Selby, and they'll try to find Luke. I wanted to ride out with them, but they left way before sunup."

"And I say if he gets to Luke and Rachael first, you'll never see your brother and sister again, Joshua," she warned.

Lacy saw by his eyes that Joshua was beginning to see the light. "You think about it and you'll know I'm right. If you don't find Rachael out there, she's been picked up by someone Jason sent to spy on her. I feel it in my bones, Josh, but there is nobody I can turn to—nobody I dare hope might believe me except you. And right now you and I and Brand Selby are the only people who give a damn about poor Rachael. You've got to help her, Josh."

He sighed deeply, rubbing his side. "You got a little food I can pack? And a supply bag?"

"I'll get you whatever you need," Lacy said, feeling somewhat relieved. At least someone was doing something. She stepped closer, grasping his wrists. "I'm sorry about what happened, Josh. I know how you're hurting, emotionally and physically. There will be time for mourning later. Right now you've got to do what you know in your heart is right. You've got to try to find Rachael, and I just know when you find her you'll find Luke, too."

He rubbed his eyes. "I don't know. I hope you're right. But I hope you're wrong about Jason Brown. It's hard to believe it could be true. And if I do find out Selby was behind any of it, I'll kill the bastard!"

"You'll see, Josh, you'll see. I'll pack some things for you."

He walked to the table to finish his coffee. "Do me another favor, Lacy?"

"Whatever you need, son."

"See if you can convince some of the men in town to go out to my place and bury Matthew. I might be gone for days, and he's probably already…" He swallowed and blinked back tears. "I didn't have the strength to do anything but pull him into the toolshed so he'd be protected from scavenging animals and birds. He's got to be buried soon. I can't let him lay and rot in the toolshed."

Her own eyes stung with tears again. "Oh, Josh, how terrible it must have been for you. Of course. I'll see if I can get someone to go out there. I'll tell them you've gone looking for Luke yourself." She walked up to him and squeezed his arm. "God be with you, Josh. You're doing the right thing. God will help you find Luke and Rachael, I just know it. You just be sure to get some help first. Don't go after them alone, Josh."

"It might take too much time to get help."

"You've got no choice, son. You can't do it alone."

His eyes teared more. "Seems pretty hopeless any way you look at it. I've lost everything, Lacy, everything—even Luke and Rachael, I expect." He swallowed, a tear slipping down his cheek. "I'll go out and water my horse," he told her, quickly leaving.

Lacy watched after him, amazed at how things could so drastically change in just a couple of days. Lives had been torn apart, and it was not going to be easy putting them back together. She was just glad Joe and Emma Rivers were not alive to know what had happened. She carried her cup to the wash pan, looking out a window and wondering what had happened to Brand Selby. He would be back, that was sure. And if Josh couldn't find Rachael, Brand Selby would!

Joshua dismounted, muttering with pain when he did so. He felt lightheaded and knew he had better rest if he expected to keep up his search. Loss of blood still left him terribly weak. He took his canteen from his gear and swallowed some water, then replaced the canteen and led his horse to a hitching post, which was about all that was left of what appeared to have been a small cabin and some outbuildings. Everything had been burned and still smoldered. There was no doubt this had happened only hours before, which told Joshua this must be Brand Selby's place. Dead horses lay strewn everywhere, and as he searched around he found the burned carcass of a horse lying among the ashes of what was probably a barn or horse shed. The animal had died in the fire.

Joshua shook his head at the smell and the ruin. It reminded him of what had happened to his own place, and he felt nauseated at the memory of poor Matthew. As he looked around, the reality of the damage that prejudice and hatred could bring began to sink in further. He knew with a somewhat guilty conscience what his father would think of his being involved in this kind of reprisal against a man who had not even had a chance to speak in his own defense.

A light breeze stirred sand and ashes, sending a puff of debris into a little whirlwind over the remains of the cabin. Crows flew overhead, squawking and circling, and Joshua looked around at a lonely land, realizing that no matter how any of this turned out, he would have to leave Texas. He had nothing left here now, and he might even be completely alone. To think he could find Rachael and Luke alive was probably hoping for too much.

He searched through the ruins of the cabin and barn, terrified he would find the charred remains of a woman's body. But he found nothing. He had searched the land all the way here, hoping maybe he would find Rachael just lying hurt somewhere, but again he had found nothing.

He walked to a rise at the north end of the sight of the

ruins and gazed out at the long, rising plateau far off in the distance. It was then he thought he spotted a lone rider coming his way. He watched for several seconds while the man kept coming. From this distance Joshua could see only that it was a big man, and the way the sun shone on the horse it appeared to be gray and white spotted. Selby? Lacy said he would come back, but Joshua could not believe it. The man's neck was a sure bet for a noose.

Joshua turned and limped back to his horse, too sore to actually run. He took his rifle from its boot and cocked it, deciding to face Brand Selby down then and there. He would know the truth, one way or another. Seeing the man riding back led him to think maybe Lacy had been right about Selby after all. The man was risking his very life returning like this.

He moved to lie down behind some of the smoking debris and waited. After what seemed like hours he realized Selby might just have seen him standing on the ridge and had decided not to come in. He winced with pain as he got up again, walking cautiously toward the ridge. He climbed it, then hesitated when a large figure loomed from the other side of it. Brand Selby stood there holding a rifle on him.

"Looking for somebody, Josh?"

Twenty-One

"You're awful damn quiet, Selby," Joshua said, facing the man squarely. "I never even heard your horse."

"I'm part Indian, remember?" Brand smiled, but it was a vicious smile, not a friendly one. "Drop your rifle, Josh. I don't want to shoot you, but I will if I have to. I'm aiming to get some explanations for last night. Were you with the men who came out here and burned my place?"

Joshua tossed his rifle aside. "No. And I didn't come here to kill you, Brand. I just came this way from Lacy's to see if I could find Rachael, that's all."

Brand frowned, feeling as though someone was letting the blood out of him. "What do you mean? What's happened to Rachael?"

Joshua felt his heart quicken. "You don't know then? She's not with you?"

"The last I saw of Rachael, I left her off in Austin Wednesday night, after we got back from your place. What the hell is going on? Why did men come for me last night?"

Joshua swallowed. Today, with so much hatred in his green eyes, Brand Selby looked much more Indian than white.

"It's partly my fault what happened here," he answered honestly. "My place was raided by Comanche. They burned everything, stole my stock and made off with Luke. And they... they killed Matthew... chopped him up like firewood." His voice choked and he swallowed again before continuing. "I figured you had something to do with it because of the things I said to you, because I got in the way of you marrying Rachael. I rode to Austin for help." He took a deep breath before continuing. "I went to where they were having the dance and accused you of

294

setting the raid."

Brand just stared at him, gripping his rifle angrily. "Rachael was there? You told everyone about me and Rachael—in front of the whole town?"

Joshua swallowed again. "I did. I think maybe now I was wrong, but I'm still not completely convinced I was."

Brand closed his eyes and took a deep breath, then stepped a little closer, speaking through gritted teeth. "Do you know what you've done!"

"I'm sorry about your place, Brand—"

"It's not this place!" Brand shouted. "It's *Rachael!* Jason Brown knows about me and Rachael! Damn it, Josh, don't you understand the kind of man he is? Is she gone? Is Rachael missing?"

Joshua nodded slowly. "Lacy says she rode out last night to warn you. Her horse came back a couple of hours later with all her supplies still on it."

Brand groaned, throwing his rifle aside and stepping closer. "I ought to *kill* you with my bare hands!" Brand growled, grabbing Joshua's shirt.

Joshua cried out with pain and broke into a sweat. "It... wouldn't be hard," he answered. "I'm not in much shape to fight you."

Brand let go of him. He had been so upset at the sight of his ruined buildings and dead stock that he had not truly taken a good look at Joshua. Now he noticed the bruises and scrapes on the young man's face. Joshua bent over slightly and grasped his side when Brand let go of him. "You are wounded?" Brand asked.

"The raid," Josh answered.

Brand reminded himself what Joshua had been through, realizing that the young man had faced him squarely with the truth. And in spite of his wounds he had come looking for Rachael.

"Come and sit down," he told the young man, taking his arm. Josh followed Brand to a tall pine tree, where he eased himself down onto a soft bed of pine needles. "Where are you hurt?" Brand asked him.

Joshua smiled nervously. "Everywhere. You name it. I took an arrow in my rib—cracked it. It knocked me from my horse and my foot caught in a stirrup—dragged me quite a ways. I've got scrapes and bruises every place you can name. When my foot came loose I was thrown into a washout by the toolshed. I guess the raiders figured me for dead. They never came back and checked. I saw them killing poor Matt, but I couldn't get up and do anything about it. Then they burned everything—stole my stock and rode off with Luke."

He leaned back against the trunk of the tree, holding his ribs. "When I got to Austin, I found out there had been some other raids. Jason Brown had already been blaming you for them, said you only came to Austin to scout for your Comanche friends. I reckon I sealed the lid on your guilt when I came in accusing you of having my place raided." He met Brand's eyes. "But I guess if you were really guilty, you would have kept on riding. You wouldn't have come back."

Brand went back and picked up his rifle, taking a look around. Joshua watched, thinking that Brand looked like some kind of cunning wild animal, listening and watching for its enemies. He seemed to actually be smelling the wind. When he seemed satisfied that no one else was about he came back to Joshua's side, carrying his rifle. He stood near Joshua, looking down at him.

"I came back for Rachael. Now you tell me she is gone. Jason Brown found out about us. I don't doubt he had one of his men watch for Rachael, knowing she might try to warn me men were coming for me. My guess is Comancheros have Rachael—Comancheros who work with Jason Brown."

Joshua closed his eyes. "I can't believe that, Brand."

"Believe it." Brand gripped his rifle, looking around again, raging inside. Rachael! God only knew what Jason would do to her! "We have to go after her."

Joshua frowned. "Just the two of us?"

Brand kept watching the horizon. "I could do it alone," he sneered.

Joshua watched him, the look on Brand Selby's face giving him a chill in spite of the already hot day. "Where do we look?" he asked Brand.

"I spent years as a scout. I know every gully, every canyon, every tree from here to Indian Territory." He moved angry green eyes to Joshua. "If Jason has Comancheros raiding locally, there is only one really good hiding place for them around here, and that's Hell's Canyon. Where is Jason now?"

"He rode out this morning... him and his men... to look you up and kill you."

Brand closed his eyes, his head aching at the thought of what might have happened to Rachael. "My bet is he'll head for the Comancheros first—where someone is probably holding Rachael for him." He turned away. "My God," he muttered.

"Is it really all true—the things you and Rachael told me about Jason?"

Brand breathed deeply to stay in control. "They are true," he answered, agony in his voice.

Joshua sat up straighter. "I'm a good shot, Brand. I'll help all I can."

Their eyes held and Brand nodded. "I have two young Comanche boys who helped me around the ranch. Some of my horses were saved last night because Standing Horse and Gray Bear were camped far out in the hills with them, grazing them on better grass. They will help us find Rachael and Luke."

"What about your horses?"

Brand looked around at his ruined buildings and the dead stock. "It doesn't matter anymore. I can always ride out and round them up at a later time. The important thing now is to find where the Comancheros are camped and get Rachael and Luke out of there."

"How can you be so sure it's Comancheros?"

"Because the raids were too convenient. And Jason Brown was too quick to blame me." His eyes blazed as he knelt down beside Joshua. "This is my chance to prove Jason is mixed up with them. Hell's Canyon is less than a day's ride from here."

"But the men who attacked my place—they looked and

sounded like Indians. They shot arrows and—" He stopped, reaching into his pocket. He handed over an arrowhead, a stub of broken shaft attached to it. "Here. I kept the arrowhead the doc took out of me."

Brand took the arrowhead from him and studied it, then grinned in a sneer. "This is no Comanche arrow!" He met Joshua's eyes. "If you had been hit with a Comanche arrow, you would not be sitting here now. Comanche arrows have barbs in them that make it very hard to get them out. They dip them in horse dung to make them dirty so that even if you survive being hit, a man usually dies from infection. And look at the shaft. It is wood. We make our arrows from bone, so that it is almost impossible to break the shaft or even chop it off." He tossed the arrowhead aside. "It was white men who did this, Joshua, not Comanche. I spoke with the Comanche who ride these parts myself, and they would not break their promise to me not to bother the Double 'R.' Even old Rotten Mouth, one that I do not get along with, would not break a promise. If you would have realized what was really happening, you would have come to *me*, not to Jason. He is behind this. I would bet my life on it."

"But why would Jason have my place attacked?"

Brand shook his head. "I don't know."

"Do you think he'd have us all killed just to get Rachael?"

Brand held his eyes. "Now do you understand? Jason Brown will do anything he has to do to get what he wants. Marrying Rachael was all part of it. It would make him look better married to a bright and beautiful woman like… Rachael." His voice broke at the name and he turned away. "We have to find her," he groaned.

Joshua frowned. "You really love her, don't you?"

Brand turned, his eyes red and watery. "I would die for her. That just might happen before this is over, but we have no choice. If we go to other Rangers for help, they will not believe us. Besides, there isn't time. Wherever Rachael is, Jason is probably with her by now. It tears at my guts to even think of it!"

Joshua got up, wincing with pain. "Let's get going then."

Brand breathed deeply, turning away and wiping his eyes.

"What about your wounds?"

"I'll make it somehow."

Brand noticed a spot of blood on his shirt at the side. "You are still bleeding a little. We had better keep an eye on that. I had to ride off with no supplies, but if the bleeding gets any worse, I can make a poultice from plants that will help stop it and will help keep the wound from being infected." He looked Joshua over. "You must be in a lot of pain. Are you sure you can do this?"

"I don't have any choice. I've got to help my brother and sister. And don't worry about supplies. I've got plenty. You want something to eat before we leave?"

"No." Brand turned to look again at the smoldering ruins. "I am too full of hatred and worry to care about that."

Joshua studied the half-breed, wishing he had been right about the man but realizing he had been totally wrong. "I reckon you're a good man, Selby. If you can prove to me you're right about Jason Brown, I reckon I'll have to blame myself for what's happened to Rachael and Luke. But I hope you understand I thought I was doing what was best for Rachael. I do love her."

Brand turned back to face him. "That makes two of us."

Joshua blinked back tears. "I'm sorry about what happened here."

"There are many things for both of us to be sorry for. I am sorry I did not turn away from Rachael the moment I knew that I loved her and just ride away from here forever."

Joshua breathed deeply, rubbing his eyes. "I'll never forgive myself if—"

"We will find her, Joshua."

Joshua just nodded, unable to speak.

Brand walked over the ridge to get his horse. He wanted to throw back his head and scream out in agony. Rachael had surely suffered some terrible fate, and all because she loved him.

It was nearly six o'clock in the evening when Jason and his men reached Hell's Canyon, an ancient chasm among a maze of canyons and crevices and rock formations set curiously amid a vast sweep of rich plains carpeted green and yellow. There was no explanation for the several thousand acres of buttes, mesas, and low, spiked mountains in this area, other than it just being another odd result of nature's hand. Jason couldn't care less about the geological aspect of the area. All he cared about was that this area provided an array of places where hunted men could hide. He had routed out many a horse thief from this area, as well as renegade Indians. But Lobo and his men were never bothered.

Sam Greene whistled out a signal to four men who stood guard atop the canyon, signifying that those who approached were friends. Jason's heart pounded with anticipation as he headed his horse down a rocky escarpment. Jules should have gotten here by now with Rachael, if he had her. Jason figured it a sure bet that Rachael would try to go and warn Brand Selby. If she did, she would be waiting for him below. If not, he would deal with her when he got back to Austin. Rachael Rivers would pay, one way or another.

The men who stood guard waved their rifles in the air while Jason, Sam, Dan, Hank, and Wendel headed downward, rocks slipping and sliding before them. The open plains led to a confusing mingle of rocks and buttes that led to this canyon, and outlaws who used it seldom worried about getting trapped inside. For one thing, no one ever got past the guards. And if one needed to make a quick exit, it was a simple matter of stampeding stolen horses or cattle through the entrance Jason now used, chasing back any would-be intruders and opening the way for the outlaws to escape. And there was another exit, narrower and harder to reach from the outside. But Lobo and his men knew about it and felt perfectly safe in the canyon, which was so deep that smoke from their campfire dissipated so much by the time it floated out the top of the canyon that it was seldom detected by outsiders. Besides that, the whole area was so rocky and desolate, few people ever came into the vast, confusing land of rocks and heat.

Below Jason could see herds of cattle and horses, many of

which he knew had been stolen from Joshua Rivers. A wagon of hay stood beside a canyon wall, also stolen for temporary feed until Lobo could leave and herd the animals south into Mexico. Then they could feed on buffalo grass as they made their journey. There was some grass below, at a place where a few pine trees clustered around the bottom of a waterfall. The water splashed out of the middle of one wall of the canyon, from some mysterious source. It splashed over smooth rock and into a stream that ran through one corner of the canyon, then disappeared underground, probably reappearing outside the canyon in a stream somewhere, but no one really knew. The water made Hell's Canyon a perfect hiding place, providing nearly everything needed for men like Lobo and his kind.

To anyone else, the canyon would be beautiful, secluded, peaceful. But men like Jason Brown and the outlaws he was riding in to greet cared little about such things.

"Greetings, Señor Brown!" Lobo called out when he saw Jason coming. He waved his arm, and Jason removed his hat and waved back. He saw Jules walking toward Lobo and his heart quickened. He was here! Surely that meant Rachael was here, too! He rode a little faster, dismounting before his horse even came to a full halt.

"Lobo, my friend!" he said, putting out his hand.

The handsome, mustachioed Mexican shook his hand. "Hey, amigo, it is about time you came. We must get going in no more than two days. There is not enough feed for the cattle and horses. And with all this raiding, other Rangers might be searching for us—ones who want to kill us, no? Not ones who are our friends, like you."

Lobo laughed, displaying even, white teeth.

"You're probably right about others being alerted, Lobo," Jason answered. "But I am glad you waited."

"Ah, your friend Jules, here, he tells me I should wait so that you can see the white woman he brings before I take her to Mexico." He grinned even wider. "Señor Brown, that one—" He made a kissing sound. "She bring much gold in Mexico. Jules say you want to marry her, now you want to sell her." He frowned. "He say she sleep with the half-breed, Brand Selby? This is true?"

The hatred came back into Jason's eyes. "It's true. And she'll pay." He looked at Jules. "She tried to warn him then?"

Jules nodded, grinning. "Just like you said she would. I had to knock her around a little to get her to cooperate, though. She's a feisty one."

The other men with Jason rode past him, hooting and hollering, greeting Lobo's men, who offered them whiskey. A white woman sat tied to a wagon wheel, her dress torn open from the waist up, the skirt of the dress in shreds. Her face was bruised and dirty, her hair hanging in strings. Her wrists bled from the rope around them and her fair skin was burning from the Texas sun.

Jason looked over at her, feeling no sentiment for her, seeing her merely as part of the spoils of Lobo's raids. She was apparently the woman settlers claimed had been stolen away, and she obviously had already been the brunt of pleasure seeking by Lobo and his men. They were good at using a woman just enough to get what they needed from her, but keeping her alive and healthy enough to get good money for her in Mexico. Seeing her made Jason ache with anticipation. Soon it would be Rachael's turn. He turned his eyes to Jules Webber. "I hope you kept your hands off Rachael Rivers. I told you to save her for me."

Jules robbed his privates. "I saved her."

Jason moved his eyes to Lobo. "You keep your men away from her?"

"*Sí*, señor, just like you ask."

"Well, you didn't do a few other things I asked. You were supposed to kill Joshua Rivers, and Luke, too."

Lobo frowned. "The young one, he is good and strong. We can sell him. My men told me the other one was dead."

"Well, they didn't check to be sure. He lived. Where is Luke?"

"He's tied to a tree by the stream," Jules answered. "He's a might beat up, but none the worse for the wear. He'll make it to

Mexico. Right now he's plum wore out—fell asleep awhile ago. What happened with Selby? You get him hanged?"

Jason glowered with a mixture of hatred and worry as his eyes scanned the rim of the canyon. "No. The bastard got away."

"Got away! Jesus Christ, Jason, he'll be looking for Rachael Rivers. When he finds out she's gone, he'll put it all together and come looking for us."

"He's just one man!" Jason snapped, moving his eyes back to Jules. "There are six of us and ten in Lobo's gang."

"Eight," Lobo corrected him. "That Joshua Rivers, he killed two of my men. We buried them on the way here. Another was wounded, but he will live."

Jason checked the canyon walls again. "It doesn't matter. That still leaves us fourteen men counting the wounded one. Whatever option Brand Selby takes, he's a dead man. He won't get any help from his Comanche friends because you and your men sell weapons to them. They don't want you dead. If Brand Selby comes here for Rachael, he'll take so many bullets you'll be able to see through him. My guess is he'll keep right on riding north, the direction he lit out in the night we burned him out. In the meantime, I'll have had my turn with the bitch and after that she's yours."

He glanced at the white woman who was tied to the wheel. Sam Greene was untying her. She made weak, whimpering protests as he half dragged her toward a rock, carrying a blanket under his arm. The woman glanced at Jason and her eyes widened.

"Ranger Brown!" she blurted out through lips swollen from the sun. "It's you! Help me, please!"

"Shut up!" Sam told her, giving her a jerk. "Can't you see we're friends of these men, you stupid woman?"

"But... I don't understand—"

"You'll understand soon enough, when I get you behind this rock."

Her eyes widened with shock as reality hit her. Jason Brown was helping these outlaws! A look of pitiful disappointment moved through her eyes before Sam pulled her behind the rock.

Jason and the others heard a sharp crack as Sam slapped her hard. They heard no more protests from the woman.

"I can't wait 'til you're through with that uppity bitch of yours," Jules told Jason. "It's gonna feel good watching her cry and beg. She always treated me like I was scum."

Jason met Jules's eyes. "Well, now *she's* scum!" be answered. "She'll pay for humiliating me in front of the whole town of Austin!"

There was laughter and drinking among the other men as they spoke. Jules nodded toward a canvas-covered wagon. "Lobo and his men stole that in one of their raids. I put the bitch in there so's the sun wouldn't get to that pretty skin."

"Did you tie her good so she can't get her hands on any weapons?"

"Didn't need to. She give me such a fight when I was puttin' her in she cracked her head good on the wagon gate. She's out cold."

"Out cold!" Jason shoved him aside. "You idiot!" he shouted as he headed for the wagon. "I want her *conscious*."

He jumped up onto the wagon gate and peered inside. Rachael lay there on her side, her dress slightly torn, her hair a tumbled mess. Jason climbed inside, pushing her onto her back and shaking her. "Wake up, you bitch!" She made no sound or move. He grasped her by the hair. "Wake up!" He threw her back down and ripped open the front of her dress. "You'll wake up, my pretty Rachael," he hissed. "And when you do, you'll be begging me to stop hurting you. Before I'm through I'll know every inch of you, inside and out! There will be nothing left hidden from Jason Brown!"

He stared down at her, his whole body on fire for her. He wanted her badly, but he wanted that first time to be as humiliating for her as possible. He wanted her awake. He climbed reluctantly out of the wagon, storming up to Jules. "How long has she been out?"

Jules shrugged. "Since we got here—maybe six hours."

"Six hours! My God, man, she might never come around! She might die before I get to have my way with her, you sonuvabitch! Can't you do anything right?"

"I couldn't help it. The little bitch fought me like a wildcat. It was an accident. I didn't hit her or anything."

Jason hauled off and landed a fist into the man's face, and Webber flew backward, landing hard on his rump. The rest of the men laughed.

"One of these days I'm going to get tired enough of your mistakes to kill you, Webber!" Jason growled. He looked at Lobo. "Have somebody dump water on her, slap her around a little, try to get her to come around."

"*Sí*, señor. We will try."

Jason looked over at the stream, then walked closer. He could barely see Luke by the light of the distant fire. He approached the boy, who lay awkwardly on his side at the base of the tree to which his hands were tied. Jason kicked him and Luke groaned, slowly coming awake. Even in the darkness Jason could detect bruises on the boy's face.

"Jason!" Luke cried out when he realized who was standing over him.

Because of what Rachael had done, Jason hated her brothers, too. They were too much like their father, and Joe Rivers had never had much use for Jason Brown. When he was alive, Rivers was a big, solid, hard-working man who never seemed to quite trust Jason, and Jason blamed the man for Rachael's initial dislike of him.

Jason was glad the Double "R" was destroyed. Josh had always been friendly enough, but he was still a Rivers, and in Jason's mind they all thought they were better than everyone else.

But, Rachael Rivers had proven that the Rivers name was no better than scum.

Tears stained Luke's freckled, dirty face, and his dark hair stood out in all directions. "Untie me, Jason," he sniffled. "You gonna take in those bad men? You gotta get Rachael out of the wagon before they do bad things to her! That one man hit her, and—"

"Shut up!" Jason snapped. He looked Luke over as the boy sat there in wide-eyed shock. "They keeping you fed?"

Luke nodded, more tears coming as he blinked in confusion.

"Good," Jason told him. "If they keep you good and strong until they get you to Mexico, you'll be worth more."

Luke shook his head. "Worth more?"

Jason grinned. "When they sell you—maybe to work in a gold mine—or as a slave to some rich family—or maybe to a ship's captain, where you can swab decks all the way to China."

Luke blinked, watching the strange, dark eyes of Jason Brown, a man he had called friend, a man he had trusted, a Texas Ranger who used to come by and check on them to be sure they were safe. And Jason loved Rachael—wanted to marry her, just like the half-breed Brand Selby wanted to do. Surely Jason wouldn't want her to be hurt.

"Aren't you gonna untie me, Jason? Aren't you gonna help us? These men are bad. They killed Matt and Josh and stole all our horses and cattle and burned down our house. Now they've got Rachael!"

Jason leaned closer. "You don't understand, son. I'm working *with* these men. I told my own man to bring Rachael here—" He grinned. "For me. Now when your sister comes to, I'm going to that wagon, and I'm going to have some fun with your sister. Then the other men will have their fun with her while they herd you and Rachael and all these cattle and horses to Mexico. Understand?"

Luke swallowed and sniffed again, feeling like he was going to throw up. Jason Brown was a bad man. He could hardly believe his eyes and ears, and he tried to tell himself this must all be an act on Jason's part, maybe to win the confidence of these men before he attacked them. But when Jason reached out to tousle his hair, then pulled at it painfully, Luke knew he was wrong. This was no trick on Jason's part.

Luke didn't want to cry like a baby, but he couldn't help the tears as Jason walked away, heading straight for the wagon where Rachael was tied. He remembered that Rachael used to say she didn't like Jason, that he frightened her. She had been right. He tugged harder but fruitlessly on his ropes as Jason returned to the campfire, laughing and joking with the hated outlaws. He cringed against the tree, overwhelmed with the reality of what was happening. Yesterday and today had been a rude awakening for Luke Rivers to the evil side of man, and he wept harder at the realization that if Jason Brown was working with these men, there was absolutely no one to help him or his sister. He had seen the other white woman raped right out in the open. Would they do that to Rachael? She was so pretty, so good. The thought of the men touching his sister brought a rage to his soul that made his chest hurt. He hung his head and wept as the men at the fire joked about Rachael being unconscious.

"You got a need, Jason?" Sam Greene asked, coming out from behind a rock and buttoning his pants. "The white woman behind that rock there will take care of you."

"Shut up, Greene!" Jason snapped. He glowered at Jules again, who slunk back into the shadows with a bottle of whiskey. "There's only one woman I want. And she'd better come around pretty soon or Jules Webber will pay for screwing this up for me!"

Luke hung his head. "Please, God," he prayed. "Don't let her wake up."

Twenty-Two

Standing Horse and Gray Bear slithered down the rocky embankment to where Brand and Joshua waited in a thick cluster of scrub bushes. Joshua was astounded at how Brand and the two young Comanche had found their way to Hell's Canyon. Darkness had fallen before they reached their destination, and the lay of the land approaching Hell's Canyon was rocky and dangerous, full of crags and crevices. As they got closer, just before night fell, Brand and his two companions had come across the tracks of several horses. They had followed them over rocky areas where Joshua was sure no human could possibly track anything. But Brand and the two Comanche boys seemed to almost be sniffing out their prey.

Joshua didn't even know this place existed, for he had never dared stray this far north. This was Indian and outlaw country, but Brand Selby seemed to feel perfectly comfortable and confident wherever he was. It seemed ironic to Joshua that men he had considered his worst enemy were now helping him in his hour of need.

Brand and the two Comanche boys spoke to each other in low whispers, using the Comanche tongue. Then Brand turned to Joshua. "Wait here," he said quietly. "Gray Bear and Standing Horse say there are many men below. By the firelight they recognized Jason Brown. They know him. They saw one white woman, but she had dark hair. They couldn't see a young white boy, or a white woman with light hair. But my bet is they're both down there somewhere. Even if they aren't, the fact that Jason is with them should be proof enough to you that he's no good. By the light of a second fire they could see some horses and cattle—probably yours and whatever settlers they raided."

"What should we do?"

"I'm going up to take a look myself. They're sure to have some lookouts up there someplace. The ones on the other side of the canyon can't do us much harm before we get through—most likely they'll run off. Either way, we can't get to them in time, but if there are any on this side, we can take care of them."

"But they'll hear the gunshots."

"We'll use our knives."

Joshua shivered, glad he was not the one this man and his Comanche friends were after.

"You wait right here," Brand told him. "I'll try to see how many there are and we'll try to get rid of a couple of them up here. Then we'll move in closer. You hold the horses." Brand reached out and squeezed Joshua's shoulder before disappearing into the darkness.

Joshua waited, his heart pounding. Were Rachael and Luke down there? How many men were there? It didn't seem to matter to Brand, and that helped Joshua's own courage. Brand seemed even more fierce when he borrowed war paint from Standing Horse and Gray Bear. All three of them had smeared the dyed clay across their cheeks, foreheads, and down their noses in black and red, and tonight Brand Selby was Running Wolf, the Comanche warrior.

They had ridden all day and half the night to get here. Until now Joshua had not wanted to believe Jason could really have anything to do with outlaws, but he was here in this godforsaken place amid stolen horses and a captured white woman. That only meant Brand Selby had been right all along. Even Rachael had been right long before this. Joshua felt sick. He could only pray now that Rachael was alive and still untouched, and that Luke was down there, too.

The next few minutes seemed like hours, until Brand and the Comanche boys returned. Joshua could almost smell death in their excited state.

"We found two guards. They are dead," Brand said matter-of-factly. "My own knife gladly tasted the blood of one of them when I pulled it across his throat. Standing Horse severed the spine of the other." Brand told of the killings as though it was no more than cutting a blade of grass. He had not lost the Comanche way of boasting about his conquests. "*Keemah*," he said to Joshua then, indicating he should follow.

Josh crept up the slope to the top right behind Brand, then flattened himself, his eyes widening at the sight of Jason Brown below, sitting around a campfire and arguing about something.

"Maybe you can bring her around," someone was saying. "A few slow slices down the bottom of her feet might do it. Sure would wake me up."

They all laughed, and Joshua's fists clenched. "Let's get the bastards!" he whispered, starting to get up.

Brand grabbed him and shoved him back down. "Wait! Let's make sure everybody knows what he's doing. I count eight men around the fire. There are sure to be a couple more guards on the other side of the canyon, and there are probably a couple of men in the shadows over by the stock, keeping watch on the herd. The one with his shirt off is all bandaged up—must have got wounded in one of the raids."

"Some look like Comanche," Joshua whispered.

"They're Mexicans who let their hair grow so they can paint themselves up and make people think they're Comanche when they raid. I don't doubt they're the same ones who raided your place, and I'll bet both Luke and your herd are down there. There are four of us, so we each have to pick a man and get off good shots first round—make sure four go down right away. The rest are going to scatter as soon as we shoot, so the first shot means a lot—brings the numbers down to more even terms. And don't kill Jason. Save him for me."

Joshua watched as Jason rose then. "You can't kill him, Brand."

"I have to," Brand whispered hoarsely. "He's got to die, and die slowly."

"Use your head, Brand. I want him dead, too, but we should keep him alive so we can take him back to Austin and prove to everybody what he's really been up to. Isn't that what you've always wanted to do?"

Brand watched the men below. "I don't think I can let him live," he said.

"You have to, for Rachael's sake! If you let him live, you'll be showing the people in Austin that you aren't the savage they say you are. If you cut Jason up, you'll only verify what they think; and with him dead, they might not believe any of it. You've got to take him in *alive*, Brand. They'll respect you more for it. We can both get our revenge when we watch him hang! Rescue the white woman and she can testify against him—tell everyone the truth about Jason Brown. I can tell what I saw, and so can Luke and Rachael, if they're down there. Make him face the people, Brand. Make him pay publicly."

Brand sighed deeply, watching Jason climb into a wagon. "The wagon!" he whispered. "That's where they've got her!" He turned and spoke to the Comanche boys in their own tongue, then turned to Joshua. "I'll try not to kill him. We'd better move closer and pick our targets. Jason's in that wagon with Rachael! Follow me!" He turned to the Comanche boys. *"Keemah!"*

Below Rachael began to stir, something hurting her foot. She screamed out, the pain suddenly excruciating. Her eyes popped open, and by the light of a lantern inside the wagon she saw Jason Brown sitting near her feet. He looked at her with eager brown eyes, holding up a bloody knife.

"Well, Jules was right," he said, his voice gruff with delight. "A few pricks of the knife did wake you up. It's about time."

She blinked and just stared at him a moment, trying to gather her thoughts. The last thing she remembered was Jules Webber slugging her while she struggled to keep him from throwing her into a wagon. Reality began to set in when Jason grasped her right ankle. She tried to pull it away, but his grip was too strong. She screamed as Jason held her foot tightly and ran the knife deep down the middle of the bottom of her foot. She began shaking with pain and horror as he came closer to her face, holding the bloody knife in front of her eyes, then moved it lightly between her breasts, leaving blood on her skin.

"If you weren't worth so much the way you are, I'd carve these pretty things off for tobacco pouches—while you're fully conscious," he said softly, grinning. He fondled her breasts and she grabbed the wrist of his knife hand with both her own hands and pushed upward. Jason only laughed, backhanding her with his free hand. He held her down by pressing his forearm against her throat until she could not breathe. In moments she was forced to let go of him for lack of air. He threw the knife aside.

"That's better," he sneered. "Now we're going outside and show the other men just how pretty you are. The rest of these clothes come off, my little white squaw, for all the men to see the fine prize they will be taking to Mexico—*after* I've had my fill of you. That could take several hours!" He took his arm from her throat, and she gagged and gasped for breath.

Jason bent closer, touching a breast. Rachael found her breath and scratched his eyes, making him cry out.

"Coward! Brand Selby will kill you for this!" Rachael screamed.

They fought as Jason jerked her up, and he hooked one arm through both her own, pulling hers behind her and squeezing her face painfully in the other hand, holding his face close to hers.

"Brand Selby is *dead*!" he lied, grinning. "By now the good folks of Austin have hanged him."

She shook her head. "No," she squeaked.

"Oh yes, my sweet," Jason answered, running his hand back down over her breasts. "Your half-breed lover is dead, and you, my lovely Rachael, are going to pay dearly for humiliating me like you did at that dance! There is no one to help you now, Rachael," he sneered. "I am going to do all the things to you I've only dreamed of doing until now. And then I'll turn you over to the rest of the men. You wanted to be a slut, so now you'll *be* one. When they're through with you you won't be fit for any decent man." He enjoyed the way she trembled, the terror in her eyes. "And then I am going to take the skin off the bottom of your pretty little feet. After all, you have to be punished for what you did to me. I would rather use my whip on you, but I decided against it. I don't want to put scars on your pretty skin."

She could not stop the tears. "You… stinking coward," she whimpered. "And you call yourself a man!" She sniffed and glared at him boldly. "Is this the only way you can get a woman, Jason Brown?" she sneered.

His jaw flexed with rage, and he literally threw her to the back of the wagon, then kicked her off the gate so that she landed hard on the ground. The pain in her badly cut foot was close to unbearable, and through misty vision she could see several men looking at her, laughing at her. She struggled to find the sleeves of her dress so she could pull it back on and over her breasts, but someone hauled her up then, pulling her arms behind her.

"Here you go, boys. Not a bad prize, is she? Didn't I tell you?"

There came hoots and whistles and dirty words, and Rachael felt faint from the pain in her foot for having to stand on it.

"Hurry up, Jason, so we can have our turn," someone spoke up.

Joshua and Brand watched in horror from above. "My God, it *is* Rachael!" Joshua groaned.

Brand cocked his rifle. "We've got to move fast. It's now or never."

"But she might get hurt in the gunfire!"

Brand slowly lowered his rifle. "We'll draw their attention first, get Jason to let go of her." He took a bow from around his shoulders, then pulled an arrow from a quiver on his back. He said something to Standing Horse and Gray Bear, then turned to Joshua. "Be ready. I'm taking the one closest to the fire. You take the bandaged one." They all took aim. "Wait 'til my man goes down. They'll be startled at first. I'm hoping Jason will let go of Rachael then."

Brand struggled to ignore Rachael's screams and struggles as Jason jerked her head back and tried putting his mouth over one breast. Brand pulled back the bowstring and let the arrow fly. It whirred through the night air, and in an instant it landed in Wendel's back. The man grunted and rose, standing awkwardly for a moment, then falling face forward into the campfire.

"Jason!" Webber called out.

Jason looked over at the suddenly quiet men to see Wendell

lying in the fire, his flesh beginning to smoke.

"What the hell—" He looked at Webber.

"Selby?"

"It couldn't be! He's nowhere around!"

"Brand," Rachael whispered at hearing someone mention his name. She struggled to clear her head as she moved her eyes to stare at the man with the arrow in his back. Now everyone was looking up at the canyon walls. Rachael had no idea if it was Brand up there, or Comanche Indians come to do in the outlaws and steal their loot.

Everything happened in only seconds, but it seemed much longer than that. Jason was suddenly shoving Rachael aside, and the men were going for their guns.

A shot rang out as Jason jumped into the wagon, and the bandaged man went down, then another man. Rachael scrambled under the wagon as Brand, Joshua, Gray Bear, and Standing Horse charged forward, letting out war whoops as they descended toward the rest of the astonished men. As the four other men around the campfire pulled guns and started firing into the darkness, Brand fired twice more, killing one of Lobo's men and wounding Sam Greene in the leg. Greene began crawling on his belly toward his horse, but Gray Bear ran up to him, grasping him by the hair and slicing a knife across his throat. The Indian let out a yelp of victory before rising and running toward where the horses were kept.

Joshua took aim at Dan, sending the man sprawling with a bullet in his lower right side. Standing Bear headed for the man with his knife. "No! No!" Joshua told him. "Save him! We need him!"

Standing Bear looked at him curiously. Making sure the man was dead was to him the only right thing to do, and he wanted a scalp. But the white man kept waving him off, so he turned to help Gray Bear, who was shooting and Whooping around the horses.

Brand raised his rifle and fired at a figure fleeing into the dark, and just then a bullet fired from inside the wagon slammed into Brand's shoulder, sending him reeling sideways. He rolled under the wagon while Joshua ran behind a large rock to take cover from the light of the flames. The stench of burning flesh pierced his nostrils, as the first man Brand had killed still lay in the fire.

Under the wagon Brand crawled to Rachael, who sat hugging the other white woman, both of them shivering and crying.

"Brand!" Rachael squeaked, folding one arm over her breasts. "You're hurt!"

He grimaced with pain, grabbing her away from the other woman for a moment and hugging her tightly. "Rachael! My God, Rachael, I'm so sorry! So sorry!"

"It's all right," she wept. "Oh, Brand, you're alive! Jason said you were hanged!"

Two more shots came from where the horses were kept, and Hank and one of Lobo's men, who had been guarding the horses, went down under fire from Standing Horse and Gray Bear. Suddenly all was quiet.

Brand held Rachael close for a moment. "Be very quiet," he whispered. She watched in terror as he moved away from her, still grasping his rifle. Brand! He was alive, and he had come for her! Her heart swelled with love, and she turned to the other woman, hugging her close again.

The woman cried quietly as Brand stayed on his knees under the wagon.

In the distance Standing Horse sliced a piece of scalp from Hank, then hurried to where Luke was tied, cutting the boy's ropes while Gray Bear took a scalp from the other man they had shot near the horses. Standing Horse motioned to Luke to stay put and be quiet. He pointed to the distance. "Joshua," he said, using the name he had learned by now. "Brand."

Luke understood, his heart rushing with joy. Joshua! He was alive? It seemed impossible, for he had seen his brother knocked from his horse and dragged, an arrow in his side. What seemed more incredible was that Joshua was with Brand Selby. Standing Horse and Gray Bear moved off into the darkness and Luke crawled to Hank, feeling around for the man's rifle. He finally found it and moved closer to the wagon where he could see the women crouched underneath.

"Make yourself visible, Selby!" Jason was shouting from inside the wagon. "Come on, you bastard!" There was obvious terror in his voice. "Come on out from wherever you're hiding and fight like a man!"

Brand crawled to the front of the wagon, and Rachael watched in terror as he just crouched there quietly. Suddenly he spoke.

"Fight like a man?" he called back to Jason. "It didn't take much of a man to terrorize and brutalize these two women under here! I wouldn't be fighting a man, Jason. I'd be fighting a goddamn coward! You might as well come out of there, Jason. It's all over. If you fight it, you're a dead man."

"You sonuvabitch!" Jason screamed, sounding as though he was crying.

Brand crawled back to Rachael. "Head out into the shadow behind the wagon," he whispered. "Stay in the dark. Get out from under here!"

Rachael pushed the other woman, and she struggled not to cry out from the pain in her foot as she scrambled out from under the wagon and limped into the darkness, while Jason Brown began shooting wildly through the bed of the wagon. Brand rolled out from under it and stood in the shadows.

"Come on out, Jason! You don't have a chance!"

He could hear a sniffling sound inside. Jason Brown was crying from fear. Brand darted back to the side of the wagon, silent as the soft night air. Joshua watched from his hiding place and waited. Finally Jason began to emerge from the back of the wagon, sticking his hand out first and brandishing a gun. He began firing into the darkness. Brand stepped from around the corner of the wagon and slammed his rifle barrel upward against Jason's wrist. The blow knocked the gun from Jason's hand. Brand quickly reached up and grabbed the hand, yanking Jason out of the wagon and raking his arm across a nail, causing a deep cut.

At the same moment the two guards who had been climbing down from above were running toward the scene. Gray Bear jumped up from behind a stack of wood and shot one of them down. Joshua came running from behind the boulder and took aim at the second man, putting a hole in the man's right hip.

Brand slammed Jason to the ground, but fear and desperation made Jason get right back up. He lunged into Brand, slamming him against the back of the wagon.

"Brand!" Rachael screamed.

Brand was bleeding badly and his left shoulder screamed with pain, but his fury knew no bounds. Jason punched Brand in desperate fury, but he was no match for Brand Selby, even wounded. Brand grabbed the man's hair and yanked Jason's head back, then kneed him hard in the stomach. Jason doubled over and Brand brought his knee up this time, bashing it into Jason's face. There came a crunching sound as several teeth broke and Jason's cheekbone cracked. Brand shoved Jason to the ground, ramming a knee into his back and pulling his knife from its sheath. He grasped Jason by the hair and yanked his head back, putting the knife to his throat.

Panting, he growled, "I can think of a hundred ways to kill you slowly, Brown! First I start by popping out your eyeballs!"

"No! Wait!" Jason gasped. Blood poured from his mouth. "I can give you money—gold! Lots of gold!"

"Brand, don't kill him!" Joshua shouted, coming closer. "We need him alive!"

"I can't let him live!" Brand snarled, pricking Jason's skin just under the eye.

"Brand, we need him, damn it!"

"Brand!" Rachael cried out. "Don't kill him!"

The sound of her voice seemed to soften him. He rammed his knife back into its sheath, then shoved Jason's face into the gravel. He got up from the man, turning his eyes to Joshua. "He *walks* back!" he told Josh. "If he can't keep up, then he goes back dragging behind a horse!"

Luke started forward, then heard someone running. A man mounted a horse and started to ride off. Luke took aim with Hank's rifle and fired at a figure outlined in the moonlight. The man fell from the horse.

"It's all right, Josh!" Luke yelled excitedly. "I got one of them!" He ran up to the body and knelt closer to see. It was Jules Webber, the man who had brought Rachael to the camp. He felt Jules's chest and put a hand to his mouth. There was no heartbeat and no breathing. It was the first time Luke Rivers had killed a man, but he didn't feel bad about this one.

Luke ran toward his big brother, his heart leaping with joy at seeing Joshua still alive. "Josh!" he called out.

"Luke!"

The two brothers hugged, and Brand turned to Gray Bear and Standing Horse, giving them orders to make sure Jason Brown went nowhere. But that was not likely. Jason still lay facedown in the dirt, his blood staining the ground.

"You are hurt," Standing Bear told Brand in the Comanche tongue.

Brand put a hand to his wound and said nothing. He hurried into the shadows where Rachael had gone, calling her name.

"Brand!" she cried out. She limped toward him, falling into his welcome arms and weeping. "Oh, Brand, I thought you were dead! It was so awful!"

He hugged her tightly, calling over to Joshua and Luke to help the other woman, who came staggering into the firelight, her eyes staring and terrified.

"Everything will be all right now," Joshua told her, taking off his shirt and putting it around her.

Brand picked Rachael up in his arms and walked over near the fire with her. "Luke, round up what horses you can and hook some up to the wagon. We'll let the women lay in the back of the wagon on the way back."

"Yes, sir." Luke walked closer to the man. "Is Rachael okay? She isn't gonna die or anything, is she?"

"Your sister will be fine. Go on now. We've got to get her and this other woman to a doctor."

Luke ran off and Joshua walked closer to Brand after helping the other woman into the wagon. His eyes teared as he stared at a still-weeping Rachael. Her feet dangled, an ugly, bleeding cut on the bottom of one of them. "He said he was going… to cut the skin off the bottom of my feet," Rachael wept. "And he was going to sell me… to the Comancheros!" She clung to Brand, her words muffled because her face was buried in Brand's neck.

"He won't hurt you anymore, Rachael," Brand told her. "It's all over now. Everything is going to be all right. We'll take Jason Brown to town and everyone will know the truth. Then we can be married."

"I'm sorry," Joshua said. "You were telling the truth, Brand. If it wasn't for me, my sister wouldn't be here at all. When I think what could have happened if you hadn't helped me find her…" He turned away, closing his eyes against the agony of it.

"Josh? Josh is with you?" Rachael asked in a weak voice.

"Yes. We came together to get you."

"Then he knows… he understands…"

Joshua turned and grasped an arm that was wrapped around Brand's neck. "I'm so goddamn sorry, Rachael. I don't know what else to say, except that I love you. I just wanted what I thought was best for you."

She moved her arm down, keeping her face buried against Brand's shoulder but grasping Joshua's hand.

"Joshua," she groaned.

Rachael lay in a clean flannel gown, enjoying the comfort of the cool sheets of her own bed. Lacy came into the room again, fussing over her as she had done ever since Rachael's return. She re-tucked the blankets, fluffed her pillow.

"Do you need anything, honey?"

"I'm fine, Lacy. If you don't stop all this attention, I'll never be able to do another thing for myself."

"Nonsense. I enjoy it. I'm just so glad to see you back safe and sound. The doctor says there's still no sign of infection in that foot."

"Where is Brand? I haven't seen him yet this morning."

"He and Josh are down at the Ranger offices. Some Rangers came in this morning from Houston. They're taking Jason and the other two men back to Houston with them. I'll tell you, the men left to guard those three had a time keeping the people of this town from hanging all three of them. Around here there's nothing worse than white men turning on their own kind and selling them off to the Comanche or to outlaws. Brand was right smart in not killing Jason Brown. Being disgraced and hanged in public is the best punishment for that man."

"Is Luke here?"

"He's down in the kitchen finishing off some cookies I baked. I'll tell you, that boy can eat a person right out of the house."

Rachael smiled. Soon she would be well, and she and Brand and Luke and Josh were all going to leave together—head north with what cattle and horses and personal belongings they had salvaged and settle someplace new. But Matthew wouldn't be with them.

They both heard the door downstairs open and close, and Lacy went out into the hallway, looking down to see Brand and Joshua coming inside with the local preacher.

"Can we come up?" Joshua asked, looking at Lacy. "We have a surprise for Rachael."

Lacy smiled, guessing from the bouquet of flowers in Brand's hands what was going on. "You sure can," she answered.

Luke ran out of the kitchen and followed the men up the stairs, curious. Rachael put a hand to her bruised face when they came into the room. Most of the swelling had gone down over the six days they had been back, but green and yellow bruises remained. Brand came to her first, sitting down on the edge of the bed and laying the flowers across her chest. His left shoulder still ached fiercely, and he had lost some of the use of his left arm. But already he had been working with it, determined to regain full use of it. After all, if he was going to spend the rest of his life providing for and protecting Rachael Rivers, he had to be well and strong.

"For my bride," he told her.

Rachael blinked in wonder. "Your bride?"

"The preacher has agreed to marry us."

"Right now?"

"Right now."

"Oh, Brand, my hair… my face. I'm not even dressed."

He leaned down and kissed her cheek. "You're beautiful, and we've waited long enough."

"Brand!" She smelled the lovely scent of the flowers, and her eyes teared. "Oh, Brand, I'm so happy we can finally be together." Her words were choked, and he grasped her hands.

"You just hang on and say your vows and that will be it. You will be Mrs. Brand Selby." He stood up and reached into the pocket of his pants. He wore dark cotton pants and a blue calico shirt. The only clothes he possessed after being chased off his land were the now bloodied buckskins he had been wearing that night. Joshua had sold some of his cattle when they got back, and pooled the money with what Brand had on him to buy some clothes for both Brand and Josh, and for Luke. Brand had not failed to buy more buckskins, but he already talked about riding through Indian Territory on their way north and trading for some "real Indian-made buckskins," as he put it. "These skins tanned and sewn by whites aren't nearly as sturdy," he complained.

But for today he wore white man's clothing, and Rachael noticed he looked more handsome than ever, realizing it was because he was completely happy for the first time in many years. He flashed an unnerving smile as he handed her a gold wedding band.

"It's not very fancy. When I get settled someplace new, I'll get you something nicer," he told her.

Rachael took the ring, studying it with tears in her eyes. "Oh, Brand, it's beautiful," she told him. "I don't ever want another."

He grasped her hands. "Don't put it on yet. Let me do it at the right time." He looked up at the preacher. "You ready, Reverend?"

"If you are," the man answered. Brand Selby's actions in exposing Jason Brown for what he really was had won Brand and Rachael at least a few friends among the people of Austin, the reverend being one of them. He had decided it was not his place to judge these two people, who apparently loved each other very much.

Rachael could hardly get through the words, the lump in her throat was so painful. She clung to Brand's hands tightly, almost expecting something else to go wrong. But then Brand was slipping the ring on her finger. Brand was kissing her cheek. Lacy was crying. The men were all shaking hands and Lacy invited the preacher down for coffee and cookies.

"Can I have more?" Luke asked right away.

"You mean you left some?" Lacy returned.

She put her hand on Luke's shoulder and led him out. Rachael moved her eyes to Joshua, who stood near the window. "I'm real glad for both of you," he told her. Brand rose, and the two men shook hands. Joshua's eyes were red and watery. "Thanks, Brand."

Brand squeezed his hand. "You're a good man, Joshua."

Joshua nodded, then turned to Rachael. He let go of Brand and sat down on the edge of the bed, taking Rachael's hand. "I ought to tell you, Rachael, that I've been thinking a lot about something." He looked up at Brand. "I'll go north with you, but I'm thinking that after a bit I just might head out to Oregon."

"Oregon!" Rachael gasped. "Josh, we should be together."

Joshua sighed, meeting her eyes again. "You've got Brand now, Rachael. I've already got an offer on Pa's land. You already know I can't bring myself to go back there, other than us going to see the graves before we leave. Everything is gone, and with my share of the money from selling the land—I don't know. I just need to go off alone, Rachael. I've never known anything but Texas. A lot of people are heading for Oregon, and I hear there's a valley there that's pure heaven for a man who likes to farm and raise horses. You and Brand don't need me around. And maybe out in Oregon, what with so many people heading in that direction, I can find a woman to settle with. Isn't that what you've been wanting for me?"

Her eyes teared. "I'd miss you so much."

"You got along fine without any of us back in St. Louis for three whole years. You're one hell of a strong woman, Rachael.

Before you know it you and Brand will be settled, and you'll be teaching school someplace—and having babies. You'll be surrounded with a new family. I'll make sure you're good and settled before I go. And there are ways of keeping in touch. I'll write and let you know where I've settled. And if I fall in love, I'll tell you that, too."

Rachael smiled through tears. "What about Luke?"

"Well, I guess it will be up to him when the time comes. He can come along, or stay with you and Brand, whichever he wants to do."

"You know we'll gladly keep him with us, Josh, if that's what he wants," Rachael answered. She breathed deeply. "Oregon." She looked at Brand. "What do you think of that?"

Brand frowned. "I'm a Plainsman myself—have to have wide-open land underfoot. But Josh has told me enough about it that I'm thinking more along the lines of settling along the Oregon Trail, up around Kansas, where we'd be close to Independence, Missouri, where most of the travelers leave from. We could raise horses—get rich supplying the travelers with fine horses and whatever food we can raise. Let those crazy people go all the way to Oregon. We'll be counting our money."

They all laughed lightly.

"Well, I'm going to be one of the crazy people who goes all the way to Oregon," Joshua said. He leaned closer and kissed Rachael's cheek. "I'm sorry for all of it, Rachael. I'm just glad you and Brand are together now." He straightened, wincing at the pain that still plagued his ribs. His face was pink on one side from where the skin had been scraped away, contrasting the sun-darkened skin of the rest of his handsome face. Rachael had no doubt her brother would find a wife easily once he started seriously looking. His problem would probably be choosing from the several young women who were bound to be more than eager to marry her brother.

"I'll leave you two alone for a few minutes," he said then, rising from the bed. He squeezed Rachael's hand, then gave Brand a wink as he left.

Brand sat back down on the bed and leaned close to his

new wife. "Are you happy, Mrs. Selby?"

"I've never been happier," she answered, a tear slipping down the side of her face.

He met her lips, in their first truly hungry, lingering kiss since he had found her. She had been in too much pain and too upset until now to think passionate thoughts. But now Brand lightly ran his tongue over her healed lips, and he moved his arms under her, drawing her to him. The old fires of desire moved through her as she circled her arms around his neck.

"We'll sleep together tonight," he told her, moving his lips to her cheek, gently kissing the lingering bruises. "I'll hold you all night and every night for the rest of our lives."

Their lips met again, and Rachael knew that in spite of their injuries, somehow they would find a way to gently make love tonight. After all, this was her wedding night. She was Mrs. Brand Selby, and she would be his wife in every way.

Brand moved onto the bed to lie beside her, pulling her into his arms, where she nestled against him, reveling in the closeness and the safety of his strong arms. Nothing and no one could ever make them be apart again. They would go north and start a whole new life, away from all the things that brought remembered pain and heartache. She would not be leaving her mother and father and brother behind in Texas. Their spirits would all be with her, wherever she went. It was time to put the past behind her now, and look to the future.

"It's been a long time since you had a lesson, Brand Selby," she said sleepily.

He grinned. "Well, now you have all the time in the world to teach. All the time in the world. No more sneaking out to steal a few hours together. We're free to love each other and be together for the rest of our lives."

She snuggled against her new husband, breathing in the lingering scent of sage and leather.

"The man whose heart was made to love does not ask himself if the object of his love is worthy of him. The moment he loves he does not examine the past; he enjoys the present and he believes in the future..."

—George Sand

More from Rosanne Bittner

Tennessee Bride

Raised in the hills of Tennessee, Emma Simms dreams of the day she'll escape her life of poverty to start over in the excitement of Knoxville But when her mother dies and she's left with no one but her stepfather, Luke Simms, her dream abruptly becomes a nightmare. Luke plans to send Emma to Knoxville alright—straight to a notorious brothel.

River Joe, the mysterious Cherokee-raised frontiersman, knew from the first time he set eyes on the beautiful Emma that he had to have her as his own. And one glimpse at the handsome, buckskin-clad stranger ignites the flame of dangerous desire in Emma's heart.

Their passion could consume them both, but their love could very well save her life.

Oregon Bride

On a trail of danger, love follows no set path.

Traveling west aboard a wagon train with her late husband's family, young widow Marybeth MacKender wishes only to leave behind the memories of her loveless marriage, and to protect her infant son. But the dangers of the train are endless, as are the advances of her brutish brother-in-law who is resolute in claiming Marybeth as his own.

It isn't until Marybeth meets Joshua Rivers, a frontiersman both tough and tender, that her hope for the future ignites as brightly as the desire in her heart. With courage aroused by passion, Marybeth is determined to face the perils of this rugged terrain for Joshua and the love she feels as great as the odds stacked against them.

Full Circle

The last thing sheltered missionary Evelyn Gibbons wants upon arriving at the South Dakota reservation is to fall in love. Yet, from the moment she clashes with Black Hawk, the complicated man of the Sioux, she knows he's everything she could ever want, and everything she can never have.

Living in the hills with his young son, Black Hawk reveres the ways of his people and is determined to preserve Sioux traditions. But when he meets Evelyn, a woman from the society he most abhors, not even his own prejudices can smother the flame of desire that burns for her.

But in the midst of their unlikely romance is a storm tide of treachery and hate that threatens to destroy their love, and their lives.

Until Tomorrow

Addy wants nothing more than to leave her small Illinois home for the gold-rich hills of Colorado, where a teaching job awaits. But her plans are thwarted when a band of outlaws rob the very bank in which she is withdrawing her savings, taking her hostage in the process. Rogue and ruthless, her captives sweep her off to the country with evil intent, but one man stands in the way.

Ex-Confederate soldier Parker Cole doesn't understand his own fierce determination to protect the beautiful captive from his fellow bandits. Touched by her courage and spirit, he vows to prove his love to her, following Addy to a mining boomtown filled with dreamers and desperados. Fearless though he may be, Parker must summon all of his courage to beat out the line of rich and powerful suitors in the pursuit of the greatest treasure—Addy's heart.